The Ghost
of
Helen Addison

D0168113

The Ghost
of
Helen Addison

The First Leo Moran Murder Mystery

CHARLES E. McGARRY

First published in Great Britain in 2017 by Polygon, an imprint of Birlinn
Ltd, West Newington House, 10 Newington Road, Edinburgh EH9 1QS

www.polygonbooks.co.uk

1

ISBN 9781 84697 379 6
eBook ISBN 978 0 85790 347 1

British Library Cataloguing-in-Publication Data
A catalogue record for this book is available
on request from the British Library.

Typeset by Biblichor Ltd, Edinburgh

To my beloved mother

When I say, 'My bed will comfort me,
My couch will ease my complaint,'
Then You scare me with dreams
And terrify me with visions

THE BOOK OF JOB 7: 13–14

PROLOGUE

The beast walks in the night, determined to destroy something that is pure and good, and full of promise and beauty.
Leo Moran walks alongside it.

He awoke, his pyjamas soaked with clammy sweat.

The bedroom was a sick chamber, optimally arranged to soothe his influenza which in wintertime stalked him like a hunter. Water jug and beaker, paracetamol, Lemsip, hot water bottle, basin and flannel, Vicks Vaporub.

Flu invariably became a mental trial for him as well as a physical one. His customary pomposity waned as the fever tormented him, and all of his iniquities and inadequacies were laid bare and brought to the fore. The sensations of the virus – the high temperatures and the horrid flavours in his sinus – awakened unsettling ghosts of influenzas past, of long-ago eras when he had struggled to cope. Was it just he who experienced this? By God, how he detested being ill, and how he dreaded the end: 'Please, Lord, allow me to expire peacefully in my sleep – either that or let a sniper's bullet dispatch me with minimal fuss.'

Inevitably, the process would then descend into an existential crisis, his faith barely holding fast as the banality of modern life was rammed home by daytime television. 'They'd be as well putting on the bloody test card,' he grumbled, wondering why he had bothered to drag the abominable box from its closet berth.

As the day progressed his fever relented, and although his muscles still ached, they did so less painfully now. He gazed out of the drawing-room window and noticed that the weather had turned foul. He hoped last night's episode had just been a flu dream. But in his heart he knew. He knew it was real. The thrusting blade, the gouts of blood were all too convincing. He resolved to avoid the day's news bulletins; he wasn't ready yet. He was still too weak. He would digest it tomorrow, in the morning paper.

Then decide what to do about it.

I

LOCH DHONN

I

L EO ordered a taxi to drive him from his splendid Glasgow apartment to the railway station and spent the minutes it took to arrive checking – for the seventh time – that the ashes in the grate were dead, gases were turned off and electricity plugs were disconnected.

The driver was an odious, high-pitched little character, who quickly broached the subject of immigration and spat a racist word into the conversation. Leo requested that he refrain from such language, then, before the man had a chance to respond, pretended to busy himself with his mobile phone, during which he made great play of jotting down the cabbie's name and number in his notebook. Upon arrival at Queen Street station Leo paid him exactly – no tip – and took inordinate pleasure in counting out a stack of grubby coppers as part of the fare.

He purchased his ticket and stowed himself and his considerable quantity of monogrammed luggage in the foremost carriage of the Oban train, which was empty of other passengers. He rubbed his gnarled hands together as he settled down at a seat with a table, and produced a felt-lined box containing a little gold-rimmed glass with harp and shamrock motifs etched on it, and a silver flask with beautiful Celtic knotwork relief. He polished the glass with a napkin, filled it with a shot of Scotch from the flask, took a swig, and settled himself down for a snooze. After adjusting his velvet-lined slumber mask, he fell instantly into an uncomfortable sleep.

A slight jolt of the train is an explosion of light within Leo's dimmed consciousness, followed by a split-second rush of the shockwave tearing the air as it rushes towards him.

He jerked, both in his mind and in the physical world, to avoid the impact, and snapped out of the uncharacteristically brief vision. He found himself blinded by the blast. Panicked, he reached for his eyes and felt the slippery texture of his mask. He tore it off to reveal yet another level of altered reality: massive patches of blond sand deposited upon the embankments of the West Highland Line. He blinked several times, unable to compute this weird phenomenon. Was he still dreaming? Was he locked within an endless nightmare of hallucinations? Then he realised – it was *snow*. Of course – the Scottish Highlands in winter. Snow.

Leo then endured a brief crisis of hypochondria brought on by the fact that his left leg had gone to sleep during his fitful nap. Having convinced himself that he was about to suffer a fatal stroke, he popped a Mogadon, mumbled a prayer, and urgently proceeded to jot down the hymnal for his funeral Mass, regretting having put the task off thus far. The onus was unsurprisingly on the side of gravitas – Mozart and Fauré – but the sentimentalist in him couldn't resist 'Hail, Queen of Heav'n, The Ocean Star' and then 'Be Still, My Soul' for the exeunt to the hearse. That'll have them weeping in the aisles, he mused morbidly, before realising that the feeling had by now returned to his lower limb and that the magic bullet had calmed his anxiety with its soporific charm. Despite that, he wondered with trepidation what the turnout would actually be at his funeral; he had fallen out with so many friends and associates over the years. He tried to number those who loved him, and pictured one of those melancholy, pitifully attended affairs: a rainy November day, a few old acquaintances shaking hands in the porch of a cold church and murmuring uneasy platitudes for the deceased, politely promising to meet up for a drink one of these days, a white lie at the ready to excuse themselves from attending the wake. Too much gravy and not enough meat in the steak pie.

Leo popped a consolatory segment of Fry's Orange Cream into his mouth, put his earphones in and switched on the radio, but the mountains blotted out the signal. Suddenly, he regretted his parsimony in not having invested in an iPod. 'Join the twenty-first century,' he could hear his friend Stephanie Mitchell, a procurator fiscal, tease. His phone vibrated on the table with a text alert. Coincidentally, it was from Stephanie: 'I told DI Lang 2 xpect u at Loch Dhonn.'

Bloody decent of her.

His thoughts turned to the murdered girl. The picture the police had released to the media was one of a pretty, petite brunette wearing a graduation gown, proudly clutching her nursing certificate, smiling out at the world, full of anticipation and hope. He read the newspaper story for the tenth time:

Police have named the Loch Dhonn village murder victim as 22-year-old Helen Addison. The body of Miss Addison, a recently qualified district nurse, was found early on Thursday morning by a local man. She had several knife wounds. It is not yet clear whether Miss Addison had been sexually assaulted. Police said they are questioning Miss Addison's boyfriend Craig Hutton, 21, at an unnamed Glasgow station and that Mr Hutton was 'voluntarily helping them with their inquiries'.

Speaking for the Addison family, Mrs Grace Dunn, the victim's aunt, said: 'Helen was a lovely young woman, a beloved and valued daughter, sister, cousin, niece and friend, who had returned to her home community of Loch Dhonn as a newly qualified nurse. Her career choice was testament to her caring, compassionate nature. Words cannot begin to describe the devastation Helen's mum Lorna, dad Stuart and brother Callum are experiencing at this time. Her wider family, numerous friends and everyone whose lives Helen touched have been profoundly shocked by this wicked act.

'Someone, somewhere must know who did this. Perhaps they suspect a loved one. No matter how hard it seems I urge you to go to the police. Whoever is responsible may do it again unless you act. Please, you have the power to stop another family going through this hell.'

Leo thought about how the remains of poor Helen Addison would soon be ensconced within an obscure little patch of Scottish clay. And how brutally the months and years would rush by for the people who had loved her, denied her presence at their triumphs and festivities as she was now denied her own triumphs and festivities. The pang of guilt endured at each mundane task, as though performing it in her absence was in some small way a betrayal, an act of forgetting her. And as they speculated forevermore upon what she would have been, the lettering on the gravestone would quickly fade with lichen and the weather, and the rest of the world would march on, blind to the void of her absence.

He recalled his conversation with Stephanie, which had ended in discord when she had visited him three days ago.

'I might as well tell you: I'm going up there.'

'Where?'

He had gestured towards the day's newspaper, which lay front page up on the *chaise longue*.

'Why?'

'I had a vision. If I get to the scene of the crime I might be able to work out who the bastard is. Being there might stimulate my senses.'

'When are you going?'

'I've yet to decide. I fear if I arrive upon the locus too soon after the event the police may spurn my advances.'

'You likely won't be made welcome, regardless of how long you delay it.'

He had gazed out of the window, watching the rain whirl in the orange glow of the streetlamps and fall upon the riverbank across the road. Drops tap-tapped irregularly on the pane. She was right, of course; he probably wouldn't be welcome. Furthermore, he mused, it takes a lot of pluck, or perhaps foolhardiness, to approach the authorities with information pertaining to a case. He knew from bitter experience that knowledge of a crime (pertinently, knowledge bestowed by a vision) tends to place the bearer under suspicion. But he felt he had no choice. He could not bear a repeat of the tragedy that had occurred when he hadn't spoken up.

Leo disembarked at the quaint railway station at Fallasky, which was approximately eight miles from the village of Loch Dhonn. He was the only passenger to get off. He waited for the locomotive to pull away, then teetered across the line with his cases. A minicab was parked near to the station house. Leo approached it hopefully, and the driver, an affable-looking, slightly unkempt man with oily black hair who wore sports slacks, a tired, brown leather blouson jacket and NHS spectacles, cheerfully announced he was indeed for hire, got out and stowed the luggage in the boot. Leo climbed into the rear and tried to disguise his distaste for an unhygienic faux-sheep's-wool throw draped over the seat.

After a while they were on a single-track road, snaking through wooded countryside towards their destination. At one point they passed a stand of pines upon some raised ground to Leo's right, and he could catch tantalising glimpses of the silver surface of Loch Dhonn flashing through the gaps between their poker-straight trunks. Further on, the branches of a hundred snow-coated firs protruded over the road like robed arms, their ghostly fingers pointing. For some of the journey they were stuck behind an HGV rig with no trailer, which laboured up a series of narrow inclines, its airbrakes hissing violently. The rural taxi driver remained patient, evidently a more amiable species than his urban cousin.

'Terrible business up here,' he ventured.

'Terrible, terrible,' agreed Leo.

'Are you with the papers?'

'No. I'm here on holiday, believe it or not.'

'Oh.'

Leo was seized by the sudden realisation that the driver might take him for a ghoul. 'I had already booked it. I'm up for the fishing, as a matter of fact,' he blurted, before realising that this claim was fatally undermined by his conspicuous lack of angling gear. Silence descended for the remainder of the journey, and Leo decided to browse a local guidebook he spied tucked in a storage net attached to the rear of the passenger seat.

Loch Dhonn was a narrow freshwater lake, situated just below the immense diagonal fissure that splits Scotland in two. Running for thirteen miles in a jagged slash roughly from south to north-north-east in Argyll, it was over three hundred feet deep in parts and approximately a mile in width. The northern reaches were dotted with several small islands, some of which bore evidence of prehistoric and medieval settlements. At the northernmost point sat a Munro, Ben Corrach, a giant, bleak sentinel which rose to three thousand seven hundred feet and watched over the loch's entire length. The scattered settlement that took its name from the loch was small, with little more than seventy permanent residents, although this was boosted by the transient population of the Loch Dhonn Hotel, which dominated the place. Loch Dhonn village was one of fewer than a dozen hamlets sprinkled down the loch's eastern shoreline, which boasted a slightly better road than the facing bank. Apart from the hotel, built around an ancient hunting lodge in the 1840s during the grouse-shooting boom, there was a general store, a small community hall rebuilt in the 1960s, a Presbyterian kirk and, just to the north, a lovely Episcopalian church, as though plucked from a green and pleasant English dale and plonked down like a little curio within this majestic and savage valley.

They passed through some lower, sheltered ground: an expanse of squat trees, naked but for moss, ivy and flaking bark, their gnarled branches reaching out like the limbs of prehistoric beasts petrified instantly by some sudden catastrophe. One particularly ancient dying specimen bore a likeness to a dragon, which had been accentuated by an imaginative local wit painting on a sinister pair of red eyes. It seemed to guard the northern extremity of the village. They crossed a little stone humpback bridge, negotiated a final, twisting climb, before descending into Loch Dhonn itself.

The original buildings clung mainly to the east side of the undulating road, which at this point sat well above the water level and was set quite far back from the loch itself. The clachan was permanently shadowy due to the high arbour above the road and the steep law to the east side. Other, modern abodes, some of them luxurious and in the Scandinavian style, had been established amid the young birchwood and perennial shrubbery below the road, weekend homes for well-off Glaswegians, Leo guessed. Between them and the lochside was another half mile of land, mostly drab blanket bog, the rushes withered and brown, punctuated by the odd skeletal tree, like death's crooked hand, or where the soil was loamier tracts of meadow, some of it pleasantly stocked with mature woods. Leo consulted the little book again: the land above the road, which didn't rise much above five hundred feet, was largely part of the local estate. Cutting through this was Glen Fallasky, which ran roughly north-east towards the railway village where Leo had disembarked.

The hotel's imposing Scots Baronial exterior was constructed from pale grey stone. The three-storey building had a grand portico, several craw-stepped gables, two turrets and a thin tower, all topped with steep conical roofs. The taxi couldn't pull up at the front doors because the driveway was choked with various police and media vehicles, and a brewery lorry obstructed a little lane which ran along the side of the building. Leo was deposited beneath a leviathan Wellingtonia, upon a forlorn little area of raw earth, which was the shade of cinnamon and dotted with patches of snow and ice. He paid the driver and was duly handed his luggage.

He surveyed the anaemic landscape, the colour bled out by winter's death. '*Et in Arcadia ego*,' he murmured. Yet, despite the land's dun seasonal garb there persisted a certain brutal handsomeness to the place. Leo gazed over towards the loch. A quintessentially Scottish scene. A ruined castle, wreathed in mist and clad in masses of gushing ivy, sat upon the largest island of a little archipelago. Spirals of vapour smoked off the braes on the facing bank, which were bearded by snowy brakes of native timber and serried ranks of commercially planted conifers. A mile to the south, the height of these slopes crested to almost that of a Graham then abruptly plunged, cloven by a great pass, a gateway to the west coast. A thin cataract tumbled in silvery slow motion from this distant promontory. Momentarily, the sun blinked from behind a cloud, drenching the crown of Ben Corrach in light as though it had been painted in oils, and making the water which sat in its lap sparkle. Leo felt a surge of joy in his lungs as he descended the muddy incline towards the hotel.

He tottered awkwardly with his heavy luggage, taking care not to slip, watched by two amused uniformed policemen who were glad of this mildly entertaining interlude to the boredom of guarding the crime scene perimeter. Leo was aware of their stares. He was used to people finding humour in his eccentric attire and gait, but he prided himself on paying it no heed whatsoever. He was more concerned by what lay behind the young coppers in the near distance: an extensive thicket of rhododendron from within which sprouted the branches of bare elms and rowans. It seemed chillingly familiar to him. A sense of foreboding welled up within him.

At that very instant the beast, sitting alone in the darkness of its cellar, amusing itself with thoughts of its dire deed, opened its eyes wide, as though disturbed by an awareness of Leo's arrival. His coming had already been foretold in code by its dark ancestor on the other side, by means of the strange runes. It would observe its adversary carefully, and consider what steps need be taken.

Nothing was off limits.

The hotel lobby was splendidly furnished and presented a predictable Highland interior. Some logs burned cheerfully in the grate, dwarfed by a magnificent mantelpiece constructed from carved, varnished maple. A couple of newshounds sat in the lounge area, chattering loudly and unselfconsciously to their editors through their mobile phones. Leo walked to the unattended reception desk. He placed his cases down and pinged the bell with his open palm. The cold air from outside lingered in the folds of his coat like an energy. As he waited he noted a just-about passably decent rip-off of Landseer's *Monarch of the Glen*.

'Do you like the painting, sir?' came the voice of a man who had arrived behind the counter.

Leo turned to face the speaker, a friendly-looking fellow in his seventies. His socialist sensibilities were always offended by being addressed as 'sir' by an older person.

'It has real character,' replied Leo diplomatically.

'It is by a locally based fellow. They have a kind of artistic community, just down the road.' He reached out his hand. 'Bill Minto,' he said. 'You must be Mr . . . ?'

'Moran,' replied Leo as he shook the hotelier's hand. 'Leo Moran. I telephoned earlier.'

'Of course,' said Minto, checking the book. 'Apart from a few of the newspaper chaps you're our only new guest this week. As you can imagine.'

Leo raised his eyebrows in acknowledgement.

The man glanced at Leo's hands and felt a pang of sympathy. The melted skin reminded Minto of the burns on his torso, which he had sustained on active service.

'How long have you had the place?' enquired Leo, changing the subject. He didn't wish to be drawn into a conversation about his reasons for being in Loch Dhonn. Apart from anything else, it would antagonise the police if he suggested to anyone that they had resorted to using psychics.

'Since nineteen-eighty.'

'It's most impressive.'

'Thank you,' replied Minto gratefully. He had narrow grey eyes, an earnest smile, and his Borders accent had a slight whine to it. 'It wasn't always like this. When we arrived – you should have seen the state of it. The business was barely ticking over. A few more years of neglect and the whole damn structure would have perished from damp. Now we've got two hotels – we also own the Ardchreggan, on the opposite bank.'

'How wonderful,' said Leo.

'Bill! Bill!' rang out a disembodied female voice. A tall woman wearing a green woollen twinset and a pearl necklace, her greyish hair coiffured into a bird's nest, poked her big face into the lobby from the back office. Irritation was written on her masculine features.

Gosh, thought Leo, she'd scare the weans.

'Oh, I'm sorry, I didn't realise you were with a guest. Welcome, Mr . . . ?'

'Moran, dear,' said Bill Minto, finishing the woman's sentence.

She glared momentarily at him. 'Well, I'm Shona Minto, Bill's wife,' she said, proffering her hand to Leo. She shook with a hearty, almost crushing, grasp. 'Sorry for interrupting, my husband has forgotten to unlock the cellar trap for the drayman. Again.'

'Excuse me, sir. My wife will see to you,' said Minto, smiling apologetically before scurrying away.

Shona's affected accent grated on Leo as he completed the formalities of registration. He had the feeling that she was less interested in the reason behind his visit than the fact that his credit card hadn't expired. He insisted on finding his own way to his room, slightly anxious that she was going to offer to carry his luggage for him in her manly grip. She would have been a farm girl originally, Perthshire stock perhaps, a big, strapping lassie able to hold her own with the menfolk before she headed to Edinburgh and worked on her diction. Leo speculated that in her earlier days she had doubtless been a Girl Guide leader, adept at camp, her strong arms unrolling canvas and hammering in pegs, her watchful eye lingering a little too long on the lassies in their bathing costumes as they emerged from the river.

Leo's room was suitably grand: dark-stained furniture, a high double bed, an en suite bathroom. He noted approvingly the neat pile of logs in the hearth. A framed series of watercolours of local wildflowers and fauna decorated the walls. He placed his luggage at the foot of the bed. His window looked northwards over the loch; he glanced down at the police activity below, noticing with a shiver the thicket of rhododendron. He drew the heavy curtains. It would be dark soon, and he wanted to seek out Stephanie's detective. Leo felt slightly nervous; he had an ambivalent view of the police. He recognised that there were many excellent, well-intentioned people in the ranks, but he distrusted their increasingly militaristic training and could never forgive their being deployed as an arm of the state against organised labour and the disturbing relish many coppers seemed to take in assaulting decent working men. Also, Leo worried excessively about the pervasive influence of Freemasonry within the police. Furthermore, he had good reason to know that certain officers would enthusiastically mount anyone who remotely fitted within the frame. And then hang them upon the wall.

So before setting off he took an immodest swig from his hip flask, then sprayed a jet of cinnamon-flavoured breath freshener into the back of his mouth.

2

OUTSIDE, the police had rigged up some arc lamps which illuminated the increasingly gloomy surroundings as the brief winter dusk fell. Leo strode over to the crime scene tape and addressed the constables who had been amused by his arrival earlier.

'Excuse me, gentlemen. I wonder: could you enquire if Detective Inspector Lang is available, if you may be so kind?'

'He's busy right now, sir,' replied the shorter of the two. Leo could remember when the Glasgow polis wouldn't recruit a fellow under five feet eight, and had to draft in big Hieland laddies from the country who weren't undernourished like their city peers. 'Who should I say wanted him?'

'My name is Moran, Leo Moran. I believe he's expecting me.'

'Just one moment, please, sir,' replied Constable Shorty dubiously. He turned away and made a call into the shortwave radio that had been clipped to his utility belt, then turned back to face Leo. 'You're to come through, sir. I'll walk you over to the incident room.'

The taller cop was clearly surprised at Leo's admittance, but politely lifted the tape in order that he could pass underneath.

Lang came out of the Portakabin before Leo and the constable reached it.

'Sir, this is the gentleman who asked to see you,' said Shorty.

'Mr Moran?'

'How do you do. Please, call me Leo.'

'Detective Inspector Lang,' replied the cop as he performed a perfunctory handshake. He was a quiet-spoken, straightforward, tired-looking Ayrshire man in his late forties, whose once red hair had been washed to a sandy grey by the passage of time. 'Good journey?' he asked automatically.

'Fine.'

'Let's get away from here,' said Lang as he ushered Leo in the opposite direction from where the press pack were milling around, obviously not wanting to stir their interest with his eccentric new acquaintance. They strolled along some shadowy red-blaes paths flanked by rhododendron thick with shiny green-leather leaves. They rounded a corner and Leo clasped his shooting coat around him tightly, feeling an inexplicable surge of cold. He stopped.

'This is where it happened, isn't it?'

Lang deliberately narrowed his eyes at his companion and flashed him a knowing smile; even in the dying light Leo could easily have guessed the locus from the plethora of forensic kit dotted around. In fact, the twine that had been pegged out on the soil where Helen Addison's body had been found was visible from where they stood.

'Look, it's just a formality, but would you mind telling me where you were during the early hours of Thursday?'

Leo stiffened, momentarily reliving his adolescent trauma when cops, piqued by his knowledge of a certain serious (although non-fatal) crime, had grilled him mercilessly, thinking him an accomplice. He hoped that Lang didn't suspect him regarding Miss Addison; he probably just wanted to assert the power dynamic between them at the outset. In truth, the detective had only reluctantly agreed to entertain this oddball because there were no strong leads in the case. He was a pragmatic man at heart; however, the canteen chat about Leo's astonishing insights at the time of the Monday Murders case had intrigued him, and he was open to the slim possibility that certain people possessed unorthodox powers as yet unexplained by science. He had consulted his colleague Carolan, who had led that investigation and whose judgement Lang trusted, to vouch for Leo before he acceded to Stephanie's rather left-field request that he speak with him.

'That's easy – I had taken to bed with influenza.'

'Can anyone corroborate that?'

'No.'

'Would you be willing to take a DNA test?'

Lang's breath was stale, that of a man who had worked hard for a considerable period of time without enough food. Leo timed the rhythm of his breathing so as to avoid inhaling the worst of it.

'Certainly.'

Lang smiled thinly. 'There was no alien DNA. Neither were there any prints or anything else of forensic interest.' He produced a packet of cigarettes from his gabardine and offered Leo one.

'No, thank you.'

'Do you mind if . . .' began Lang, already lighting up.

'Go ahead. Passive smoking is one of my few pleasures in life these days,' said Leo, slightly disingenuously, considering his fondness for a good cigar.

They walked on.

'So, this . . . power of yours, how does it manifest itself?'

'I see images, when the mind is in an unconscious or semi-conscious state.'

'When you're dreaming?'

'Usually. But also when my mind is idling in an alpha state, during daydreams, meditation, spiritual contemplation, general reverie. Or some-times an idea can just bubble up into the conscious mind, as clear as day. My peepers needn't be shut. The vision can be of an event past or present, and it may recur, oft-times with different details or from a different perspective.'

'What about seeing the future?'

'Yes, there are certain visions that I have experienced that I believe were of things yet to come. Precognition, as it is known.'

'And with this case?'

'It came to me in a dream.'

'What did you see, precisely?'

'First I was walking through a dark wood, as though alongside the killer. Then I saw a black-gloved hand thrusting a blade into a white nightdress, again and again. There was a great deal of blood.'

'Anything else?'

'Apart from that initial vision, just some random images when I was in church, none of them obviously helpful.'

'Such as?'

'A dark figure standing by a loch, upon which was an island.'

'Can you give me a description of the individual?'

'No. It was just a dark figure in the middle distance. Except . . .'

'What?'

'It was wearing some sort of robes. And oddly-shaped headwear; it was a bit crooked, and came to a point.'

'What else?'

'I saw a smith working at a furnace. I had the sense of two young men, their features obscured, wrongly suspected of the crime. One of them was in a police station; the other one, slightly older, possessed not the wits to cope with his predicament.'

'It's not much to go on,' said Lang, sighing out a stream of cigarette smoke.

'I'm afraid not,' replied Leo, a look of disapproval flashing across his face as Lang casually cast his fag end to the ground. He had to resist the urge to stoop down and bury it. 'The visions are usually oblique, their content often symbolic. The trick is reading between the lines, detecting the gist, working out what Providence is trying to impart. For example, the solitary dark figure suggests we are only looking for one man. Look, Detective Inspector, I realise that this sounds outlandish, but I believe that Helen wants me to help her. And she deserves my help. I'm hopeful that my being here at Loch Dhonn will stimulate my powers. In the meantime I must beg of your forbearance.'

'I've checked you out. Carolan said you were of some help with the Monday Murders. Although if you ask me anyone could have worked that one out.'

'Nonetheless, Detective Carolan will also have told you that there were details I had knowledge of, details that no one – not even the killer – could have possessed.'

'Carolan said something else about you.'

'If it regards charges brought against me for lying down in front of a lorry on the M8, that was a peaceful protest against the invasion of Iraq. I take the view that rather than breaking the law I was supporting it – international law.'

'No, not that.' For a dreadful moment Leo thought that Lang was going to dredge up his interrogation from 1976. He needn't have worried – all police memory and record of the teenage Leo's interviews were long-since lost, not least because his inquisitors had in fact become convinced of his innocence. Instead, Lang said, 'He told me that you drink far too much.'

'I have taken more out of alcohol than alcohol has taken out of me,' quoted Leo.

'Well, get this – if you wish to remain around here then know that I will permit no drunkenness. The whole of Scotland's fixated on Loch Dhonn at the moment.' Lang stopped and gazed distractedly into the sky. 'Although this case would drive Samson to drink. As a detective you become somewhat hardened to violent crimes – a wee bitty callous even – but some . . . some stay with you for ever. You wouldn't be human otherwise.'

'And this is one?'

'Yes. This is one. For certain offences, extreme ones such as this, well, I'd have the scaffold, quite frankly.' Lang eyed Leo and punctuated his next words with jabs of his index finger. 'You can have no official capacity in this case whatsoever. The press would have a field day. As far as everyone is concerned you are simply a tourist staying in the local hotel, here to enjoy the scenery. If we happen to converse from time to time then let's keep it discreet. If they identify you as a soothsayer I'll disown you as a crank and have you removed. Understood?'

'Understood.'

'And you are not to go near the family.'

'Why not?'

'Because they're upset enough without finding out we've had to enlist the services of Mystic Meg.'

'So, what happened?'

Lang sighed. 'The murder took place in the middle of the night, approximately between the hours of two and four according to the pathologist who attended the scene. No one knows why the victim was out, no one knows why she was clad only in her nightdress on a cold night. There were no late-night text messages summoning her from her bed, or calls to her mobile or the family's landline, nor did anyone hear shouting or knocking for her. According to her parents she had occasional bouts of sleepwalking during childhood, but not, as far as they were aware, during adolescence or adulthood, and there is no record of mental illness or any recent upset within her personal life.'

'It seems extraordinary that she was abroad in the dead of night, almost as though she was summoned to her doom under some vampiric influence,' interjected Leo.

'She lived with her parents and teenage brother up in the village. She was last seen by her parents, bidding them goodnight and going up to her bedroom at just after ten the previous night. She was a the new district nurse at the local surgery, enjoying her job, enjoying being back home.'

'And enjoying her romance with Craig Hutton?'

'Yes. He's being questioned in Glasgow.'

'He didn't do it. I suspect the boyfriend was one of the innocent young men from my second vision.'

Lang didn't reply. He was a good man, but in many ways a typically suspicious, world-weary cop. Yet his cynicism didn't extend to treating the world and his brother as a suspect, and he disliked the groupthink that pervaded the force. It wasn't 'them and us', he believed; it was criminals and everyone else – or rather, serious, violent criminals and everyone else. Lang couldn't help but like many of the fly men he had encountered earlier in his career. He would process them diligently and help put them away if required – that was what the law demanded – but he wasn't about to get high and mighty about people who often stole only to feed a desperate addiction, or because they fell hopelessly into bad company and bad habits. Craig Hutton was innocent, he felt sure, and he was slightly ashamed of the way his fellow officers had bullied and manipulated the lad when he had been brought in to be interviewed. They were lacking in compassion and devoid of either intelligence or instinct.

'The modus operandi smacks of someone who knows the area well, but we have to keep an open mind as to the perpetrator being an outsider who could be miles away by now,' said Lang. 'There was no evidence of a pursuit, which suggests the victim wasn't initially frightened at meeting the murderer, and probably knew him. There was no sign of a struggle on the ground at the murder scene; neither did the victim's hands show any evidence that she had fought back. She was struck on the head with a blunt instrument – probably first, and which may, hopefully, have knocked her unconscious – then stabbed twenty-three times to the chest and abdomen. All the wounds were inflicted by the same long blade. It was a frenzied attack, with lots of blood on the immediate surroundings. Some must have splattered onto the killer, and we found a couple of droplets nearby where it must have dripped from his hand or garments or the weapon. The body hadn't been moved. There was rowan bark residue in the victim's hair, and contusions to her throat consistent with the grip of a large, gloved left hand; we reckon the killer pinned her upright by the neck against a tree while using his other hand to stab at her. There were abrasions and a couple of the victim's hairs upon the tree. Neither weapon has been located, despite an extensive search.'

'Was she sexually assaulted?'

Lang raised a finger. 'This is the bit we've held back from the press so far, so if it gets out, I'll know it was you. She was violated with an as yet unidentified hard cylindrical object, probably metallic, very possibly the same item that she was struck on the head with. Now this part of the attack was very brutal, and post-mortem. It seemed almost ritualistic. We ran a nationwide cross-comparison of the entire MO but there were no matches. This is someone with a profound hatred of women.'

'You said there was no DNA?'

'There was the boyfriend's DNA – he says they were together the evening before and there are witnesses to that fact. And that of two patients, both elderly and housebound. If the perpetrator wasn't the boyfriend he was extremely careful not to leave a particle of evidence on the victim or the crime scene.'

'So he was probably someone local, who knew he would be swabbed, or someone on a database.'

'Maybe.'

'Did you use bloodhounds?'

'We brought a couple of tracking dogs up from Pollok, but they failed to pick up a precise trail from footprints we found at the murder scene which we believe belong to the killer. The rhododendron paths are well used and the whole area would be awash with scents, especially after two dozen polis swarming all over the place. Also, a breeze had picked up and time had elapsed because the dogs were delayed getting here, neither of which would have helped. By the way, there was a distinct scarcity of clear footprints due to the compacted blaes used on the paths around here.'

'Who found the body?'

'James Millar. Forty-year-old loner. He lost his wife suddenly a few years back, and has had psychiatric problems as a result. Since then he's stayed way up the glen in a little but 'n' ben. He found the body just after five a.m. He was one of the victim's patients.'

'What was this fellow doing strolling around so early?'

'He's something of a night owl. Apparently, it's not unusual for him to go for nocturnal walks. And the body was quite visible from the path. It was a bit misty over the loch, but the cloud was broken and there was a full moon.' Leo raised his eyebrows. 'Aye, he's a suspect, sure. We're keeping tabs on him,' said the policeman.

'Was the killer definitely a man?'

'We believe the footprints and the angle of the wounds indicate a strong male, between five foot nine and six foot one, acting alone. Right-handed with a size nine shoe. The trouble is, that description, give or take a shoe size either way, fits numerous men living around here, including Millar. It does, however, pretty much rule out the victim's father and brother, and the GP with whom Helen worked.'

'What about the hotel guests?'

'They've all been interviewed, but I couldn't keep them prisoner any longer and they were understandably keen to get home. I'm fairly satisfied that our man wasn't among them. With it being off season the hotel was quiet. There was a young professional couple from down south, a middle-aged couple from Aberdeen and a young family from Ayrshire. Oh, and an elderly couple from the States.'

Leo suddenly raised his left hand to silence the detective and used his right to smother three violent sneezes. He then plucked a mono-grammed Irish linen handkerchief from his pocket with which to blow his nose; an extended, dissonant trichord. He lowered his left hand and replaced the hanky.

'Forgive me. Do continue.'

'The only remaining guest is a bachelor who you'll no doubt meet around the hotel at some point. I gather he's virtually a permanent resident. As for employees, they're all female apart from the chef and the barman. They were both on their days off, and we've verified that they were in Glasgow partying the night away. Everyone else's alibis are some-what less watertight: they all claim to have been asleep in bed. Apart from Millar, of course. It's a pity these trusting rural types don't seem to believe in CCTV; we might've picked something up.'

Lang withdrew a business card with his name, mobile phone and land-line numbers printed on it, and handed it to Leo. 'Text me so as I have your number. And get in touch if you come up with anything. It's nearly dark – come on, I'll walk you back to the hotel.'

They set off. The policeman, who had set quite a brisk pace, fell into a sullen silence. At the edge of the grounds at the rear of the hotel he stopped.

'This is as far as I go.'

The men shook hands.

'The perpetrator of this crime will face justice,' said Leo, sensing the detective's despondency, 'and one day the awesome judgement of God. Evil does not have the final word in human affairs. Good will always prevail. In the end.'

'Well, let's hope it prevails before the bastard decides on a second helping.'

'Evil has a way of obscuring the truth, but things will become clearer.'

'So, you believe in evil, do you, Leo?' enquired Lang, who had lit a cigarette. 'As an actual, living force?'

'On the contrary, I take the Augustinian view that evil is precisely the absence of an actual, living force – the absence of goodness and the rejection of God's will; a kind of void, if you will. That may all sound rather neutral, but within that void, when man becomes his own god and gives in to lust, envy and the unrestrained pursuit of power, terrible things can happen, even torture and genocide. However, concerning the dark metaphysical host wandering the world engaged in the proliferation of that void – primary evil – I believe in that as profoundly as I believe in sound waves or sunshine or electricity or love. I believe in it because I've stared it in the eye.'

Lang was unimpressed by Leo's potted theology lesson. 'You work in this job long enough you find out that convenient labels of good and evil just don't wash. Most murders I've investigated have involved a scared-shitless, drunk teenager from a dysfunctional background, a few words of bravado, a blade and a lifetime of regret.'

'Precisely my point; horrendous things happen when the conditions are conducive.'

'So, you're a churchgoer, Leo?'

'Yes, I am a professing Catholic.'

'Ah, a Holy Roman.'

'You gotta believe in something,' replied Leo, rolling with the mild jibe.

'I don't,' said Lang as he exhaled smoke. 'Apart from the law. But I still envy you religious lot, having that certainty.'

'Faith doesn't work like that. Show me a man who has certainty and I'll show you a fool, and a dangerous fool at that. Even I, who has oft-times been confronted by the legions of darkness, have been assailed with doubt as to the existence of the forces of light. But there's one thing I remember, Detective Inspector, even during those dark nights of the soul. That as a society we've got ourselves into a whole mess of trouble precisely because we've lost sight of the difference between good and evil.'

3

WHEN Helen had been alive she had racked herself over the slightest confrontation. Regardless of whether she was right or wrong in the matter, the very experience of outward conflict made her feel anxious, guilty and exhausted. She would witness with wonder other people falling out and then becoming easily reconciled; she herself was terrified of the prospect. What had been said could never be unsaid and she simply did not believe that for her the wounds would heal quickly, or indeed ever. It was not so much what was said to her that would injure her – she could forgive easily enough – more what she might say to others.

She recalled the day she had come home from school, aged ten, in an uncharacteristically foul mood, and lashed out verbally at her mother over a trifling matter. When her mother responded Helen cast up to her a malformed, long-held belief that her parent would occasionally deliberately humiliate her due to some strange, primal resentment. Even as she revealed the secret she felt a surge of self-disgust and pity for her victim which swelled up like nausea, but some perverse impulse made her press on with the cruel accusation which only now, by being uttered out loud, was denuded as unfounded. Eventually, with her beloved, aproned mother standing speechless and pathetic in the kitchen, Helen ran upstairs and threw herself onto her bed in complete despair. She gazed up at the early summer teatime sky through her window. She wanted to put out the sun.

The memory would haunt her over the years. Nothing indeed could unsay what had been said, nothing could wipe away the human stain of ill will she had unveiled on that June day. Yet death had now released her from such frivolous guilt. 'The Waiting' – that was what she had termed this new metaphysical state. Perhaps it was a transitional dwelling, a holding area where souls could come to terms with their new situation while a place was prepared for them, or until some critical issue connected to violent or sudden death was resolved. Or maybe it was that thing called Purgatory she had heard old Mrs O'Donnell, her late grand-mother's friend, once speak of (Helen had enjoyed the semantics of the word – Purgatory – *Purge*-atory; a place of purging, of purification, of restoration; it instinctively made sense to her). Anyway, perhaps setting out on her career and the romance she had found with Craig had already given her a fledgling certitude about herself, and perhaps being denied the natural opportunity to fully realise these and the many other joys of adulthood – because she had been brutally murdered – meant that right-eous indignation now reinforced this hardening of the will. And as she wandered this new, waking limbo she rediscovered a long-forgotten child-hood pugnacity that had been gently crushed by her parents' tendency towards public humility, and also by other dramas that afflict far too many children and which she had taken to heart more than she would ever know. She thrived upon this refound confidence now, celebrated it. She was no longer the typecast Miss Shy, with memories of the play-ground bullies' taunts blooming like a heat rash on her chest and neck and face. She found that underneath she was insightful, witty and even cutting. And now it relieved her boredom and provided her righteous anger with a proper channel.

The trouble was, she had no one to try it out on.

The restaurant was empty by the time Leo arrived for his evening meal, having taken his time unpacking and freshening up with customary fastidiousness. He was glad; he wanted some time alone, to focus only upon fine dining and a bottle of robust Burgundy. It was a magnificent cliché of a traditional Scottish dining room, the walls adorned with the heraldry of various local clans, some tasteful Highland landscapes and the inevitable deer-head trophies. A welcoming fire crackled in the hearth and a Scottish longcase clock tick-tocked reassuringly.

Leo sat between a baby grand piano and a window which looked out onto the black yonder, his back facing the rest of the room, indicating his desire for privacy should any diners tardier than himself arrive.

He ordered a Campari and soda as an *apéritif*, and politely requested a fresh knife – the existing one was slightly spotted. He started with some exquisite Oban scallops with braised pig's cheek, followed by mock turtle soup, braised halibut, and then saddle of venison in a beetroot and sloe gin jelly, all washed down with a bottle of 2006 Chambertin. It was a satisfying repast, so much so that he didn't quibble over the fact that the meat had been cut slightly too thinly such that it had lost its optimally gamey flavour. He abjured dessert for some Hebridean Blue cheese before ordering his espresso and Cognac. While he was waiting he savoured the powerful fruity structures of his last mouthful of wine. Leo remembered too well the 1960s. The last days of old Glasgow. The end of old poverty and the shame of the slums. Spam on the dinner table, strips of the *Evening Citizen* on a nail, a shaft of morning sunlight through a dirty window pane revealing peeling Edwardian wallpaper. Yet he was proud of his humble origins. Proud of the stoical and dignified way his parents had borne the struggle brought about by his father's chronic illness. Proud of the values and manners and culture that had been instilled in him which so greatly outweighed material possessions in a world in which every ha'penny had to be accounted for. It all made him more appreciative of the finer things in life now that he could afford them. He signed the bill to his room and unfolded a crisp ten-pound note for the Polish waitress on account of her pretty smile.

He wandered towards the bar, past the splendid drawing room with floor-to-ceiling windows which during daylight hours afforded grand views of the lawns and the loch beyond. Leo felt recharged and ready for social intercourse. Like the other rooms in the hotel the bar was furnished and decorated in solid Caledonian style, and Leo noted a mini humidor with approval. The place was empty of patrons but for a trio of hard-drinking newspapermen huddled together around a corner table. Bill Minto was on duty.

'No rest for the wicked,' joked Leo lamely, after ordering a Rob Roy – dry, no cherry.

'No, indeed.' Minto smiled, partaking only of a lime cordial at Leo's pleasure.

He was a clean, somewhat cowed man, who smelled of Pears soap and wore steel-rimmed spectacles and a zipper cardigan, and his remaining white hair clipped short. Leo speculated that his only vice was the occasional half pint of real ale (he was wrong – Minto was teetotal). Yet Leo couldn't help liking him and soon unearthed a bit of his background. The defining period of his life occurred after he had been called up for National Service. Expecting an easy, boring couple of years of half-hearted manoeuvres in Aldershot and the Rhineland, instead he found himself in some godforsaken, frozen valley in Korea, being used by Chinese riflemen for target practice. He returned from the peninsula singed and shaken by friendly-fire napalm but unbowed, until his harridan of a wife inexorably ground down his spirit (not that Minto expressed himself in such overt language). He slaved away for years as an actuary for a commercial financier, then as a wine importer, finally as a hotel entrepreneur, and he was still slaving away in that capacity today.

Minto and his wife had bought the Loch Dhonn when it was crumbling to a slow death. It had been owned by a pair of English alcoholics whose attempts at maintaining or improving the hotel came in occasional half-hearted spurts amid an ocean of gin. Things came to a head after the man of the house befriended members of a quite popular progressive rock band, who had travelled to the area in order to get in touch with their folk roots as they struggled to write the traditionally difficult third album. After one evening of particularly indulgent revelry, the hotelier decided it would be a grand idea for the boys to expand their consciousnesses by experiencing the haunting night mists of the loch, and promptly rowed the entire band, replete with assorted folk instruments, into the middle of the water. The trouble was that they were all high on a heady cocktail of Courvoisier brandy and cocaine, and the band's renowned bass player, who had earlier been mainlining the narcotic, stood up in a fit of hubris, lost his balance, toppled into the water and was promptly drowned by the weight of the hurdy-gurdy he had strapped over his shoulder, an instrument he had thus far singularly failed to master. As the years wore on increasing numbers of the drowned bassist's fans would make pilgrimage to the hotel, bolstering the coffers. Enterprising local businesspeople created a mythology that his spectre could be seen hovering above the loch at the same hour he had perished. Bogles are great for tourism, but the initial impact upon the hoteliers was one of shame. Therefore, not long after the tragedy the Mintos bought the Loch Dhonn for a song, and Shona's grand plan swung into action. The progressive new owners took a hands-on approach, renovating and extending the building, and rediscovering its grand interior. Marcel, a down-at-heel but brilliant chef from Grenoble, was unleashed upon the newly installed Falcon gas range with dramatic results. He was fired by his domineering mistress after six months over 'culinary differences', but the hotel's gastronomic reputation had been secured, and was subsequently maintained by a succession of low-paid Gallic magicians whose skills became the stuff of legend and helped upgrade the establishment from a two, to a three, then a four-starred attraction. This funded the purchase and renovation of Ardchreggan House, a derelict stately home on the loch's western shore. After the fall of the Berlin Wall came the availability of cheap, willing tradesmen from the east, and that house was re-imagined as an exclusive spa retreat with an exquisite art deco bar as its centrepiece, a monument to the Mintos' growing fortune which earned them the nickname 'the Minteds'. There wasn't resentment as such, just mild envy; Bill and Shona weren't locals but they were Scots, and even if he was just a Lowlander at least they weren't 'white settlers' who had sold up a terraced house in the south east of England during the Thatcher property boom and bought a castle up north.

In spite of all this auspicious enterprise Bill hinted at his quiet desperation. Somewhere along the way he and his wife had lost sight of the original purpose of their ambitions. He was an old man, for goodness' sake. His pals had retired a decade ago. Yet here were he and Shona, childless and increasingly disconnected from each other, slaving away. And for what, exactly?

Leo and Minto's chat turned to the hotelier's extensive wine cellar, which he promised his guest a tour of, before they were then interrupted by the influx of the usual evening suspects, two of them, anyway.

Leo's antennae detected one was a malt whisky bore and so, in an effort to avoid a conversation about 'peatiness', he quickly pretended to study a wall map of the Inner Hebrides while the man deliberated over the top shelf. Once he had been served, Leo attempted to return to his conversation with Minto, but the fellow interrupted with overbearing gregariousness. He introduced himself as Lex Dreghorn with a crushing handgrip, and immediately proceeded to dominate the conversation. He was approximately fifty years old, a handsome man, Leo grudgingly noted, who actually suited his baldness, with tanned, outdoors skin and sparkling blue eyes. He was dressed in a tired-looking pea jacket, and at his side was a bonny Border Collie, perhaps a conversation piece to draw the pretty ladies in. Dreghorn was someone who had cultivated his own self-mythology, readily informing the company that he was 'easily bored', or in some way nonconformist, adventurous or ruggedly individualistic. 'No mortgage, no pension, no health insurance; all I have is the shirt on my back – but that's the way I like it.' He was a former Royal Navy sailor, and he told self-glorifying yarns of saloon bar disputes in various ports around the globe in which he was never the instigator, and always the victor.

Leo guessed that Dreghorn was in fact a rather cynical man, a barfly wearied by the world's failure to realise his greatness. Occasionally witty, but not as witty as he thought he was. He was indeed a failure, nowadays eking his living out of various illegal and barely legal practices.

The pretty Polish waitress who had served Leo at dinner walked through the bar to fetch her coat.

'Hey, beautiful!' called out Dreghorn. 'When are ye gonnae marry me?'

The waitress flashed a smile as she walked out, to where a constable was waiting to accompany her to the staff quarters, which lay a couple of hundred yards down an unlit lane.

'Boy, does she love the bold Lex!' Dreghorn confided conspiratorially in the third person. 'Well, she's got to, I suppose.' He grinned.

Leo doubted that she did, in fact, have to.

Dreghorn was accompanied by a local labourer by the name of Robbie McKee, a phlegmatic man aged approximately thirty with a big dome of prematurely receding black hair. He had unshaven, fleshy jowls, a pug nose and an upturned chin. He had hands the size of hams, strong arms and a powerful chest, but a beer gut flopped over his beltless jeans. He wore a faintly medicated air and Leo wondered if he was ninepence short of a shilling, yet there was an anxious edge to him which was a little unsettling. He smelled strongly of testosterone and too many cigarettes. His and Dreghorn's clothes were soiled from some manual job. McKee had let Dreghorn buy him a pint of heavy, with which he had washed down a pill from a little vial he carried.

Next to arrive was the type of individual Leo generally detested: a posh Anglicised Scot, who was dressed in trews, a tweed hunting jacket and a canary-yellow flat cap. He removed this last item to reveal thinning blond hair that barely covered his skull, which, like Leo's, was on the large side. His small grey eyes were rather closely set. His chin and belly had been expanded by too much good wine and rich food, and this, combined with his shortish stature, lent him a portly bearing.

Leo refused to be cowed by these Crawfords and Torquils from Edinburgh, with their Hooray Henry accents, their unconscious sense of entitlement and their big, tartan-clad arses which had got fat on the back of the Act of Union and the slave trade.

'Hello, Fordyce Greatorix,' said Posh Boy, offering his hand.

Fordyce? Bloody hell!

'Leo Moran,' Leo replied tepidly, performing a perfunctory handshake.

'Very pleased to meet you. Always grand to see a new face up here. Can I get you a dram?'

Leo, whose glass was empty, was blindsided by the offer, and couldn't think of a reason to refuse it. 'That's most kind. I'll have a J&B and soda with you, thank you.'

'Two large J&Bs and soda if you please, Bill, and one for yourself, and whatever these chaps are having,' said Fordyce, with a pleasant smile.

In fact Fordyce, who was the hotel's resident bachelor whom DI Lang had mentioned, proved to be a perfect gentleman: beautifully mannered, diffident and happy to take a back seat in the conversation. He enjoyed the company, and was fastidious in making eye contact with all present when he did speak, even the humble yeoman McKee.

Gosh, he seems a really nice, straightforward bloke, thought Leo guiltily, twenty minutes or so after the man's arrival. He inwardly chastised himself for his prejudiced initial reaction. *You're* the snob, Leo Moran – an inverted one. He tuned back into the conversation, grimacing as he endured Dreghorn's chat, which had evolved into a particularly boring tale about how he had been 'the best physical specimen his petty officer had ever seen'. Once he had finished, Leo managed to turn proceedings around to the murder, and subtly enquired as to who, if anyone, the assembled suspected.

Fordyce was for once eager to speak. 'Oh, it wouldn't have been anyone local, old man. Folk round here are decent; fine, fine people. We're a lovely, peaceful community up here in Loch Dhonn – just ask any of these chaps. No, whoever did this . . . unspeakable thing was an interloper. Some madman who came across our little corner of paradise and shattered it with their wickedness.'

'That's about the size of it,' agreed Minto.

'But the police must have their suspects?' suggested Leo.

'The lassie's boyfriend is in the jail,' said Dreghorn, gesturing towards the gantry at a framed photograph of a smiling youth with a buzz cut holding a massive trout.

'He's not in the jail,' protested Minto. 'He was released without charge. He's staying at his mother's in Glasgow, attending the police station voluntarily.'

'And it wasn't Craig,' interjected Fordyce firmly. 'That poor young man wouldn't have harmed a hair on Helen's head. The stoutest of fellows!'

'Well, the cops must be interviewing him for *something*,' remarked Dreghorn, with a sly, suggestive look on his face.

'Is he the only suspect?' asked Leo, liking Dreghorn less and less as the evening unfolded.

'I heard they paid thon James Millar another visit,' said Dreghorn.

'Who's he?' asked Leo, feigning ignorance.

'A bloody freak o' nature, that's what he is.'

'Lex, I really must protest,' said Fordyce. 'James is a rattling good chap, a gentle soul who's had more to cope with than any man ever ought. He's not a freak by any stretch of the imagination.'

'What – biding a' the way up at yon Witch's Cauldron on his ain like Ben Gunn?'

'It takes all sorts,' proposed Minto.

'The Witch's Cauldron?' enquired Leo.

'It's a hollow, a natural shelter further up Glen Fallasky,' explained Fordyce. 'Poor James is something of a hermit. His wife died tragically some years ago, and he has never been the same. He became more and more withdrawn. He took to camping out in all weathers, in remote places. The laird – Lady Audubon-MacArthur – took pity on him and permitted him to build a blackhouse on her land. James is accomplished at drystane dyking, and he constructed it with his own hands, from local materials. He has lived there ever since, and only ventures down here on occasion, during daylight at any rate. It was he who found poor Helen's body.'

'And there's Bosco,' snorted Dreghorn. 'If the polis are looking for a prime suspect they'd better start talking to him.'

'Who's Bosco?' asked Leo.

'The Grey Lady's footman,' said Minto.

'The Grey Lady?'

'That's what we call the laird,' said Dreghorn. 'Another bloody oddity if ye ask me. Keeps herself to herself, *don't you know*, does her ladyship.'

'Now, Lex, that's not fair, Lady Audubon-MacArthur is a fine woman,' started Fordyce, but Dreghorn blustered on, ignoring him.

'She owns a' the land above the clachan, a' the way to the Fallasky–Oban road. And plenty mair besides. She stays up in the big hoose; ye'll see the gates on yer way south. She seldom deigns to pay us peasants doon here a visit, is that no' right, Robbie?'

The taciturn McKee grunted in vague agreement, then said, 'They say she's a spaewife,' in a strange, guttural voice.

'So, what about this Bosco individual?'

'He's a Malteser,' said McKee.

'Pardon?'

'It means he's from Malta.' Dreghorn laughed loudly and derisively.

Leo swallowed his pride along with a gulp of whisky soda, choosing not to correct the error. Despite his buying an unreciprocated round of drinks and his best attempt at the pally Columbo routine, the wiseacre Dreghorn had already chosen to dislike this Glaswegian intruder, concerned that he might in some way pose a threat to his position as local character-in-chief.

'But he doesnae speak a word,' Dreghorn continued. 'He's corned beef, a mute. Aged about forty-five. They say he's shagging her ladyship.' Fordyce groaned. 'A big, strapping heifer he is too . . . could snap a wee lassie like Helen Addison in two.'

'Lex, *please*!'

'Oh, come on, Fordyce. Don't say ye havenae wondered. Him being sent away to Glasgow just after Helen was killed. Awfy suspicious, don't ye think?'

'Lex, you don't have a shred of evidence against him. Not a shred. This is all conjecture, and I don't think it's helping things at all.'

'Ach, a' I can say is that the next time I see Bosco I'm gonnae hand him a pencil and a piece o' paper. And if he doesnae start writing, telling me where he was that night, I'll need to go to work on him wi' old southpaw,' announced Dreghorn, rubbing the knuckles of his left hand. 'And while I'm on the subject, I'll pay thon Millar a visit too. Find out what he was doing daundering around at that time o' night.'

'James often goes out walking at night when there's nobody around,' said Fordyce.

'Hardly normal behaviour, is it?'

Eventually the conversation lulled, and the impecunious Dreghorn and McKee, realising that neither Leo nor Fordyce was going to fund their drinking campaign any longer, sloped off home.

Bill Minto retired to bed, happy to entrust the bar to Leo and Fordyce, both of whom had begun to slur their words. They partook of a couple of whisky macs as a nightcap, and Leo's final addition to his chitty was for a Montecristo No. 1 which he had liberated from the humidor. The next day he would dimly recall lecturing his new and politely forbearing drinking buddy about the essence of the class system, before Fordyce had bid him goodnight and then stumbled off, pleasantly greeting a suit of armour he had mistaken for a hotel employee before ascending the stairs.

Leo, who had borrowed Fordyce's topcoat, smiled to himself, then stepped outside to trim and light his cigar, the cold, misty air suggesting to him how drunk he was. He noticed a squad car parked up ahead, the hunched silhouettes of two coppers inside, sipping from a flask of hot coffee. Leo nodded vaguely in their direction, then walked round the hotel's gravel apron so that he could get a view of the loch. The waning gibbous moon and a couple of police arc lamps lit his way. The rear of the building faced the loch, the bar's locked glass doors leading onto a grand terrace with a stone balustrade and high arches of white-painted metal lacework which clung to the hotel's granite walls. Leo savoured the thick, sweet-flavoured tobacco and decided to stroll down some worn steps to a lawn, which was dotted with classical statues, and then through some trees towards the water, which was still a good few hundred yards away. He paused at a charming Victorian folly which was covered in moss. His smoke had gone out so he relit it, bent down to bury the match in a patch of soil, then straightened up and looked skywards.

The ghost of Helen Addison sat on the parapet of the folly, her nightdress translucent in the moonlight. She smiled down at him.

II

GLASGOW

4

THE day after Leo had awoken from his first vision, Stephanie had visited him at home.

She breezed in gallusly, small but self-assured, glowing with beauty and experience, her chin set at its permanently pugnacious angle. She was wearing a fragrance he had almost certainly never heard of, a stylish faux-fur coat, and new, multi-toned hair. It occurred to Leo that he wasn't actually sure of her natural colouring.

'How's the man flu?'

'It was a wretched bout, but the worst of it has passed and I believe I will see out the winter after all. I'm not given to complaining, but I am left with a persistent rasping cough – a consequence of too many cigarettes in my youth – and I am also stricken by a peculiar insomnia which afflicts me towards the end of an illness, despite my fatigue. Only a good deal of alcohol can coax me off to sleep.'

Stephanie would never tell him, but she always enjoyed Leo's rich, resonant, educated West of Scotland baritone. While his voice was subtly authoritative, hers was husky and consequently quite sexy.

'Well, after that speech I think you'll be glad to hear I've brought you some medicine.' She held up a litre bottle of J&B, then tossed it towards Leo, who just managed to clutch it to his breast.

'Thank you. Most kind.'

She shrugged off her coat and casually cast it onto one of Leo's sofas, then followed her host into the dining room. She fetched two Waterford crystal tumblers from the sideboard.

'Would you care for some supper?'

'I've had my tea, thank you.'

'Do you mind if I . . .'

'Not at all.'

He sat down at the table to finish his evening meal. She regarded the remains of tinned stew and tinned potatoes on his plate, which was illuminated rather absurdly by candlelight and accompanied by a half-eaten buttered slice of plain bread which sat by itself on a side plate. Her working-class-come-good unrestraint contrasted with this clerkish frugality, the impression of which was accentuated by the meagre coal fire glowing weakly in the grate.

'Why don't you splash out on some decent grub? The war's over, didn't you hear?'

'Oh, believe me, Stephanie, I indulge myself most extravagantly from time to time.' This was true. Leo's spells of proletarian puritanism were merely occasional intervals between extended culinary binges, and he favoured acquiescence to the contradictions that nestle within every man's soul. 'You must have forgotten that I can be quite the *gastronome*, quite the *bon vivant*. Indeed, I recall this dreadful little usurer with whom I was once slightly acquainted. He was one of those vulgar *nouveau-riche* types who measure people's merit entirely by their income, and he let it be widely known that he was well remunerated by whichever counting house it was that employed him.'

'You're *nouveau-riche* yourself,' observed Stephanie.

'True, but I am not vulgar. Anyway, on one occasion he accused me of being a champagne socialist. I simply agreed with him, replying, "Indeed, why should the Tories get all the champagne?" He was quite dumb-founded. And yet, while I enjoy the finer things in life, I also believe that one must experience the humble, precisely in order to then properly appreciate the sublime. And so, for tonight, this is perfectly adequate, thank you very much. Particularly with a nice bit of piccalilli on the side.'

Yet it was with feigned relish that he returned to his plate.

'Bugger adequate, live a little,' said Stephanie, walking towards the kitchen to fetch some ice. 'You remind me of my late grandfather. You'd make a good old-school Prod. You're so puritanical.'

She retrieved the ice tray from the freezer compartment in Leo's refrigerator, and stopped to regard the plain white label of the empty tin that was lying on the counter: *EEC Surplus. Stewed Beef in Gravy. Use by 09/92.*

'Yuck – that stuff's *years* out of date!' she exclaimed, when she returned to the dining room.

Leo set aside his plate and cutlery with a clatter. 'Stephanie, one of the few consolations of bachelorhood is that I get to eat precisely what I choose, when I choose. And anyway, I abhor waste while there are people starving in the world. And did you know the US Army estimates that tinned food is good for a hundred years?'

'Why ration yourself, that's what I say. We could all be dead tomorrow,' Stephanie replied as she dropped the cubes into the glasses. She poured two shots of the whisky and squirted in some soda water from a siphon. She stood behind Leo and began massaging his shoulders. 'For example, did you know that fucking is *such* an invigorating part of life?'

Leo shrugged off her hands, resenting her teasing him. 'I can assure you I am quite uninterested in your mad pilgrimage of the flesh,' he declared, before downing half his Scotch and soda in one gulp.

'It's a pity you aren't so temperate when it comes to the sauce.'

'The greater the man, the greater the weakness.'

'What's so great about being a boozehound?'

Leo didn't respond.

'I think you need to get out more. There's an opening night at GoMA we should go to. It's this mad minimalist video installation by this *über* art school grad. There's a wicked Detroit techno DJ on after.'

'How *dreadful!*'

'Come on, you can't keep moping up here like Miss Havisham.'

'I go out often.'

'Oh, really. Where to?'

'I went to an Association Football match last month, at Celtic Park.'

'Why do you say things like "Association Football"? Why not just say "football"? It's just that people might take you for a complete pompous ass.'

He ignored her remark and proceeded to paint a false picture as to the extent of his exploits. 'I go to galleries, to the cinema, to concerts, to the lunchtime organ recital at Kelvingrove Museum. In November I took the tour of the City Chambers – marblework of magnificence I've not seen outside Italy.'

'Yes, but you go with your mother, or by yourself. You've been single for far too long. You should try and meet someone nice. You're a reasonable catch. You're not *bad*-looking, and you possess *some* charms.'

'Damned with faint praise indeed!'

'Oh, come on. What I mean is that you're an asshole, but you're not an entirely unlovable asshole.'

'That's better,' he said, draining his glass. 'I'm afraid it is too late for me,' he added a little mournfully. 'One becomes inured to solitude. Do you know what I realised the other day? That I am nearer to the traditional male retirement threshold than I am to the age of thirty. Can you *imagine*?'

'You're not old,' she sighed as she plonked herself down on a chair. 'You're just no fun any more. And I would suggest you retired years ago.'

'When was I ever fun?'

'At uni.'

'At university people were drawn to me because I was brilliant, not because I was fun.'

'You could easily meet someone. You don't know what you're missing. And I'm not just talking about the bedroom. I'm talking about having a partner. An ally. Someone to share your troubles with.' Stephanie splashed some more Scotch into his glass, then a long spurt of soda. 'I mean your . . . gift. It must take its toll,' she ventured.

'It is a burden I bear without complaint,' Leo said serenely.

'I imagine you haven't had much opportunity to employ it. In a practical way, I mean.'

'On the contrary.'

'Well, give me an example. You never seem to talk about it.'

'Modesty forbids.'

'Oh, go on!'

'Well, there was the case of the Monday Murders. It occurred during the period in which you and I had . . . lost touch. I was of some considerable assistance to the CID. Do you happen to know a Detective Frank Carolan?'

'Yes, yes, I remember. Your name was leaked to the papers. But your involvement was denied completely by the polis. What else?'

'Well, most of my other work has been for private clients. For example, I found a young man once. He had fallen out with his parents and buggered off down south. He had written a letter to tell them he was safe and well, but someone had forgotten to post it. I kept "seeing" him outside this effete café in Brighton. Locating him was rather straightforward, actually; I recognised the charming late-Georgian architecture.'

'Did it pay well?'

'You think I do it for the money?' Leo snapped.

'No. But did it pay well?'

'It paid sod all. They were poor people who were worried sick about their son.'

'So, how come you don't need to work? After all, a joint like this doesn't come cheap,' Stephanie said with a sweeping gesture of her arm towards the lavish interior of Leo's apartment.

He poured a further dose of J&B into his glass, unimpressed by the alcohol-to-soda ratio his friend had served up. Fair play to Stephanie, he thought. She always brings the decent stuff.

He got up and walked through the arch into the drawing room, his silk Paisley dressing gown swishing over his clothes. He sat down in his rattan chair, facing the window with his back to her. The room was shadowy, lit only by firelight and two beautiful Tiffany table lamps with leaded, coloured-glass shades. He took a long sip before speaking. 'There was another case. A wealthy family; their daughter had gone AWOL. It involved quite extensive travelling on the Continent. The case put a great strain upon me, for various reasons, both physically and metaphysically. Thankfully, it had a happy conclusion, and the family were most grateful.' He coughed slightly. 'And generous.'

'How much?'

Leo didn't reply but simply smiled sedately.

'Typical bloody Scotsman: never wants to let folk know how much he's got.'

'Let's just say it was enough to provide a stipend sufficient to protect a creature of my sensitivity from the rigours of labour.'

'I thought socialists were supposed to extol the dignity of work.'

Leo took another sip. It was at this point that he discussed with Stephanie his intention to visit Loch Dhonn.

'You likely won't be made welcome, regardless of how long you delay it,' she concluded.

He gazed out of the window pensively for a while. A Japanese Imari vase sat proudly on a shisham table, a defiant splash of colour in the face of the louring Glasgow winter a pane's thickness away. To his annoyance, out of the corner of his eye he noticed a rogue sliver of wallpaper that had unstuck itself. Impatiently, he stood up and tried in vain to paste it back with whisky and soda. Stephanie came through the arch with the bottle, to regard the windswept scene with him.

'Heavens release us from this ghastly weather!' said Leo, dabbing his nose with a linen handkerchief he had produced from a pocket. 'I often think I should follow the example of the Victorian gentlemen who would take laudanum and go into hibernation for the winter.'

'At least it'll be February soon.'

'Actually, in a way I prefer January.'

'Really?'

'Yes. For all its tumult, at least it is an honest month. February is a pretentious month.'

'What *are* you talking about?'

'February has delusions of early spring. It lulls you in, then kicks you in the you-know-whats with a bloody snowstorm. When January bequeaths a splendid, sunny day – which it occasionally does – one feels truly blessed.'

Stephanie topped up his glass again. It was time to broach the subject she had come to discuss. 'So, did you read my note then?'

'Yes.'

'And, *will* you help?'

'It's not something I can turn on like a tap. And anyway, I lack . . . empathy for your predicament.'

'And why is that?'

'I believe . . . I *know* that you have been unfaithful to him, too. I fail to see why Jamie's indiscretions should be uncovered in a blaze of self-righteousness, while your own unconscionable behaviour remains a secret.'

'That's low.'

'I hardly see why.'

'To cast up that one time. Jamie and I had barely met.'

Oddly, Leo hadn't actually been referring to their night together. It did often loom large in his mind, but he had momentarily forgotten about it and its massive pertinence to the current conversation. Leo disliked Jamie, and even though he regretted his transgression with Stephanie, not only on moral grounds, sometimes he spitefully hoped that the handsome sod suspected he had slept with her.

He took a few paces, then ventured, 'But that wasn't the only time, was it?' Stephanie made an exclamation of protest, but Leo rounded on her. 'Well, deny it then. Deny that you haven't been intimate with at least one other man while you were in a relationship with Jamie.'

She slumped into the rattan chair, defeated by his challenge. She resented Leo when he was judgemental like this. He had become so despondent, so devoid of passion that he couldn't begin to understand. Couldn't understand that sometimes stuff just happens. Her concern about Jamie was that something *serious* had developed with someone he had met down in London, where he spent so much time working. Or, perhaps even worse, that nothing had happened, and that her husband's recent withdrawn state was because he had simply grown tired of her.

She sighed, aware of her hypocrisy, aware of how flimsy her argument would sound to a third party. She'd had to try hard to get to where she was in life. All was effort, from filing off the rough edges of her Lanarkshire accent to seeking therapy when her self-esteem had been low. And as for study! She was testament to the egalitarian Scottish educational system which had been extended to the lass as well as the lad o' pairts, to the ethos that if you endeavoured enough you would gain your just rewards, no matter what your background. She had known Leo during her initial Arts papers: Early Medieval European History and the Philosophy of the Enlightenment (a memory flashed through her mind: the autumn light flooding through the stained glass of the tutorial room, her friend eviscerating an obnoxious young doctor with his superior grasp of Hume's religious critique). Later, she had resolved to do her LLB. She was going to succeed. To do something with her life. To make a difference. Nothing was going to stop her. She would take full advantage of the opportunities previous generations of women had been denied. And what had *he* achieved, exactly? Eased to the inevitable First, every avenue open to him, then drifted from one dead end job to . . . to doing nothing at all! Riven by morbidity and introspection because of some medieval outlook. Now she was rightfully reaping the fruits of her labours, and putting bad guys behind bars, to boot. She loved her life these days, and she hadn't always loved it. And she loved her pleasures. Sometimes Leo could be so bloody sanctimonious. Why should she allow a curmudgeon such as him to make her feel shame? Yet, drawn as she was to his intelligence and the rich seam of humanity that resided beneath his dyspeptic exterior, somehow he still managed it. Or perhaps the shame already lurked within her, and Leo had merely shone a light on it.

'It's not as simple as you make out,' she replied sulkily. 'Everything's so black and white in your pious Catholic world. I can't relate to it.'

'And neither is your world – or rather your situation – one I can or wish to relate to.'

'Wish to.'

'It would be an inappropriate use of my talents. It is impossible to explain. I cannot hope to make you understand.'

'Thanks for the favour, pal.'

'Don't be like that.'

'You know what your problem is, Leo?'

'No, but I've got a funny feeling you're about to fill me in.'

'You're a coward.'

'Gosh, that's a new one!'

'You're cowardly and proud. You're so afraid of rejection that you would rather spend eternity alone than take a risk. The only love you are capable of is for these fucking *trinkets*,' she said, indicating Leo's richly ornamented abode. She stood up, grabbed her coat and headed for the door. 'Enjoy what's left of your whisky,' she added.

He made to shout something unkind after her but fortunately the words caught in his throat. On her way out she left the front door open, and almost immediately regretted the childishness of the act.

Pompous ass, she thought.

Leo strode into the hall and slammed the door angrily at Stephanie's descending footsteps. He flicked the Bakelite switch up to leave the lobby in darkness. He brought some more ice from the kitchen and went into the dining room, fumbled at the back of a drawer in the sideboard, and produced his late father's leather cigarette case, which contained the cherished items that had slowly killed him. Apart from allowing himself the occasional cigar, Leo had officially quit smoking years ago, but he petulantly lit one of the fags from the table lighter in the drawing room, piled a quantity of ice into his tumbler and drowned it in Scotch. He sat in the rattan chair and watched the rain drive in from the North Atlantic. The cigarette tip glowed orange in the gloom. The smoke was noxious and caustic to his inflamed lungs, but he inhaled it anyway.

All had come so easily to her, he thought bitterly. Good looks, a natural way with people, easy confidence. Everything laid out. Never a doubt in her pretty head.

He sank the Scotch, then went to the kitchen and took a large bottle of milk stout from the refrigerator. He sat on one of his oxblood sofas and used the stout to chase down another half gill of whisky. He gazed around his apartment, furnished in an elegant, old-fashioned style; a stubborn redoubt against the forces of modernity.

'I'm drinking myself sober,' he said out loud. He was mildly amused at the blunt sound of his voice breaking the oppressive silence. 'I'm drinking myself sober,' he said again.

He regarded the raindrops drearily running down the window pane. He became aware of the sound of the wind scouring the back courts. His sulk started to give way to creeping doubts.

Perhaps he *was* craven. Perhaps he had developed a problem with intimacy. Incredible as it would have seemed to his younger self, he increasingly considered the very notion of a relationship, of sharing one's time and space with another human being, as wholly an inconvenience.

As well as drinking more and more he seemed to become more misanthropic with each passing week, trapped within the prison of his own subjectivity. The simple truth – of which Leo was dimly aware – was that he was too often alone with his thoughts, and too willing to follow them into convoluted, futile ruminations, like a traveller who is led into the quagmire by jack-o'-lanterns. For some reason numerous memories of ancient humiliations and sufferings had surfaced of late, wounds which kept him awake at night brooding with resentment. And these thoughts then made him feel isolated and inadequate. Could there be anyone else in the known universe who wasted their time in such an ignoble fashion?

He worried that he was now set in his ways and had come too much to appreciate his home comforts. More and more he preferred his own company, talking loudly in long conversations with himself or shouting grumpily at the wireless during the news. He would often amuse himself with different words or phonetic sounds, even staring at his reflection in a mirror while he mouthed exaggeratedly,

'Unterseeboot . . . unterwasserboot . . . unterwasserbooten . . . unterwassermaschine . . . hunterwassermaschinen . . . hunterhosenmaschinen . . . hunterpantenmaschinen . . . hunterpantenwassermaschinen . . .'

Perhaps he was just plain bored.

Despite his outward air of imperturbability and flamboyance he actually felt a growing desire to withdraw from the world, and often made excuses for not leaving the flat or else carefully planned each trip in order that he could chalk off as many tasks as possible in one go. He would invite old Arnstein, an antiquarian bookseller with whom he was acquainted, up to play chess at his apartment, rather than meeting him at the tearoom in Otago Lane or at the Star and Garter in Garscube Road. He no longer visited the Billiards Hall at the University Union for a few frames of snooker, and he had let lapse his membership of a famous Victorian bath house in Woodlands. There, he used to luxuriate in the torpidity of the ornate Turkish suite, stark naked but for his plum velvet smoking cap, gesticulating expansively as he engaged in stimulating social intercourse beneath the spangled dome. Or he would lounge on a draperied daybed in the cool room and read the newspapers, passing languid comment to acquaintances upon the day's affairs. Nowadays, he barely went to so much as the supermarket, unless it was a time when he knew it would be quietest. When a Waitrose had opened nearby he had rejected it outright, ostensibly out of loyalty to his usual Sainsbury's, but really because he was allergic to change. Indeed, sometimes he was so disinclined to venture outside that he would telephone Sanjeev's Dairy and get the eponymous proprietor to send his son up with a boxful of groceries. He could volunteer for the Society of Saint Vincent de Paul or the Mountain Bothies Association, but something always held him back. For this self-quarantine was a recurring habit and the spells of gregariousness ephemeral, a process which Leo blamed on the increasing uncouthness of the modern world, but its origins actually lay in his avoidance of catcalls and suspicious glances after a false accusation had been levelled against him a long time ago. He knew his fear was by now irrational, but trauma embeds itself so deep as to become reflexive. Therefore, even all these years later part of him still feared that business being dredged up again in some chance encounter on the street, and though he generally prided himself on being immune to other people's opinions of him, that specific allegation retained the latent power to cut him to the marrow.

However, Leo remained resolute in going out to attend to his solemn duties: Mass and visiting his mother, who had taken a bad turn a few years back. He had suggested that they share a house, but she had demonstrated an independent spirit similar to that of her son, and maintained a degree of autonomy by opting for sheltered housing. She also held out hope that Leo might still meet someone and marry, and she didn't want to cramp his style.

He was going to have to snap out of this mode sharpish, now that a new case had arrived for him to solve. And anyway, ensconcing himself at home brought only a temporary sense of security. As Leo knew only too well, all it meant was that reality would be harder to face up to when it arrived. So when he did go out he checked things anxiously – the fire, the gas hob, the electric heater, the front door mortise – again and again. And why did humming 'Happy Birthday to you' twice, as was recommended, when washing his hands after visiting the lavatory not suffice to assassinate all the little germs? No, he had to hum it *four bloody times*! He obsessively kept the flat clean and tidy, with everything just so. In a misplaced orgy of *feng shui*, ornaments now even had to face a precise direction. Stocks of all provisions were assiduously maintained, as though there was about to be a nuclear attack. He was a Scotsman of Irish blood, yet where was his Celtic passion? What had happened to his spontaneity, his poetry, his romance? My goodness, how had he become so governed by rules, so cold and sterile?

Yet his time wasn't entirely wasted. He read copiously. He listened to the live concerts on Radio 3, despite disapproving of that station's diminished adventurousness as it chased listener ratings. He wrote (in elegant but flawed penmanship – an art he had to relearn after his hands were damaged) letters to MPs, chastising them for their abandonment of socialist economic policies, or to foreign tyrants politely requesting the release of political prisoners or an end to torture, and signed fat cheques for various good causes. And at least now, unlike back then, during his disintegration, he could live with and largely enjoy his own company, even if the fire in his soul had gone out. Yes, at least simplicity had emerged from the fevered chaos of complexity. Yet clarity had been accompanied by something less palatable. A hardening round the edges, an unarticulated cynicism, a rather unsettling casting off of sentimentality.

He thought again about his sybaritic visitor, his mood towards her having softened slightly. On the face of it, their friendship would have seemed the unlikeliest to endure from those sunlit undergraduate days, because they were very different people in many ways. Yet Stephanie, uniquely, had remained a faithful friend to Leo (if not a faithful wife to

Jamie) during his time in the wilderness, only finally falling away after his umpteenth refusal of her hospital visits. What had become of the rest of their fellow alumni? Conspicuous by their bloody absence. Leo had never once told Stephanie how much he had appreciated her concern, her compassion. He could just have said, 'Thanks for your kindness back then, and I'm sorry I told the nurse to ask you to go away. I simply couldn't face visitors.' He counted them. Twenty-four little words. Twenty-four. But that would have meant bringing up the whole hellish business, and there are aspects to madness best forgotten, that other people needn't ever know of.

'Damn it!' he uttered, as he stubbed out his third cigarette.

At least he had drunk enough to sleep.

The next morning, mercifully, he had no headache, just a nausea sitting in his belly like a familiar friend. His nerves were frayed, but his carnaptiousness returned as the hangover set in and he watched the liver salts fizz up inside the beaker. Stephanie's culpability for last night's conflict was restored entirely. If she was unable to appreciate the delicacy of his talents then that was her problem. He had no say in the matter of whom he could or would not help, anyway.

5

I T was two days later, while at church, that Leo had the next vision.

The morning had started off unremarkably enough. Having forced himself over the threshold, he felt somewhat refreshed at being out and about, although he still felt quite weak as a result of his recent flu bug. He had gone into a little dairy to buy a roll of Victory Vs and a Fry's Orange Cream. An elderly female customer conversed with the overweight woman behind the counter: 'A bloody disgrace so it was, right outside the close, in full view. Knickers at her ankles, him no' caring a jot, as bold as brass!'

'Some folk have nae shame,' muttered the shopkeeper.

Leo felt an odd sensation of lustful envy at this wildly dissolute couple, and then a feeling of self-disgust. He was glad of the forthcoming sacraments. Afterwards, he would visit his mother, then the grave of his father.

A freezing fog had descended which rasped at Leo's lungs like an emery board and gave the city a surreal, ghostly veneer. The odour of boiling tar from a road gang mixed sweetly with the thick atmosphere and Leo had to pause before entering the church as he struggled to clear his chest. A passing gaggle of street kids, who were sharing a cigarette as though in a vain effort to keep warm, mocked his elegant attire – tasteful two-piece charcoal Sunday suit, topcoat and hat, polished leather-soled shoes, scarlet cashmere scarf and pigskin gloves – which contrasted starkly with their inevitable tracksuits.

'Away and play in the traffic,' he suggested to them.

The church, which was not the one Leo usually attended, was a Dumfriesshire red sandstone oblong topped by several glass domes, with a bell tower upon the north-east corner. The façade, although Baroque, was somewhat restrained compared to the richly ornate contents. Leo read the inscription above the entrance: '*Ego sum ostium; per me si quis introierit salvabitur.*' I am the gate; if anyone enters by Me he shall be saved.

He wondered if the inside had been inspired by that of Santa Maria della Vittoria, one of his favourite churches in Rome. Pillars of verd antique from Connemara dominated the nave, the capitals carved ornamentally and painted brilliant gold. Colourful mosaics depicted the Stations of the Cross and certain Celtic saints: Ninian, Kentigern, Patrick and Columba. Beautiful stained-glass representations of New Testament episodes cast a fragile-coloured light into the cold marble gloom of the side aisles. To the right of the altar was a large statue of Saint Joseph (Leo's favourite saint) gently cradling the infant Christ. Of the various side chapels the Lady Chapel was the jewel in the crown. Based on the altar in the Florentine church of San Miniato, its centrepiece was a statue of the Virgin – a faithful reproduction of the Black Madonna of Montserrat – flickering in the light from the two dozen votive candles below. Leo lit one and prayed to Our Lady of Good Success for his forthcoming endeavour. The main altar table and screen were hewn from white marble inlaid with red. The centrepiece was a gold crucifix, set beneath an arch and between two graven pillars. Above this was a semi-dome of emerald green, spangled with silver stars. There were also the words '*Christus Rex et Redemptor Mundi*' and the Greek letters alpha and omega in gold leaf. Above this again was an arch decorated with a mural of the Last Supper. Directly above this was the largest of the church's domes, which had stained-glass depictions of several saints including Augustine, Alphonsus, Aquinas and Ignatius. Elsewhere in the high-vaulted ceiling, exquisitely colourful abstract Eastern-style patterns maintained the Byzantine theme of the domes.

Leo remained kneeling for a while after saying his penance, feeling a palpable sense of calmness and relief, as though a clutch of devils had taken their leave of him. To kneel before another human being and utter one's sins aloud is the ultimate act of humility – and the dark one hates humility more than all the other virtues. And then to be assured that one was forgiven and still unconditionally loved was catharsis beyond catharsis. How palpable the sacraments could feel to him nowadays, a thousand miles from the ritualistic habit of his youth when he would skulk away before the final blessing. And how alive the gospels and Paul's letters, and indeed the psalms, sermons and hymns were to him, offering shards of pure wisdom to soothe some current anxiety so as to seem Providential. He resolved to try harder to make his faith count in his day-to-day life, to truly see Jesus in his fellow man.

The High Mass, with a choir clad in fine purple robes, was sublime. The sermon addressed the Beatitudes, and Leo felt fortified by the steely conviction and intellectual subtlety that only a Jesuit can deliver. Palestrina's *Credo*, the one from the Pope Marcellus Mass, was particularly moving: '*Deum de Deo, lumen de lumine, Deum verum de Deo vero, genitum, non factum . . .*'

Leo considered how Catholicism had bequeathed the world its greatest artistic glories, imbuing an elevated aesthetic sensibility which conduced to moral enlightenment, but as he knelt for the Liturgy of the Eucharist his mind wandered briefly towards more sensual gratifications. He considered how, with his soul cleansed and nourished, he would prove the lie of Stephanie's accusation of austerity. He planned the forthcoming culinary indulgence. *Release the 12oz sirloin from the fridge, season it and let it reach room temperature.* The priests' vestments seemed gloriously vivid, the chasuble of a most gorgeous jade. *Get to the Polish deli before it closes at two, for shallots and tarragon. Oh, and a vanilla pod for the dessert. And a pot of that lovely beluga caviar as a special treat.* The incense smelled heady and delicious, almost intoxicating. *Eggs and butter from Sanjeev's.* The ancient Latin words of the sacred ordinances were like hypnotic poetry. *Liberate the Bourgogne pinot noir – no, the '06 Château Margaux – from the cellar.* He gazed at the candles on the altar. The tongues of flame seemed to merge into a single entity.

An island set upon a lake of black water. A dark figure, its outline broken by robes and wearing crooked, pointed headwear, standing by the shore, features indistinguishable, watching him.

Then a smith wearing a welder's mask, working at a furnace. As the smith toils, Leo senses others nearby, their faces hidden to him. A family devastated by grief. A desperate young man, his heart ripped out by bereavement, falsely accused. Weeping with sorrow and frustration as he languishes in a police station miles from home. Another man, a few years older and slow-witted, drowning in a sea of innuendo yet somehow rendered mute. Suffocated by trickery; panicking, sweating, gasping for breath.

Leo came to, he himself sweating and gasping for breath. He glanced around, glad that he hadn't obviously disturbed anyone, relieved that the vision was over. He inhaled deeply, recovering himself, and focused upon the priest's words.

At that very moment, about forty miles to the north-west as the crow flies, the beast sat among other human beings and aped their decency, moving its head slowly from side to side in feigned sorrow and uttering platitudes of outrage. It was in some way pleasing to witness this portion of the anguish it had inflicted.

The beast wasn't entirely sure how it had come to this. How the poison had drip-dripped into its soul over the years. For most of the time it had been grudgingly willing to live in some semblance of outward peace with the world, to hide the true measure of its cynicism behind a façade, while limiting itself to the occasional act of petty savagery, such as torturing a stray animal or terrifying the living daylights out of an unfortunate street prostitute; just enough to temporarily sate its hatred for humanity.

But failure with women, that was a different matter. That was simply unacceptable.

It was all so clear now. The trap that had been laid. To humiliate it, to provoke its rage. But it would conceal its rage. It would be cunning. It was better than all of them. Stuck-up bitches.

Leo decided that the soundtrack would be the ultimate – the Ninth. Von Karajan, Berliner, 1962, very loud. That treat he granted himself only rarely, for fear of rendering it mundane. As though that was possible. Yet it was a tiny chance he was unwilling to risk.

He reverently withdrew the precious, heavy original pressing from the sleeve, blew a particle of dust from the vinyl, placed it gently upon the 1972 Technics SL-1200 turntable, carefully set the needle and listened to the low murmur of the empty grooves, the tantalising anticipation of the greatest artistic accomplishment in history. Then the opening bars: the unsettling initial key, the hopeful gathering of the following notes and the first burst of sheer splendour. The masterpiece always struck Leo as strange as well as sublime; experimental to the point of *avant garde*. So revolutionary, so modern that it could have been composed yesterday and still have sounded as though it had just arrived from outer space.

He replaced his necktie with a scarlet and mauve Paisley-patterned cravat, poured himself a Ricard and water preprandial, and set to work.

After the caviar *hors d'œuvre* he tackled his version of *moules marin-iere*. A pound of the Loch Fyne blighters which an enterprising fellow in the Carnarvon Bar near St George's Cross (Leo had stopped by for a half-and-a-half on his way home after Mass) had pulled up and sold at a fraction of the tourist shop's price. One or two were a wee bit gritty, but who cares when they are wild and excellent? Leo steamed them open with butter, wild garlic (which he had picked from the banks of the Kelvin the previous May and frozen), finely chopped shallots, flat-leaf parsley, a bay leaf, the juice of a whole lime and a generous slug of Frascati. He drank the remainder of the white with the mussels, before attempting his famous (famous to him, at least) *sauce béarnaise*, to top an organically reared steak which he had bought from the local family butcher at no little cost, served *saignant* after having been momentarily seared above a terrifying heat. He served this with creamed potatoes, glazed carrots, asparagus and baby onions. He gazed at his reproduction of *La Belle Ferronnière* as he masticated, while Beethoven stormed heaven from the next room.

'And so the ascetic becomes the aesthete,' he announced, as he lifted a large glass of Margaux in a toast to an imaginary Stephanie.

He spied his mobile phone, the camera facility of which he had only recently mastered. 'Sod it,' he said, and took a picture of his half-cut self with his food and drink in the foreground and his da Vinci in the back-ground, and text-messaged it to Stephanie with the caption, 'And so the ascetic becomes the aesthete'.

Later, when he had almost finished consuming the dessert he had prepared – *crème brulée*, his favourite – the iconic four-note phrase from the Fifth Symphony's *Allegro con brio* informed Leo that a text had arrived.

'Amazin wot u can get out of a tin these days. When u headin up?' read the reply.

'On the morrow. Can you help me out?' he responded.

But no further message arrived.

For Leo, a good cigar was indispensable to completing an epicurean experience, and so he trimmed his Fonseca and lit it from the applewood (never from butane), having first removed the little paper band, as was decorous. He splashed some 1983 Armagnac he had been saving into a goblet for a perfect *digestif*. He settled into his rattan chair in the drawing room, feeling vaguely foolish at having contacted Stephanie. He checked the photograph he had sent; instead of a suave gourmet he saw a jaded, middle-aged man with a lonely supporting arm outstretched towards the camera, eyes glassy with booze, teeth tinged vampiric crimson with claret and bovine blood.

Something else – an emotional memory – disturbed him. The *sauce béarnaise* had transported him to that stolen, halcyon summer with Maddi in Biarritz.

It felt like a lifetime ago; several lifetimes ago, when anything had seemed possible. How thin in comparison were the flavours of the subsequent eras of his life. Smiling, he closed his eyes and breathed deeply though his nose, as though to drink in the essence of that sacred time, the texture of it, the way it had felt.

They had stayed at the Hotel du Palais, a nineteenth-century grand hotel. How gorgeously the sunlight flooded into their bedchamber in the mornings, he recalled, with the sublime soundtrack of the Atlantic in the background.

They watched the Bastille fireworks from the terrace, sipping vermouth and bitters with an elderly gentleman who had won the Legion of Honour, and his wife, as the scent of honeysuckle drifted up from amid a grove of tamarisk and hydrangea, mixing with the salt air. In a whisper, the man captivated Leo as he described his experiences in the trenches. The endless column of nervously smiling youths clad in unblemished blue serge marching up the Voie Sacrée, France's sacrifice for the altar of Verdun, while in the opposite direction lurched the muddied procession of gas-blinded and shrapnel-maimed.

Leo recited Verlaine's '*Clair de Lune*' as they strolled alongside the Grande Plage in the moonlight, past wonderful *belle époque* villas. She wore a cocktail dress which matched her sable-black hair, and a cream bolero jacket. Her dusky complexion, a result of her part-Indian extraction and browned deeper by the sun, meant that people kept mistaking her for a woman from southern France. She looked like a film star.

Later, at the Barrière, after playing *trente et quarante*, they found themselves at the same roulette table as a real film star, a veteran of French cinema whose kooky charm and simple beauty had not deserted her despite her maturing years. She was rather taken with Maddi, whom she asked to place a large bet for her. Maddi chose *manque* correctly and the actress gave her a one-thousand-franc chip by way of celebration.

Leo and Maddi attended Mass together with various famous émigrés at the splendid Russian Orthodox Church, then visited Albert's, where they ate oysters from their shells which had been cooked in champagne.

They rented a silver cabriolet and drove through the mountains to Lourdes, then over to Pamplona, Bilbao, then the B-roads to Lekeitio and San Sebastian. Prior to recrossing the border they detoured to take in the coast, where they made love beneath a million stars, amid weird, tumorous rock formations by the wine-dark sea.

He had felt so certain that they would spend the rest of their lives together. My goodness, how foolish that misplaced notion made him feel now. Sometimes, in order to torture himself, he imagined an alternate history in which he retained Maddi's heart and also somehow maintained his sanity. But he wondered whether he could have sustained the affair even if he had kept the rudest of mental health; it would inevitably have succumbed to his eccentricities: his obsessive rituals and habits, his tendency to live inside his own head. His drinking.

Following his descent into the abyss, he had been resolute in spurning Maddi's well-intentioned attempts to reach out to him. That was for other, feeble men, and what was left of his human dignity Leo had guarded jealously. And thereafter he had been scrupulous in his efforts to avoid any details of Maddi's life; to have heard of her inevitable next love affair – one which doubtless would have lasted – would have been too painful. She, unlike him, had experienced relationships before they had been together, and their encounter had been relatively brief, barely the lifetime of a lit cigarette when compared with the hours that make up a single day. Doubtless her life would then have shifted tectonically – romance, the gilded wedding, motherhood – while his existence had calloused over and shrivelled up. He imagined Maddi's offspring, perfect amalgams of her and her partner, products of their profound closeness, their unimaginable and impenetrable love. And what he dreaded – what terrified him more than just about anything in the world – would be to discover that if she ever did reminisce about him it would be like remembering a day trip down the coast you had once gone on, or a DJ you had once danced to, or an old acquaintance who had once made you laugh but who now seemed a quaint anachronism in this era of mortgages and dinner parties and school fees; something transitory and in the bigger scheme of things trivial. Better never to know, he mused.

Nonetheless, he had believed back then, during that golden summer when everything was exalted, that they would indeed spend the rest of their days as one, as surely as he believed that dawn followed night. At times it had seemed effortless, like a dream; at times he had been spontaneous and utterly in the moment. But if truth be told, the cracks in the dam had already begun to appear. In fact, all the while he had been with Maddi a sense of being unworthy of this happiness had gnawed at him. Not that he had let on to anyone, not even properly to himself and least of all to her. His increasingly heavy drinking, for instance, was passed off as recreational, rather than a response to the damage that had been inflicted upon him when the stigma of an unjust accusation subsequently caused him not to act when he could have prevented something terrible from happening. Until one day the background noise suddenly rose to a crescendo and overwhelmed him.

Leo took a meditative draw on his cigar. Future nostalgic remembrance would require that he gloss over this uncomfortable fact, he realised – inasmuch as romance is a quality most often conferred upon events in retrospect – because everyone needs their glory days to look back upon. Yet the young woman murdered at Loch Dhonn would be denied even that. Leo cursed himself for his selfish introspection. He gazed glumly out of the window as the deep blue January Glasgow night descended, a surge of loneliness overcoming him. Time for whisky, he decided.

6

L EO's usual seltzer remedy had failed him. He tried some Scotch as the hair-of-the-dog, but it only succeeded in giving him heartburn. He tried mixing some brandy with milk but that nostrum too had little effect. He resolved to endure the hangover manfully.

With some flourish he used his antique letter opener, a nineteenth-century German silver production with a beautiful leaping hart and oak leaf terminal, to unpeel a handful of envelopes, all junk except for one from the council, a final warning regarding his burning of coal, a prohibition he refused to observe due to his conviction that smokeless fuel gave off inadequate heat. Furthermore, he adored the smell and crackle of a coal and wood fire. He scrunched up the letter contemptuously and cast it, fittingly, onto the grate for later. He coughed a raw, barking cough. It was strange, he thought, how with age one began coughing exactly like one's father.

He stirred in some emollient and checked the water; it was hot – very hot, enough for Leo to play his traditional bath game in which he would lower himself slowly in at as near to scalding point as possible. As the surface lapped his dangling scrotum he knew that he could bear the temperature, and gradually immersed his entire body, enjoying the scent of the lavender bath oil as he did so. The rising steam softened his stubble, making for the perfect shave, which he executed with a modern safety razor ('Don't push down, let the blade do the work,' he heard his father gently advise; it's funny, the little things you remember) – an ivory and badger-hair brush, and luxury shaving soap he had picked up in Knightsbridge. He carefully checked his chops with his fingers for any stubble he might have missed, rinsed and dried his face, patted his neck and cheeks with Italian aftershave, then applied some expensive balm. He combed Macassar oil through his thinning hair and applied talcum powder to his armpits, feet and to Benjamin Franklin, who afterwards put his owner in mind of a sugar-dusted pastry in the window of a *pâtisserie*.

Having completed his toilet Leo strode to his bedroom, disrobed and cast his dressing gown upon the bed. As he did so he caught a glimpse of his paunch in the full-length mirror, a gross totem to middle-aged bachelorhood. He paused to survey himself – precisely the sort of pastime that can instantly disabuse a man of any vain notion that he has uniquely preserved his youth and dilute his theory that he is still handsome in his own rough way. At least his tallish bearing made the gut more forgivable, and his chest and shoulders had retained some defiant pride amid the entropy. His hands looked peculiar and artificial as they hung pendulously from his long arms. They had been badly burned in a house fire a number of years ago. One of them – the left, which had sustained some fourth-degree injury – would have been a mere purple claw had it not been repaired to almost full functionality by a brilliant NHS surgeon, yet they remained unsightly, and sometimes when undertaking menial tasks Leo experienced a familiar twinge. One aspect of ageing was the hypertrophy of the cranium – the effect accentuated by the hair's glacial retreat from the Moranite bluffs and valleys. Leo therefore preserved that of the wiry stuff which still flourished at the fenders and brow at a length just shy of unkempt, producing an emblematic triad which further intensified focus upon his visage. At least it had retained its dark brown pigment, but recent invasions by burgeoning legions of powder-white bristles into the shaving basin were harbingers of decline. The slightly bulging jowls and thickening neck amplified his default demeanour: brooding. By some genetic miracle the booze hadn't done for his beak yet (an item acutely imperilled given its naturally drooping posture), but a close inspection revealed that the onset of mutation was in fact underway: an Orinoco Delta of tiny broken capillaries, the surface beginning to rupture and raddle, a slight swelling to asymmetrical bulbosity. The expansion of the features meant his keen hazel eyes had retreated somewhat into their furrows. Once, when in company, he had described these peepers, housed beneath the noble arches of his eyebrows, as 'hawklike'; 'piggy,' a wag had demurred unkindly.

Once Leo had dressed, he packed his vintage dressing case, then began looking things out for the trip, taking regular breaks to rest upon the *chaise longue* on account of his hangover. At one point he went into the dining room and carefully slid volume two of Gibbon from his bookcase, then removed a false panel and withdrew his money box. He counted out fifty twenty-pound notes, rolled them up and slipped them into an empty cigar cylinder which he put inside his jacket pocket. There was a knock at the front door. Leo hurriedly replaced the money box, the false panel and the book, then rushed through to meet his visitor. Probably a neighbour, as he would have needed to buzz someone from outside into the building first. His heart leapt a little excitedly as he undid the bolt, suddenly realising how eager he was for some human company. It was Rocco from downstairs, and it was unusual to see him abroad at this tender hour. Leo unslotted the chain and hospitably ushered him inside. He walked to the kitchen, lit the gas burner and put the kettle on, while Rocco, barefoot and clad only in tracksuit bottoms and a vest, padded into the drawing room and sat down.

Rocco had enjoyed modest success as a guitarist during the Britpop era and still wore his trademark mop top, although it now clashed with his prematurely aged face in a faintly comical way. His band, The Insects, had been heralded as Glasgow's answer to Oasis, but their minor chart hit 'Suburban Dreams' was withdrawn from sale after a songwriter in the States initiated legal proceedings claiming plagiarism. Rocco – and The Insects – went downhill after that. He developed addiction problems and spent some time in prison for passing forged banknotes (he had 'previous' for certain drug-related offences). He came out fairly chewed up, but at least he now had the flat, which he had inherited, as a nest egg. Leo liked to look in on him from time to time, to check that he hadn't turned into a marijuana plant. If ever he was cooking a pot of soup he would make enough to fill a couple of extra Tupperware dishes, one for Rocco and one for Mrs Godomski, the misanthropic cat woman from 3/2, thus doing his bit to keep alive a neighbourly Glasgow tradition. Rocco was rather in awe of Leo, and eternally grateful for his kindnesses. Whenever he was invited into his apartment he would gaze around and marvel at his neighbour's excessively uncluttered, aesthetically pleasing rooms (Rocco himself was a hopeless hashish slob). Today, however, the usual order of the flat was somewhat thrown asunder by Leo's packing.

'You goin' then?' enquired Rocco, nodding at the oxblood leather suitcases lying opened in the middle of the room as Leo served the tea.

'Indeed.'

'Why do ye need so much stuff?'

'My sense of sartorial elegance isn't just for personal gratification. Others put great stock in appearances, whether they realise it or not. And it is crucial that I impress the local constabulary.'

'Are ye goin' today?'

'Yes, despite it being a great sufferance upon me. But *carpe diem* and all that. Ideally, I would spend the day digesting last night's flesh, like a boa constrictor.'

'Ye mean ye have a hangover?' Rocco grinned.

'I must confess I did imbibe a little too much sherry. Anyway, regardless of the reason, today I would really much prefer to rest my brainium.'

'Ye mean cranium?'

Rocco's voice had a nasal quality, as though he was permanently suffering from a head cold, and Leo always enjoyed the way it accentuated the earnestness of the man. Leo had once enquired if his name was owed to some Italian lineage; in fact its convoluted origin occurred in a Glasgow playground. His real forename was actually Maurice, which was tenuously, by merely the common initial syllable, converted by his imaginative school pals to Morocco Mole, a 1960s Hanna-Barbera cartoon character. This was abbreviated to Morocco, which was in turn abridged to Rocco.

'No, brainium. It is an appellation I devised for my head, which is essentially an immensely powerful brain within a bone chamber. I felt brainium somewhat apt.'

Rocco seemed to consider this for a moment, nodding his shaggy-haired head thoughtfully as he chewed and swallowed a mouthful of tea bread. 'I brought ye somethin'.' He solemnly placed the gift upon Leo's Regency table. It was a flick knife.

'I thought I asked you to get rid of that for me.'

Years ago Leo had been employed as a night dispatcher for a taxi firm, and a security guard who worked at a nearby parking lot used to pop into the office for a cup of tea and to get out of the cold. He was an old navy salt who had sailed on destroyers in the Atlantic and Russian convoys. He regaled Leo with stories of the gangs in Glasgow during the 1930s. The old-timer had refused to join with his local team, and that had made him a marked man. He told terrifying tales of being chased by mobs of razor-wielding hooligans. 'But ye could leave your front door open in those days,' the old guy would muse wistfully. Once, while docked in

Brooklyn, he had bought this flick knife from a street pimp. When he had returned to Glasgow after the war, the gangs had temporarily gone into abeyance, but the weapon still had its uses within the tough old city. The man then bequeathed it to Leo who, for certain reasons, was being pursued by members of the National Front at the time. Leo despised knives, bringer of countless tragedies to his beloved hometown, but he didn't want to hurt the old tar's feelings, so reluctantly accepted the present, then cast it into the back of a drawer. Years later he came across it and requested that Rocco dispose of it safely for him.

'I hung onto it. Ye never know when such a thing will come in handy.'

'If you carry a weapon you are more likely to become a victim of violence.'

'But I'm old enough in the tooth to recognise that these are unusual circumstances. Whoever killed that wee lassie is one brutal bastard.'

Leo sighed as he eyed the wretched item disapprovingly.

'I kind of had this feelin' . . . that ye might be in danger up there,' continued Rocco, rubbing the bristles on his chin. 'Will ye take it with ye, for my sake?'

'If it will keep you happy,' replied Leo, tossing the thing into the front compartment of his case.

After Rocco had left, Leo resumed packing. He fetched his father's *Golden Treasury*, his electronic chess machine, a couple of Graham Greene novels, a box of linen handkerchiefs and his tortoiseshell clothes brush, shoe brush, hairbrush and hand mirror. He had already looked out his Harris Tweed herringbone sports jacket (he would wear this on the journey up), his Blenheim shooting coat, his walking shoes, an evening suit, a couple of Fred Perry polo shirts and two V-necked lambswool jerseys, along with a silk necktie, a cravat, two pairs of silk Paisley-patterned pyjamas, a dressing gown, his deerstalker, a couple of pairs of flannels, several shirts, long underwear, a dun cashmere scarf and his fleece-lined black pigskin gloves. He polished his versatile Oxfords – comfortable enough for travelling, smart enough for dinner. He located his cigar cutter, his multi-tool, his knapsack, his World War II Barr & Stroud binoculars, his Stanley torch, a box containing his (filled) hip flask, his aluminium water flask, matches, his tinder box, two notebooks bound in crocodile leather, a tin of shoe polish and enough drugs to fill an entire apothecary's shop. He would wear his more robust Swiss

Army Infantry wristwatch rather than his Cartier. He looked out two bottles of Ballantine's blend, three packs of mini Cohibas, a box of Orange Creams and a quarter-pound bag of Pan Drops he had bought at Sanjeev's. Finally, he checked that his detective's kit was in order; it was all contained within an electrician's pouch which fitted beautifully into the large pockets he had ingeniously fashioned into the insides of his overcoats.

Leo surveyed his packed luggage with satisfaction. He glanced at the mantle clock and called a local taxi firm, a slight sensation of anxiety resonating in his stomach as the impending adventure beckoned.

III

LOCH DHONN

7

'I HOPE you're not afraid of ghosts,' said Helen.

Leo started violently. His immediate reaction was that he was being hoaxed; then he quickly realised the absurdity of the notion of a young woman, who looked exactly like Helen, abroad with a murderer on the loose on a freezing cold night wearing nothing but a thin nightie simply to prank a perfect stranger. Then he wondered if he was hallucinating. He instinctively dispelled this idea. And so he came to the rapid conclusion that this was, in fact, the phantom of Helen Addison. In spite of his previous personal experiences of the supernatural a chill ran down Leo's spine and his skin tingled with fear as the effects of alcohol retreated rapidly within his brain. He made to speak, but the words choked in his larynx, such that he had to clear his throat and start again.

'I-I've never b-been harmed b-by one in my l-life,' he stammered, 'thus far. Permit me to introduce myself . . .'

'I know who you are. And I know about your magic visions. I heard you talking with that policeman earlier.'

'So you are able to . . . spy on folk, and listen in to their conversations?'

'Only some of the time. Why haven't they caught him yet?'

Leo gathered his thoughts, keen to adjust himself to the surreal nature of the situation. It was crucial to make the most of this extraordinary opportunity.

'I don't know. Tell me who did it and I'll tell them.'

'I don't know who did it. I couldn't see his face. It was covered.'

'*Damn!*'

'Yep.'

'Helen, I'm so sorry about what happened to you. The police, and myself, we'll do everything we possibly can to catch this character and make sure he's punished.'

'He'll be punished, one way or the other. Eventually. I'm just afraid he's going to do it again.'

'I understand.'

'Well then?'

'I only arrived today. Yesterday, rather,' he said, glancing at his wristwatch.

'So what will you do?'

'I'm hoping that my being here, at Loch Dhonn, will help stimulate my visions. In the meantime, now that we've connected, you must tell me everything you can about your ordeal. There must be some purpose behind your not having fully passed beyond the veil yet. I know it's not easy, but please try. Just start at the beginning.'

'It was like I was watching myself in a movie. Like I was there, but that I wasn't really there. I don't remember leaving home. The first thing I can remember was standing down there, not far from the water, and seeing a little rowing boat on the loch getting nearer and nearer. I watched him reach the bank and drag the boat up. I knew it was really cold but some-how I didn't feel it. I was watching him from the trees down there. I was transfixed by him. It was like I was rooted to the spot.'

'I wonder what the devil he was doing out on the loch.'

'I've no idea. I think he was coming from Innisdubh. That island over there,' she said, gesturing towards the loch. 'I bet there are clues there.'

'The police must have conducted a search.'

'Well, look again.'

Leo gazed out at the misty surface of the loch, over to the little island with the keep on it which he had seen earlier. It seemed ugly and sinister to him in the night-time. Helen leapt down from her position on the folly and landed soundlessly beside him. She was pretty, slim, petite, small-breasted. Her chestnut hair looked as black as liquorice in the night, and her eyes shone with a strange, furious candescence. She had elfin features and freckles, which in the pale light looked as though they had been tattooed on with henna.

When she had been alive Helen had always dreaded moments of silence between herself and others. She felt that for a conversation to go into abeyance proved a deep-seated fear of hers: that she was a dull and unin-teresting person. She had overestimated what conversation actually required, often wondering what people filled their sentences with – what on *earth* were they talking about? Therefore she had been anxiously inclined to fill blank spaces with little outbursts of tangential chatter. Yet over the last few days she had overheard several conversations, invisible as she was to the participants. And she had gained the knowledge that folk had been largely talking a lot of blethers all along. And because of this revelation this moment seemed pleasantly novel; she felt totally centred, comfortable in her own skin (such as it was), happy to let the silence play out between her and this strange man, towards whom she was for some reason able to physically manifest her spectral self.

She sighed, taking in the moonlit view, then continued relating her terrible tale. 'It was misty over the loch, just like this. He was wearing gloves. Black leather ones, I think. And this weird hood.'

'Weird in what way – can you describe it to me?'

'It was black. It had two little slits for eyeholes. You know, I couldn't even see his eyes. They were just two deep shadows. It came to a point at the top, like the ones those racists in America wear.'

Leo recalled the oddly shaped headwear worn by the dark figure in his second vision. 'The Ku Klux Klan?'

'Yes. And he was wearing some sort of robes; they were black, too. The robes and the hood had these weird patterns, in red.'

'Describe them, if you please.'

'A kind of a star with something superimposed on it, like an animal's head.'

'A goat's head?'

'It could've been a goat, yes. There was other stuff too. Geometric shapes . . . like diagrams.'

'Can you remember what?'

'A pyramid, some interlinked circles – no, ovals – and another star, inside a circle.'

'A pentacle?'

'I don't know what a pentacle is.' She turned to face him. 'I can't remember any more shapes.'

'Then what happened?'

'We walked up, towards the rhododendron paths.'

'Did he force you to come with him?'

'No. I was in, like, a trance. I couldn't *but* follow him. It was as though it was all kind of fated.'

'What did he have with him?'

'A stick.'

'What was it like?'

'Quite thick; it looked quite heavy.'

'Could it have been made of metal?'

'Yes. Like copper or brass. He also had this bundle over his shoulder.'

'Did you see the blade?' Leo felt desolate upon uttering this sentence in so callous a manner.

'Not then. He had it under his robes. He bashed me over the head with the stick. It hurt like heck and I nearly passed out. Then he put the bundle and the stick down, pulled out the knife, grabbed me by the neck and started stabbing me.'

'What height was he?'

'About six foot. More or less.'

'What was his build like?'

'It was hard to tell because the robes broke up his shape, but I think he was quite broad-shouldered. And he was strong . . . I could tell by his grip when he had me by the throat. I thought it might be that mute who worked for the Grey Lady.'

'Bosco.'

'He always scared me a bit. But maybe I'm being unfair; he never did me any harm.'

Suddenly, Helen turned on her heel and raced away, into the shadows, out of sight.

Leo made to yell after her, but his voice came out faint and broken: 'Helen, I'll catch him for you. I promise.'

And then he sat down upon a mossy tree stump and wept.

8

UPON wakening the next day Leo sat upright in bed for a while, still deeply affected by the spectral encounter. He sought solace in his morning prayers, and then performed a perfunctory toilet to make him respectable enough for breakfast. He was glad of his dinner the evening before; it had lined his stomach and curtailed his hangover to just a thirst.

He arrived in the dining room to be waved enthusiastically over to Fordyce's table. Leo ordered a pot of coffee, an entire jug of grapefruit juice, a rack of toast, and a full Scottish breakfast, with double egg (one fried, one scrambled), double sausage (one link, one Lorne) and double Stornoway black pudding. He devoured the lot voraciously, then slipped the waitress a fiver to bring him a dram ('a mere curer').

Fordyce, meanwhile, only picked at a poached egg on toast, as he was feeling last night's alcohol consumption a lot more keenly than Leo. 'I've something of a delicate constitution, I'm afraid to report,' he said.

Nonetheless, Fordyce retained his cheery disposition, and Leo was silently impressed to notice that he had already worked his way through the majority of the *Times* crossword; he himself couldn't get on with such things at all.

'What's the plan for today, old stick?'

Fordyce had endearingly started referring to Leo by this sobriquet in the light of the intractable political views his new acquaintance had proclaimed late the previous night. The adjective 'old' was affectionately employed despite the fact that they were the same age.

Leo remembered that he had been circumspect the night before, not telling Fordyce his real purpose in visiting Loch Dhonn, instead murmuring something about a rambling holiday. He felt a little guilty about this apparent mistrustfulness, but he had been obeying a long-standing vow never to discuss sensitive matters while inebriated. He was sober now, and he knew in his heart that he could depend upon Fordyce. He resolved to confide in him that very morning; apart from anything else he could prove a useful ally. DI Lang need never know.

'A bracing walk around the environs. Won't you join me, as a guide?'

'It would be a singular pleasure, old stick!'

Leo clad and equipped himself appropriately, and having restored Fordyce's overcoat to his possession the duo set forth into the cold morning. Leo noticed his companion was wearing his canary-yellow flat cap, and felt bad for having been irked by it the previous evening. Wisps of low cloud persisted over the water, and Ben Corrach could barely be discerned at the northern end of the loch, just as a sinister black shadow lurking behind a veil. Their breath came out as mist, and the freshness of the day was invigorating, heightened by the quarter pound of Pan Drops Leo supplied.

They made their way northwards along the road a little distance, past a quaint red telephone box, towards a track that cut off to the left and would eventually lead them down to the loch. Before taking this they passed two rather outlandish-looking young women wearing knitted ponchos and bright woollen Peruvian *chullo* hats to defend themselves against the chill. Fordyce greeted them warmly and they returned tentative smiles.

'They're from Kildavannan. It's a community about two miles south of here,' explained Fordyce, once they had passed by.

'What's that – some sort of hippie commune?'

'Not really. They describe themselves as an eco community; there's accommodation for meditation retreats and whatnot, and studios for artists and writers. Marvellous, really.'

The men presented a rather curious sight as they walked towards the lochside; two country gents dressed for the winter season of 1950, Leo with his deliberate, long stride, Fordyce with his jaunty, almost skipping gait. Fordyce chatted pleasantly as they went along. His parents were both deceased. He was unmarried, and when he wasn't at Loch Dhonn he lived with his sister in Edinburgh's New Town or in Galloway, where the ancestral pile was. Leo guessed that this wasn't a room and kitchen, but Fordyce, with fastidious decorum, never directly referred to the wealth or station of his kin. There was also an elder brother who split his time between Scotland and London.

'We used to take our childhood summers up here,' he continued. He paused to take in the air. 'This place gets into one's blood. Now I spend much of my time here. For periods I'm a permanent resident at the hotel – like the major in *Fawlty Towers*!'

Leo laughed at the reference.

'Have you read much of Scott, Leo?' asked Fordyce as he surveyed the prospect.

'I adore him. Apart from his politics.'

'Then you are a Scottish romantic, like me?'

'And proud of it!'

'Scott eulogised Scottish history and the Highland clans, and cynics have been quick to deride him as quixotic. But he tapped into something real. There truly is nothing like this land for romance. And for legend and heroism. It makes one feel *alive*, to be a Celt!'

'We are truly blessed,' agreed Leo. 'In spite of the grim timing of my visit here, it is always refreshing to leave behind the urban sprawl for these wild and enchanted glens.'

'How right you are – how *right* you are!'

Encouraged, Leo theatrically addressed the braes on the opposite side of Loch Dhonn, and declared, 'Land of the mountains – my beloved home!'

Leo really did feel a renewed sense of vigour, having been released from the confines of his apartment, and it felt thrilling to be in wide open spaces among new company, so soon after having craved only solitude and seclusion.

Further down the path, amid a little grove of firs, was an ancient Pemberton caravan, painted army green, its windows filthy. Junk littered a scruffy little yard and a couple of neglected vegetable plots. Derelict cold frames and greenhouses sat nearby, the glass long since shattered or removed, and a rusted hatch led to an old root cellar.

'That's where Lex lives,' remarked Fordyce.

Leo noted that no other abode lay in the expanse between Dreghorn's place and the murder scene.

Near the loch much of the land was intersected by deteriorating drystane dykes, evidence of long-forgotten enclosures. They came across a coppice of various conifers amid a larger wood of bare alder, lime, oak, rowan and apple, and Leo voiced his appreciation of the rich medley.

'They're the remnants of parkland from the old estate,' Fordyce informed him. 'The current baron of Caradyne's grandfather sold this land off after the First War. You should see this area in autumn – it's a perfect riot of copper and gold!'

They entered a walled garden, ruined and overgrown. Leo stopped to regard some strange, large specimens, with long purple protrusions extending from a nest of huge, rubbery leaves.

'What's the Latin for that one – *Phallus Phallus?*' he joked.

'Rather!' said Fordyce, enigmatically. 'The twelfth baron was a regular botanist; he imported lots of exotic plants from the Empire. This odd fellow seems to flower at the strangest of times.'

Leo decided to get down to business. 'Fordyce, I have something to tell you. I'm afraid I was rather insincere last night, when you asked why I had chosen to visit Loch Dhonn.'

'That's all right,' said Fordyce, with his usual equanimity. 'I didn't mean to probe.'

'I'm perfectly happy to confide in you, but you must swear to keep what I am about to tell you within your own breast.'

'I swear it upon my honour, old stick.'

'The truth is I'm here to help the police with the murder case. You see, I am blessed with a certain type of extrasensory perception, a power which I have put at their disposal.'

'Extrasensory perception! Are you joshing?'

'I am in deadly earnest. I possess a sort of second sight. I see things, in visions. Academic researchers in the US termed one comparable phenomenon "remote viewing", but I am unsure if they are referring to my specific gift.'

'Well, more power to your elbow, old stick!'

'You're not a sceptic?'

'I'm open-minded about such matters. And don't worry about me – Mum's the word. Anyway, I'm honoured that you would see fit to take me into your confidence.'

'I wouldn't be too flattered.' Leo smiled. 'You see, I know for sure you aren't the murderer.'

'Why's that?'

'You're the only man round here who's under five foot nine.'

Fordyce laughed good-naturedly, although he didn't actually get the reference.

They walked out of the walled garden, through a rusted old gate that hung languidly from its hinges. The land sloped steeply towards the water below in a pleasant, tree-covered bank.

Leo examined a grim building on the far shore of the loch through his binoculars. This, no doubt, was Ardchreggan House, the other property the Mintos owned. It was set against a beautifully wooded hillock, and alongside this to the north was a stretch of more open parkland, the sparser, brown-grey, leafless trees ghostly in the slight mist. A lovely old boathouse sat on the waterside. Leo adjusted the focus and scanned the little islands on the loch. His gaze rested upon the jagged profile of Innisdubh. It was enclosed by rocks and trees as though to conceal its possessions.

'Fordyce, do you happen to possess a boat?' asked Leo.

'Why, yes, as a matter of fact I do. The *Fairy Queen*.'

'I need to ask of you a favour. I wish to take a dekko at those isles, in particular Innisdubh.'

'Certainly, old stick. Let's head along forthwith and release the old girl from her winter bondage. She's just a dinghy, but the outboard's been serviced recently.'

'Splendid.'

They ambled along the lochside, a series of pebbly little bays lined with young birch, hazel and alder crouching over the waterside. Past a soggy paddock in which were a pair of fine, caramel-coloured colts and a flock of noisy peewits, towards the little boatyard and jetty, at the end of a track which came down from the hotel. Halfway there, just adjacent to Innisdubh, at the place where a path led up to the folly and then to the hotel, Leo suddenly halted, rooted to the spot.

'What's up, old stick? You look as though you've seen a ghost!'

'This place – I've seen it before. In a vision I had, in church,' replied Leo, recalling the image of the dark, robed figure standing by the water. 'Yes, and this is where the killer's boat was landed,' he continued, noticing the telltale impression of a shallow draft upon a muddy area at the water's edge, and several sharp indentations from where the police must have staked out the scene. Leo observed that the groove the boat had left had a particular texture within it: a little tramline caused by some tiny flaw in the fabric of the keel. 'Helen would have been somewhere over there,' he said, pointing towards the path. 'Watching him.'

'Good God, man, how on earth can you tell such things?' exclaimed Fordyce.

'It's all simply a question of opening the senses.'

Leo took out the bespoke detective's kit he kept stowed in his coat and crouched down to take some measurements with a little tape. Next to a particular shoeprint, which had been made by a deep criss-cross grip, he noticed a few blobs of solidified agent, used by the police to take a cast. He produced his mobile phone and after fiddling with it for a while positioned it and took a photograph of the print and then the impression the boat had left. 'Take a good look at this shoeprint, Fordyce. When we visit Innisdubh, I want us both to have our eyes peeled for any similar ones.'

Just before the boatyard they came across two men working a splash net at the mouth of a burn. One was McKee from the previous evening, who wore a vacant expression, his eyes red and his face ugly from lack of sleep. He was clad in oily overalls and a little unlit roll-up cigarette was tucked in the corner of his mouth. The other was apparently one George Rattray, a large man in a Barbour jacket, who was aged about sixty, as bald as a mushroom and who had a broad, pleasant face.

Leo was curious about the men's task, which involved fishing out fat brown trout and depositing them in a large tub of water. A long kit bag lay across the path. Rattray seemed to hold a distinct authority over McKee, whom he instructed with barely a word. McKee obeyed, lifting the tub with his strong arms and placing it onto a barrow. He wheeled this off towards a beat-up old Land Rover pick-up which was parked in the boatyard.

Rattray noticed Leo's interest and explained: 'We take out the pregnant trout so that we can hatch the eggs, and make sure the loch is well stocked.'

'Isn't it a bit late – or early – to be doing that?' enquired Fordyce.

Rattray smiled good-naturedly. 'Hark at the expert!' he joked. 'What brings you to Loch Dhonn?' he then enquired of Leo.

'I'm up to see what I can catch,' Leo replied, obliquely.

'Well, you've come with the wrong guy. I've yet to see Fordyce land so much as a stickleback!'

'Liar,' joshed Fordyce. 'What about that brace of trout last October?'

'Ach, he'd been to the shop in Fallasky,' whispered Rattray, tapping the side of his nose conspiratorially. 'You should've seen them; they were already filleted – and smoked!'

Leo laughed politely, but he reckoned that Rattray was one of these mildly annoying people who would inanely milk a lame joke. He reproached himself for his irritability. Why couldn't he be more like Fordyce, who seemed only to see the best in folk and celebrated their myriad facets?

'Robbie seems to be taking things rather badly,' noted Fordyce, after a pause.

'Yes, poor soul,' sighed Rattray, shaking his head as he stood up.

'He was recently made homeless by a fire,' Fordyce told Leo. 'But George here did the decent thing and put him up.'

'Ach, he's just living in my old converted washhouse. It makes no odds to me.'

'Still, that's very kind of you,' said Leo, wincing slightly at the man's coffee breath.

'Do you know the police haven't even spoken to me yet?' said Rattray, suddenly frowning. 'Did they interview you?' he asked of Fordyce.

'Yes. It wasn't very pleasant, I can assure you. Although that Detective Inspector Lang strikes me as a very able man.'

'Well, they haven't talked to me. It's not as though I stay far outside the clachan, so what the heck are they playing at? They should be grilling every male around here, straightaway. I overheard two of them blethering about Robbie.' Rattray broke off momentarily to glance over his shoulder and check that his companion was still out of earshot. '*Robbie McKee* – I ask you! He thought the world of Helen. A bit of an oddity but he wouldn't harm a fly. Well, apart from that bad business – but he was just a boy then. Och, I don't know anything any more,' he concluded despairingly.

'If you think you can help the police, you ought to approach them without delay,' said Leo, who was unimpressed by the offhand way the man had referred to McKee as 'an oddity'. 'Otherwise, I'm sure they will speak with you directly.'

'It's not that I know anything *specific*. It's just that I live here, I know the family. I even babysat for Helen when she was wee. They might be able to get a clearer picture of Loch Dhonn, of the folk here. I might know a clue without even realising it.'

*   *   *

75

After they had said their goodbyes, Leo and Fordyce walked past a little memorial cairn dedicated to the drowned bassist, and on to the boat-yard. A row of motor boats for hire bobbed on the water, tethered to a pontoon. Numerous vessels sat idle on trailers, some under tarpaulins. Others were kept in wooden sheds, and Fordyce, being a trusting type of soul, generally left his unlocked. They wheeled the *Fairy Queen* out, down the gentle slope and into the water, before loading the outboard and the oars. Leo was glad of his waterproof walking shoes. He noticed a rigid inflatable police launch moored alongside the rickety little jetty, the twin Evinrude engines latent with power. The duo clambered aboard, and after Fordyce had fastened the outboard to the stern, they set off, using only the oars at first.

'Poor George,' said Fordyce, quite affected by their encounter. 'And poor, poor Robbie. He looks dreadful. Simply dreadful.'

'This McKee fellow – George said he'd been in some sort of trouble in the past?'

'It was years ago. He was only fourteen, for goodness' sake. And he was never charged with any offence.'

'What happened?'

'The story goes – and it is just a version of events – that he got a bit rough with a local girl, after a date. Apparently, it took him a while to take no for an answer, if you take my meaning. Which would have been very wrong, of course. But there was no suggestion that he actually, you know . . .'

'Forced himself upon her?'

'Precisely. What he did do, and this is beyond doubt, is stalked her for a while after that. He camped out in the woods behind her house, spying on her. I know because I saw it with my own eyes and suggested to him that he go on home. But he wasn't to be dissuaded and the police had to have a stern word with him.'

'What was the upshot of it all?' asked Leo.

'The family were moving away anyway, down south, so the whole business just blew over.'

'I wonder if DI Lang knows about this.'

'He does – he probed me extensively about it when I was being inter-viewed. I'm afraid the police seem to be taking a keen interest in Robbie. Now, I believe – I know – that he has had certain mental problems: he gets depressed and suffers from anxiety. But I don't believe Robbie is capable of this. Not for a moment.'

Leo didn't answer as he pulled the ripcord on the outboard and fired up the motor first time.

9

THE islet Innisdara took its name from the Irish hermit saint who lived there in glorious contemplation for twenty years during the seventh century. Its main features were the remains of Dara's cell and the ruins of a twelfth-century chapel dedicated to him. It was here that Fordyce and Leo visited first. They half-beached the little dinghy on a pebbled southern shore and secured it to a nearby tree. Scrub and young woodland bordered the little bay, and a burn ran into the water.

'We can follow this stream up to the chapel,' suggested Fordyce.

A little track took them up a steep incline, and the burn tumbled through a mossy gorge a dozen or so feet below to their right. Despite the time of year there was still enough coniferous foliage to obstruct their passage and they had to be careful not to slip on residual patches of snow and ice. They happened upon the remains of the odd man-made fire, one of which was strewn with rusted lager cans, evidence of teenage tippling. Leo tut-tutted in disapproval, and scooped the cans into a neat pile with his shoe.

Further on, the track flattened out and the trees cleared. Down a gentle slope of rough grass sat what was left of the chapel, and beyond that what Fordyce would identify as Dara's cell, which was merely a scattering of white stones.

'The church was in use right up until the Reformation,' Fordyce said. 'If you look inside you can see the Latin inscriptions on what was the altar stone.'

The nave was muddy, and clotted with heather and blackened bracken. A large Celtic cross, about eight feet in height, was propped up against the northern wall. A plaque explained that it was one of the finest examples of late Dalriadan carving in existence, and that it had originated in Kintyre. At its centre was a raised spiralled boss, from which low-relief knotwork stretched out through the limbs with no beginning and no end, because all things belong and are interconnected.

Leo wondered aloud how they had managed to transport it all this way north and across the water. 'It must weigh two tons!'

According to the plaque, the cross had been broken maliciously during the time of Knox and brought here for safekeeping. Leo ran his fingertip along a jagged scar of cement, where the fracture had been.

'Anything?' asked Fordyce.

'Pardon?'

'I mean regarding your powers . . . are you feeling anything, any vibes about this place?'

'It doesn't always work like that.'

'Oh, sorry.'

'I do think that this is a sacred place, Fordyce.' Leo smiled. 'I think Saint Dara was a good man; he imbued this island with good feelings.' And you are a good man too, Fordyce Greatorix, Leo thought to himself about his newfound companion. They wandered past some ancient graves and through a charming little meadow, then through a screen of pines and onto the northern shore. Leo's attention was arrested by the sound of a horn emanating loudly from the other side of the loch. He glanced up to see a diesel locomotive, which was hauling two dozen empty timber wagons, carefully negotiating a sharp curve in the line which led into the great pass he had noticed upon his arrival.

'That's Stob's Bend,' explained Fordyce. 'It's the only point at which the railway skirts Loch Dhonn, as it enters the Lairig Lom. It's a blind corner, so the trains have to go dead slow in order to enter it safely. They always sound their horns.'

They walked a complete circumference of the island, before returning to the boat by crossing via a different, lonelier path than the original one.

Leo launched the *Fairy Queen* by planting an oar on the loch bed and pushing downwards. 'Right. Now for Innisdubh,' he declared.

Fordyce started the engine and took the tiller, and steered the boat round Innisdara and towards Innisdubh, about a half-mile away. Leo looked over at the mainland, noticing an ugly scar of stubble on the hillside above the village where commercial forestry had recently been harvested. A mood of nautical whimsy overtook him and he couldn't resist making a series of light-hearted references to the 'aft' and the 'foc'sle'. A snell wind suddenly whipped up the strait's surface and the little outboard protested, whining like a buzzsaw as they rode the waves.

Leo and Fordyce instinctively pulled their headgear down to shield their faces, and hunched their shoulders to keep warm. Leo produced his hip flask and unscrewed the cap. Fordyce, who was still hungover, took a tentative swig; Leo took a long draught.

Other than Innisdara, Innisdubh was the only island of significant size on Loch Dhonn. It was slightly the larger of these two and sat rather by itself to the north, whereas Innisdara had the close companionship of several calf isles, some of which were virtually linked by sand spits. Innisdubh was a forebidding prospect. Unlike Innisdara it was surrounded by rocks, which made the waters there treacherous, and it took an experienced helmsman to negotiate a landing at the only possible place, at the south-eastern corner. Much of Innisdubh's coast comprised steep slopes of black quartz, and at its western end the land came to an ugly jagged peak which jutted out pugnaciously over a sheer drop below. It was no accident that the ancient chieftains of Caradyne chose this for their citadel, Fordyce told Leo, such were its natural defences. The medieval keep was the chief man-made feature of the place, which was more thickly wooded than Innisdara. Dotted around these woods were tombs and mausoleums of various dead lords and their kin. The islet was also notable for several Iron Age standing stones.

Fordyce had to take care to avoid a colony of ill-tempered Canada geese, before cutting the outboard and skilfully ferrying them to shore using the oars. They landed at a small strand of dull flint which was fouled by decomposed vegetation and aquatic weeds. Leo stood upright in the bow, scanning the ground in front of him. A little apron of dark sand between the water and the flint was disturbed by different human visitations, footprints and also the marks left by various boats.

'Looking for something, old stick?' enquired Fordyce.

'Yes: an indentation similar to the one we just saw on the mainland. An indentation made by a boat – the same boat – having been hauled ashore. And behold – there it is!' Leo announced excitedly, pointing at a groove which bore the distinctive tramline pattern. He leapt ashore, withdrew his little tape measure and bent down to confirm the match. He then produced his phone and took a photograph of the evidence. 'However, there are no shoeprints on this sand which match the one we saw earlier, the ones the police had taken a cast of.'

Leo and Fordyce had to get their shoes wet again in order to drag the dinghy beyond the waterline and away from the hazard of the rocks. Leo withdrew a box of miniature Cohibas, a little luxury to compensate for his cold extremities, and offered one to Fordyce.

'No, thank you. I can't seem to take to the things.'

Leo lit his and set off through the trees into the dark heart of Innisdubh, his flesh creeping at the ancient malevolence that seemed to inhabit the place.

The keep was in remarkably good condition considering its antiquity. A portion of the inland-facing wall had collapsed, affording one a partial view of the tower's interior.

'It was built by the Green Lord in the thirteenth century.'

'Pardon my ignorance, Fordyce, but who was the Green Lord?'

'Sorry, old stick. He was a notoriously cruel clan chieftain who, legend has it, impaled several of his enemies and left their bodies to rot on the stake for months on end, as a warning to folk to toe the line. One day the locals turned against him and hanged him from the rafters of the keep. First, they slit his belly open so that his innards would spill out when the rope tightened.'

'Why was he called the Green Lord?'

'Because it is said that they left him hanging up there so long that his face turned green. It was their means of revenge. You see that stone over there?' Fordyce indicated a large, rough-hewn slab. 'That's where he's buried. As I mentioned, all the chieftains and barons of Caradyne are buried around here.'

They walked over to the slab, and Leo examined the faded Latin inscriptions and rudimentary caricatures of gargoyles, serpents, griffins and dragons.

'It's really odd,' said Leo.

'What is?'

'Why they chose to be buried over here, rather than on Innisdara, where the church is. A holy place.'

'Perhaps the locals didn't want the Green Lord buried on consecrated ground.'

'Good thinking. And in doing so started a tradition, such that all his descendants were laid to rest on Innisdubh.'

Next to the Green Lord's grave was a hideous modern tomb of black marble and granite which stood about seven feet tall. It was devoid of

Christian markings, and upon the frontage was carved a long and complex series of runic lettering, surrounded by occult symbols including fylfots, trapeziums and skulls. Leo was intrigued, and traced his fingers over some of these strange hieroglyphics. A couple of them were similar to ones described to him by Helen, which had been on her killer's robes.

'That, I believe, is where the thirteenth baron is interred,' said Fordyce in a low voice.

Leo took several photographs of the engravings. He realised that some of the symbols were Masonic, and he wondered what degree of the Craft the old baron had attained and what dire initiations he had fulfilled.

A little further on was the most impressive sepulchre of all, a proper, walk-in mausoleum belonging to the tenth baron who had died in the year 1801. Fordyce hesitated, then followed Leo down a short flight of stairs and stepped into the vestibule which smelled of dampness and old masonry. Leo tried the iron double doors that sealed off the main chamber, but they wouldn't budge. He withdrew his pencil torch from his detective's kit, which revealed a padlock on a hasp.

'The lock looks recent: late twentieth or twenty-first-century,' he noted. 'Oh well, nothing ventured.'

Fordyce exhaled and hurried back up the stairs, secretly relieved that Leo's quest to enter such a ghastly place had been frustrated.

They walked further round the island, through some woods which opened into a stagnant little heath. Towards the loch the ground fell away sharply, and below there was a grove of melancholy ash trees, flooded by water which was brown with deposits. A deep fungal smell assailed the men's senses and Leo took in an impressive circle of druidic standing stones.

'Innisdubh indeed has a dark past,' said Fordyce. 'If Innisdara is the island of the blessed then this is its delinquent sibling. Archaeologists have speculated that it was used by the Celts as a place for human sacrifice. They excavated a part of the shore which was once below the waterline and found human bones. The ancients believed that where land met water was a mystical place, a junction between this world and the other world.'

The largest stone had long since collapsed and lay on its side like a mammoth building block. Leo stooped to examine its surface. He withdrew a little plastic bag from his detective's kit and picked the item up with a pencil.

'What have you got there, old stick?'

'Signs and wonders, dear boy, signs and wonders.'

'It's just a dead toad,' observed Fordyce, crouching down alongside Leo to examine the item dangling from the end of the pencil.

'Not quite. It is part of a dead toad,' said Leo, dropping the thing into the bag and slipping it into a pocket before again scanning the huge stone. He noticed something else, withdrew a magnifying glass, and held it between his eye and the face of the rock.

'*Et voilà!*' he exclaimed.

'What's that? It's just a blob of tar.'

'Wrong again, I'm afraid. It's candle wax. Someone's been dabbling in things they shouldn't be dabbling in.'

'Gosh, it must be hellishly ticklish to be a dick!'

'I beg your pardon?'

'You know, a dick – a private eye, a detective.'

'Oh. Yes, it is rather,' said Leo a touch smugly, as he stowed away his glass and sealed the wax in another little plastic bag.

'And you do resemble Sherlock Holmes somewhat with that eyeglass and that deerstalker. Anyway, what do you mean when you say someone's been dabbling illicitly. Dabbling in what, pray tell?'

Before Leo had a chance to explain, a distant, angry voice arrested their attention. They both looked northwards, out over the loch, where a sailing dinghy not dissimilar to the *Fairy Queen* bobbed upon the swell. There were two men on board. One, a florid-faced character wearing the tweedy outfit of the country gent, shouted over urgently. Leo strained to hear.

'Pardon?'

'I said you, arsehole, what are you doing on my island?'

So affronted was Leo that he was rendered speechless. And so he turned his back to his antagonist, unbuckled his belt, unbuttoned his waistband, unzipped his fly, peeled down his trousers and underwear, and bent over, to provide a full and magnificent view of his arse. He even patted his white rear cheeks as though to further establish the point.

Leo resumed his dress and his dignity, a little shocked by his own ungentlemanly riposte. He placed his binoculars to his eyes and gazed out at his slack-jawed antagonist. Now it was his turn to be rendered speechless. The other man, however, a heavy-set, middle-aged, evil-looking customer with shadowy jowls and deep eye sockets, looked quite impassive. Amused, even. He grinned malevolently at Leo as he gripped the oars in his enormous hands.

Fordyce's initial astonishment gave way to mirth, and he dunted Leo on the back to congratulate him on his unorthodox victory. They watched as the sinister man pulled the oars inside the boat, started the engine and steered the vessel in the direction of the boatyard.

'You do realise that was the fifteenth baron of Caradyne?'

'No.'

'No prizes for guessing which clan his house is liege to.'

'I am glad for having offended this man. I have heard of the Caradynes; they owned land in Glasgow. They grossly insulted my family, more than a century ago. Of course his people wouldn't record a slight against a bunch of ignorant Micks, but our memories are more enduring.'

After a further inspection of the area proved fruitless, they headed back towards the boat. On the way Fordyce filled Leo in about the feudal baron.

'He lives in the great house above the village of Caradyne, which is a few miles south on the other side of the loch. He still owns much of the land over there, but he only *thinks* he owns the islands. In fact, they were sold to the MacArthurs – the so-called Grey Lady's lot – by the thirteenth baron. Yet the Caradynes think themselves the rightful masters of all they survey and have been trying to wangle out of it ever since, saying that the deal was only for the walled parkland and gardens on the eastern bank – where we were earlier. The baron has powerful blood allies, but they haven't been able to trick the islands back into their possession.'

'Why are they so keen to keep folk off?'

'Family pride, I suppose. He's always hated the fact that Lady Audubon-MacArthur granted the public free access to the islands, even in the days before the right to roam Act.'

The return crossing, rather choppy due to the squall, combined with the whisky from the hip flask, the cigar smoke and the excessive portions he had consumed at breakfast, made Leo feel slightly dizzy and a little nauseous, and he was glad to step back onto terra firma. He took a few minutes to rest by the lochside. The baron's boat, *Argus*, was already fettered to the jetty, and there was no sign of its owner or his manservant. Leo helped Fordyce reinstall the *Fairy Queen* in her shed and then stated his intention to provide DI Lang with an update. Fordyce said he would take the opportunity to finish some tasks at the boatyard. Before he left, Leo turned to his companion.

'Fordyce, one thing: this hermit fellow . . .'

'James Millar.'

'Yes. How did his wife die?'

'It happened in Turkey, while they were on holiday. It was in the papers and everything. She was murdered.'

10

'IT looks like a piece of a frog,' said DI Lang, when Leo showed him his first evidence bag at the incident room.

'Wrong. It is a piece of a toad. The question being: where is the remainder?'

'I'd say it's inside the belly of whichever beastie ate it.'

'No creature on God's earth makes an incision as perfectly as that. I put it to you, Inspector,' Leo announced, with a self-important flourish of his right hand, 'that the rest of this toad was cut away and imbibed as part of a Satanic ritual.'

'You mean, like a Black Mass?'

'In the Black Mass a toad is used as a parody of the Eucharist, a profane surrogate for the Communion host. Also on Innisdubh was this fragment of candle wax,' he said, brandishing his second little bag. '*Black* candle wax,' he added portentously.

'And you think this has something to do with Helen Addison's murder?'

'I'm certain of it. Also, my theory of black rites would fit in with the strange robes worn by the sinister figure in my vision. And you said yourself that the violation of Helen seemed ritualistic.'

Lang, looking altogether unimpressed, remarked that surely a toad would poison whoever ate it, but he took the items from Leo and examined them cursorily. Leo suspected that the bundle Helen had seen the killer carrying contained whatever instruments had been used in the ceremony on Innisdubh, but he was hardly about to share this information and lose credibility with the policeman by attempting to convince him that he had engaged in social intercourse with the discarnate spirit of the victim the previous night.

'Do you think your forensic scientists would be able to tell if the toad was cut by the same blade used in the murder?' asked Leo.

'Unlikely,' replied Lang, tossing the little bags on a shelf behind him, 'and the thing is too decomposed anyway.'

'Detective Inspector, was there a rowing boat found by the water, down from the crime scene?'

'Yes, as a matter of fact there was. It had been dragged ashore on the night of the murder. How did you know that? You never said you had seen a boat in one of your visions.'

'The perpetrator arrived on that boat,' said Leo, ignoring the question. The boat Helen had mentioned had indeed been missing from the vision he had experienced in church, but this was not unusual because his powers often only bequeathed incomplete visual approximates of reality. 'He must have left on foot.'

'We know all this.'

'Why didn't you tell me? Were you testing me?'

It was Lang's turn to ignore a question. 'A few partial shoeprints on some softer patches suggest that the killer headed in the direction of the tarmac at the side of the hotel, and we were unable to track him further. He may well have changed footwear at that point.'

'Whose boat was it?'

'The Mintos'. Anyone could've taken it. It was tied up at the jetty. The rope was cut, possibly with the murder weapon, probably to save time because the knot had been clumsily tied. Forensics have finished with it, and it's been returned to the boatyard.'

'I wonder why he bothered to haul it ashore.'

'Because the rope wasn't long enough to tie it to a branch. And perhaps he figured a lone, crewless boat drifting on the loch would have aroused people's attention sooner than he wished, so he dragged it onto dry land where it was hidden by trees, unless you happened to walk right by it. I doubt he reckoned on the victim's body being found so quickly.'

'Or perhaps it was simply sheer force of habit. Perhaps he was a man so accustomed to using boats on the loch that he brought it ashore out of harm's way, quite unconsciously. Were there any prints aboard?' enquired Leo.

'Bill and Shona Minto's, unsurprisingly. And some other unidentified ones which haven't showed up on the national database, probably belonging to tourists who they'd hired the boat out to. We're fingerprinting everyone in the area. We also found a single woollen thread. But that could have belonged to anyone who had used the boat recently.'

'Black, if not red?'

'Black,' replied Lang. 'Good guess,' he added.

'I'll tell you something else: that boat was at Innisdubh first. Prior to the murder, I mean.'

'For the Black Mass?' Lang said rather wearily.

'I don't wish to be impertinent, Detective Inspector, but I take it your men searched Innisdubh?'

'Of course.'

'It's just that I found an indentation on the landing shore there which correlates with the one made by the Mintos' boat down from the murder scene.'

Leo took out his phone and showed Lang the relevant photographs.

'Any number of vessels would have a similar hull,' said Lang.

'No – observe the distinctive little tramline pattern, common to both grooves.'

'OK, but a nosey tourist could easily have landed the Mintos' boat at Innisdubh at some point in the recent past. Now, listen, you're being indulged up here because of your alleged special powers, not so that you can swan around like Hercule Poirot. And I'm confident that my men conducted a sufficiently thorough search of all the surrounding country-side, including the islands.'

'And you say it yielded no further shoeprints matching those of the killer?'

'No. Not on Innisdubh or anywhere else.'

'I didn't find any either. But as you indicated, being the careful type, he may have used certain footwear specifically and only for the murder itself.'

'It's a distinct possibility. Incidentally, the imprints were of rubber-soled shoes with a slight instep and a man-made upper, widely available from a popular high-street chain for some time, and could have been bought years ago. Forensics say they were in perfect condition, and prob-ably never previously worn.'

'So the murderer was savvy enough to know that you lot can lift clues from used footwear.'

'Indeed. Look, Leo, I don't doubt that there are weirdos around who believe in the devil and are into worshipping him, but surely you don't think that this stuff – Black Masses and all – has any actual power?'

'It is my personal belief that the rallies at Nuremberg were akin to a Black Mass on a grand scale, a kind of monstrous incantation. Just look at the power Hitler wielded. Yet good prevailed in the end; always does, always will. My theory is that Helen was in some way entranced and drawn out from the safety of her home that fateful night by a specific ceremony based on the Black Mass, conducted upon Innisdubh.'

'Och, stop havering, man!'

'Well, let's agree to disagree on that point, and allow me to propose simply that the killer came from Innisdubh. How else do you explain the use of the boat? Why would the killer use it to transport himself the modest distance between the boatyard and where he landed, when he could simply have walked?'

'Because to have walked might have left a trail – the lochside path can be quite muddy – or some clue or other. It's quite ingenious when you think about it; everyone and his dog round here uses the boatyard, it's covered in foot traffic, so he had no worries about leaving evidence of himself there. But by nicking a boat, perhaps even on the spur of the moment, he could arrive at his destination having broken the trail. It would have given him an opportunity to change footwear, assuming that's what he did, putting distance between any of his other footprints. And anyway, even if the culprit did come via Innisdubh, it is of little consequence to us unless it throws up some meaningful material evidence as to his identity. And a dead toad and a daud of candle grease just doesn't cut it, I'm afraid.'

Leo paused deliberately before changing tack. 'You never told me about Millar's wife being murdered. Was it ever solved?'

'No.'

'Was Millar a suspect in it?'

'Briefly. I applied to the Turkish police for more details. Apparently, he found the body.'

'How was she killed?'

'Multiple stab wounds.'

Leo whistled unconsciously as he sucked some air through his teeth. 'And what about this Bosco fellow?' he then asked.

'What about him?'

'Is he a suspect?'

'We haven't ruled him out. He's in Glasgow. His employer, Lady Audubon-MacArthur, sent him away. She feared there would be a storm of accusations, on account of the fact that he's a scary-looking customer. He and the victim would have been familiar with one another; I'm told she visited the house fairly regularly, because of Lady Audubon-MacArthur's blood pressure. We're keeping tabs on him. Come on, let's go outside. I need a smoke.'

Lang cupped his hand to light a tipped cigarette. He exhaled the blue smoke, a faintly amused expression forming on his face. 'Tell me, Leo, do you often display your rear end to members of the aristocracy?'

'Never, sir, he was mere petty gentry!' Leo joshed. 'I see that news travels fast up here.'

'He's just left. Thought your bahookie worthy of complaint.'

'Poor, sensitive soul.'

'I didn't think you were a fellow outcast,' Lang said, as he observed Leo lighting one of his little cigars.

'Only ever to focus the mind, Detective Inspector.'

Lang nodded. 'Leo: that's quite an uncommon name. Were you named after some pope or other?'

'Indeed. My parents were inspired by the Great and Saintly first pontiff of that appellation, upon whose then feast day I was born. However, my mother was then drawn towards the particular elaboration of Leomaris.' Leo noticed Lang almost smile. 'You'd have to ask her why she liked it! Generally, I am known by the humble abbreviation, Leo.'

'Are you married?'

'No. I am part of the modern disease. I am one of the legion of miserable singletons who while away their lonely lives in dreary flats.'

'In what way is it a modern disease?'

'Because in days gone by people at least had the common decency to while away their lives in miserable marriages,' Leo joked blackly. 'What about yourself, Detective Inspector?'

'Married with two kids. Girls. Fourteen and ten.'

'How wonderful.' The sun, which Leo had assumed would be absent for the day, unexpectedly broke from behind the cloud cover, just enough to kiss the far bank of Loch Dhonn with its wan winter light. Leo stood transfixed. 'Oh glory!' he announced unselfconsciously.

'What are you looking at?'

'Just the way the sun shines on the pines. Noblest of trees! The land up here . . . I just love the way it *is*. A theologian I know once told me that

Eden existed once, quite literally. An earthly paradise inhabited by noble savages, in the time before history – the Golden Age, the Dreaming, whatever you wish to call it. He told me that many religions recall that splendid era. Then the Fall came along to spoil things. I think I pine for it. For heaven in nature.'

The detective was no philistine; he was well read, had a broad vocabulary and loved articulating ideas, all of which, along with his professional studies in criminal psychology, lent his official reports a distinctly erudite air. However, he was keen to steer the conversation to a less esoteric territory. 'Would you like to live in the countryside, Leo?'

'At heart I believe we all belong to the land. It is our natural habitat. We are nature's gentlemen, corralled into the foul and crowded cities against our will. The trouble is we become set in our ways, enamoured of the conveniences of urban life.' He turned to address Lang directly. 'Why are you shutting me out, Detective Inspector, keeping information from me? Let me help you catch this fiend.'

Lang looked thoughtful for a while. 'OK. We have found something.'

Leo raised an eyebrow.

'The same rules apply,' urged Lang. 'About discretion.'

Leo nodded vigorously in reply.

'We've found Helen's diary. It was concealed in her bedroom, and it's written in code; a rather ingenious one, so I'm told. Most of the stuff in it is irrelevant, but for one paragraph.' The policeman withdrew an A4 photocopy from his inside pocket and held it out so that Leo could see. Lang read aloud: '"October thirteenth. Tark cornered me in the woods today. Must have seen me and Craig making love. Gave me the creeps. Said we are meant to be together. Could not fathom my refusal. Assured me is not pathetic, but we know differently, don't we?!"'

'Who in God's holy name is Tark?'

'We've no idea. We've tried everything on the computers – acronyms, old cases – but we came up with nothing meaningful. Google it and you'll find everything from an obscure town in Iran, to an Orkish word from Tolkien, to an American slang expression for an arty type of youth.'

'Do any arty youths live in the area?'

'Apparently not. They're a more outdoorsy lot, into fishing or horse riding.'

'And did she like Tolkien?'

'Not especially, according to her family, although she read the books when she was younger, and watched the movies when they came out.'

'So, what is a tark in Orkish?'

'It's a derogatory term for a man.'

'Intriguing,' said Leo.

'You can hang on to this,' said Lang, handing Leo the sheet, 'in case you come up with any ideas. But ensure no one else sees it. We discovered something else, or rather the victim's father noticed it when we were searching his daughter's bedroom. Her favourite childhood toy was missing. A little rag doll which she apparently cherished even into adulthood.'

'Do you think Helen might have instinctively brought it with her on the night of her death?'

'Yes.'

'And the killer kept it, as some sort of a trophy?'

'It's a possibility. Oh, and another thing: I believe the boyfriend is back up at Loch Dhonn. We've pretty much finished interviewing him, for the time being.'

'Have you ruled him out as a suspect?'

'Not quite; we've got to keep an open mind. Look, I've got to call in with my boss, so I'll catch up with you later.'

'Be seeing you,' said Leo. Before Lang had opened the incident room door he added, 'You know something, Detective Inspector, for all the tawdry things about our society – and there are many – the way our police forces treat murder, I think it's a fine testament to us. The way we won't rest until justice is done.'

Lang shrugged his shoulders to acknowledge what was to him a prosaic fact.

II

L EO walked back to the hotel; his stomach had settled now and he
would order a light meal in the bar to tide him over until dinner.
However, through the French doors he could see Lex Dreghorn perched
upon a stool, devoted canine companion at his feet. He noticed the gleam
of pewter as the deadbeat surreptitiously replenished his tumbler from a
hip flask to offset the four-star prices.

Regular little barfly, aren't we? thought Leo, irritated by the prospect
of the man's company. The brasserie was closed due to the lack of guests
so he would order room service instead, thus avoiding another bout of
Dreghorn self-hagiography.

Having enjoyed a Caesar salad with a carafe of youngish and agreeable
Sangiovese in his room, he headed down to the hotel's free internet port,
housed in a little telephone alcove across from the dining room. He
wished to pursue his theory of black rites being used to entice Helen
from her slumber. Despite trying different criteria his searches yielded
nothing enlightening. He searched for 'ancient Germanic alphabets' and
found a site where he discovered that the runes he had photographed at
the thirteenth baron's tomb were of the Scandinavian variety. A table
translated them into Latin characters, but jotting them down in order
revealed only a random mishmash of letters. Perhaps the meaning of the
inscription was encoded.

He returned to his room and telephoned his mother, then ran a bath
with some oil, closed the door to the en suite, and sat at the dressing table
to call Stephanie. He was relieved that she picked up.

'Any result yet, Sherlock?' Her tone seemed a little derisory. She was
breathing hard, as though she had been exerting herself. Some Olympian
sexual feat, no doubt. Leo cast the image from his mind.

'Nothing solid yet. But thanks for setting me up with Lang. It's been a
great help.'

'He's a good cop.'

'Look here, another small favour is required.'

'*Quid pro quo*, Leo.'

'Come, come, Stephanie, there's a murderer to be caught. Remember, we're the good guys. We're both on the same team.'

'You do realise that almost all homicide cases are entirely predictable? The police will probably already have strong suspicions as to the killer's identity. Someone known to the victim, I'll bet. I heard the boyfriend was in the frame.'

'No. He wasn't charged.'

'Oh.' She took a sip from a drink. 'I tried you earlier, by the way.'

'I was out and about; most likely there was no signal,' he said, vowing inwardly to master the missed calls display on his mobile phone.

'It was just to let you know I looked in on your mother, and she's fine.'

'I know. I've just spoken with her. She was most grateful for your visit. As am I.'

'What were you up to?'

'I was on the loch with Fordyce.'

He immediately regretted providing the details.

'With *who*? Since when did you start cutting about with guys called Fordyce? I thought you were an avowed friend of the working man?'

'He's just a bloke up here.'

'Not Fordyce Greatorix, by any chance?'

'Yes. That is his name.'

'Posh Edinburgh Fordyce? Fettes-educated Fordyce? Fordyce whose family own half of Kirkcudbrightshire? Fordyce who speaks so cut-glass you think he comes from England?'

'Stephanie, you must understand that not everyone judges other people by their class or outward appearances. It is the essence of a man that counts.'

'Don't paraphrase Burns to me! But on that theme, you do realise Fordyce is *Scots wha hae*?'

'Yes,' Leo lied. 'And I couldn't care less. We have a great deal in common – although not that, of course. He loves Beaujolais Nouveau. He's big on Mozart. In fact, he has an original pressing of the seventy-four Leppard-Alldis recording of the Great Mass in C Minor. He's going to play it to me when I visit him. Although I sense that he is keener on opera.'

'*Visit* him?'

'Why not? And anyway,' said Leo, giving in to his curiosity, 'how do you know him?'

'His cousin's a QC.'

'Oh, it's a small world.'

'No, just a small country. So, how's it going?'

'I have my work cut out. There are numerous dubious characters up here.'

'Well, be careful,' she said, in spite of herself.

Leo thought he could discern a male voice in the background. 'My senses can detect a malign force up here.'

'What utter twaddle.'

'Oh, so it's twaddle now? Funny, it wasn't twaddle the other day, when you wanted me to uncover your spouse's indiscretions in your hypocritical fit of self-righteousness.'

She had hung up before he could ask her to go to the Mitchell Library for him, in order to research certain aspects of Satanism in rural Scotland.

Leo, exasperated with himself for having allowed the conversation to heat up, launched himself onto the bed and lay on his back, staring at the ceiling, meditating upon his unlikely female friend. She was a paradoxical sort of Proddy; disarmingly fair when discussing Irish history, then scathing about the Catholic Church. The fact that she surrounded herself with Tim friends and had indeed ended up marrying a Tim was oddly typical of the type. Stephanie had already started seeing Jamie when that liaison between her and Leo occurred. It was years into their friendship yet somehow inevitable, and afterwards it remained (usually) unspoken between them. But it had been very real at the time. Leo cringed as a memory of her taking part in a live broadcast debate flashed through his mind. Her hapless opponents were feminists who wished to persuade Parliament to curtail the sale of pornography. Stephanie, the consummate lawyer, argued brilliantly for her and her partner's unequivocal right to enjoy dirty images as part of their healthy, vigorous sex life. It was fairly eye-watering stuff for Sunday morning television and Leo hoped desperately that his mother wasn't watching. 'Gosh!' he said out loud as he thought back to their night together. 'The very *idea* of us as a couple!'

As for Stephanie, she soon regretted hanging up the phone. What if she could have been of real assistance? It was a murder inquiry, after all. She would text him tomorrow to find out what he wanted.

12

Leo had invited Fordyce to dine with him as his guest, a proposal that had been most enthusiastically welcomed. They had arranged to meet in the bar at half past four for a few preprandials, and, as Leo had hoped, Dreghorn had already run out of funds and buggered off. However, Robbie McKee was in situ. He was acting rather strangely, staring dead ahead, his lips moving as he mumbled to an unseen companion. Leo considered that it was as though there was some planetary influence working upon the man.

The sunset gilded everything with a weird and bonny purple blush, and Leo felt quite uplifted as he ordered his first drink of the evening, feeling dapper in his classic-cut evening suit. He felt renewed by his hot bath; it had taken the outdoor chill from his bones and eased the stress he felt after his telephone conversation with Stephanie.

Fordyce soon arrived wearing a faintly eccentric brown and cream houndstooth dinner jacket with a chocolate collar and matching bow tie. He was apologetic despite being only minutes late, and ordered a libation from Shona Minto, who was on duty, and a top-up for Leo. He noticed the notebook his friend had been studying, which was laid upon the bar, revealing the jumble of letters Leo had jotted down earlier.

'Ah, I love a good puzzle!' Fordyce said, before remembering himself. 'Sorry, old stick, didn't mean to pry.'

'Not at all, Fordyce. It is a translation of the runes we saw inscribed upon the thirteenth baron's tomb. I reckon it's some sort of cipher, and I can't make head nor tail of it.'

'Do you mind if I have a go?' suggested Fordyce. 'I hate to blow my own trumpet, but I'm not completely useless when it comes to puzzles and brainteasers and such like.'

'I'd be only too happy,' replied Leo, remembering his chum's speedy solving of the *Times* crossword that morning. He tore out the page and handed it over. 'Fordyce, this solitary, James Millar – is his place easy to find?' He took a sip of his vodka martini.

Fordyce sighed, a pained expression on his face. 'Look, old stick, I wouldn't get a bee in your bonnet about poor James. He's not what you'd think at all. Losing his wife didn't make him angry; it just made him incredibly sad. Timid, actually. He's a very gentle fellow. An absolute first-rater.'

'Tell me about how he took to the wilds.'

'He's a big fan of all things Appalachian. So, after Carole died he decided to live the life. He plays his banjo, traps and hunts, distills moonshine. He may be deemed rather peculiar by some people's standards, but he's perfectly harmless. Finding poor Helen like that . . . it's been really hard on him. It brought back a lot of dreadful memories.'

Leo gazed out of the French doors. The lovely purple light had drained from the sky, which was marred with vast blots of charcoal, and the landscape had suddenly become incredibly gloomy, as though it was about to tip its ink-dark melancholy into the beholder's heart. Leo thought of the north, of the lonely lights of Klondykers and extraction superstructures perched upon the deep, blackening water, of shadow rolling up the great sea lochs. Something impossibly desolate about the images brushed against his soul.

'You're not thinking of visiting him now, are you?' asked Fordyce. 'It's *miles* away.'

'No, no. The shadows 'gin to loom, such are the ephemeral days of this dismal season. I'll go up tomorrow. For tonight, there is only warm company, excellent food and the finest wines with which to rinse our lusty palates. *Slàinte!*'

'Bottoms up!'

They raised their glasses and chinked them together, glad of each other's companionship in this darkest of winters.

13

L EO had aimed to breakfast early before setting off to visit James Millar. However, as usual his best-laid plans were frustrated by the soporific effect of the previous evening's alcohol. He still laboured under the illusion that he only required seven hours' sleep per night; in fact he needed nearer ten after boozing, which was almost always. He devoured a plate of kippers, then sat reading the *Guardian*, tutting at the impenetrable commentaries therein, more and more of which seemed to be concerned with gender politics. Leo would often plagiarise an adage by declaring that his socialism was more rooted in Methodism than Marx. For one thing he tended to like Methodists; Marxists generally chilled him to the marrow.

Ludwig informed him that he had received a text message. It was from Stephanie: 'Wot is it u wantd me 2 do?'

He replied: 'Could you please visit the Mitchell Library for me? I require you to do some research.'

In what seemed like a moment Stephanie, who could knock out a text at several times the rate of Leo, responded: 'Closed for refurb. Soz.'

'Damn and blast!' he exclaimed.

He came up with an alternative strategy, and called the operator who put him through to the University of Glasgow's Medieval History Department, but it transpired that the professor with whom he was acquainted was on sabbatical, and unreachable at some remote Canadian mountain retreat.

Defeated, he made his way through a rack of buttered toast and marmalade, and an entire pot of coffee (as well as a restorative early tot of The Glenlivet), glancing up occasionally to see if Fordyce had surfaced. By half past ten, as the dining room was being cleared of the breakfast things, he decided to call his friend's room from reception. The phone rang several times before Fordyce answered with an indecipherable sound.

'Still abed, Fordyce? Come along, the day's a-wasting!'

'I'm sick, old stick, sick!'

'Have you come down with something?'

'Yes, alcohol poisoning. I should never have started so early.'

'I'll be right up.'

By the time Leo had arrived bearing a glass of fizzing liver salts, Fordyce had propped himself up against his pillows. He looked deathly pale, but also faintly comical in his lurid emerald and chartreuse green silk pyjamas. He sipped the effervescent tonic gratefully then gasped slightly.

'Better?'

'A little.'

'Excellent. So you'll be ready to accompany me to the Witch's Cauldron?'

'Not that much better,' Fordyce groaned. 'I'm sorry, old stick, and I hope you don't think me the most frightful bore, but you'll have to make your own way. Do pass on my most affectionate regards to dear James.'

'No matter. Just give me directions and, if you don't mind, a loan of that stout walking stick,' Leo said, pointing at an elegant staff leaning against the wall.

'Of course, old stick, you may borrow my old stick,' Fordyce said, with unintentional humour.

Thus armed, Leo set off towards Glen Fallasky. He wore a knapsack containing a cold luncheon prepared by the hotel kitchen, a water flask and a bottle of Wild Turkey Kentucky sipping whiskey he had purchased from Bill Minto as a blandishment for Millar. Kentucky was in Appalachia, Leo believed.

Robbie McKee's Land Rover sat outside the hotel, the keys in the ignition. Presumably its owner had been too drunk to drive home last night. The morning was raw enough to rasp Leo's lungs, which were still recovering from flu, but it wasn't as cold as it had been, and quite bright, with the sun occasionally filtering through the cloud. Leo crossed the main road and noticed a little wooden plaque mounted on a garden gate bearing the carved lettering 'EDEN'. He entered the tree line. A startled red squirrel looked up from rummaging through the carpet of dead leaves to reveal his pearl-white breast. Upon seeing Leo he raced up a bare lime trunk, his bright tail swishing behind him like a chestnut feather boa. Leo passed through some richly wooded parkland, catching a glimpse of the white rump of a fleeing roe deer. Many of the trunks were robed in thick layers of moss, and one mighty Scots pine lorded over the coppice like an aged monarch, draped in kingly verdant folds. Nearby ran what was presumably the perimeter of the Grey Lady's grounds. This ancient, crumbling wall, crowned with masses of ivy, blushed lime with lichen in the thin sunlight. Huge wrought-iron gates guarded the entrance, beyond which a cinder track ran into oblivion amid a mass of laurel and rhododendron, and bare rowan and ash. Leo walked on, over the cold, spongy turf, taking care not to tread upon a clump of early Candlemas bells. A flock of visiting redwings sounded cheerfully above, their thin, high-pitched call heralding the coming season.

Spring. Leo longed for it, with the virgin light of its hallowed days culminating in the great mysteries of the Holy Triduum. He loved the symbiotic manner in which the Church's calendar mirrored the rhythm of earthly life while holistically paying due tribute to the great saints and seismic biblical events. Christmas, the Word coming into the world, the light of hope defying the death of winter. The Easter miracle resplendent amid nature's own annual resurrection. The Church as a constant throughout fad and whim, a beacon in life's stormy sea, mankind's lamp of sanctuary, Waugh's 'small red flame'. A memory flashed into Leo's mind of a golden tabernacle in a shadowy church on Holy Thursday: unclothed, starkly empty, the lamp put out, its fully opened doors somehow challenging the beholder to consider the Paschal Victim, like the Madonna in Michelangelo's *Pietà*. Perhaps this time round he would finally cleanse himself of drink during Lent, which would come early this year, and feel entitled to celebrate the victory all the more once it came. Perhaps not.

Leo then thought about Fordyce for a while. He imagined how liberating it would be to possess his temper. He would see Christ Jesus, and not potential hostility, in any stranger. He would be tolerant and understanding of folk, instead of seeking fault, which was his great sin. However, he consoled himself, it was easier for some people to be holy than it was for others. Probably the way one's DNA is arranged defines one's default mode of irascibility. Every individual human being had their own unique journey, and the key was in the striving to be a better person, to overcome whatever darkness was found within one's soul. Furthermore, Leo's loneliness, his perpetual hangovers and the pain he often endured from his damaged hands lent him a dyspeptic outlook, and his visions had lain bare too much of the beastliness in men's hearts to permit him a particularly benevolent disposition.

The woods gave way to the glen proper, which was a rather bland piece of Scottish countryside. It was a shallow strath, boggy and inclining at its sump, and punctuated only by sheets of snow and clumps of heather or gorse. The perennial flower of the latter species, a little miracle of the natural world, cheerfully scorned the washed-out pall of the season. The drab rattle of a hidden ground-nesting bird sounded from a laroch. Leo chose a natural path which ran up the left side of the bog. The odd stone or piece of planking wrapped in chicken wire had been strategically placed to bridge the soggiest parts. He trudged through a dense plantation of conifers – larch then Sitka spruce. It completely enclosed him for a while, but for the central mossy strip which trickled with water, and gave him a sense of being in an endless, mystical forest.

Cursing his lack of fitness, he toiled up the gradient and had soon drained his flask of water. However, further on the country became somewhat prettier and the contour of the land less steep. The odd tree dotted the horizon and the water flow which had dissolved into the bog further down was a veritable torrent up here, running merrily along the valley floor. The views became better, too. To the west a white curtain of rain soaked a distant glen, and the sun blinked through and kissed the magnificence of Ben Corrach, highlighting its ravines and scaurs and corries like lines on an old man's face.

Eventually, Leo could see a spur on the hill ridge ahead, which Fordyce had instructed him to look out for, and he knew he was near the Witch's Cauldron.

James Millar spent his days smiling. Smiling with sadness, or smiling with joy at the honour of having known her, of having been married to her, of having loved her. Of having been loved by her.

Sometimes she would visit him in his dreams, the gorgeousness of the experience always counterbalanced by the desolation he would feel when he woke up alone in the haggard pre-dawn light. Yet Millar still smiled, more often than not. Smiled with bittersweet sorrow, smiled with gratitude. But most of all he smiled in the certain knowledge that they would meet again, just as surely as the gloom of night would be pierced by the rays of sunlight that gently crept over the mountains like the caressing fingers of a lover.

Leo heard Millar before he laid eyes upon him. More precisely he heard his skilful plucking of 'Cripple Creek' on a five-string banjo.

'Earl Scruggs, eat your heart out!' announced Leo.

Millar was perched on a boulder next to a little camp fire, a man of forty wearing a lumberjack shirt under a sheepskin coat, blue denim jeans and outdoor boots. A milky blond fringe protruded from beneath a red and black tartan hunting hat, its ear flaps dangling loose. He had misty blue eyes and wore round-framed spectacles. He had a certain dreamy, distracted air and slow, deliberate movements. After a moment he smiled in greeting towards his visitor.

'Leo Moran. Delighted to meet you.'

'James Millar,' the man replied in a mild voice, shaking Leo's proffered hand. 'But you already know that, I suppose?'

'I came up here to see you. I'm a friend of Fordyce Greatorix.'

'Fordyce is a special man. Such beautiful manners.'

'He thinks very highly of you too.'

The Witch's Cauldron was a perfect hollow, generously embroidered with trees and shrubbery, its steep natural walls protecting its inhabitant from the worst of the wind. The stream had been dammed here to cause a cistern from which Millar could draw his water, and at the back of the hollow was his blackhouse, a simple but beautifully built abode complete with thatched roof. In places much of the undergrowth had been cleared and a patch of rich, fecund black earth had been tilled and planted.

'Gosh, when I heard of the Witch's Cauldron I imagined a sinister place, but this is quite beguiling!' said Leo. 'What a wonderful home you have made for yourself.'

'Thank you. Perhaps she was a good witch, whoever she was. Are you here about Helen?'

Leo was taken aback by Millar's directness, and wished he had prepared what to say in advance. He decided honesty was the best policy. 'Yes. Look, I'll level with you. I'm an amateur sleuth, and as such I don't have any right to ask anything of you. But I just wondered if I could put to you a few questions.'

'Of course. Can I get you some coffee?' Millar offered, gesturing towards a pot that sat upon the fire. A greasy skillet sat on the grass, smelling of bacon fat.

'Actually, I'd just love a glass of water, if you may be so kind. I'm fair puggled.'

Millar ambled off and came back with a jam jar filled with water and a little wicker chair for Leo so that he could sit by the fire.

'Thank you,' said Leo, sitting down and surreptitiously wiping the rim with his handkerchief when his host's back was turned, yet feeling somehow honoured at being bequeathed the man's humble hospitality.

'Fresh from a mountain stream.' Millar smiled. 'I don't blame folk, you know.'

'For what?'

'For suspecting me. I mean, I understand that people find my way of life somewhat peculiar. And, of course, there's what happened to my Carole and the fact that I found poor Helen's body.'

'As a matter of fact I am myself somewhat predisposed towards private, quiet living. Also, I have a personal allergy to throwing around unsubstantiated accusations. So I am not here to accuse you, Mr Millar.'

'James.'

'James. Believe me, there are plenty of suspects in this case. To an extent every man of military age in a ten-mile radius is one.'

Millar noticed Leo's nose twitching at the sweet smell of liquor on the air, and grinned. 'Mum's the word. Perhaps not the most prudent habit for a man with my medical . . . issues. But it keeps the cold out.'

At that Leo withdrew the bottle of Wild Turkey, much to Millar's appreciation. He proposed that they take the top off it there and then.

'Actually, I'd love to try the homemade stuff, if there's any ready,' suggested Leo.

Millar rubbed his hands together gleefully and came back from a little outhouse armed with an earthenware jug and two little tumblers. He poured two measures of rust-coloured liquid into the glasses, and handed one to his visitor.

Leo had sampled homemade *raki* in Turkey, *ouzo* in Greece, *grappa* in Italy and *poitín* in the Connemara hills, but nothing came close to James Millar's *peatreek* for sheer, throat-scalding potency. Millar laughed good-naturedly as his guest coughed and spluttered, his face flushed, his eyes glazed.

'Well, that's a fine drop!' Leo croaked, before leaving an appropriate pause in the conversation. 'James, I believe Helen used to come up here to visit you?'

'Yes, even when she didn't have to. She would visit lots of isolated people: the Grey Lady, the Kildavannan lot. She'd come up here on horse-back. Bring me my prescription, various wee gifts and provisions. She was a lovely lassie. And for her age she had real wisdom, real empathy. But there was something else about her, a kind of vulnerable quality.'

'How do you mean?' enquired Leo, intrigued.

'It was as though she was a little . . . damaged, by something that was buried deep.' He paused, the colour draining from his face. 'There was so much blood!' he gasped. 'Just like with Carole . . .'

Millar blinked the tears from his eyes and gazed down towards the distant loch. Leo felt moved by the sadness that filled his innocent features, and ashamed that he momentarily begged God never to permit him to suffer the profound and incomprehensible agonies that had befallen this gentle creature. He instinctively sensed that James Millar was a human being incapable of a single act of cruelty.

14

O N the way back down Glen Fallasky Leo paused at a forlorn, turbid little pool called Lochan nan Nathrach, 'Pond of the Serpents'. His perspiration had gone cold but he couldn't be bothered stripping down and removing his damp singlet. He consumed his packed luncheon and brooded upon James Millar's extraordinarily bad fortune. When he got to the foot of the glen he took a different, roundabout route back to the hotel, wishing to explore a little lane he had spied on the way up that ran in front of the Grey Lady's walled abode before cutting through some pinewoods. It proved of little interest, but Leo followed this to the road, crossed over, and wandered down a narrow dirt path to the lochside. From here he negotiated the rocky way back to the Loch Dhonn.

He soon regretted his choice of route, such was the difficulty of the terrain. Every headland deceived him that it was the final one prior to the hotel; it was akin to climbing Ben Lomond, with its numerous false summits. Just as he was about to opt for the easier route of a narrow beaten path he had noticed which skirted the worst of the shore, Leo reached yet another little bay and there was Craig Hutton, Helen's boyfriend, unmistakable from the photograph he had seen behind the hotel bar. He was sitting upon a dilapidated little pier, smoking a roll-up. A fishing line, which was dipped in the water, swayed languidly in the almost imperceptible breeze. Hutton had sharp youthful features and a number two cut. He wore an olive-coloured field cap, a drab army-surplus shirt and body warmer, khaki combat trousers and safety boots. He turned and acknowledged Leo with a nod.

'Any luck?'

'I think I caught the cold about half an hour ago.'

Leo smiled politely at the old joke. Already he knew by the expression on Hutton's face that this was a straightforward country laddie who was struggling to find a way of processing the trauma that had so suddenly and indecently descended upon him. He had resolved to tough it out. He was too inexperienced and immature to know any other way.

'I owe ye one,' said Hutton.

'Why's that?'

'I overheard the polis sayin' ye'd vouched for me.'

'I doubt that I had very much clout.'

'Well, thanks, anyway.'

Leo paused for a moment, then said, 'I know what it feels like to be falsely accused of a crime, although apart from that I can't imagine what you have been through. I am truly sorry for it all.'

'Cheers.' Hutton took a drag on his roll-up, then exhaled. 'Ye must have an idea who he is?'

Leo shook his head solemnly.

'I know who ye are, why ye're here,' Hutton continued. 'I saw ye talkin' wi' Lang, found out yer name. Googled ye.'

'It's edifying to discover I am so famous. I just hope the press don't realise my identity quite so quickly, or DI Lang will dispatch me on the next train back to Glasgow. But I'm afraid I don't know who did it. Not yet.'

Leo looked out at the fishing float. He could feel the young man's gaze on the side of his face.

Hutton's green eyes flashed as he spoke. 'When ye do I want ye to kill him.'

At these words blackness flickered in front of Leo's eyes, not a vision but a peculiar sensation of premonition, a feeling that something profound and deadly augured. His legs almost gave way and he just managed to steady himself.

'Are ye OK?'

'Yes.'

Leo sat down upon a mossy stump, panting, loosening his collar. Hutton handed him a bottle of water. Leo took a long draught, then withdrew his hip flask and brazenly gulped from it. He offered it to Hutton who took a nip.

'What happened?'

'I don't know. Perhaps killing someone isn't a very fair thing to ask of a man.'

'I dinnae feel very much like being fair these days. He's done it once, he may have done it afore and he'll certainly do it again. Folk deserve to be protected. Ye'd be doin' society a favour – destroyin' somethin' evil.'

'Craig, you're a young man. Don't let him get inside your head like this. We'll catch this devil and throw away the key.'

'She was the best person I ever knew. We were talkin' about gettin' engaged. If ye dinnae have the stomach to do it, tell me who he is and I will.'

15

B Y the time Leo reached the hotel the streetlamps that lit barely a hundred yards of Loch Dhonn village had been switched on, and whirls of black vapour had started to congregate in the cold, deepening blue sky. All was gloomy and shadowy. The meeting with Hutton had shaken Leo and he resolved to take dinner in his room alone and have a soak in the bath and an early night.

Leo noticed that the population of the hotel had swollen somewhat, now that the initial horror of the murder had subsided. The incident room and a heavy police, and indeed media, presence remained, but the tape that had surrounded the crime scene had been taken down and no longer could polythene-clad forensic officers be seen crawling around in the undergrowth. Some tourists who had booked in advance and didn't want to lose their deposits were milling around the lobby, and couples who had saved up a few bob for a slap-up meal had driven in from Fallasky, Inveraray and even Oban and Crianlarich to dine at the renowned restaurant. Leo retrieved his key from its hook in reception, also picking up a note inviting him to dinner from Fordyce, who even in this digital age rather charmingly insisted that invitations should always be handwritten. Leo used the desk telephone to call his friend's room and respectfully postpone.

'Not at all, old stick, think nothing of it.'

As Fordyce rang off, Leo spied, through the doorway into the office, Shona Minto dressing down the pretty Polish waitress. Neither party was aware of his presence and Leo was struck by how unpleasantly the hotelier threw her weight around. When she had finished the waitress came out to the reception area and hurried off, not looking at Leo, with tears welling up in her eyes. Shona followed her out and saw Leo standing there with the telephone receiver in his hand. She gave him a look that said, 'You can't get the staff nowadays', but Leo simply regarded her coldly in return.

*   *   *

He was glad of the warmth of his bedchamber and poured himself a large whisky. He rang down an order for salmon mayonnaise, Cullen skink, and roast duck and green peas, with a bottle of Château de Beaucastel. He consumed his meal with some considerable voracity after the exertions of the day. He padded into his room after his bath, noting approvingly that the dishes had been removed and that the siphon and ice bucket he had ordered had arrived. He opened his portmanteau and withdrew his little chess computer. He tried a Budapest Gambit but played badly, his mind preoccupied by thoughts and theories about the murder case. He decided to say his night prayers and go to bed.

Leo lapsed into a troubled, fevered sleep, his body twitching, his eyes moving rapidly as images bombarded his consciousness. These were largely random and banal, the type of dreaming that is common to all people, but soon certain visions permeated his psyche which were characterised by a familiar sense of potency and significance.

Helen and Craig together in a wood. He chases her playfully through the trees. He catches her. They laugh, then he regards her fondly, strokes her cheek, kisses her passionately. He spreads his coat. The sylvan lovers lie down, thinking themselves concealed. But something is lurking in the undergrowth, watching. The beast. Leo can feel its envy, its hate; hear its breathing quicken as the animal anger rises in its throat. Leo's vision turns a hundred and eighty degrees but the beast's face is in shadow; something is jamming his signals, something is muddling his perception.

Then Leo is on Innisdubh. He sees the serpents and griffins and gargoyles and dragons that are carved into the Green Lord's gravestone come to life, and spit fire and whirl around a lead-grey sky which is bruised with intense Tyrian purple and vermilion. Then he sees pseudo-religious rites being performed upon the standing stone which had collapsed; repellent, obscene ceremonies. Then he sees the double doors of the tenth baron's mausoleum. His vision zooms in upon the padlock, slowly at first, then faster and faster. Now he is inside the sepulchre, terrified yet somehow compelled to press further into its gloomy depths. He rounds a corner where a figure dressed in the robes Helen had described floats off the ground, wearing the ghastly, pointed hood on its head. The figure produces something, a wand perhaps, from the folds of its robes and raises it. It is black. There is an explosion of light yet there is no sound.

Leo flinched as though to avoid the shock wave of the blast, and instantly woke up, overheated and unnerved, his sweat-sodden pyjamas clinging to him. He switched on the bedside light, got out of bed, and walked into the bathroom. His tongue was incredibly dry, like a fat piece of leather. He heard a two-note horn, strikingly loud in the still night air as it echoed mournfully across the loch's surface. He supposed it was the milk train at Stob's Bend, exiting the Lairig Lom as it headed for Glasgow or Perth.

He rinsed and spat the sourness from his mouth. He held forth Benjamin Franklin, who looked rather distinguished in the half light.

'Hail to thee, noble, redundant fellow,' said Leo, keen to dispel the incubus with humour as the stream began tumbling noisily into the pan. He washed his hands thoroughly with soft soap, his mind heavy and indescribably bleak, as though his consciousness had been immersed within an ocean of the weird evil abroad in the world. Leo's visions were often fragmented or oblique or symbolic, but in this investigation they all seemed to be particularly incomplete. 'What is Your path for me, Lord?' he wondered aloud. He recalled a line from the diary entry DI Lang had given him: 'Tark cornered me in the woods today. Must have seen me and Craig making love.' It chimed with the initial part of this latest vision, of the watcher in the woods. He would ask Helen about Tark, assuming he ever encountered her again.

Leo peeled off his night clothes and sponged the clammy perspiration from his torso with a towel. He rummaged in a drawer for his other pyjamas, then slaked his thirst with two glasses of water followed by a slug of Scotch for his nerves. He caught sight of his tired likeness in the mirror. Something about the padlock had captured his attention at the time: its relative newness. Of course that could mean nothing of consequence; perhaps vandals or decay had broken the original lock. But generally these details recurred in his visions for a reason. He looked directly into the reflection of his eyes and resolved to return to Innisdubh that very day. He was going to find out what lay inside that tomb.

16

LEO slept only fitfully after that, and was comforted when he heard the mundane hum and clatter of life from below as the staff prepared for breakfast. He shaved, showered and dressed for the day.

Downstairs a number of hacks were checking out, their editors presumably having baulked at the exorbitant expense claims being filed from the luxurious hotel and told them to find cheaper accommodation. Leo entered the dining room and was helloed loudly by Fordyce, who looked far healthier than he had the previous morning, and was tucking into a hearty Scottish breakfast.

'Grab a pew, old stick. Gosh, did you have a rough night?'

'Does it show?' asked Leo.

'You just look a little tired,' said Fordyce, backtracking tactfully. In truth he had just witnessed a flashing image of Leo as an old man.

'Bad dream,' Leo said, massaging his forehead as he watched Bill Minto wait upon the tables at the far side of the room. Something servile in the hotelier's manner irked him. 'I don't have any appetite.'

The Polish waitress stood by Leo's right shoulder, checking herself for staring at the livid skin of his burned hands. Leo noticed her gaze but didn't seem to mind.

'Good morning, sir.'

'Good morning. Just coffee, please.'

'Bring him some toast and scrambled eggs also, if you please, Ania,' interjected Fordyce.

'And a wee dram, dear,' said Leo, 'as a pick-me-up,' he added, noticing his friend's look of disapproval.

Ania first brought the coffee and Leo sipped disconsolately from his cup.

'Fordyce, I need to go back to Innisdubh. May I borrow the *Fairy Queen*?'

'Something to do with your dream?'

Leo nodded solemnly.

'Right. We'll go over once you've rested a little more.'

'I appreciate your concern, but I need to press on. I've been in Loch Dhonn almost three days and I haven't a clue who the killer is. If he were to strike again I'd never forgive myself.'

'But it isn't your responsibility.'

'Using my God-given talents to the best of my ability – yes, that is my responsibility.'

Fordyce sensed Leo's determination and relented with a shrug.

'There's something else I need to ask you.'

'Anything, old stick, just say the word.'

'Is there any way you could discreetly source me a hammer and a chisel? My wire cutters will be too flimsy for the job I have in mind.'

Fordyce, remembering Leo's interest in the padlocked tomb of the tenth baron, read his friend's intentions. 'You're not thinking of breaking into that ghastly repository, are you?'

Leo was silent.

'But why not tell the inspector and get the police to investigate it? After all, he must take your powers seriously if he was willing to have conferred with you.'

'Because DI Lang will play it by the book and time is of the essence. Even if I can persuade him to apply for a search warrant, and even if the sheriff was to issue one – which would be difficult because the baron would likely hire a top Edinburgh lawyer to prevent it – too much time would have elapsed.'

'All right. I have a hammer and chisel in my boatshed. I'll take us over to the island after breakfast.'

'No, Fordyce. I'm going alone.'

'Why, my dear fellow?'

'Because what I am to do is illegal. You have to live up here; I'm not going to get you into trouble.'

'Oh, what rot. We'll go together and be damned together. Besides, those rocks are treacherous, and I'm used to them.'

'I'm saying no, my friend. This is something I need to do myself.'

Fordyce nodded slowly in defeat.

*　　*　　*

From the high turret window of the Loch Dhonn Hotel someone watched Leo and Fordyce walk down to the boatyard after they had finished breakfasting. The watcher watched as they wheeled the *Fairy Queen* from her shed and set her afloat in the water before lugging the outboard and fitting it to the boat's stern. The watcher watched as Fordyce handed Leo a tool bag, mouthed advice on how to best operate the vessel, and Leo fired the engine and set off towards the dark isle of Innisdubh.

Then the hand of the watcher – the manly hand of Shona Minto – reached for the telephone.

17

THE morning was grey and unforgivingly cold. Sound seemed to travel further in the frigid air. Leo, strung-out and tired from stress and lack of sleep, had great difficulty beaching the boat at Innisdubh. He struggled to haul it up the shore, and slipped and fell upon some ice. He recovered, secured the *Fairy Queen*, then slung the tool bag over his shoulder and headed for the mausoleum.

All was as he remembered, and it seemed strange to be there so soon after his vision. Leo's damaged hands were numb as he began hammering the chisel at the hasp. The vestibule was gloomy, so he held his pencil torch between his teeth and it shed enough light for him to work. The noise within the semi-enclosed space was terrific, and gradually the metal began to give way, before fracturing and shooting off in two jagged pieces. Leo tried the heavy iron doors. They were still jammed. He put his shoulder to where they met but still there was no give. He examined them using the torch and to his exasperation found another, smaller padlock and hasp, further down from the first one.

'Someone is keen to keep this place firmly shut,' he muttered out loud as he positioned the chisel once again.

Then he felt an explosion of pain in his skull like a sheet of white light and a sickness in his belly as his legs turned to jelly and gave way. The last thing he remembered was a sensation like being cast into a fast-flowing river, a rushing torrent, the black water boiling and deafening.

Fordyce gently called him out of his coma. His friend was cradling his head, pressing a white handkerchief to his scalp in order to stem the bleeding. Behind him towered Detective Inspector Lang, who looked on from atop the vestibule steps.

'Oh, I feel *terrible*,' croaked Leo.

'You'll be all right, old stick.'

'Why did you . . . come over?'

'After you left I went back to my suite. Just after one o'clock I wandered down to the boatyard and you evidently still hadn't returned. I started to get a bit worried about you, so I sought out Detective Inspector Lang and he kindly agreed to take me over in the police boat.'

'Did you see anyone approaching or leaving the island?'

'No. As I said, I had repaired to my hotel room.'

'The hammer and chisel?'

'Gone,' confirmed Fordyce.

'I'm sorry, I'll get you new ones.'

'Don't be silly, old stick, as long as you're all right.'

'Come on,' said Lang. 'Let's get you back. Any ideas as to who it might have been?'

'It could have been the baron's man,' proposed Leo.

'Well, it wasn't McKee, Dreghorn or Rattray. They've been in the hotel bar since opening time,' stated the policeman.

Lang and Fordyce each hooked an arm under Leo's shoulders and half dragged, half lifted him towards the boats. Lang took the police boat while Fordyce piloted the *Fairy Queen* with the stricken Leo languishing in the bow. As they ploughed the grey water he had begun to shiver uncontrollably, having been lying in the cold for some considerable period of time, and Fordyce stopped to drape his coat over him. Once they had landed, Lang drove them the short distance from the boatyard to the hotel. He was unimpressed by Leo's escapade, and before dropping them off he murmured some vague threat in legalese about 'violation of sepulchre'. The policeman had already briefly assessed the scene for clues with an eagle eye. The only items of note were fresh male footprints leading to and away from the top of the vestibule steps which were too large to match those of the killer. Two of them were superimposed upon Leo's recent imprints, meaning they doubtless belonged to the assailant. Lang said he would have Forensics come over to take a look at them.

Leo was made comfortable in his bed by Fordyce, who insisted that he call the local GP. Dr Fitzpatrick was a small, quietly-spoken Englishman who inspected Leo's head through severe black-rimmed spectacles. The patient winced as he applied iodine to the cut and mended it using butterfly stitches before swathing his head in bandages. The physician recommended going to Oban for an X-ray but Leo stubbornly refused. Leo enquired about Helen, who had briefly been the doctor's colleague, but received no information of value from the taciturn man, who then left without ceremony.

A concerned Bill Minto dropped by with some beef tea. They chatted pleasantly and Minto happened to mention the fact that the baron had dined in the hotel at lunchtime with his manservant.

'You're sure the baron's man was with him – that tough-looking fellow?' checked Leo.

'Yes, Kemp was there. I know because I served them myself, in our private dining room.'

'So,' said Fordyce, once Minto had gone, 'it doesn't sound as though the baron is to blame.'

'Hmm,' agreed Leo reluctantly.

'Could it have been the murderer who attacked you?'

'Possibly. Although Lang said the shoe size won't be a match. I'd like to find out what's so special about that tomb.'

'Well, you won't be doing any more finding out today, laddie!' commanded Fordyce.

Leo was happy to obey. He felt groggy and nauseous and his head hurt, and even he struggled to concoct an excuse for taking a drink. He did however see an opportunity to use the situation to his advantage and make peace with Stephanie. He texted her, informing her of his mishap.

She responded within two minutes. 'OMG! RU OK?!!!'

'I am beaten but unbowed,' he replied after a while. 'The doctor wishes to hospitalise me in Oban but I will resolutely stick to my task.'

'FFS! Was it the killer?'

'Possibly.'

'U shld cum home!'

'I never realised you cared,' he teased, detecting real anxiety in her abridged messages.

Fordyce proceeded to nurse his friend attentively for the remainder of the afternoon and early evening. Leo fervently wished to avoid having to reject his rather clumsy overtures. He didn't want to hurt Fordyce's feelings, but also, if truth be told, he felt rather flattered by the interest. And so their mutual, unspoken little game endured: Fordyce – subtly, so as to allow deniability should it be required – playing the incorrigible flirt; Leo either pretending not to notice, or else coyly fending off the advances.

Just after eight in the evening an official-sounding knock at the door announced Lang's arrival. Fordyce left the room.

'How's the head?' enquired the inspector.

'Its magnificent exterior gives me complaint, but thankfully its precious cargo is undamaged.'

'Why were you trying to break into that tomb?'

'I had a vision,' replied Leo weakly.

'Two days ago you reproached me for not sharing information on the case. Now you tell me you've had one of your hallucinations and decided to act upon it alone – and illegally, I might add – without telling me. I'm decidedly unimpressed, Mr Moran.'

'I am legitimately rebuked. It's just that you would never have been granted a search warrant on the strength of a man's dream.'

Lang paused. 'You're right. But you could still have let me know what you had planned.'

'I give you my word, Detective Inspector, that from now on I will be fastidious in sharing everything with you, even items of apparently the least significance.'

'All right then, in that spirit, tell me the exact content of this latest vision.'

'I saw Helen and Craig together in the woods, being watched by the murderer, which chimes with the diary entry you found.'

'Perhaps the diary entry invoked the dream,' suggested Lang.

'I saw black rites being performed on Innisdubh,' continued Leo, ignoring the detective's interruption, 'which correlates with the theory I expatiated to you two days ago. Then I was inside the tenth baron's mausoleum, where I again saw the figure dressed in robes and hood. It smote at me with some sort of talisman, conjuring up an explosion of light. In none of these images was the key protagonist's identity revealed to me.'

Lang seemed to consider this data for a moment, then said, 'I wonder if it was the baron's man who attacked you. He'll be of a large shoe size, and the old boy did seem awfy offended at your presence on that island the other day.'

'No,' replied Leo. 'Bill was here earlier and informed me that Kemp was dining at the hotel with his employer.'

'Right. Well, I'll need to have a good think about today's events. If it's got anything to do with Helen's murder then I want to know everything about it. I've asked around, to find out if anyone saw a boat approaching or leaving Innisdubh while you were over there, but I drew a blank. I've also had some men search the vicinity of the mausoleum, for any other clues as to who attacked you, but they found nothing.'

Lang left, and Fordyce came back in, and once he had been persuaded to stop fussing and leave his patient in peace, Leo clicked off his bedside lamp and fell into a deep and unusually dreamless slumber, which soothed his wound and troubles like a heavenly balm.

18

THE next morning Leo felt slightly hungover, and had to remind himself that he had been unusually abstemious the night before. His skull continued to ache somewhat, but the sensation had reduced to a dull throb, and he felt steady on his feet when he got up to use the lavatory. He caught a glimpse of himself in the mirror as he washed his hands: the wounded hero with the picturesque dressing on his head.

He ordered a late breakfast in bed, just porridge drizzled with golden syrup and a pot of strong coffee. He also took an immodest nip from his hip flask – purely medicinal, he assured himself.

Fordyce looked in on him. 'How's the patient?'

'Much better, thank you,' replied Leo, foregoing his customary hypochondria.

'You certainly look a bit brighter. You should take it easy today, old stick.'

'Hmm. I'm thinking of getting out and about. The fresh air will do me good.'

'Sorry, old man, I can't permit that – doctor's orders, don't you know.'

'I need to speak with the Grey Lady.'

'You mean Lady Jane Elizabeth Charlotte Audubon-MacArthur, Laird of Fallasky.'

'Do you know her?'

'They're old friends of the family.'

Leo harrumphed. His allegiance to left-wing ideals was typical of West of Scotland Tims; socialism was imbibed with their mother's milk along with the other two aspects of the holy trinity: the Roman Catholic Church and Celtic FC. If there was one aspect to Britain Leo despised it was the class system, and sometimes this objection spilled into inverted snobbery.

Fordyce, meanwhile, decided for once to resist the usual sense of guilt for his wealth and status, and enquired: 'What's up?'

'I should have known.'

'Known what?'

'That you privileged lot are all pals together.'

'Don't be like that, Leo.'

'Like what?'

'Like you are filled with class hatred. It is unworthy of you.'

'I've always been a great champion of the underdog. I'm well known for it,' Leo ventured feebly, suitably chastised.

'Anyway, I'll let her know you're planning to call,' said Fordyce. 'She's a very private person. She doesn't like to be taken by surprise by unexpected visitors.'

'Thanks,' Leo said grudgingly. 'I'm hoping to find out more about this Bosco character.'

As Leo washed and dressed he ruminated over the events of the last few days: the attack upon his person, the people he had met, the places he had been. And he brooded over how speculative his efforts at finding the killer seemed. It was as though his unconscious was leading him a merry dance.

Fordyce, exasperated by his friend's insistence that he get out of bed and go about his business, had struck a compromise whereby he enlisted Robbie to drive Leo to and from his destination in his beat-up Land Rover, despite the Grey Lady's abode, Fallasky House, being a mere knight's move from the hotel. Fordyce escorted Leo as far as the hotel portico and took his leave of him.

Leo felt rather peculiar as he faced the morning and waited for McKee to arrive. The day was filthy and drab. A cruel wind, which threatened to swell to gale-force, scourged his face with drops of rain. To the west, a cumulonimbus incus cloud formation stacked up ominously against the horizon.

Shona Minto happened by, and enquired as to his wellbeing.

'I'm perfectly all right, thank you for asking,' replied Leo politely.

'Off out, are we?'

'I'm waiting for Robbie.'

'Oh, tell him I have a job of work for him, would you? I need some things moved. Mind you, the way he's been acting lately I'm not sure he's fit for it.'

'I'll be sure to pass that on,' Leo said stiffly.

'I saw you heading up towards the glen the other day. Visiting James Millar, were we?'

'Just taking my constitutional,' fibbed Leo, irked by the woman's nosiness.

'It's easier walking up there since they put in the stepping stones, though they put me off somewhat. I much prefer the wild country for hiking. Too much of a free spirit,' she declared with a false smile, before disappearing into the hotel.

'Free spirit indeed!' muttered Leo, 'you're a bloody *Tory*!'

McKee duly arrived in his ancient vehicle, the bodywork of which was a rust-lined patchwork from different paint jobs and panel replacements. The inside of the cab had a musty smell like stale breadcrumbs, and the journey was conducted in silence, but for the monotonous thudding of the windscreen wipers, which were on at a higher speed than was necessary and only served to spread grime over the glass. Leo's head was still cloudy from the attack and from being so absorbed of late in intense meditations regarding the murder case. Therefore he simply could not come up with any topic for conversation. The saturnine McKee, meanwhile, wore a haunted expression on his face and remained quite oblivious to convention's demand for social intercourse. He seemed somewhat anaesthetised to the cold, wearing only a sleeveless jerkin on top of a faded Rangers away top, which was a size too small for his bulky chassis, and he had evidently forgotten about the dead roll-up cigarette tucked between his lips. In spite of his driver's foibles, Leo felt sure this fellow was innocent of Helen's murder. He had by now equated McKee with one of the people from the vision he had experienced at church in Glasgow: the slow-witted man, the man who had been drowning in a sea of false accusations. And apart from anything else, the real killer had covered his tracks with great effectiveness, and Robbie surely lacked such guile. Also, the crime clearly had an occult element, and McKee just didn't fit the bill. Leo therefore worried about something Fordyce had told him a few days ago: that the police seemed to view Robbie as a prime suspect.

McKee dropped Leo at the impressive gates of Fallasky House, which were entwined with two wrought-iron serpents. Fading coats of arms were embossed upon the gateposts. He tried the handle and the right-hand gate opened with a creak worthy of any Hammer film. He walked up the cinder path towards the house, beneath a louring sky, taking in the environs as he went. Within thickets of rhododendron, laurel and holly he could discern a grotto shrine to Our Lady of the Snows with a perfect-white statue in ecstatic contemplation. Set upon the splendid lawn were dormant display beds, various classical statues, a bird bath, a lectern-shaped sundial and, by a pond, a weeping willow which Leo imagined would look magnificent in summertime. He had a sense that acres of enclosed policies stretched out from the opposite side of the mansion. The breeze hissed in a chase of huge fir trees which overlooked the south-ern side of the lawn and house, and a pair of hooded crows croaked irascibly as they hopped around, patrolling their territory. The brisk wind seemed to add a melodramatic edge to Leo's mission; he fancied for a moment he was being filmed in movie close-up.

Fallasky House itself was beautiful if rather creepy. The façade was of blond stone which had been aged by more than a century and a half's exposure to weather, and further darkened by spreading tendrils of ivy. The south wing was a square tower with parapet, from which extended the main spine of the edifice. Off this projected three front gables with the original sash windows still in place. These gables were craw-stepped in a paler stone from the facing, and ten magnificent chimneys and several dormer windows protruded from the roofs. Leo pretended not to notice the figure watching him from one of these. He must have presented rather a curious customer as he strode forth armed with Fordyce's walking stick, his head swathed in bandages, a tuft of unmanageable mouse-brown hair sticking up, his expressive face betraying his every thought as he surveyed the scene.

The rain had intensified, so Leo was glad to make the porch and pull the bell. As he waited he scraped his shoes and admired the fine, dark-red wrought-iron lacework. In a while the door opened.

Leo could barely discern the person framed by the gloom of the hall-way, but after a pregnant period a voice called out stridently, at last putting him at his ease: 'You must be Leo! Do come in out of that beastly dreich weather.'

'Thank you, madam.'

'Please, call me Jane – any friend of Fordyce's, and all that.'

Once in the hallway Leo's eyes quickly adapted to the light. It was a fine, late Georgian chamber, the floor tiled in an oblique geometric pattern of gold, rose and violet which shot off down corridors to either side. A stunning chandelier filled the stairwell. A grand staircase with heavy mahogany banisters curved up from the left to a half-landing, beneath which was an archway leading to the rear quarters. Above the landing was the hall's, and indeed the entire house's, centrepiece: a marvellous window depicting the birth of spring, and Leo, ever the aesthete, couldn't help but stare at it in awe.

'You like the window?'

'I don't believe I've ever seen anything so perfect!'

'You are most kind. Grandpapa, like his father, was a Victorian Romantic and polymath, and among other architectural items he championed stained glass. He had it commissioned after we lost the original – a far plainer affair – in a storm. When the sun shines in through it on a summer's morn it is like standing inside a Kandinsky.'

Suddenly, Leo could feel his father's eyes upon him, and he resolved not to be seduced by the opulence and glamour of nobility. Such is how the Establishment recruits its minions and perpetuates itself, he chided. Instead, think upon the poverty wages that built this mansion. Think upon the crime behind every great fortune. Think of the skilled, hard-working craftsmen who were paid a pittance as the rich luxuriated amid splendour they hadn't lifted a finger to create.

Yet Leo couldn't help but like the Grey Lady. She had the inevitable Anglicised accent, with a slightly husky smoker's catch, but something about her demeanour was down-to-earth and not in the least stuffy. She was aged approximately seventy and wore her grey hair, which was straight and quite long, down. Her eyes, too, were grey, and sparkled with wit and intelligence. She was attired in a mocha long-sleeved dress with a crocheted bodice. However, these muted tones clashed eccentrically with her bright stockings and loud silk scarf, printed with images of botanical blooms, under which she wore purple heliotrope beads and a yellow-gold Celtic cross. Such vibrant colours were converse to her local sobriquet, Leo noted.

She led him down the corridor, which was lined with renderings of various solemn, long-dead ancestors, scowling absurdly under effete tartan bonnets, and alcoves housing fine busts of the principal Stoic philosophers, towards the south wing.

'There was a time when this poor old house was fully staffed,' she informed him as they walked. 'Now it is just Bosco, when he's around, two Ugandan women who come in once a fortnight, and a whole lot of dust covers. Many of the rooms haven't been opened in years.'

The Grey Lady's voice was forthright and authoritative. Leo enjoyed the clipped way in which she pronounced her syllables. She led him into an exquisite drawing room which, unlike the cold halls, was properly heated by a blaze of fir heartwood burning merrily between two fine Jacobean firedogs. This was surrounded by a huge fireplace carved from Carrara marble, which towered above Leo. The room was decorated in two-tone turquoise, which contrasted with extensive white-painted wooden panelling and delicately moulded stucco forms and medallions on the ceilings and walls. The south window, which looked out on to the chase of fir trees, was dressed with huge satin drapes, and flanked by two magnificent Grecian columns, finished with cloudy pale-blue ersatz marble and topped with ivory-painted scrolled capitals. Upon the north wall was mounted a large canvas, *Stag Hunt in the Snow*, by Jan Fyt.

'Do sit down,' implored the Grey Lady, gesturing towards an elegant rosewood suite upholstered in Persian-blue fabric. Leo guessed it was a Chippendale reproduction by Edward Tolly, the renowned nine-teenth-century Edinburgh cabinetmaker.

The Grey Lady busied herself at an antique Russian samovar converted to run with an electric element which was set upon a fine mother-of-pearl-inlaid cabinet.

'It is a shame we are required to bear it alone,' she said obliquely.

'I beg your pardon?'

'Our gifts. I foresaw your visit, prior to Fordyce's telephone call, and the fact that you are a seer. Who first noticed that you possessed *darna shealladh*?'

'A holy man.'

'A priest? A minister?'

'No. A Muslim mystic. We were holidaying in Baghdad when I was a five-year-old child during a tour of the Near East. My upbringing was a humble one, and this uniquely exotic trip was funded by a not-inconsiderable win by a Pools syndicate, of which my mother was a member. Anyway, we were browsing the *souk* when a dervish picked me up in his arms and declared to my father – may God rest his soul – in Arabic (our guide later translated): "This child is my beautiful brother. We both enjoy God's special blessing, the power to see that which the eye cannot. May he be an instrument of truth." I remember the fellow had wild, shining eyes, a dazzling smile, a bushy beard and a tall *sikke* hat. He smelled of tallow and cannabis, and had a charisma to him that spellbound everyone in the place. He performed a ritual about me, as my parents looked on rather nervously.'

'How marvellous! My mother was a clairvoyant. She knew I was too, even when I was in the womb. Yet neither of us was blessed with your extraordinary faculty, Leo: the power of visions. With us it was just feelings, you know, intuition. And information we possessed that we had no right to know . . . it was just *there*. You're Catholic, aren't you?'

'*Via, Veritas, Vita.*'

'Good. It will fortify you for the trials that follow.' Leo felt a shiver run down his spine. 'I sense that you are here to investigate poor Helen's awful murder.'

Leo didn't answer. 'Are you Catholic, Jane?' he enquired, recalling the statue of Our Lady he had seen outside.

'Yes,' she said. 'Another aspect that keeps me apart from the folk . . . down there.'

'I'm sure they don't hold it against you.'

'No, but we Papists will always feel something of the outsiders in Scotland. Anyway,' she began, suddenly shifting tack, 'my man is innocent . . . he was with me all night.'

Leo was slightly taken aback by the abrupt change of subject. 'How do you know for sure? He could have left his room.'

'I mean *with* me. In my room. In my bed. I am a chronic insomniac, and that night I hardly slept a wink. Therefore I can testify for certain to Bosco's innocence. Although I already knew him incapable of such an outrage.' She noticed Leo struggling to mask his disapproval. 'Does it shock you that the gossips are correct about my sex life?'

'No,' Leo fibbed. *Great Scott*! he thought. Everyone's up to it these days apart from yours truly.

'We aren't recusants, you see: I converted to the old faith because my late husband was of French extraction. I was brought up and schooled in a very liberal fashion, and one doesn't entirely shake off such ways. Anyway, after all of this dreadfulness occurred I dispatched Bosco to Glasgow, as soon as the police had interviewed him.'

'Why, might I ask?'

She raised her voice above the hissing of the samovar as she filled the teapot. 'Because he is a strange foreigner with strong hands and a mute tongue. He is also my link to the outside world and I couldn't bear the thought of him being the target of tittle-tattle and sideways glances.'

'But surely the police wanted everyone to stay put?'

'Yes, but they have no right to insist upon it,' she replied, turning off the valve and walking over to him with a tray upon which sat the teapot, crockery and a little plate of arrowroot and Abernethy biscuits. 'Anyway, I assured them that he would check in at a local station once he arrived in the city. Also, I told the police everything that I have just told you, about Bosco being with me that night. It's just so difficult to gauge if those people believe one or not.'

'I gather that Helen visited you in her capacity as a nurse. Do you think Bosco might have unintentionally . . . frightened her a little?'

'It is possible. He certainly admired her – she was an entirely admirable person – but in a perfectly appropriate fashion. He thought her peculiarly beautiful and good. He told me so, in writing, which is how we communicate. What possible objection could there be to that?'

'None whatsoever.'

Leo sighed inwardly as he felt the Bosco lead crumble to dust. He had come to another dead end. Loch Dhonn was quite evidently reluctant to give up its secrets. His heart sank and a feeling of frustration rose in his chest. He could hear the hooded crows cawing outside, mocking him.

'She was indeed a fine person,' continued the Grey Lady. 'Kind and thoughtful, if a little unsure of herself at times – if anything that added to her charm somewhat, and self-assurance would have come with age. Youth can be so infinitely selfish and frivolous, but Helen seemed to bypass all of that.'

She poured the tea.

'Thank you.'

She took a slice of lemon, Leo a sugar lump. He held the delicate china and took a sip, glad of the pause. The Grey Lady tactfully pretended not to notice his disfigured hands.

'Jane, is there any history of occultism in these parts?' asked Leo.

'I was once told that certain residents at the Kildavannan community practised Wicca. I believe the parties in question have since moved on.' She noticed Leo's countenance flash with disapprobation. 'Harmless enough, don't you think – a couple of white witches?' she mused, proffering a white-tipped Turkish cigarette from a cedarwood box which was lined with red felt. He decided to accept as a special treat and tapped its end gently on the tabletop. She lit it for him from a silver-plated table lighter, then one for herself. She smoked elegantly, her arm crooked and her fingers splayed.

'Not according to Deuteronomy,' said Leo.

'Ah, but doesn't that chapter also forbid divination? Surely, therefore, you and I are equally guilty?'

'I am quite assured that our gifts are meant to serve God,' replied Leo, 'for it is written: "I will pour out of my Spirit on all flesh, And your sons and your daughters shall prophesy—"'

The Grey Lady interrupted him, completing the verse from Acts: '"And your young men shall see visions, And your old men shall dream dreams."'

'Quite. Anyway, I was thinking more of Satanism than mere witchery.'

'The Baron of Caradyne's grandfather was an occultist and a necromancer. A horrid, lecherous man by all accounts, quite infamous around here; dear Grandpapa wouldn't utter his name. He also dabbled in alchemy and astrology. As for actual consorting with the devil, it wouldn't surprise me in the least.'

Leo took a meditative drag on his cigarette and exhaled two thin streams of smooth blue smoke from his nostrils. 'Do you think there is any possibility it might have continued?'

'Within the family, you mean? I don't think so. Douglas, the present baron, is an inveterate twerp, but I don't think he's in league. Anyway, the thirteenth baron used to lock himself away in Ardchreggan House on the other side of Loch Dhonn, casting his vulgar little cantrips. Apparently, one could see flashes of weird-coloured light for miles around. Meanwhile, the estate fell into neglect, so he was forced to sell his lands on this side of the loch and the isles to my family. He then tried, unsuccessfully, to renege on the deal for the isles using legal chicanery, citing obscure, ancient charters that allegedly gave his lot ownership until the end of time. There has been bad blood between our families ever since.'

'And the current baron sold the Mintos Ardchreggan House, which is now the Ardchreggan Hotel?'

'Yes. By the time the thirteenth baron died it had fallen into grave disrepair. No one particularly wanted to venture there, after all the evil that had taken place, and the Caradynes kept to their main ancestral pile, which is a bit further south. There was one particularly awful story . . . but there's no evidence.'

'What was it?'

'The baron had procured for himself a young woman – some foreign unfortunate, from Eastern Europe I believe, someone who didn't speak English or Gaelic and therefore couldn't gossip locally. He claimed that she was his housekeeper for when he was spending time at Ardchreggan. Anyway, she stopped being seen about the place, and a legend grew up that he had murdered her, as part of one of his rituals. Apparently Grandpapa was deeply concerned and the police were eventually persuaded to question the baron, but he was adamant that the girl was lazy and had been sent back home.'

'What about the current baron ? You don't seem to like him.'

'I don't. And he's my second cousin, I'm afraid to say. The Caradyne barons are one of the few houses in Scotland who remain openly proud to have stood alongside Butcher Cumberland at Culloden. He actually asked me to marry him, would you believe, years ago. Transparent little toad; it was glaringly obvious all he wanted was to regain his family's former lands.'

Leo took a contemplative sip of tea.

For its part, the beast had become enthralled when it first researched the thirteenth baron's history. It seemed seismic that a spirit so kindred in every sense should have roamed these glens a mere two generations ago. And it had been initially terrified, then thrilled when it came to believe that the old sorcerer was communicating from the other side and guiding it in the ways of Satanism. Up until then the beast had occasionally felt a pang of shame at its own wickedness. Its lust for cruelty could seem barbaric and tawdry even to itself. Now that it was ordained by a power beyond the veil it was legitimised, somehow. And on the island of Innisdubh the magick was particularly strong, the dark power rooted deep. What an indescribably visceral thrill it was to summon it up from the ground in the dead of night.

19

L EO was delivered to the hotel by McKee just as the storm closed in, and he felt overcome by a wave of lassitude and a burgeoning sense of disillusionment with the case which threatened to overwhelm him. While still half clothed, he collapsed upon his bed where he instantly fell asleep. Such was his fatigue that he had even left his Oxfords in the little depository in the service corridor, a practice he normally abhorred as it offended his socialist principles to have another human being clean his footwear. He had left his door unlocked, and at one point Fordyce tapped lightly upon it before entering. He gazed at the slumbering Leo for perhaps a minute, with great affection, before composing a note in beautiful handwriting inviting him to dinner, and leaving it on the bedside table.

Leo was awoken by the sound of the wind rampaging through the glens and shaking the window-panes in their frames. His sleep hadn't improved his state of mind but he was reluctant to refuse another of Fordyce's invitations and he telephoned his friend's room to accept. He had plenty of time until dinner, which allowed him to take a shower he barely required. Leo's fastidious regime of personal hygiene had prevailed for as long as he could remember; he recalled even as a young child being irked by the sensation of having sticky hands, and, much to his playmates' chagrin (on the scarce occasions when he actually had playmates), he would often take time out to go home and wash them.

He dressed for dinner, telephoned his mother, and then headed downstairs slightly early, carrying with him his precious Palgrave's *Golden Treasury*, a lovely, crimson cloth-bound edition which had belonged to his late father. It would provide him with some spirit-lifting stimulation until Fordyce arrived. As he descended the staircase he could hear Bill and Shona Minto arguing in the reception area. At the foot of the stairs, beside a fifteenth-century suit of plate armour with a fearsome-looking halberd gripped in its right gauntlet, the Mintos had installed a Sheraton sideboard, upon which sat racks containing leaflets for various local visitor attractions: a botanical garden and a hydroelectric dam, a working steam locomotive and a country house. Leo put down his poetry book and chose one at random (for the nearby St Fillan's Kirk, an eccentrically designed Victorian church) and pretended to read it as he tuned into the conversation round the corner. Shona's tone was bullying, Bill's supplicating.

'We should just tell them.'

'It is out of the question, Bill. I'm not having our good name dragged into the mud.'

'It won't get out.'

'Of course it will! These policemen would sell their grannies to make a few shillings. And anyway, it won't help them at all.'

'Look, dear, it would be for the best –'

'No!' shouted Shona, before checking herself and lowering her voice to a snarl. 'That's final. I am not, I repeat, not, discussing this again.'

She stormed off into the office. Bill Minto watched her go, then wandered towards the kitchen to oversee things, unaware of his guest's presence nearby. Leo absent-mindedly stuffed the leaflet into an inside jacket pocket before departing – forgetting to pick up his book. He walked towards the dining room, oblivious to the presence of Kemp, the baron's man, who was sitting in the telephone alcove. He noticed Leo passing, smirking as he glanced up from his newspaper.

Leo pretended not to see George Rattray, who was going into the gents, then entered the dining room, which was half full – busier than it had been since the murder – and was offended by the Baron of Caradyne before he had even set eyes upon him.

'Fucking useless Polack,' muttered the puce-faced, portly nobleman as Ania the waitress fled from his table in tears.

The baron sat alone, a platter of oysters before him, the virgin white of the tablecloth despoiled by a gout of Burgundy, doubtless the cause of the altercation.

'What did you call her?' demanded Leo, fury rising within him like poison, his anger unfettered due to his already black mood.

The baron looked round, grunting a vague noise of surprise.

'I said, *what* did you call her?' spat Leo, reaching for and missing the lapels of the baron's Harris Tweed jacket.

'Kemp!' the baron ejaculated in a high pitch, a look of terror flashing in his eyes as he tried to fend off Leo, who was a few inches taller than he, with a cirrhotic hand.

'That's right, call on your fucking gorilla,' said Leo, instantly regretting using the profanity.

The conversation around the room, which had already been muted by the baron's treatment of Ania, now ceased altogether. Leo felt a restraining arm on his chest. It was Fordyce. He ushered him back a yard. Leo felt a pang of shame as he realised the physical inadequacy of his antagonist.

'Everything all right, sir?' boomed a deep Doric voice.

The doorway framed Kemp's huge figure. A cringing Bill Minto appeared, dreading a further scene.

'Everything's fine now, Kemp,' said the baron, in his pipsqueak accent. Then he spoke in a quieter voice to Leo: 'I remember you. You're the arsehole who was on my island.'

'Evidently it takes one to know one,' said Leo. 'Come on, Fordyce, we can sup in my chambers. I only ever dine in the company of gentlemen.'

'He's a big fucker, isn't he?' the baron hissed as he indicated Kemp, who had resumed reading his newspaper through the doorway in the telephone alcove. 'He's also a sadistic bastard, and he's getting restless. So if you molest me one more time I will set him loose upon you.'

Let it slide, son. Leo remembered his father's gently chiding words. *Choose your battles carefully; keep your powder dry. There will be another time.*

Leo took a deep breath, turned and walked out.

'How's yer head?' enquired Kemp sarcastically as Leo and Fordyce passed by, his massive hands making his tabloid seem the size of a mere pamphlet.

Leo stopped to regard Kemp's smirk, then thought better of it and walked on.

'That'll teach ye to stay off his lairdship's island in future.'

Leo, unable to contain his ire any longer, whirled round. 'Look here, Mr Kemp. It's nothing personal, but I should inform you that I am subject to an ancient disinclination towards your employer's house. I realise that the locality doubtless overflows with innumerable resentments against them, so just to explain, my specific one is rooted in a certain long-dead chief's refusal to sell a plot of land to a fellowship of poor Irish immigrants who wished to build a place of worship in a Glasgow parish. The reason he baldly gave was that they were Roman Catholics. Now, my people – my flesh and blood – were among those unwanted, kindly folk. So, no, I will not keep off his bastardship's damn island.'

Leo and Fordyce strode off towards the stairs, but a few paces on the former stopped abruptly.

'Shithouses!' he cursed.

'What's up, old stick?'

Leo bounded towards the Sheraton sideboard where he exclaimed, 'Blast and buggeration!' before anxiously checking the floor and the surrounding area.

'I say, whatever's the matter?' pleaded his perplexed friend. 'What on God's earth are you looking for?'

'A poetry volume. My Palgrave's *Golden Treasury*. I left it here earlier – now it's gone!'

'I expect the Mintos will have it in their possession.'

'I certainly hope so – it belonged to my late father.'

But upon enquiry it transpired that the Mintos did not, in fact, have the precious book, nor did any of the staff, nor did a thorough search of the stair and lobby area, and a thorough racking of Leo's brains, produce it. Bill Minto promised they would keep their eyes peeled; Leo, meanwhile, was inclined to believe that Kemp had pinched the cherished item in order to spite him, but he wouldn't give the big bully the satisfaction of a confrontation.

They decided to dine in Fordyce's heavily furnished rooms rather than Leo's because the former consisted of an entire suite and was therefore more spacious. Fordyce looked rather foppish in his canary-silk neck scarf and Roselli smoking jacket. Bill Minto served dinner as the wind soughed outside and rattled the window frames.

'I don't know why you put up with him,' Leo said to Minto. 'Such a *dreadful* little man.'

'Och, I'm afraid it was part of the deal for Ardchreggan House,' replied Minto, as he poured juniper gravy over the haggis and clapshot. 'He is entitled to dine here, at our pleasure, fifty-two times a year. Between ourselves, I'm beginning to wonder if we got such a bargain. He comes over regularly, generally causes a fuss, and I swear he deliberately orders the most expensive items on the menu.'

'The hallmark of a true barbarian!' opined Leo, before stuffing a copious quantity of sheep offal into his mouth and washing it down with a long draught of claret.

20

LEO slept reasonably soundly that night, and woke up early. He used the bathroom, noting that Benjamin Franklin had expanded a little (as was his wont during the early hours), then returned to bed for a further ninety minutes or so of sleep, this time fitful and filled with fragmented, unsettling dreams.

When he awoke his mind had descended into a familiar guddle, whereby it took him an inordinate amount of time to process and synchronise any simple strand of information. And typically by the time he had processed it he had forgotten the original purpose of the computation. He was also disappointed that he had not encountered Helen again in order that he could probe her about certain key aspects of the case. A proposal Fordyce had made the previous evening for a bracing spot of trout fishing could be just the tonic he required. His friend had a spare rod he was welcome to borrow. Gingerly, Leo peeled the bandage from his head, wrapped it in newspaper, cast it into the little pedal bin in the bathroom, and prepared for the day.

The storm had moved eastward to terrorise the Trossachs, then Fife, then the trawlermen and roughnecks of the North Sea, leaving a fair amount of debris in its wake. The air, which was fresh and cold, was still apart from the occasional gust, reminders of the previous night's violence. The tepid late winter sun lit the sky an anaemic blue.

Leo, feeling like a prize clype but wishing to remain faithful to the latest promise he had made to DI Lang, visited the incident room to relate the fragment of conversation between the Mintos he had over-heard the previous evening. The policeman nodded slowly as he listened, wearing an inscrutable expression. He looked stressed and seemed drained of vitality, a washed-out man, a ghost. Leo couldn't help but wonder which one of them would win the race to meet his maker first.

'By the way, we've finished fingerprinting all the locals: there was no match with any of the prints found on the boat,' said Lang, once Leo had finished.

'No surprise there; the killer would have been wearing the gloves I saw in my original vision.'

'Unless he wasn't a local at all.'

'He's from round here all right,' said Leo. 'The whole case reeks of it.'

'I'm inclined cautiously to agree. And if this Tark individual from the victim's diary is the killer then he is even more probably local. I've some other news for you. Now this is strictly off the record.'

'Understood.'

'I took a turn over to Innisdubh yesterday. And let's just say that a set of special keys I had in my possession gained me access to that charnel house you dreamed about.'

'The tenth baron's mausoleum! And?'

'And, nothing. There's bugger all there apart from the old boy's tomb. I got soaked in that bloody storm for nothing.'

Leo sensed it was time to leave, but as he neared the door he turned around to address the policeman once more.

'Just one last thing, Detective Inspector. Did you know that Robbie McKee was rendered homeless by a house fire some time back?'

'I heard that, yes.'

'Could the blaze have been started deliberately?'

'I've really no idea. And I don't see the relevance. What are you getting at, Leo?'

'Oh, nothing. Just a whim.'

Leo communed upon a Pan Drop as he tottered down to the boatyard to meet Fordyce. Surprised and impressed as he was by Lang's maverick conduct, he didn't much care that the policeman's search had yielded nothing. He had to get inside that sepulchre for himself, have a look round. *Experience* it.

'First sport of the season!' announced Fordyce cheerfully as he arranged his tackle. He had a Kelly Kettle on the go, which gave off a comforting smell of coffee and burning twigs. 'The loch is bound to be teeming with bounty, and they'll be rising to feed now that the freshets caused by the storm have abated. George caught a huge ferox trout last April; it was twenty pounds if it was an ounce. However, we, my friend, shall target its colonial cousin, *Oncorhynchus mykiss*, the little ol' rainbow trout – yet still a noble and worthy adversary! We'll try the wet fly, and if we have no luck we'll move on to the nymphs.'

They made their way to the end of the little jetty and set up.

'The Mintos are hiding something,' Leo told Fordyce as he cast. 'What's more, I'm getting nowhere with this case. I need to get back over to the island, to check the mausoleum. But first I'm going to speak to the Addison family.'

'Are you sure that's wise, old stick?'

'Perhaps not. Gosh, Loch Dhonn is full of such bloody weirdos!' said Leo. 'Present company excepted, of course,' he added apologetically.

'Not at all, old stick. We are rather a rum lot, I grant you.'

'I am in a constant torpor. Perhaps it's the after-effects of my recent influenza. Also, my mind's all a fug. It is as though a cataract has formed over my frontal lobe; I can't seem to think straight.'

'Perhaps your . . . levels of indulgence . . .' began Fordyce falteringly.

'It's not the drink; something's impeding my powers.'

'What do you mean, *something*?'

'A malign force.' Fordyce regarded his friend solemnly. 'I just can't get a handle on the fiend,' continued Leo. 'Celtic mythology speaks of the *ilchruthach*. Shape-shifters, faeries who can metamorphose at will. Perhaps that's what I'm up against.'

'Perhaps, old stick. Perhaps.'

Craig Hutton had already informed Stuart Addison, Helen's father, about Leo and his purpose at Loch Dhonn, so it wasn't entirely a surprise when he called by.

After their fruitless fishing expedition – Leo hadn't had so much as a bite; Fordyce had landed a couple of baggies, then sentimentally released them, in spite of the directive that all non-native specimens be despatched when landed – the friends had returned to the hotel for a late luncheon of poached salmon and asparagus. The 'locally caught' prefix served to mock the failed anglers. Having receiving directions to the Addison home from a reluctant Fordyce, Leo had retired to his room to take a steadying nip from his hip flask, and used some cinnamon breath spray to disguise the odour.

*　　*　　*

After Helen's murder, her two maternal aunts had come up, from Musselburgh and Edinburgh, to help the family cope. Today, one had driven to Oban to shop at the supermarket there, and the other, Grace Dunn, who had made the family's statement to the media, answered the door to Leo and regarded him rather coldly. She was in her mid-fifties, her short grey hair and black-rimmed spectacles serving to increase the severity of her countenance, which, quite understandably given recent circumstances, was lined with stress and suspicion. Leo, untypically, hadn't prepared what to say in order to gain access, but upon stating his name an adult male voice called upon Mrs Dunn to send him through.

Leo walked reverently into the Addison home, a white-roughcast 1970s bungalow that sat alongside Loch Dhonn village's main drag of original cottages, although slightly further back from the road. It was the house bearing the little plaque 'EDEN' upon its garden gate that Leo had noticed before. He felt strange, almost guilty, at entering the family abode of an individual he had communicated intimately with on the other side. But intruder or not, he had to hold his nerve and proceed, and try to discover a way of vanquishing whatever force was frustrating his efforts.

The house had an odd, smothered atmosphere, as if a veil had been drawn over all usual activities. These were now conducted at a slower, more definite pace, and at a lower volume. It was as though the pall of bereavement had physically dampened the very essence of the household. The interior itself was familial and unremarkable, filled with flat-pack furniture and ornamented by glass animals and little statues of straw-hatted rustic folk doing rural things, such as snoozing upon hayricks or leaning rods upon 'NO FISHING' signs. Had he been in his usual critical mode Leo would have decided that his and the Addisons' tastes didn't concur, but such matters seemed pitifully inconsequential to him today. These were ordinary, decent people, Leo would soon observe. The salt of the earth. In a way he wished they hadn't been. He would have preferred that they had been cold-hearted or in some way obnoxious. As though anyone could deserve what they had been through.

From time to time Stuart Addison would blink in a moment of complete incredulity; then he would gaze down at his opened palms, as though he would find an answer there as to why his lovely family had been torn apart. His son Callum, a pleasant, diffident lad of fifteen years, sat on the floor by his side, allowing himself to be petted by the absent-minded brush of his father's hand. Grace Dunn went into the kitchen to make tea.

'Mr Addison, Callum, I'm so terribly sorry for your loss.'

'Thank you,' replied the father in a broken voice. 'Please, do sit down.'

Leo lowered himself into a wing-backed chair.

'Everyone's been so kind,' smiled Mr Addison weakly. 'The police have been marvellous.'

'There is a lot of good in the world, Mr Addison,' said Leo, choosing his words carefully. 'We've got to focus on that.'

'It's just that they haven't released . . . Helen, yet.'

'I'm sorry to hear that. I expect they have their reasons. I wonder, if you don't mind my asking, where is Mrs Addison?'

'She's in bed. I'm afraid she isn't coping at all well.' Mr Addison let a long breath go. 'To think I used to worry myself sick about Helen when she was training in Glasgow. So for her to come back home to us . . . and then *this*!' It was a scenario Mr Addison had outlined two dozen times already, to various listeners who didn't know where to look.

Leo nodded sympathetically.

'So, you're here to help us?' asked Mr Addison, forcing a smile.

'I certainly hope so.'

'Good. Getting the . . . getting whoever did this won't bring Helen back. But it would help, I think. Bring some sort of satisfaction. Maybe some peace, eventually.'

'I shall do my utmost, sir, of that you have my word.'

'So, I believe you're some kind of a medium?'

'Not really,' replied Leo gently. 'I have the gift of what is called second sight. Things that are unfolding occur to me as visions, within dreams and such like.'

If Mr Addison was unconvinced by this elucidation he didn't show it; perhaps he was simply willing to grasp at straws. Anyway, evidently DI Lang's anxiety that the family should discover Leo's involvement with the case was misplaced.

'Any leads as yet?'

'No, I'm afraid I've drawn a blank so far. The visions haven't been all that revealing of late. That's why I came round. I really didn't want to disturb you, but I thought if I could meet you all, and get a better idea of what Helen's life was like, it might help to . . . stimulate the flow of ideas.'

Mr Addison didn't require further encouragement, and instructed Callum to retrieve a box of photo albums from the hall. Thus armed he produced his spectacles and gladly proceeded to detail much of the Addison family's history, especially regarding Helen, and informed Leo about her character traits: her foibles, her likes and dislikes, her compassionate nature.

If only he knew, Leo thought to himself rather guiltily, just how familiar I already am with his daughter, on a one-to-one basis.

As Mr Addison commentated on the photographs and the family's chronology, Leo drank in the scene. His host, a man of roughly his own age, was of average height and slim build, with a bald pate and a naturally amiable way, who would try to inject positivity and humour into proceedings as a coping mechanism, and in order to help those around him bear their burden. Leo wondered if the collar and tie he wore underneath his green tank top was to fortify his family, to display the fact that he was keeping it together. He was a clever man, a sewerage engineer at Argyll and Bute Council with an instinctive knack for all things technical, from electric circuitry to the internal combustion engine. He and his wife were not natives but came originally from Edinburgh. They had moved to Loch Dhonn as newlyweds before Helen was born. It had been their mutual dream to forsake city life for the rural idyll and they had adored it until the morning it turned into a nightmare. Now Stuart Addison's eyes would be red-rimmed forevermore, and folk never knew if he was about to start laughing or crying whenever he reminisced about his daughter. Usually it was a mixture of both. As for Callum – a sensitive and thoughtful boy with a Liam Gallagher mop top and the same clever hazel eyes as his sister – he had lost his hero, and was simply wrecked by the whole tragedy, but possessed the selflessness to hide the worst of his despair from his grieving parents.

One photograph of Helen was taken when she was four years old, and it evoked laughter from the assembly – Grace Dunn had now joined them, along with tea and digestive biscuits. In it, Helen was standing in a sandpit at a play park, her arms folded, a comically cross expression on her face as she stared defiantly into the camera.

'It was time to go home, but she just plain refused to come out,' laughed Mr Addison.

The relief was short-lived, however, as the disembodied voice of a person broken by sadness and pain called out, 'Stu-art! Stu-art!'

Leo looked up to see Mrs Addison, Helen's mother, pad into the hall-way, calling on her husband, either oblivious to their visitor's presence or uninterested in it. She wore a faded red housecoat and her hair was matted from lying down. She was mournfully pale yet even without make-up one could detect her daughter's similar elfin beauty. She looked painfully thin and was hunched over with grief, and her eyes betrayed a dejection that had by now gone beyond sensation into a dull limbo of numbness, breached by sharp stabs of brutal anguish.

Mr Addison got up to see to his wife and Leo recognised upon Grace Dunn's features the suggestion that his visit should end.

'Thank you for your time, and for the tea,' he said to the aunt as she accompanied him to the door once Mr and Mrs Addison had disap-peared upstairs. 'And do thank Mr Addison for me.'

'You're welcome. Please don't think it's not appreciated. It's just that things are obviously incredibly difficult round here. I'm sorry if I seemed stand-offish.'

'Please, my dear lady,' protested Leo from the doorstep, 'I beg of you, do not apologise. Only know that my heart and my every effort goes with your family.'

As Mrs Dunn was closing the door, a thought occurred to Leo. 'Mrs Dunn,' he called out, and the door opened again. 'I noticed, in one of the photographs of Helen, she was wearing a servant's uniform?'

'She was a chambermaid, briefly. At the Loch Dhonn Hotel.'

'Oh, really,' said Leo, unable to disguise his interest. 'When would this have been?'

'Och, she was just young, not long out of school,' said Mrs Dunn, clutching her grey cardigan round her to keep out the chill as she cast her mind back. 'It would be four or five years ago. She didn't like it, mind. Didn't like that Mrs Minto much. Told her to stuff it, I believe. Which wasn't like Helen. She was quite a shy lassie really.'

'Thank you, Mrs Dunn. Thank you very much.'

Leo began walking the short journey back to the hotel, absorbed by his thoughts, and was thus unaware that Shona Minto herself, who happened to be out for a stroll and a general nose around, had from a distance witnessed him emerging through the Addisons' garden gate. Leo was intrigued by this last morsel of information, and overwhelmed by the need for a stiff drink, after having set eyes upon Mrs Lorna Addison.

He speculated about the dreadful moment when a pair of kindly officers from Fallasky braced themselves and then knocked upon the Addison front door that cruel morning. He imagined the initial disbelief that Helen was anywhere but upstairs, safe in her bed, giving way to ever-increasing circles of horror as the terrible reality dawned.

A Royal Mail van passed by, and Leo could hear a two-stroke engine spluttering in the nearby forestry. And he wondered how life can proceed in its banal way at such a time.

21

THE brief sunset was intense, casting Ben Corrach in the most vivid garnet. The entire Munro glowed in the most extraordinary way, like a colossal ember. Leo felt a mixture of unpleasant emotions as he sat in the lounge, morosely chasing a large J&B with a glass of Irish stout. Further down the bar Lex Dreghorn kept a safe distance, sensing that he would not be made welcome in the Glaswegian's company. Leo had been rather curt in response to George Rattray's couthy anglers' humour, and the fishing enthusiast seemed to take the hint and sauntered over to where Shona Minto had arrived, perching herself on the other side of the bar like Queen Bee, turning not a stroke of work. She laughed affectedly at Rattray's sycophantic chatter. By now Leo reckoned – correctly – that the locals had an inkling as to his purpose at Loch Dhonn. If they had not become aware of his mystical abilities then they at least suspected that he was there in some form of investigative capacity. It was in the way he caught them regarding him, or now avoided engaging in conversation with him about the murder.

Part of Leo felt that he had intruded upon the Addisons' grief, and that he had possessed no right to knock upon their door empty-handed, without so much as a clue as to who had brutally killed their beloved daughter. Another part of him felt a glimmer of the immensity of what the Addisons were enduring. He also felt a not entirely unfamiliar gnawing at the edge of his faith, such was the senseless and appalling nature of the crime.

Eventually, Fordyce joined him from the dining room; Leo had earlier turned down his suggestion that they dine together because he had no appetite. As far as Fordyce could tell, Leo was sober. If he had asked Paul the barman, a pleasant, conscientious fellow aged approximately twenty-five with the dark hair and handsome features typical of the Glasgow Irish, he would have discovered that his friend had already drunk his way through four pints of Guinness and two gills of Scotch. If he had asked Lex Dreghorn, he would doubtlessly have received a more modest and less truthful estimate, such was his preciousness at maintaining champion-drinker status in Loch Dhonn.

'During a dark time,' Leo confided to Fordyce, 'when I was struggling to cope, I went to stay in a monastery for a while. As a guest, you understand. Looking back, it was there that I started to heal, within my soul. One of the monks there, this Brother Francesco, he was sort of my buddy, my *consigliere*. He had been a psychotherapist prior to taking Holy Orders. Anyway, one day we were chatting about where I was in my life and what I had been through, and he said something that I always remember. He said that God never asks more of us than we can endure. But looking into that poor woman's eyes today and seeing nothing but desolation, it made me truly wonder.'

Fordyce could think of nothing to say in response; any words of intended comfort would be inadequate and inappropriate, and he could tell that Leo had no stomach for platitudes. Instead he kept his counsel, took a sip from his port and ginger, and then inwardly chastised himself for letting his mind drift to contemplation of the youthful Paul's lissom rear profile. Meanwhile, Leo stared out at the pouring darkness. He detested these short days; everyone scuttling around like beetles in the gloom. He thought about the bleak, obscure muirs of bitter grass that lay beyond the window, and he wondered if the beast was out there, traversing the cold, wet ground as the birch woods and the drab, snow-streaked mountains turned to shadow. Watching. Waiting.

'One almost feels helpless in the face of such pure, unadulterated evil,' he muttered.

22

THANKFULLY, Leo had allowed Fordyce to persuade him to have a roasted cheese supper, in order to soak up at least some of the booze (he had ended up drinking a good deal more stout and Scotch), and this, accompanied by a pint of tap water, made for a more bearable morning ahead. And Leo, in spite of the amount of alcohol he had imbibed, did have a vision during his sleep, albeit on the face of it an unremarkable one.

An old coach house, early nineteenth-century, with whitewashed harling and quaint dormers protruding from the roof, their frames and sills painted a pleasant shade of green.

The scene recurred and recurred, such that it had made an indelible impression upon Leo's consciousness by the time he awoke. It was disappointing, however, that the dream had disclosed so little. Again it seemed as though his visions were being frustrated, impeded by some unknown adversary. It was also disappointing that it was Sunday, and he had no prospect of keeping the Sabbath. But he felt sure that a dispensation was justified, such was the importance of his being around Loch Dhonn at this particular time.

Leo prepared some liver salts and took a bracingly cold shower before dressing for the outdoors, driven on by some vague but compelling urge. He slipped into the dining room only to drain a glass of orange juice and procure several oatcakes and some Jarlsberg, which he would munch as he journeyed southwards, the direction his antenna seemed to suggest. He found Paul the barman outside, chaining his bicycle to a drainpipe, and checked with him that it was all right to borrow a gnarled walking stick topped with a piece of antler he had spotted in the hotel hat-stand. Having donned his deerstalker, he looked a singular sight as he strode forth, rather like an Edwardian ghillie leading out a gang of beaters.

The sky was overcast, yet it still felt extremely cold, and Leo wondered if they would have snow soon. A scrawny kite hovered above, despondently scanning the ground for pickings. Leo walked along the road with the higher, forested ground to his left, and strips of meadow and virgin woodland to his right, beyond which was the loch itself. He cut down at one point in order to walk along the waterside. In a field a pair of magnificent thoroughbreds stood close together for mutual warmth, and Leo took a moment to admire them. He found a little beaten path which skirted the ragged shoreline and followed it due south. Each bay hemmed an enclave of contrasting topography. A little green faery dell with a tumbling white linn. A silent and enclosed valley utterly invaded and subdued by moss – everything clad in the stuff: the drystane dykes, the trees, the boulders, the blanket bog – a weird, verdant, alien world. A peat flow, all dun and drab, the bunch grass withered, a forest of tall rushes brittle and dead. A dense wood of spruce, the aspect of their tops against a charcoal band of sky somehow depressingly evoking the sensation of an indeterminable time lang syne.

Leo then had to negotiate a burn which crossed the path, and he did so by taking a run and jump. This effort was initially successful, but unfortunately he landed on a patch of glaur, slipped and then fell on his bottom, strangling an expletive. His coat had ridden up and the rear of his light grey trousers was soaked and muddy.

Kildavannan was situated near to the point where the Uisge Dearg drained Loch Dhonn and flowed eastwards to eventually irrigate the idyllic pastures of southern Perthshire. It sat on the northern bank of that little river, and consisted of a hotchpotch of eco homes, barrel houses, trailers and outbuildings, all focused around the original dwellings of the clachan of Kildavannan, which had been officially abandoned in 1960 and had lain derelict until the community was founded in 1979. Along the steep ridge behind the settlement stood a series of modestly-sized wind turbines, and many of the buildings were crowned with solar panels. Across a bland stretch of haugh, beyond which was the river mouth, sat the community's biological sewage treatment installation.

Leo ambled past some neat kailyards, then down an avenue of polytunnels which took him to the main Loch Dhonn road. It seemed queer to see the coach house of his vision so abruptly and so soon after having dreamed of it. There seemed to be nobody around.

The building was on two levels. The lower one, which would originally have been used to stable horses, had evidently been converted to provide workspaces for various resident artists and craftspeople. Their living quarters were in the roof space which in bygone days had housed travellers on their way from Oban to Glasgow.

Leo followed the sound of metalwork to the furthest unit. The large, arched wooden doors were ajar, in order to let fumes escape. He peered inside. A slender female figure clad in a dark blue boiler suit and a welder's mask was hammering a white-hot piece of steel against an anvil. Leo was immediately put in mind of the image from the vision he had experienced in the church in Glasgow, of a smith wearing a welder's mask, working at a furnace. The woman picked up the piece with a pair of tongs and immersed it in a tank of water. With her other hand she turned a valve and the rushing sound of her propane forge ceased.

Leo called out hello.

The woman started slightly, turned and flipped up the visor of her mask. She regarded Leo for a moment, then raised the tongs out of the water and placed them and the metal on a firebrick. She peeled off her mask and shook loose a mane of shoulder-length, wavy brunette hair, some strands of which were gathered in tiny cylindrical beads. She was in her mid-thirties, and her whole face seemed to smile good-naturedly at Leo, who was immediately taken with her overall impression: her informal bearing, the whiteness of her teeth, the largeness of her hazel eyes, her strong jaw-line, the little ridge of freckles over her cute nose. She wore no make-up, but her slightly weathered skin somehow suited her, its slight duskiness increasing the appeal.

'Hi!' she replied.

Leo ensured he kept himself mostly outside the premises, concerned that a lone female would be made anxious by a strange gentleman caller, in the aftermath of Helen's murder.

'Sorry to bother you while you're hard at work. My name is Leo Moran. I'm staying up at the Loch Dhonn.'

'Yes, I saw you when we drove by the other morning. You were standing outside the main doors. You had a bandage on your head.' She had a tranquil energy and spoke with a rich, confident tone, in a middle-class Home Counties accent.

'Indeed. I was waiting for my lift. That was just before the storm – gosh, I was nearly blown away!'

'It's odd, I spent the entire duration in here, so engrossed in my work that I was hardly aware of it.' She gestured towards a work-in-progress, a tall, skeletal structure that looked something like a plesiosaur built from a giant Meccano set.

'Very impressive,' said Leo politely.

'I'm Eva Whitton,' said the woman as she jauntily walked over and extended her hand. 'Please, do come in. Do you like modern sculpture?'

'I do admire Archipenko's work,' Leo lied as he stepped inside.

Eva smiled pleasantly and Leo inwardly reproached himself for the mendacity of his statement.

'Feel free to take your coat off.'

'I will, thank you,' said Leo, forgetting about his soiled behind which the outer garment had concealed. 'It is a touch tropical in here.'

'What happened to your hands?' Eva asked with an uncommon yet endearing forthrightness.

'They were burned in a house fire,' replied Leo, a little taken aback.

'Sorry, I didn't mean to be nosey. I just thought you might be a fellow smithy. Many of us bear battle scars.'

'Not at all.'

'So, what brings you to Loch Dhonn?'

'I'm here in a . . . professional capacity.'

'To do with the murder?'

'I'm afraid I can't say much more.' Leo's face flushed slightly at his words. For once, he didn't mean to sound self-important.

'You're not a *journo*, are you?'

'No, no.'

'I thought not. Thank heavens for that!'

'I'm just trying to get a feel for the place. For the people round here, especially for those who knew Helen.'

An expression of doubt flashed across Eva's face.

'The police know about my being here – I kind of have their blessing, actually,' blurted Leo, keen to assuage her fears. Leo prided himself on being a man of his word, and he wondered what was so enamouring about this sculptress that it had made him risk breaching his promise of discretion to Lang. A feeling of unworthiness welled up inside him, familiar from other times when he had felt attracted to a woman. 'I'm afraid I'm sworn not to divulge the precise nature of my involvement, and I must beg of you to keep what I have told you to yourself, if you please.'

'Certainly,' replied Eva. 'I did know Helen, rather well, actually. I've been at the community for, oh, seven years now.'

A surge of romantic bravado, which had lain dormant within Leo for a decade, suddenly sprang forth.

'Well, then, perhaps you would do me the honour of being my guest for dinner this evening, at the hotel. It could be very useful to get your local insights.'

'I'd be delighted.'

'Excellent!'

A rush of excitement rose in Leo's chest, and he fought hard not to betray it in his expression or intonation. Trying to look cool he gazed round the workshop. As he turned, Eva noticed his muddy posterior and smiled. Leo saw a pile of scrap metal nearby. Alongside this, sitting upon a worktop, was a little stack of several foot-long, two-and-three-quarter-inch diameter rods of high-grade brass. Leo wasn't initially sure why, but he felt compelled to step over and stroke the surface of the topmost one.

'Brass. Must be expensive.' Then it occurred to him. 'Have any gone missing?'

'I don't think so. I really should keep stock control. Why do you ask?'

'Oh, nothing.'

23

THE mere sight of Lex Dreghorn was enough to raise Craig Hutton's hackles. He had always disliked the older man, whom he considered a phoney and a deadbeat with a fair conceit of himself, but had only come to despise him after he had made a pass at his beautiful Helen. Dreghorn, of course, would later insinuate that Helen had thrown herself at him, but Hutton had instinctively known the truth as soon as he happened upon them together in the lobby of the community hall. What he didn't know for sure was whether or not the guy was capable of murder. Certainly, Dreghorn had worn a black look on his face that night after the village ceilidh as he stalked off, leaving the two young lovers holding hands as they watched his ignominious exit contemptuously. Dreghorn was proud, no doubt about it, and rumour had it that his two marriages had failed because of his egotistical need to cheat with younger women. But, pondered Hutton, what constituted a woman hater? At what point did chauvinism descend into something darker, something more violent? After all, *someone* had killed Helen, and as often as not a murderer turns out to be an individual who had previously been regarded as perfectly normal – and known to the victim. Why not Lex Dreghorn? Plus, the man lived quite near to the murder scene, and could easily have nipped there and back unnoticed in the dead of night.

Hutton was aware of the whispered suspicions against Robbie McKee and he knew where they stemmed from: his increasingly erratic behaviour and his withdrawn moods. Hutton also knew that McKee had been strongly attracted to Helen, but he could hardly blame him for that. Helen hadn't ever seemed the least bit intimidated by McKee's interest, and had behaved sympathetically towards him. Therefore Hutton, as always impressed by his girl's compassion and quiet wisdom, had followed suit. Sure, there was the unpleasant incident from his past, but he had been fourteen years old for goodness' sake, and it's not as though he had gone on to repeatedly bother young lassies.

No. Hutton felt sure of McKee's innocence. As for Dreghorn, he would spy on him, as he was spying on him now. Watching as he loaded scrap metal into the back of McKee's Land Rover – he was aye borrowing it; he probably had McKee under his thumb. Indeed he was always hanging around the little homestead where McKee and Rattray lived quietly in adjacent buildings, as though he owned the place. And right now he was glancing around in a manner surely too suspicious for a man who was merely shifting a bit of hooky lead.

Hutton would watch, and he would learn. Then he would act.

24

UPON returning to the Loch Dhonn a restless Leo had been unable to locate Fordyce, and so he had lunched alone (a light Caprese salad in order to preserve his appetite) and had little with which to occupy himself for the afternoon ahead. The sky cleared somewhat but the day remained too ugly to merit any further exploration of the countryside and the wireless informed him that the mercury was to plummet even further. However, Leo felt in better spirits now, not only because of his forthcoming dinner date, but also because of the fact that a vision had borne forth a tangible lead: one of the brass cylinders at Eva's workshop could have been stolen and be the very item used to violate Helen post-mortem. He would pass this piece of information to DI Lang when he returned from Glasgow, where the short constable had informed him he had been summoned by his superiors.

Leo built a fire and drew a bath, which helped take the chill from his bones. He then telephoned his mother and pretended to read some pages from *Travels with My Aunt*. He whiled away the remaining hours gazing out of his bedroom window, resisting the temptation to drink, and wearing out the carpet by pacing up and down. He dressed far too early for dinner, and by the time Eva was due to arrive he was too wound up to properly enjoy the occasion. Booze would indeed be required to relax him, but also, if he had been being totally honest with himself, to dispel the little demons of self-loathing that had been haunting the edges of his consciousness ever since he had met the sculptress earlier that day. Why, he wondered in exasperation, did the default flavour of his psyche have to be so negative and ungentle towards his own self? Also, there was a nagging feeling that his excitement for the forthcoming engagement was because some unknowable but vital aspect to Miss Whitton reminded him of Maddi, his long-lost love.

Leo descended to the dining room, where Eva had already arrived a few minutes early. She widened her eyes slightly when she noticed the formality of her date's attire. She had chosen a simple charcoal woollen dress, but such plain clothing was more than adequate to draw out her easy natural beauty. Her hair spilled gorgeously from a green chiffon headscarf, and she wore an attractive antique jade brooch on her bosom, which, given her slim frame, was surprisingly ample. As they were being seated, Leo happened to glance towards the doorway and noticed Lex Dreghorn ambling through the hall on his way to the bar. He paused to stare in nosily. Leo fancied that he saw a look of envy register upon the man's features as he noticed the identity of his comely dining companion.

Fordyce had woken that morning in one of his melancholy moods, and had decided to switch off his mobile phone and kill the day by taking some provisions up to James Millar at the Witch's Cauldron. Having returned to the hotel, he booked a table for one and went to his suite to freshen up. He strolled towards the dining room where he was presented with the sight of Leo and the delightful Eva Whitton from the Kildavannan community at table together. He felt a familiar sinking sensation in his heart. Yet unrequited love was no longer an agony to him. Had it been a decade before, it would have cast him into a depression so black he would have taken to his bed for several days or even weeks. Still, he mused over a large glass of port wine, after he had cancelled his table in favour of a bar meal: he and Leo's friendship could endure, given their common interests and mutual familiarity with loneliness.

After a round of spritzer *apéritifs*, chef furnished the diners with an exquisite *amuse-bouche* of pickled pig's trotter stuffed with chestnut and chicken liver mousse. It was at this early point when it emerged that Eva didn't eat meat. She explained this a little apologetically, omitting to send the item back lest she seemed ungrateful. She would have quite happily permitted Leo to consume her trotter, which sat glistening and forlorn upon the perfect white glaze of her untouched plate, and Leo would have readily obliged, but didn't want to ask for fear of coming across as gluttonous. Eva waited patiently while her dining companion guiltily munched away. Leo avoided the citrus sorbet due to his vinegary starter, opting for the champagne variety instead. Then it was the soup: she minestrone, he oxtail. Leo naively presumed that Eva's vegetarianism wouldn't encompass seafood, and so he was forced to consume an entire platter of sea scallops by himself, washed down by the lion's share of a bottle of Chablis. Eva, meanwhile, was simply relieved that he hadn't chosen the Thermidor. Leo's livid burns put her in mind of crustaceans, and for him to have set upon a dish of lobster with those hands was an image too far. She chastised herself for such an unkind thought, and felt a little ashamed. Leo, Eva noted, seemed gloriously and defiantly unself-conscious of his scars, a characteristic which she admired. As for Leo, he was delighted to have met such a colourful and attractive creature amid the gloom and horror of this winter. For now he was content to lose himself in the moment, and not to speculate as to whether his initial stir-rings of desire were to be reciprocated.

It transpired that Eva was aged thirty-seven, and came originally from Canterbury. After studying at Glasgow School of Art, she had spent most of her twenties living the artistic life in London, often enduring acute penury. In the wake of the millennium something altered within her, a kind of spiritual yearning, and she pined for wide-open spaces. She started to look back upon the weekend breaks she had taken with her student chums in the West Highlands, times which she had enjoyed immensely. That lush and grand landscape seemed to be calling her. So Kildavannan proved the perfect answer, its ethos and spirit coinciding precisely with where she wanted to be in her life, although sadly her long-term relationship with Toby, her former partner, didn't survive the move very long: he was driven back south by torrents of rain and legions of midges. Which proved it wasn't meant to be, Eva supposed philosophically.

By now Leo felt relaxed by the wine and energised by the fine cuisine, his senses stirred by the good conversation, the spiders of self-doubt back in their nests, for now. His carnivorous voracity extended into a fowl *entrée* of *poulet sauté aux truffes* (Eva's fortuitously timely expression of disapproval towards the *foie gras*, an option which Leo had been silently considering, had aided his choice), and a main course of pork, black pudding, warm ear and tongue salad (he stopped himself just in time from ordering the Limousin veal in case it offended Eva's sensibilities). As Eva picked at her roast aubergine and counted the number of species that passed down Leo's gullet, so did she observe her dining partner's capacity for alcohol (she herself was at most a moderate drinker, prefer-ring a grass joint to mellow her out, or, now and again, a cheeky pill to take her up or down). After his spritzers and Chablis, a bottle of Château Latour was ordered – of which she, despite Leo's coaxing, consumed a mere glass, and, after a sumptuous *Nougat de Montélimar* dessert washed down with a glass of Riesling and a platter of cheese accompa-nied by a largish port wine, he sank an Irish liqueur followed by a double brandy. Eva was still rather astonished, not to mention amused, by this eccentric who had crashed into her life like a wrecking ball, who unself-consciously crossed himself before heartily devouring each course while quaffing glass after glass of alcohol.

'You seem to enjoy good dining, Leo,' she observed.

'Indeed! I say let us praise the Lord, "Who satisfieth thy mouth with good things; so that thy youth is renewed like the eagle's."'

Eva smiled. Leo seemed to belong to a bygone era, yet she couldn't help but like this generous, cultured man with his earnest expression, who listened so intently and who had such beautiful manners. If Leo could have known that Eva wasn't entirely unattracted to him it would have been of some considerable consolation. Yet, while she noted his undoubted charms, Eva was too experienced to overlook incompatibility when she saw it, and Leo Moran had it in spades. Best not to give him any ideas, she concluded.

Once they had finished, Leo generously tipped Ania, complimented the food, but politely requested that she inform chef that *les légumes* had been too crunchy. Leo's latest culinary campaign was against this irritat-ing modern fad. Apart from anything, undercooked veg made him flatulent, an observation he just managed to stop himself from sharing with Eva.

'So, you knew Helen well?' he asked rhetorically as they settled into the deep, luxurious armchairs beside the dining room's grand fireplace.

'Yes. She used to come down to the community, on horseback, to do her nursing duties. But I also knew her before. Before she went away to Glasgow. She liked to hang around the workshop. I guess she kind of looked up to me a little, like you would a big cousin or something. We shared a love of horses.'

'A noble beast, the horse,' observed Leo irrelevantly.

'God, I can't believe I'm doing that.'

'Doing what?' asked Leo, his face glowing with alcohol and heat from the log fire as he gently swilled his cognac in its snifter.

'Using the past tense to describe Helen.'

Leo looked into the flames. 'I didn't realise she had worked at the hotel,' he said.

'She barely did; just for a few weeks, until she was sacked.'

'Sacked? I was told she left.'

'That's what she told her folks. But she confided in me that Shona had sacked her.'

'Why?'

'She didn't say exactly. Just said they had disliked each other. Which was unusual – for someone to dislike Helen.' Eva paused, suddenly in need of a sip of her brandy. 'So, who are the chief suspects, in your opinion?'

'I have no firm idea as yet. But I expect the police will take an interest in Robbie, such is their chronic lack of imagination. But, as a matter of interest, did he ever bother Helen?'

'No, but he certainly fancied her. Made some clumsy attempt at a Valentine's card, I seem to recall.'

Leo paused as he removed an after-dinner mint from its sleeve, before continuing: 'What do you know about that Lex Dreghorn creature?'

'He fancies himself, and he used to try and flirt with Helen, but he's no killer.'

'How do you know him?'

'Let's just say he's a good source of various metals.'

'Illicit metals, I'll wager.'

'Ask no questions. You don't seem awfully keen on him.'

'Let's just say I admire him about as much as I admire Gershwin,' Leo replied dryly. 'Pardon my asking, but did he provide you with the brass rods I saw in your workshop?'

'No. I bought those commercially.'

'Does he ever have access to your workshop?'

'Yes, but lots of people do. We're very trusting at the community. Often suppliers and customers will drop things off or pick things up without my being there.'

Leo reached over to stir the fire, a thoughtful expression on his face.

* * *

As the evening progressed, Eva twice dropped heavy hints that she was romantically interested in another member of the community by the name of Ryan, a half-truth spoken to forestall any amorous proposals her dinner date might have planned. She needn't have concerned herself; Leo could read the familiar signals of rejection and had no intention of making a fool of himself. Nonetheless, ever the gentleman, he insisted upon walking Eva home. He tottered upstairs, feeling bloated from food and alcohol, to retrieve his shooting coat and torch, then they left the hotel and walked towards Kildavannan by the road, keeping to the right so as to face any oncoming traffic.

The night was bitterly cold, the clear winter sky revealing the sparkling cosmos in all its glory. A couple of policemen, huddled round an oil brazier, eyed them as they went by.

'Gosh, it's absolutely freezing,' said Eva with a shiver.

'"This cold night will turn us all to fools and madmen",' said Leo.

'Is quoting from *King Lear* supposed to impress me?'

Leo smiled.

They walked by the Grey Lady's house, then, about a mile down the road, about halfway to the community, they passed a public house, the Innisdara Inn. It was set in a little cutting just back from the road and glowed welcomingly with warmth and light. Just ahead of there the road turned sharply at a blind corner. They had not yet encountered any vehicles, but Leo and Eva instinctively stepped onto the verge and went in single file for safety's sake. At this point a large knowe now obstructed their view of the lochside, and just as they came abreast with it they saw a dark figure, barely three yards ahead, who was studying the ground in front of him with a flashlight.

'Great Scott!' exclaimed Leo.

Eva gasped and grabbed Leo's sleeve. Leo shone the torch upwards to reveal the face of George Rattray.

'Sorry, folks, did I startle you?'

'Just a bit,' said Eva.

'I got a bit of a fright myself,' said Rattray with a smile.

'Out for a stroll?' asked Leo.

'Sort of. I lost my grandfather's fishing knife earlier. It was clipped to my haversack and must have fallen off. I'm retracing my steps with the flashlight. I'll never get over it if I've lost it. Where are you headed?'

'I'm just escorting Eva back to Kildavannan.'

'Quite right – you never know what strange types you can meet on the road. This place is full of weirdos, and they don't come much weirder than me,' said Rattray, milking the joke.

'How is Robbie keeping?' enquired Leo.

'Ach, he's not too great, I'm afraid. I looked in on him earlier,' replied Rattray, vaguely gesturing towards his half-lit home, which sat directly down from where they stood, near the loch. 'Sometimes it's as though his mind is in another world. He's awfy upset about poor Helen. He's a sensitive soul. He's got some idea in his head that he could have protected her. I keep telling him it's not his fault.'

Eva sighed sympathetically. 'Well, it's good of you to look out for him,' she said. 'Such a terrible business.'

'Such an evil act . . . it's quite beyond my comprehension,' agreed Leo.

'Aye,' continued Rattray, shaking his head sorrowfully. 'That poor, poor girl. I can remember her as a lassie, she was such a sweet wee thing. You know, it was always her intention to come back to Loch Dhonn after her training. She loved this place, loved her family, loved the people here.'

He wiped his sleeve across his eyes.

'How is that fix holding up?' Eva enquired, keen to break the awkward silence that had descended. She turned to Leo to explain. 'I do little welding jobs for George; recently I replaced the rowlocks on his boat.'

'Fine, fine,' said Rattray cheerfully, glad of the change of subject. 'It was a sterling bit of British craftsmanship, or rather craftswomanship! Anyway, I won't keep you young lovers out here in the freezing cold any longer. No winching on the way home, mind!'

They said their goodbyes, Leo inwardly reproaching himself for feeling irritated by Rattray and his harmless humour. After all, it wasn't George's fault that Eva didn't find him attractive. Occasionally, Leo was appalled by the amoebas of spite that lurked at the edge of his consciousness.

They walked on. 'Poor, sweet George,' said Eva. 'How could this awfulness come to Loch Dhonn?'

25

Leo deposited Eva at the coach house and, as expected, received only a chaste peck on the cheek as a farewell. Despite the inevitability of this, something inside him still sank. Romance had eluded Leo for some considerable time – Maddi had been an epoch ago. He seldom seemed to meet anyone he was interested in any more, although there had been one woman whom he had been keen on a couple of years back. Leo had met her during a rare spurt of self-motivation when, uncharacteristically heeding Stephanie's advice, he had taken to attending various extramural evening classes. The vivacious and in her own way rather fetching lady in question taught intermediate German at a college in town. She was younger than he but not improperly so, and Leo was self-deluded enough to fancy that his tender feelings were reciprocated and that some sort of unspoken connection existed between them. Therefore it came as something of a shock when she mentioned a boyfriend, who it transpired was of the live-in variety, and the announcement of their engagement had felt quite crushing. Thereafter, in order to avoid her innocent pre-class chatter about wedding arrangements and house hunting, Leo had taken to waiting in the railway station after alighting from his train until the optimal moment, in order that he could arrive exactly when the lesson was due to start. However, as someone who stood firmly against tardiness, invariably he would quicken his pace too much and still arrive a few minutes early, or else the class wouldn't start on time and he would have to endure some discussion of the impending nuptials anyway. His dejection wasn't even permitted the balm of self-pity, because he felt ashamed of his jealousy and lack of generosity, and embarrassed by the extent of his infatuation. After the course finished, despite passing his examination, he didn't bother signing up for the advanced level.

Before she went inside Eva turned and said, out of the blue, 'Leo, I hope you don't mind my asking, but why do you drink so much?'

Leo paused for a moment to think. It was a simple question, yet the answers were truly manifold and befuddling. Most prominent was probably the fallout from failing to act upon information divulged to him by his second sight when he was a teenager; as a consequence a vulnerable person had been destroyed. But he hardly wanted to rake up such ignominy, so he plumped for a different answer instead, only because it was one particularly pertinent to recent experiences. And it was an answer which Eva could hardly have expected: 'Because when I fall asleep I stare into the heart of darkness.'

He turned on his heel and disappeared into the bitter night.

The tarmacadam sparkled as the cold took its full icy grip, and Leo wobbled slightly on its treacherous surface before adjusting his gait appropriately. He cheered himself by lighting a cigarillo and with the prospect of a consolatory glass or two at the pub he had passed on the way down. He paused for a moment at the knowe where they had met George, to take in the scene. The crescent moon, although slim, gleamed like quicksilver, enough to make for a spectacular panorama. From here, Loch Dhonn was a perfect mirror but for the black tumour of Innisdubh, its crooked outline resembling the silhouette of a hag riding a broomstick.

Leo gazed upwards in wonder at the infinity of galaxies, sprinkled across the firmament like multicoloured powder. There to the south was the diffuse gorgeousness of the Orion nebula; the giant accompanied by his hunting hounds Canis Major and Minor, with Sirius, the night sky's brightest star. There were Castor and Pollux, the heavenly twins of Gemini; there was Auriga the charioteer and the distant Lynx, blinking out from the timeless abyss. He spun round to take in the ancient light of Andromeda and her mother Cassiopeia, the bears Ursa Major and Minor, Taurus the bull, and Perseus the hero, incorporating Algol, the dead eye of the decapitated Medusa.

Leo spontaneously exclaimed aloud: '"The heavens are telling the glory of God!"'

He was abruptly brought out of his astral meditations by a nearby voice.

'How was your dinner?'

Helen sat upon the knowe, her nightdress as white as a bone.

'F-f-fine,' Leo spluttered as he collected himself.

She turned her head to gaze up the loch. 'I don't think she fancies you.'

'Thanks.' Leo walked over to be nearer to the insouciant spectre. 'And how are you?' he enquired, softening as he recalled meeting her grief-stricken family. The experience had made him feel more bonded with Helen.

'Oh, not so bad. Still dead. I have found some friends though. They're lovely, even though their English isn't terribly good.'

'That's nice. Who are they?'

'The girls the thirteenth baron killed.'

'Girls? Girls plural?'

'Yes. There are six of them.'

Leo exhaled a long sigh of misty breath. 'Six . . . sweet Jesus.'

'Why don't you have a girlfriend, Leo?'

'How do you know I don't?' he replied.

'It's obvious. You're so miserable and unloved.'

'Well, you've certainly got me pegged,' he replied disconsolately.

'I rather think I do. In fact, if you've got a mo, I'd say that you live a sad little life in a sad little flat in Glasgow. Probably the dutiful son. Neat and tidy, moments of moral resolve and renewal, but then you drink too much and think dirty thoughts you oughtn't to think. Friends all married now, and sometimes it seems such an effort to keep in touch. Affairs fewer and further between these days – "Oh, if only she could see the *real* me!" – but all of your romances were damp squibs anyway. I think you still cherish one of them – "The very *thought* of bumping into her at Tesco with her undoubtedly handsome husband and perfect children." You're a churchgoer, but with barely the faith to get you through regular dark nights of the soul. Because you're haunted by something, although I haven't worked out what. Mild depression kept in check by Prozac, another week speeds by and you've grown seven days older, and you realise that, apart from your mother, the only people you've spoken to are the grocer, the postman and the nice lady at the Bank of Scotland call centre.'

Leo paused to clear his throat, trying to disguise the shock and hurt he felt at Helen's words. 'Just my luck – an uncivil ghost,' he retorted lamely. 'And anyway, I don't have a Tesco. I go to Sainsbury's. And I don't take Prozac. Justerini and Brooks is quite adequate.'

'It's OK,' said Helen, as she leapt to her feet, skipped down from the knowe and stood in front of him. 'I'm not actually down on the notion of you at all. In fact, I think we rather connect.' She seemed to give off a strange, cold energy. 'I would have been your girlfriend,' she added coyly, a puckish glint in her eye. 'If I was single. And alive.'

Leo cleared his throat again, uncomfortable in the silence that followed, but also a little flattered by the girl's change of tack, if slightly unsure of her sincerity. But she gazed into his countenance with such deep admiration that he decided that she was not, in fact, teasing him. He remembered an offbeat theory he had once heard, that in the afterlife our visual form is beautified, and we all resemble Hollywood film stars. And at this moment Helen Addison certainly did look supernaturally beautiful, robed in luminescence, as though she was composed of light. Leo had to stop himself from reaching out and affectionately stroking her porcelain cheek.

'I went to see your parents,' he began. 'And I spoke with Craig.'

The words had an immediate and profound effect on Helen. The warmth drained from her face, and was replaced by a look of profound grief and anxiety. Her apparition started to fade.

'I don't wish to discuss them,' she said, her voice breaking with emotion. 'I'm not ready.'

He shouted her name in vain but she was gone, disappeared into the ether, before he was able to ask her who Tark was.

26

THE Innisdara Inn had stood for over two centuries, and new owners had faithfully restored a measure of its original ambience. The walls were lined with gypsum and painted white. The ceiling was low, with exposed joists dark-varnished to contrast with the emulsion. The room was tastefully decorated with framed watercolour scenes from Sir Walter Scott's *Waverley*. The bar itself stood in the centre of the room, a square island of polished hardwood and sparkling glass, its gantry stocked with a formidable array of regionally distilled amber-coloured liquids; a veritable Aladdin's cave for the inveterate boozer.

The inn's focal point was a fireplace on the north-facing wall, to Leo's left, set within a stone chimney breast. Peat burned cheerfully within the grate, and enthroned upon the hearth seat was, as far as Leo was concerned, an unwelcome patron: Kemp, the baron's man. He nursed a pint of lager in one of his massive hands as he chatted lazily with a pair of farmhands who propped up the bar, the establishment's only other guests. He noticed Leo come in and flashed one of his trademark grins in his direction. Leo didn't react, and ordered a large Old Pulteney with a pint of the local heavy to accompany it from the landlord, who had an English Midlands accent and a bushy moustache. Leo then retreated to an alcove which was out of the draught of the front door but on the other side of the room from Kemp. There he deliberated upon the evening's events for a while.

Well-oiled, and with the landlord calling 'Time', Leo set off for the hotel, leaving Kemp and his cronies still drinking; presumably licensing hours didn't apply to locals.

The cold air did little to sober Leo up, such was the massive quantity of alcohol he had now consumed. He veered a little across the road as he walked the mile or so back to the Loch Dhonn. Not far from the gates to Fallasky House, the road was bordered by thick coniferous woodland, a dark place which gave Leo the creeps. What the cold air did do was contract his bladder, such that he felt an urgent need to pee. Leo stepped to the side of the road and found that Benjamin Franklin had shrivelled somewhat with the temperature, and that the flow was feeble and sporadic. As he performed he fancied that he could discern sprites and nymphs watching him from the wood's shadowy glades, mocking him.

Leo zipped up and set off, focusing his eyes on the lights of the hotel in the middle distance. Just over a gate to his left he noticed a figure with a torch in the meadow there. Leo directed the beam of his flashlight to reveal George, still out searching. Poor bugger must be bloody freezing, thought Leo, noticing now the man's inadequate, archaic country attire. He greeted him, but Rattray didn't seem to hear, or perhaps didn't feel like chatting, and he turned and walked in the direction of his home. Leo called out again, and such was his distraction that he was unaware of a Land Rover, its headlamps off, creeping up behind him.

Suddenly, the engine roared, and Leo spun round to be blinded by the lights, which had now been switched on to full beam, as the vehicle was driven towards him at speed. In an instant he opted to leap, rather than run, out of the way, a decision that prevented him death or serious injury. He ended up tumbling down a bank, into the dreaded woods, his torch falling from his grasp and dying from its impact with the turf. He had the wind knocked from him and felt pain in his left shoulder and both knees, but a quick flexing of his extremities told him that nothing was broken. He heard the gearbox whine as the vehicle reversed too quickly. Leo instinctively stayed perfectly still so as not to give away his position; he had fortuitously landed among thick cover. Against the starlit backcloth he could make out the unmistakable outline of a Land Rover pick-up. The driver, who was wearing what looked like a flour sack over his head with a slit cut for vision, got out and shone a flashlight into the woods. It looked somehow obscene, the yellow beam of artificial light picking out the midnight detail of an obscure thicket. The hooded man had what resembled a shotgun crooked in his other arm, and Leo murmured a prayer. The miracle duly arrived. The man got back into the vehicle and drove off. Leo lay for a while on the black soil, which smelled cold and rich, listening out for the sound of an engine, lest his stalker return. When he felt quite sure that he was alone, he retrieved his torch – a quick shake restored it to functionality – and crept along the apron of the wood for a while, then dashed the final few hundred yards to the hotel.

27

Leo's sleep was wrecked by the trauma of what had been the second attack upon his person since arriving in Loch Dhonn. His dreams presented him with a recurring image.

Two thoroughbreds galloping, in slow motion, through a pasture by a loch. He sees the beasts from several angles, their manes being tossed proudly, their chestnut flanks shivering with exertion, steam rising from their flared nostrils.

After breakfast Leo, whose hangover was remarkably mild, wasted no time in entering the steel-grey, bitterly cold morning and seeking out DI Lang, who was sitting behind his desk in the Portakabin, looking as though he hadn't slept in a week. He had evidently taken to flouting Scotland's ban on smoking in the workplace, and his reception was little warmer than the temperature outside.

'Were you bevvied?' enquired the cop blithely, after Leo had related the events of the previous day and night, including the theory that a brass cylinder had been stolen from Eva's workshop and used to violate Helen. He also told Lang that Shona had fired Helen from the Loch Dhonn Hotel, but, of course, he kept his audacious visit to the Addison home to himself.

'I was well fortified against this infernal cold, I'll grant you. But he was trying to kill me, guaranteed. Assuming it was the murderer, it would prove that our man is indeed a local, Detective Inspector, as we both suspected.'

'Who could have known you were on the road?'

'Any number of people would have seen myself and Eva dining earlier, and surmised that I would escort her home to Kildavannan and then walk back to the hotel myself. We met George Rattray on the way down, and that arse Kemp was in the Innisdara Inn, where I stopped for a night-cap on my way home. He could have followed me out.'

'Are you sure it was McKee's vehicle?'

'Yes . . . I mean, I think so. It was dark, obviously.'

'Did you see it up by the pub, where Kemp was, beforehand?'

'No. But it could have been parked round the back.'

'Have any of your apparitions been about McKee?' asked Lang as he lit his third consecutive filter cigarette of the conference.

'You will recall my telling you of the second vision I had back in Glasgow, involving the unintelligent man wrongly accused. I now believe that fellow to be Robbie McKee. I take it he is a suspect?'

'Well, you yourself say it was his Land Rover that tried to run you down.'

'But that doesn't mean he was driving it. He's known to leave his keys sitting in the ignition overnight. The driver was wearing a hood. It could have been Kemp. Or, more likely, the murderer. Or perhaps they are one in the same. Although Kemp's shoe size will be bigger than a nine, the size of the killer's footprint.'

'Where did this take place, exactly?'

'By the woods just south of Fallasky House, the Grey Lady's place.'

Lang raised an eyebrow.

'What?'

'Her man Bosco is back in town.'

28

L EO, discouraged by Lang's rather dismissive tone, headed back to the hotel for a brief respite from the hard frost and to take morning coffee. He felt comforted to sit in the lobby by the huge fireplace, content to be in proximity to the low hubbub of the hotel's activity. Leo had missed Fordyce at breakfast, and withdrew his mobile phone in order to call him. He noticed a rather oblique text from his friend: 'Gone back to the 'Burg for a few days, old stick. Be back up soon.'

Leo felt rather troubled by the message. Was something wrong? Had he offended Fordyce in some way? He had wanted to obtain his assistance, so that he could visit Innisdubh again and try to open the sepulchre he had dreamed of and been violently denied access to.

Then Leo's thoughts turned to the image of the previous night, the magnificent horses running free. It put him in mind of a scene he had witnessed recently, in a meadow by the loch; he felt sure that his powers were urging him to visit this place. Therefore he returned to his room to dress properly for the outdoors. He then borrowed the walking stick from the hotel hat-stand and popped a Pan Drop into his mouth before heading outside. He strolled up the drive, by the colossal frosted trunk of the Wellingtonia, then set off southwards through a crystal realm, the countryside majestic under its pale dusting, his footsteps making a satisfying crump-crump sound on the hoary turf. He hoped that his choice of direction was genuinely instinctive, and not some forlorn subconscious attempt to bump into his dinner date of the previous evening.

Soon, Leo came across that rarest of Loch Dhonn sights – James Millar at ground level during daylight hours. However, the recluse was hardly making himself conspicuous as he wove a path through the trees that bordered the roadside. Leo hailed the hermit and Millar walked across the tarmacadam to meet him.

Apparently, he had only been smoked from his hinterland retreat by an urgent need for camphor to treat a nasty abrasion he had sustained.

'Do you happen to know why Fordyce went back to Edinburgh?' asked Leo.

'I would guess he needed a bit of time to himself.'

'Oh,' said Leo, unsatisfied by this answer.

'He won't thank me for telling you this, but he's very keen on you.'

'I'm keen on him, too.'

'Don't play dumb. You know what I mean.'

'And you tell me this why? In some cavalier attempt to convert me to sodomy?'

Leo immediately regretted his words, blurted out in a moment of embarrassment; he actually felt overwhelming concern for Fordyce.

'That's unworthy of you, and of Fordyce.'

'I . . . didn't mean it,' mumbled Leo.

They came abreast of the village store, a timber-log affair which probably coincided with Millar's mountain cabin aesthetic. Two doves remained where they sat with their heads partially buried in ruffs of feathers, too cold to bother concerning themselves with the arrival of humans.

Millar faced Leo and placed a hand on his arm. 'Be gentle with him.' He turned and went inside the shop, the ping of the bell announcing his rare visit.

Thoughts of Fordyce tormented Leo as he walked on. He reckoned that helping Leo with the case – not to mention watching his back in case of danger – had meant a great deal to him. Therefore his heartache must have been acute for him to leave for Edinburgh so abruptly.

Things would be so much simpler – and infinitely better – if only Eva fancied him instead of Fordyce, he speculated.

A commanding view of the lochside now presented itself. Down in the pasture beyond the boatyard, beyond George Rattray's home and across from Innisdara, stood the two chestnut thoroughbreds – undoubtedly the animals he had foreseen in his sleep a few hours ago.

Before the knowe where Leo and Eva had been startled the previous evening, and where Helen had appeared, was a path which led its way down towards the loch, passing through some boggy land, then skirting the rear of Rattray's property to the right, with an area of woodland to the left. Down further still was the pasture itself, to the south of which were stables and some agricultural buildings. While passing the woods Leo became aware of a figure in the periphery of his vision. It moved stealthily through the trees, and at first Leo thought it might be one of the locals hunting for wigeon or snipe. But something about the person's furtive body language suggested it wished to remain undetected by human, rather than avian, eyes. Leo crept into a brake of firs for cover, and fixed his Barr & Stroud binoculars to his eyes. There! He saw a flash of colour as the figure moved into the open. There again! But not a long enough exposure to identify the individual. Leo hunched down and quietly stole forward, taking care not to snap any twigs and give himself away. He knelt by a decayed stump and again raised his binoculars. This time he got a good look at the creeper – one Lex Dreghorn.

Just like a hunter he had a .22 rifle and a game bag strapped over his shoulder, but this could have been a cover to disguise his real purpose. Further into the woods went Dreghorn, and Leo followed his progression. The trees were a little thicker now, although many of them were denuded due to the season. Dreghorn stopped in a glade and began scanning the surface of the loch with a pair of field glasses. Leo wondered what vessel he expected to see upon the water. Dreghorn suddenly brought the glasses down, spooked by some unknown sound. His bald head darted around anxiously in every direction, and Leo instinctively dropped to the ground and kept perfectly still. By the time he peered back out into the glade, Dreghorn had vanished.

So intently had Leo been watching Dreghorn that he was oblivious to the huge, lurking figure watching him from the shadows. And when Leo turned round to head back towards the path he found himself looking straight into the face of an ogre.

Yet the ogre did not strike; it merely babbled a few indecipherable sounds from his wet red mouth. He had a large, oval-shaped head upon which his sleek black hair was cut so short that it looked as though it had been painted on. His eyes were as small as raisins, set deep within a large copper-coloured face.

So this is Bosco, deduced Leo.

He was tall enough, yet it was his girth that was truly impressive. He had a beer barrel for a body, his arms and legs were arboreal limbs corded with steel, his hands blunt and brutal bludgeons.

It became apparent from the man's simian gestures and idiom that he wished to show Leo something. Leo took a deep breath, tightened his grip on the walking staff, and followed. Bosco's massive back seemed to ripple with power, and stretched the fabric of his suit jacket to bursting point. Leo wondered what the Grey Lady was attracted to in this brute other than raw manliness (and the event that his anatomy was all in proportion), then admonished himself for judging the fellow so by his appearance.

Once at the path Bosco led Leo down its slope towards the pasture, where he stopped. The horses trotted over to the barbed wire and regarded the duo curiously. Leo wondered if Helen had ridden these fine animals. Bosco pointed at something nestling in the long grass by a little ditch which drained the run-off from the path. It was a 100ml pharmaceutical vial, its seal unbroken, the trade name Anesket printed on its label.

Leo withdrew an evidence bag and lifted the vial into it with a pair of tweezers from his detective's kit. He mouthed his thanks to Bosco, who replied with a nod of his massive rugby-ball head.

29

'KETAMINE hydrochloride,' declared Leo, brandishing the evidence bag in the police incident room like a trophy.

Lang whistled. 'And in liquid form! Where did you find this?'

'By the pasture adjacent to Innisdara. Last night I had a vision that drew me to the location, except Bosco had already found the item. He directed me to it.'

'Did he now? Hmm. Perhaps a vet dropped it.'

'No. I'll wager you'll take George's prints off that vial. When I saw him last night he was looking for something.'

'Yep, that would make sense.'

'I beg your pardon?'

'George helps manage the loch – fish stocks and such.'

'So?'

'Some ghillies use ketamine once they've netted fish for egging. Apparently, a few drops in the tank and they lay like billy-o. Strictly speaking, it's illegal, but as long as he's not selling it to kids . . . well, frankly, I've got bigger fish to fry at the moment – pardon the pun.'

Leo looked rather downcast at this prosaic but convincing explanation.

'Ketamine is a powerful animal anaesthetic, and causes hallucinations in humans. Could it have been used to dope Helen?'

'No. Apart from an over-the-counter antihistamine taken for an allergy her TR was clean.'

'TR?'

'Toxicology Report. Try again, I'm afraid.'

Leo suddenly slapped his head in exasperation.

'What?'

'I'm being a damned fool. Assuming it was the killer who tried to run me over last night, that rules George out altogether.'

'How?'

'Because I saw him, still out searching, just before the Land Rover was driven at me. By the way, I just saw Lex Dreghorn creeping around, near the lochside. Pretending he was out hunting.'

'How do you know he was pretending?'

'Just a feeling I had. Is he a suspect?'

'We're keeping an eye on him, but most of all we're keeping an open mind.'

Leo left the Portakabin, pondering the growing suggestion that his efforts were akin to urinating in high winds. And he suspected that DI Lang was becoming less and less enthusiastic about his being around Loch Dhonn. He walked back to the hotel, shivering in the cold, before taking a disconsolate luncheon of chicken confit in duck fat with *sautéed* potatoes. The hock he had ordered was overly chilled, the meat was a little teuch, and the fat had congealed around the potatoes to create an unsightly accompaniment. Yet Leo couldn't be bothered complaining to chef and instead wearily padded off to his chamber, feeling rather deflated.

He missed Fordyce's company, and at some level he felt vexed over the possibility that he had somehow led his friend on. He comfort-ate his way through an entire layer of Orange Creams and then felt rather sickened by the sugar overdose. He would open a bottle soon enough, then it would be room service for an early dinner, following which he would drink enough Ballantine's to coax himself off to sleep.

He built a wood fire in the grate, loaded Levitsky versus Marshall 1912 into the chess engine and marvelled at the poetry and audacity of the majestic queen sacrifice. He visualised the spectators showering coins of gold onto the table as Levitsky conceded. Such chess embodied something Leo hugely admired in human endeavour: the ability to combine craft with artistry. He was never quite comfortable with the manner in which western academia clung to the classical division of arts from sciences, and the way that psychology still felt it necessary to marshal personalities into some latter-day version of the humours. To him, God's creation had to be understood in terms of its sublime beauty as well as its awesome scale and complexity. Another great player, Marcel Duchamp, proved the point: the great surrealist artist turned chess master.

Leo gazed into the dancing flames in the fireplace, then lay back on the bed, and fancied for a moment that he was Marshall, playing some Faustian chess match against whichever diabolic foe had killed Helen. And he lamented the fact that, unlike the grandmaster, he couldn't seem to see one move ahead, let alone five. And he wondered what the endgame would be, fantasising that it would involve a decisive thrust, a glorious flourish of genius on his part which would go down in history and be studied for years to come.

30

THAT night Leo dreamed of a massive, golden bird – an eagle, in flight over a midnight sky.

The cold firmament is illuminated by starlight, and the bird glides effortlessly and majestically. It scans the ground a mile below, not for prey, but for its destination. This is the eagle of Saint John the Evangelist, a messenger to mankind. It happens upon a loch, long and jagged, like a shard of broken glass. The eagle's eye glints with recognition. It swoops lower now, the water flashing by below, over islands, towards the head of the loch. There, perched upon the steep northern bank in the shadow of a great mountain, is a church. The eagle checks its direction with a slight shifting of its wings. It hunches now to lose altitude, then plummets rapidly. The magnificent creature circles the building, then takes a final dive towards the open main door.

Inside now, the Victorian nave creepy, lit by the faint flicker of votive lights in the far aisle. A whoosh of air, the eagle enters and lands on the cold stone floor. Struts over to a marble plinth and hops onto it. It then turns a hundred and eighty degrees, folds its wings and raises them above its nape, and becomes perfectly still. A change has come over it – it has metamorphosed into a lectern of solid bronze.

The door slams shut and the resultant gust blows out some of the candles. A shadowy male figure is silhouetted in the meagre light. He is armed. He steps closer, closer, closer.

Leo woke up with a gasp, his heart racing, the knowledge that something profound was about to occur weighing upon him heavily. Again he felt that his vision had been curtailed by some mysterious and sinister influence, that it had been cut short before some final chapter had unfolded. His mind raced to where he recognised the church from. The leaflet – of course! The one he had pretended to browse while eavesdropping on the Mintos' argument. What was that weird kirk called? St Finnan's? No, St Fillan's. Leo leapt from his bed and switched on the centre light. He flung open the wardrobe and searched his evening jacket for the leaflet – bingo! Eagerly, he spread it out upon the dressing table and scanned it. It was all tourist information about the history of the building and the finer points of its architecture – not data desperately relevant at this precise juncture. Leo flipped it over; a little map detailed the location of the kirk. It was just outside a little village called Scalpsie, which sat at the head of Loch Dhonn. Leo would have to follow the road to the top of the loch, then take a left in the direction of Oban for half a mile.

Quickly, he dressed, wrapping up well. He thrust the leaflet, his torch and his detective's kit into his shooting coat and set off, closing his door softly and creeping down the carpeted corridor, under the watchful gaze of a huge mounted deer's head. It had only just gone midnight but the hotel was already still with sleep. A familiar feeling of darkness – a combination of weariness and dread – filled Leo's consciousness, exacerbated by the comedown from the previous evening's whisky.

The cold air pinched his face as he stepped into the freezing night. He strode directly over to a squad car inside which sat two policemen on sentry duty. He tapped urgently on the driver's side window. The glass, which was misted with condensation, slid slowly down. Leo found himself looking into the face of the taller of the two officers with whom he had spoken on his first day at Loch Dhonn. His short pal was dozing on the passenger seat but came round as soon as Leo began speaking.

'Look here, you've got to take me to Scalpsie, at the top of the loch,' he exclaimed, immediately regretting the unintentionally haughty cadence.

'Sorry, sir, we're not a taxi service.'

'It's important. I think someone might be in danger.'

Constable Shorty eyed him with bemusement. He spoke to Leo in a rather offhand manner: 'We're under strict orders to stay here. There's a brutal murderer on the loose, remember?'

'And besides,' said Lofty. 'The DI's fuming with you. Says we're not to cooperate. I'd stay out of his way, if I were you.'

Damn, thought Leo. Lang must have found out I visited the Addisons. Sodding, buggering, bloody shithouses.

'Look, I beg of you, couldn't just one of you splendid fellows take me there, and the other can remain to stand guard? You see, I've got good reason to believe that a serious crime is about to be committed at St Fillan's Kirk.'

'What good reason would that be, sir?' asked Shorty.

Leo realised that the conversation was pointless and stood beside the car as the window slid back up, plotting another course of action. It would take the best part of an hour to walk to Scalpsie, by which time he might be too late to foil whatever the dream had been warning of. If only he could procure some means of transportation – a car, a boat, even a bicycle. That's it – a bicycle! Leo remembered seeing Paul the barman chain his to a drainpipe at the side of the hotel. He hot-footed it round and made a small exclamation of triumph as he saw the pushbike gleaming gloriously beneath the arc lamps. He looked from left to right, then tried the lock, but it was properly fastened. Nonetheless, Paul had opted for a bottom-of-the-range security device, and Leo withdrew the wire cutters from his detective's kit and began chewing at the flimsy cable. In less than a minute he had reduced it to shreds.

'Sorry, Paul,' Leo muttered as he switched on the rear and front lamps, 'but I'm commandeering it for a higher purpose.'

The bike tick-ticked as he wheeled it into position. He mounted it in a rather ungainly fashion, wobbled for a few feet as the front wheel thrust from side to side, and then gained enough speed to glide brazenly by the police vehicle in the car park, and up the driveway towards the road, the gravel popping under the tyres.

Leo was struck by how laborious the task of cycling felt compared with his youthful days when he would take off by himself into the Campsie Fells and Fintry Hills upon the second-hand Raleigh Rebel his father had procured for him, with its scarlet frame and white-walled tyres. The thought evoked some unpleasant memories: the other youths in his street shunning him or teasing him relentlessly for having a girl's bike. It wasn't a girl's bike – it had a crossbar – it just lacked the kudos of the Grifters, Choppers and racing bicycles with drooped handlebars that they possessed. In fact, his saddle bag and basket proved extremely practical for adventuring, and he used to love leaving the melting tar and white dog shit behind as he headed off alone towards the fragrant meadows and sun-dappled dells.

Thankfully, there was a shortcut some way before the T-junction at the Oban–Fallasky highway, a path beaten for anglers that skirted the north-eastern shore of the loch and which took several hundred yards out of Leo's journey. The ground was frozen as hard as ceramic and it started to snow lightly. The slender sickle moon in the heavens shed only minimal light and it felt decidedly odd to be riding a stolen bicycle across open countryside in sub-zero temperatures in the dead of night – not to mention a little eerie. But he dutifully stuck to his task, just as he had done on many, often thankless, previous occasions. Leo was encumbered with his fair share of human flaws, yet for some providential reason he had been vested with this strange and awful power of visions. He was still haunted by the disaster that had followed the one occasion when he hadn't acted upon their content. Therefore, ever since he had been resolute in answering the call, using it for good and in the service of others. Yet he wished that he wasn't always required to undertake tasks such as this on his own. The sardonic lyrics of a World War I song came to mind: 'We're here because we're here because we're here because we're here . . .'

Suddenly, he heard a rumble of footfalls: bare soles, brogans and deerskin ghillies upon an ancient road. There, to the north, was Lachlan – who would fall upon the killing ground at Culloden – at the head of a column of his beloved kinsmen, lightly armed, and clad in green and red plaid. They marched towards the gathering at Glenfinnan, towards the true heir's rallying call. They marched into the great valley ahead, into shadow.

'Fortis et fidus!' exclaimed Leo, remembering that noble clan's motto and the honourable role it played in the '45. And the spectral vision indeed fortified him, which was just as well because he had to pedal hard to reach the road again, and even harder to haul himself over a humpback bridge which spanned a little river. He was almost at Scalpsie now, and he hoped that he wouldn't have to face any exertions once he got there; he was utterly exhausted, and last night's Ballantine's had risen in his gut to make him feel slightly bilious.

He freewheeled through the village itself, which gave him the chance to catch his breath somewhat. He then rolled into the churchyard through an open gate, stopped and dismounted. He listed his complaints: his head felt light, his mouth was as dry as a cinder, there was a searing sensation in his lungs, his legs burned with lactic acid, and his hands were sore from gripping. He leaned the bicycle against a tree, switched off its lamps, switched on his torch, and quickly scanned the leaflet again in the vague hope that it might bestow some key scrap of information about the church which might help him, before walking past a pair of graves, iron-clad against body snatchers, and going inside.

St Fillan's Kirk had been conceived by Lord Kenneth MacArthur, the Grey Lady's great-grandfather, whose own father had part-designed Fallasky House. It was located outwith their ancestral lands, but MacArthur, a keen amateur architect and antiquarian who was a devotee of the Church of Scotland, bought the plot of land with the purpose of dedicating a kirk there to the glory of God and as a gift to the locals – whose nearest Presbyterian place of worship then was in Fallasky, five miles away, this now being the beginning of the traditionally Episcopalian/Catholic end of Argyll, where the old ways had been kept alive by the heather-priests. MacArthur was keen to put his own talents to good use in the project and contrived almost all of the structure. He furnished it with fine artefacts including an ancestral tomb of carved stone in which his dead father was installed, an oversized statue of Malcolm Canmore at rest (replete with a decidedly un-Calvinistic finger-bone relic), and an array of stunning stained-glass side windows which told various chapters from Scottish history and heraldry. MacArthur even helped to cut the very granite from which the church was built with his own hands; boulders of it were rolled down from the scree slopes of Ben Corrach, which began just across the road. Yet for all of his vision, philanthropy and romance, MacArthur was also a hopeless eccentric, and tacked on various architectural styles to the gothic core of the kirk, which lent it a crazily eclectic and at some points downright ugly complexion. For many visitors such foibles, such as the exterior's series of bizarre gargoyles, merely added to the charm of the place; to purists such as Leo they spoiled it, and under different circumstances he would have pondered how much he preferred the more harmonious unorthodoxy of the European Baroque.

He walked through the gloomy chancel, passing gnarled carvings, vulgar candelabras and the eagle lectern from his dream, then entered the semi-circular ambulatory of the apse, some of his natural fear dispelled by his admiration for this part of MacArthur's folly, with its double pillars and narrow arches. Indeed, he was momentarily transfixed by the effect the thin moonlight had upon the apse, as it filtered through tall clear-glass windows and fell delicately upon the cold stone. He felt like a figure set within a Victorian steel etching, trapped in a lovely silver and black world.

Suddenly, a pane of glass to his right shattered violently, instantly snapping Leo out of his reverie.

'Murder! Murder!' he bellowed, realising he had been shot at. As he was yelling he switched off his torch and dashed behind a pillar, approximately out of what he supposed was the line of fire.

'Who the hell is down there?' sounded a male voice, from high up in the kirk's roof space.

'It is Leo Moran,' Leo began, his voice breaking with fury and fear. 'Whoever you are, the police are on their way. They know where I am. You shall be arrested. I claim sanctuary. Do you hear me? I claim the sanctuary of this sacred place!'

'Leo? Is that you?'

Leo recognised the voice and peered out. 'Craig? Come down – show yourself!'

'What the *fuck* are ye doin' here?'

'I could ask you the very same question, young man! Though I should do so without profaning the Lord's house.'

Leo came into the open, his heart slowing now, an almost ecstatic sensation of relief coursing through his body. Hutton noisily clambered down a rickety set of wooden stairs from a small choir loft. Suddenly, they both heard a motor engine being gunned outside and a vehicle's tyres screeching as it sped off.

'Shite, he must have heard us! He's gettin' away!' wailed Hutton as he skipped down the last few steps, hurdled the rail and rushed towards the exit.

'*Who* is getting away?' Leo exclaimed after him, before uttering a sound of exasperation and following.

Outside, the pair looked on as the unmistakable profile of a Land Rover pick-up roared through the village and over the humpback bridge. Hutton raised but then lowered a weapon – a fearsome-looking crossbow – quickly realising the futility of taking a shot from such a range.

'Murderer!' he yelled instead.

'What the devil is going on?' asked Leo, shocked by the rage that had suffused the young man's features. 'That's Robbie's Land Rover, and he's no murderer!'

'I know, but the man who's drivin' it is.'

'And who might that be?'

Hutton turned to him. 'Lex. I was told he was comin' here.'

'Who told you he was coming here?'

'Robbie texted me.'

'Do you mind if I see it? The text message, I mean.'

Hutton displayed the message: 'The murdering bastard Lex will be at St Fillan's Kirk at some time after midnight.'

'Can you forward this on to my phone, please?'

Hutton thumbed in Leo's number as he dictated it and pressed send. A few moments later Ludwig informed Leo that the text had arrived.

Leo regarded the crossbow which was now pointed at the ground. 'Great Scott, man, you fired a bloody bolt at me!'

'I'm sorry, I thought ye were Lex.'

'Craig, I am gravely concerned that you are going to do something incredibly unwise and quite possibly unjust.'

'Unjust?'

'We don't know Dreghorn is guilty. He may be a bounder and he's not exactly my cup of tea, but that doesn't mean he deserves to die.'

'Thon bastard did it. Robbie wouldnae lie. And anyway, I'd already suspected it.'

'You can't take the law into your own hands. You can't take that risk. Innocent until proven guilty. You need proof.'

'He tried it on wi' Helen. She was young enough tae be his daughter. A guy like Lex doesnae take rejection easy.'

'I want you to promise that you won't attack him again.'

'I cannae dae that.'

'Then I'm afraid I'm going to have to tell DI Lang about what's happened here tonight, and what you intend to do.'

'Well, fuck you, then.'

'I'm sorry, but it's for your own good.'

31

THE next morning, Leo scoffed a full Scottish breakfast in double-quick time, tossed back a discreet dram to help him adjust to the day, hastily donned his outer garments, and set out into the freezing fog that had draped itself over the countryside. His destination: the old washhouse behind George Rattray's property in which Robbie lived.

Leo found him in the yard, ventilating great clouds of steam, his bare, powerful, veined arms chopping logs into splinters as though they were matchsticks.

'Good morning, Robbie.'

McKee turned round, unshaven, drowsy-looking, red-eyed, brandishing the axe like a maniac. He made a vague sound of greeting.

'How's tricks?'

'I've to get these logs chopped for George's heating.'

Leo walked over to him, patting the Land Rover as he passed it, its surface coated with rime which prickled outwards like cat fur.

'This old girl sure gets around. I saw her last night, beating a hasty retreat from St Fillan's Kirk.'

'That wisnae me.'

'Who was it, then?' McKee shrugged his shoulders. 'Would you mind putting the axe down, Robbie? If you may be so kind.'

McKee obeyed, slamming the blade into the stump he used as a chopping block.

'I'll give you a clue, then,' continued Leo. 'Let's say it was Lex.'

McKee stared at him blankly.

'Robbie, I want to help you. And I really believe that you could do with some help right now.'

'I asked Lex if I could come along. To help him wi' the lead. But then I didnae feel well. Must've been thon curry George made; we baith had the shits. I said Lex could borrow the Land Rover.'

'Did you send a text to Craig, to tell him Lex was heading up to St Fillan's?'

'Eh?'

'Did you send Craig a text message, to tell him Lex was heading up to St Fillan's?'

'Naw.'

'Are you sure?'

'Aye!'

'Well, would you mind letting me check your mobile phone?'

McKee handed Leo his ancient Nokia, which was scored and grubby, and held together with electrician's tape. Leo took it and flicked to the sent items, wincing slightly at the stink of a man who had been living and sleeping in the same clothes for days on end. There was no such message, but, of course, it could have been deleted.

'See?'

'All right.' For some reason the ugly, abbreviated text-messaging style utilised by his friend Stephanie popped into Leo's mind, and an idea occurred to him. 'Would you mind doing something for me?' He withdrew his notebook and Montblanc fountain pen. 'Write the words "St Fillan's Kirk" down for me.'

McKee took the exquisite pen in his blunt, nicotine-stained fingers, and acquiesced, in a childish scrawl.

Leo's right eyebrow rose with enlightenment. 'Thank you.'

Leo made to leave, discreetly polishing his pen clean with his handkerchief once McKee's back was turned. Then he remembered something else he had meant to ask, and faced McKee again. 'Incidentally, I'm told you were recently made homeless by a house fire.'

'Aye, I was,' replied McKee, before lighting a crumpled little roll-up cigarette.

'How did it start?'

'Dunno. The fire brigade couldnae say for sure.'

32

L ANG had the lean, pallid look of a man who had for several days been substituting cigarettes for meals. His cheap suit was rumpled, his necktie loose and the top two buttons of his shirt were undone. He looked up at Leo, and his bloodshot eyes flashed with anger. He addressed the three constables in the Portakabin sharply.

'Right people, out! I want to speak with our Mr Moran alone.'

Lang followed the uniforms to the door and glared after them, checking that they weren't hanging around to eavesdrop. He slammed the flimsy door shut and marched back to his chair.

'How could you bother those poor people? I thought I told you to keep a low profile!'

He was spitting phlegm as he shouted. It was unusual to see Lang so stirred, but Leo resolved to hold his nerve.

'You're upset, I can tell. Perhaps the inquiry is making you overwrought.'

'Of course I'm bloody overwrought – I told you not to visit the Addisons!'

'Did Mr Addison complain to you about my visit?'

'No, but I'm complaining about it to you.'

'Who told you?'

'As a matter of fact it was Shona Minto.'

'Bloody old besom!'

'It doesn't matter who told me. I expressly forbade you to bother that poor family.'

'It's a free country. I must follow my instincts. Justice is at stake, and the safety of other women. And anyway, I didn't *bother* them and I didn't promise anything.'

Lang stood up and leaned over towards Leo. He lowered his voice threateningly. 'Don't mess with me, son, or I promise I'll have you fucking lifted for obstructing a murder inquiry.'

He resumed his seat and lit a cigarette.

'In what way have I been obstructive?'

'I'll think of something.'

'That is tantamount to harassment. I might remind you that we are both equally subject to the same rule of law.'

'OK, fine. I'll have you lifted for stealing a bicycle. That Paul fella wants to know when you're going to buy him a new lock, by the way. Now, the last train to Glasgow leaves at six-fifteen, and you're going to be on it. A squad car will be waiting outside to take you to Fallasky station at quarter to. That gives you plenty of time to pack your bags and say your goodbyes. If you're not there, you'll be spending the night in a police cell in Oban.'

Leo sighed, but did not move. He took a deep breath. 'McKee's in the frame, isn't he?'

The detective regarded him in silence, and leaned back in his chair.

'He's innocent,' insisted Leo.

Lang decided to humour this odd character, one last time, just to dispel any lingering doubts he might have about his perspicacity. 'Is he, indeed? He's been acting more and more oddly. The police shrink reckons he's becoming . . . disassociated from his surroundings.'

'I've just been round at his; he seemed perfectly all right to me,' Leo ventured mendaciously.

'Did he tell you that he was thrown out of the Innisdara Inn on Saturday night? He started babbling incoherently, then he started screaming and bawling about Helen. And, of course, there's the letter.'

'What letter?'

'We know McKee had a thing about Helen. He sent a love letter to her; it arrived at the Addisons' earlier this morning. Fairly creepy stuff.'

'This morning?'

'Yep. One of our Forensic people is up here and she's already given it the once over. It might have been lost in the postal system, but that's unlikely. Probability is that McKee sent it post-mortem, as some weird means of confession, or worse, to torture the family.'

'That stinks. Someone's posted it to transfer suspicion onto him. I'll wager it was written ages ago.'

Lang seemed to flinch slightly at Leo's guess. 'As a matter of fact it was. It wasn't dated, but Forensics confirmed it. But it's authentic.'

'So he fancied Helen, so what? If that was evidence you'd have arrested him by now. Look here, Detective Inspector, I'm telling you it's not him. You will recall how I told you of one of my visions in which a slow-witted man had been falsely accused – I still believe that person to be Robbie McKee. I reckon someone – most probably the actual killer – is trying to frame him.'

Leo fiddled with his mobile phone until the message that Craig had forwarded to him appeared. Then he withdrew his notebook and flicked it open to reveal McKee's scribble. He placed both items on the desk and turned them to face Lang.

'Last night I had a vision that something wicked was about to transpire at St Fillan's Kirk, up at Scalpsie.'

'Hence your little midnight bicycle ride?'

'Indeed. Anyway, Craig was up there, waiting to get – to *kill* – Lex. Lex and Robbie had been planning to steal lead from the kirk roof, except Robbie called off sick.'

'Did Lex turn up?'

'Yes. At least, I believe it was him, in Robbie's Land Rover. Lex was startled and drove off.'

'Christ Almighty!' ejaculated Lang in exasperation. 'And what about Craig? Did you actually see him either?'

'Saw him, spoke with him and fell out with him. Someone had told him that Lex was the murderer, and that he would be at St Fillan's at an approximate time. By sending a text via Robbie's phone.'

'So Robbie feigned sickness and then sent the text in a clumsy attempt to shift the blame from himself.'

'No, no. I don't believe he did send it. Observe,' said Leo, pointing at the items on the desk. 'The text says "St Fillan's Kirk", which is grammatically correct in that it contains the possessive apostrophe. Now, look at it written by Robbie this very hour – no apos.'

Lang looked decidedly unimpressed. 'That proves nothing.'

'No, but is it likely – to take the trouble to insert an apostrophe into a text message yet omit to insert one using a pen? Just because it came from Robbie's mobile doesn't mean it was he who sent it. I reckon he's not so daft as to send an incriminating message from his own phone. Someone else could have been aware of his and Lex's plans for the night, and they could have got a hold of the mobile and sent the text. Then Craig would strike and some suspicion would fall upon the dead Lex, and/or Robbie, whose phone had tipped off Craig, and who would then be accused of orchestrating the ambush to cover up his own guilt.'

Lang sat in silence for a moment, drawing on his cigarette, then crushing it out. His tone softened a little.

'Look, Leo, you're a good guy, but it's time for you to bugger off from here. This text message/St Fillan's Kirk business interests me, but only in that it implicates Robbie even further, and therefore I'm grateful to you for the information. Oh, and regarding your near miss with the Land Rover: Robbie says it wasn't him driving two nights ago, but he would deny it, wouldn't he? He also says he didn't lend the vehicle to anyone but he can't vouch for its whereabouts. Also, the landlord of the Innisdara Inn and two patrons have given Kemp an alibi. They said they had a lock-in that night, and that Kemp remained in the bar for at least another hour after you left. In which case it couldn't have been him who tried to run you down.'

'He could have primed them to lie, before you spoke with them.'

'But is it likely?' quoted Lang.

'*Touché*, Detective Inspector. Look, I'm not saying it necessarily was Kemp who was driving; I'm simply saying it wasn't Robbie.'

'Well, the shoeprints on Innisdubh, from when you were assaulted – they did match with Kemp.'

'But that's impossible! Bill told me he was dining at the hotel at the time.'

'He's a size twelve, by the way – too big for the murderer. Anyway, I'm afraid to say a footprint alone isn't enough for me to press an assault charge. Kemp admits he was on the island that day but denies it was he who coshed you,' Lang said flatly, clearly uninterested in proceeding with the matter.

'Of course he denies it!'

'Anything else?' asked the policeman, having already wearily moved on from the chapter of Leo Moran in his professional life.

'Craig fired a crossbow at me last night, thinking I was Lex. It narrowly missed me and smashed a window. I want you to do something about it.'

Lang sighed slightly. 'I'll bring him in and caution him.'

'You'll need to do better than that. I want him charged. That lad means business.'

'And what, exactly, is he to be charged with? Attempted murder? The poor bastard has just lost his beloved and you want me to throw him in the jail?'

'You misunderstand. I want him taken into custody until such time as this case is solved, to protect him from himself before he delivers his wild justice and kills someone – probably the wrong man. Charge him with recklessly discharging a deadly weapon, or wilful damage to an ancient monument, or bloody peeing in the street for all I care.' Leo leaned forward a little. 'Otherwise, I will go to your superiors. You have my promise on that.'

He turned and strode out before Lang could explode, and walked briskly towards the hotel, humming tunelessly in a lame effort to pretend to himself he wasn't shaken and upset by the harsh exchange.

33

AFTER lunching in his room, Leo packed and then killed a few dismal hours with his chess computer. It was never the same as playing a human being: no mind games, no feints, no getting to know your opponent's style, weaknesses and preferred tactics, and most of all it was lonely, with only a vast swathe of binary for company. Then he solemnly descended the hotel stairs to check out, but first headed into the lounge, hoping to find Paul. Unfortunately, the barman had returned to his quarters for a nap, so Leo placed his luggage on the floor and began jotting down a brief letter. He would enclose a twenty-pound note in order that Paul could replace his bicycle lock. He would also buy a bottle of twelve-year-old Bruichladdich by way of a peace offering. As Leo was scribbling his apologies Lex Dreghorn, who had been installed upon his usual stool since opening time, sidled up to him.

'Leaving us so soon, good sir?' His breath was stale with beer and hand-rolled cigarettes.

'I am.'

'Have a falling out wi' the polis, did we?'

Leo didn't reply.

'It just goes to show: never think ye can make pals wi' those sods,' he advised with false bonhomie as he brought his face closer to Leo and slyly glanced at the note he was writing.

'Do you mind,' said Leo, covering the sheet with his hand.

Dreghorn made great play of backing off, issuing a vaguely apologetic sound and raising his hands in surrender. He disliked Leo and they both knew why. Leo, with his easy wit and natural eccentricity, had constituted a threat to his station as local character-in-chief. There was also the small matter that Leo could doubtless drink him under the table, which would undermine Dreghorn's ferocious repute among his acolytes for holding his ale.

Leo waited for the next instalment.

'Who's going to look after yer wee click once yer gone?'

'I beg your pardon?' replied Leo, missing the point.

'Thon wee English bird wi' the rack,' said Dreghorn, cupping his hands in front of his chest to illustrate his off-colour remark.

Leo could have punched him. 'Oh, you mean Eva, the artist.'

'Aye, that's the one. Might have to pay her a wee visit. She's gotta love the Lex,' he slurred.

'I'll take your word for it.'

'Eh?'

'I said, I'll take your word for it. That Eva's "gotta love the Lex".'

'No need to get snippy wi' me, pal,' said Dreghorn, with bad drinker's aggression. 'It's no' my fault ye couldnae solve a fuckin' crossword.'

He sauntered off, emitting loud, false laughter for Leo's benefit.

Bill Minto checked Leo out in near silence. Leo requested a conference in private and the two men retired to the rear office where they stood facing each other.

'I'll come straight to the point: why did you lie about the baron's man?'

'Sorry?' said Minto, taken quite off balance.

'You gave Kemp an alibi for when he was bashing me over the head on Innisdubh.'

Minto was silent and his face coloured crimson, a slightly odd phenomenon to witness in one so mature.

'I think you're protecting him. He doesn't want folk on that isle because he's up to something downright wicked.'

Minto sank into a chair. 'I didn't think he was going to hurt folk, just scare them off. Believe me, Leo, none of this is what you think.'

'What I think is that there's a poor girl stabbed to death, and you're obstructing the inquiry.'

'Look, I'll admit to you there's something up. But it's nothing to do with Helen's murder, I swear to God.'

'Then tell me what it is.'

'All it is, is that the baron . . . he's very sensitive about certain aspects of his family history.'

'His grandfather?'

'Yes.'

'What, then?'

'He killed several young girls. Sacrificed them. He had them brought in from abroad. Eastern Europe, I believe. While we were in the process of buying Ardchreggan House we found this weird chamber over there, hidden in the cellars . . . some sort of occult temple. Very creepy. There were weird robes, strange books with runic lettering, and also journals detailing certain crimes. The present baron obviously didn't know about the place, but once we showed him it he made us sign a legally binding document that swore us to secrecy regarding that and anything else we might find. Otherwise, he would have pulled out of the deal.'

'So what's Innisdubh got to do with it all?'

'That's where the thirteenth baron buried the bodies, in one of the mausoleums; it said so in one of the journals. So his lairdship is completely paranoid about folk sniffing around over there. He said that if we ever had knowledge of anyone visiting that island he wanted to know right away. He said if a guest from our hotel ever poked their nose in he'd hold us personally responsible. Myself and Shona discussed it. She said that the old baron was long gone, what good would it have done dragging all that badness up, and so we signed.'

'I have reason to believe that some sort of Satanic ceremony took place over there recently. Carried out by whoever murdered Helen.'

'I know nothing about that, honestly. The baron is a lot of things, but he's not a killer.'

'What about the girls his grandfather murdered?'

'They were poor people from goodness knows where; they could never be traced anyway.'

'They were God's children, who deserved to have been given a decent burial. And the police would have at least tried to trace them.'

Bill Minto gazed at his feet, utterly ashamed.

'What else?'

'After a few years the baron started making noises that he wanted more money from us. He got jealous of the success we had made of the Ardchreggan and started going on about how it was his birthright. Claimed we had ripped him off over the deal. Said we had cheated him, not paid him enough. We, well, Shona told him to get stuffed. But then he turned the whole business about his grandfather around. He held the only copy of the contract and he started blackmailing *us* with it. Said he wanted full hospitality at the Loch Dhonn once a week, or he'd go public about the whole dirty deal. Mutually Assured Destruction.'

'Did you believe him?'

'No. I thought his family pride would probably prove too great. But I knew he'd make life more and more difficult for us. To use the Glasgow parlance, he's a complete bampot; an extremely vicious and unpleasant man. But a well-connected one. I figured one free meal a week was a fair bargain for peace of mind.'

'A few days ago, I overheard you and your wife arguing. You wanted to go to the police about something, and she didn't.'

'Yes, and you clyped to DI Lang about it. He questioned us about it, you know. It was quite unpleasant, having to pretend we didn't have a clue what he was talking about.'

'Well, stop pretending now and tell me: what was the nature of you and your good lady's dispute?'

Minto sighed. 'Helen used to work for us. Just for a wee while, part-time. As a chambermaid.'

'Yes, I know that.'

'One day Shona dismissed her.'

'I know that too. Why?'

'She accused Shona of something . . . she was quite out of line.' Minto's voice quavered.

'Well?'

Minto cleared his throat. 'She accused Shona of making a pass at her. Shona denied it, of course – she's not like that – and told her to clear off and never to come back. What you overheard was that I wanted us to be up front with the police, in case they heard a rumour and that put Shona in the frame. But Shona was having none of it.'

'That's it?'

'That's it.'

34

Outside, Leo surveyed the hotel's grand, imposing exterior with a sigh before stowing his luggage in the boot of the waiting police car.

As he was being driven through the village, he saw Craig Hutton being led in handcuffs towards a police van. One officer was carrying his crossbow.

Leo's driver, a surly constable, noticed his gaze in the rear-view mirror. 'The DI says you've to make a statement about Hutton tomorrow, in Glasgow,' he told him.

Leo admired this little piece of Eden for quite possibly the last time as it flashed by his window. Half a mile out he spied Eva, oblivious to his presence in the back of the car, as she foraged by a hedgerow. He felt a tightening in his solar plexus, a pining feeling, painful, but rather thrillingly so. A sensation he hadn't felt in years. He still longed for a last burst of passion, a brief remembrance of what joy actually was before he died. Yet romance – that very process of meeting someone you admire greatly – tended to bring all his insecurities and a sense of unworthiness to the forefront of his mind. And then he remembered that this feeling he had for Eva had not been requited anyway, and he saw a bank of cloud fix itself above Ben Corrach like a pall, and suddenly he dreaded his lonely apartment and being left there to be consumed by his infatuation. Yes, tonight he would sup upon a bowl of cold misery. The snow came on, quite heavily, and he remembered that the killer of Helen Addison was still abroad.

The train barrelled through the dark pine forest, indifferent to the flurry of thick flakes, blue in the diminished light.

Leo surreptitiously sipped from his hip flask, musing upon the case with a dreary sense of dissatisfaction. He followed a thread of logic, trying to consider all the possible permutations which crowded his mind.

The conversation with Minto – assuming he was telling the truth, and Leo felt strongly that he had been – confirmed it had indeed been Kemp who had socked him on Innisdubh, to scare him off for reasons probably not connected with Helen's murder. Had Kemp been the killer, and therefore wanted to be rid of the meddling Leo altogether, he could easily have dispatched him that day upon the island when he had him at his mercy. Unless he wanted to carry out the dire deed at a different juncture; after all, the Mintos might have blabbed to the police had he resorted to homicide. But then there was the issue of Kemp's shoe size, far too large to be that of the killer. But what if he was in fact of a smaller size and had taken to wearing bigger footwear to throw the police off the scent? No, the idea was fanciful, and surely the killer would not have risked using such a fragile ploy.

It simply seemed improbable that Kemp was the murderer. Yet there was the outlying possibility that the killer had a confederate – such as Kemp – who was helping cover his tracks. Bill appeared to sincerely believe that the baron was innocent of Helen's murder, but what if he was mistaken and the nobleman was performing some macabre tribute act to his long-dead grandfather? However, Leo's visions, which had never misled him before, gave the impression of a solitary fulcrum of evil; this chimed with Lang's assessment that the murder scene pointed to a perpetrator acting alone. Also, the baron's stature was a bit too diminutive and his gouty fingers didn't seem those of a powerful killer. And it seemed implausible that Kemp or the Baron of Caradyne could have gained access to Robbie's mobile phone in order to send the text that was designed to set up Lex's assassination at St Fillan's.

The attack upon Leo with the Land Rover two nights ago was far more serious than the one by Kemp at Innisdubh. It had quite obviously been an attempt upon his life, and the driver of the vehicle had even got out, presumably to do Leo a fatal mischief. Yes, deduced Leo, the two attacks were by different individuals with different motivations. The Land Rover had been driven by the killer of Helen Addison, wishing to put paid to Leo's interference.

Leo still didn't believe that Robbie had sent the text message drawing Craig to St Fillan's Kirk, but what if his theory about the real sender was only half right? He recalled the furtive manner in which Lex had been skulking around the lochside yesterday – what if he was indeed the murderer? However, Leo suddenly recalled something Lex had said the first time he had met him, referring to himself as a 'southpaw'; whereas the coroner had established that the killer was right-handed. Leo doubted that Lex was pretending, that he had the guile to inject such a subterfuge into the conversation. And whether he was the culprit or not, what if the sender was merely a party who, mistakenly or not, was sincerely convinced of Lex's guilt – George Rattray, for instance, who would have had easy access to Robbie's phone – and simply wanted to give Craig the satisfaction of direct justice, rather than seeing the slayer of his beloved released from Barlinnie after a ten-stretch? And perhaps the sender used Robbie's mobile in order to maintain anonymity. But that could have made Robbie an accessory to Lex's murder, had it come off, and what just person would risk that? Perhaps the sender would have taken said risk, and had Robbie subsequently got into trouble with the police, then at that juncture he would have come forward and admitted to sending the text.

Leo sighed with exasperation. At Crianlarich, with his brain aching, he managed to get a signal on his phone and make a call. The line wasn't clear and his mother had evidently not put her hearing aid in.

'That's me on my way back, Mummy.'

'What's that, pet?'

'I said that's me on my way back.'

'That's you got the sack?'

'No. That's me on my way back. Back home. To Glasgow.'

The train had creaked back into motion and the signal was lost. Leo cast the phone onto the table with exasperation, and caught the eye of a blonde dream who had boarded at the station. She glowered, offended that one such as he should dare to contemplate her beauty. Leo flushed with unaccustomed embarrassment.

As the train neared its destination the snow turned to sleet, then ceased altogether. Exhaustion threatened to overcome Leo as he gazed at the high-rise panorama of the city, which was constructed from a million little lights. Fortunately, he procured a taxi right away. He burst through the front door of his cold flat, launched his luggage onto the floor, fell out of his clothes and dived into bed. He was asleep before the clock had chimed half past nine.

IV

GLASGOW

35

THERE was something faintly tragic about the service. Ash Wednesday is properly a solemn affair, but it was the paltry attendance that night (he had slept until midday, thus missing the morning edition) which subdued Leo. He gazed up at the high 1960s ceiling and wondered how long they would be able to keep the lights on, let alone keep the place heated. Leo had recently made a substantial private donation (under the pseudonym 'The Braes of Glenlivet') to pay for a repair to the roof, but such acts of discreet generosity could only sustain things so far. The numbers at Mass were so few that the priest invited everyone to leave their pews and gather round him as he blessed the ashes. This unorthodox little assembly at the altar rail brought some sort of consolation, some small catharsis of camaraderie, like the few survivors of a pestilence gathering anxiously to survey the future together.

'Remember, man, you are dust, and unto dust you shall return,' muttered the priest seventeen times as he blotted each forehead with a rudimentary cross. His manner was indescribably sad, and later he would inform the brethren that they were free to wash off the ashes afterwards. He explained that to do so was not an act of denial, and Leo, in his depleted condition, wondered if the others, like he – who usually endeavoured not to give a stuff about what folk thought of him, were secretly relieved not to have to wear this ancient badge and explain it to a society that was becoming more and more hostile to the faith it represented.

Often during Mass, Leo would feel compelled to examine his conscience, to hold all of the tawdry, venial little compromises he made with himself up to the light. There would follow a period of vexation; then he would relax as he remembered the Divine Grace at work, how the Blood of Christ had cleansed and forgiven the world of its sins, how the Cross had delivered mankind from his sinful state. And so, Leo would refrain from throwing himself into a holier life and snugly settle for his status quo. After all, had not Tolstoy driven himself half mad trying to attain perfection?

Yet this process always left Leo feeling faintly squalid and restless, for there is, indeed, no liar comparable with the man who lies to himself. It did all the more so today, such was his dejected state, as he repressed a dread that his usual hubris and self-stupefying drunkenness had impinged upon his efforts to unmask the killer of Helen Addison. Also, the experience that afternoon of making a statement to the police against Craig Hutton for the crossbow attack at St Fillan's Kirk had sickened him, and he had started to doubt his previous conviction that it was indeed necessary to protect the headstrong young man from himself by so harsh a measure.

Part of Leo indeed longed for a purer existence, for the purging satisfaction of self-mortification, for a simple life lived closer to God. Other matters also weighed heavily upon Leo's mind, more to do with the case than his conscience. All day, and to no avail, he had been searching over and over again for unseen permutations and possibilities related to the theories he had expatiated to himself on the train home. Now his thoughts turned to all the other characters he had met over the last week and he feverishly hypothesised upon ways they might fit into the frame. There was James Millar: why had he believed in his innocence so easily? And what about Bosco? Might the Grey Lady have fabricated his alibi for him? What if Robbie McKee was indeed guilty? Or what if the murderer wasn't even a man, and instead Shona Minto acting in a fit of lesbian pique? Indeed, what if there was more than one antagonist after all, and Loch Dhonn was a veritable coven of wickedness in the grip of some Satanic cult (after all, northern Scotland seemed to abound with rumours of occult sects engaged in dark, abusive practices), and everyone from the Grey Lady to the Mintos had been conspiring to feed Leo a tissue of lies? Certainly, he believed that his visions had been impaired of late by some malign influence, so perhaps his regular senses too had been dulled by the same force?

No. He realised these speculations were a result of his being overwrought. There was no way Leo could have been so pitifully blind; he had to trust his instincts about people, and he intuitively knew, then as now, that these individuals were incapable of such an appalling crime.

36

THE next morning, which was dull and pregnant with rain, Leo walked all the way down to Dumbarton Road with the intention of going for an open-blade shave at Mehmet's Turkish barbershop. At one point, on Hyndland Street, he stopped to whip off his trilby as a hearse crawled by. Leo had been deeply moved when, on the way to his father's burial, an elderly gentleman had undertaken this simple, respectful act, and he had vowed to perform it himself thereafter whenever the occasion arose.

Leo was the only customer at Mehmet's, and he requested that the wireless, which was blasting throwaway chart music broadcast by a local commercial station, be turned down. The hot towels and pampering always revived Leo, and he would tip Mehmet generously, because he was an expert who took great pride in his work, utilising castor and grape-seed oils, menthol, eucalyptus balm, astringent, cologne and vast quantities of soft, warm lather. There were lovely little finishing touches: the napkin tucked into the rear of his collar, the wet shave of the nape of his neck, the face massage. Mehmet even used a taper, in the traditional manner, to burn off the excess hair around Leo's ears. They discussed Atatürk, and Mehmet recommended Leo read the great man's 1919–1927 discourses. But he could tell that all was not well with his customer. A good barber, just like a good barman, knows.

Someone else who knew was Leo's masseur, who operated from a private bath club in Garnethill, the heart of the city's Chinese community, even though Liu couldn't speak English and had to communicate via a series of hand claps and gestures. The trestles groaned and Leo's bare rump wobbled as Liu kneaded and pummelled with his hands, which were as strong as iron. The smell of embrocation mingled with steam from the next room, in which two elderly Chinese men played dominoes. Leo stared down at the hundred-year-old black and white floor tiles, listening to the sounds echoing up in the high ceiling. Liu could feel the tension within Leo's frame, and his muscles seemed inert with the impurities of overindulgence – or at least more so than usual.

Someone else who knew was old Arnstein, whom Leo met at the Tchai-Ovna House of Tea, a charming little bohemian retreat stuffed with curios and bric-à-brac, for chess. Arnstein had opened aggressively with the Albin–Chatard Attack, and Leo, quite distracted, had walked into the trap.

'Leo, your mind is not on this game. You have broken biscuits in your head today,' said the elderly man with a kindly smile, his heavy Russian accent still intact after all these years.

It was true; Leo was more interested in fantasising that the teapot that sat between them contained something stronger than Jin Jun Mei. He made his excuses and headed off to Costcutter, instead of his usual Sainsbury's, in order to stock up on whisky.

He found the experience of shopping among ordinary, decent people somehow cathartic. But, of course, as C.S. Lewis observed, there is no such thing as ordinary people, 'mere mortals'.

37

L EO took the bus home and trudged up Spring Gardens from the stop in the gathering darkness. The weather was turning foul, the orange glow of the streetlamps already on, the cobbles slick and filthy. August, soot-stained Victorian tenements towered gloomily above him and the sweet, thick perfume of coal smoke mixed with the damp air. He decided that it was a night for the fire. He walked up the little flight of steps that led to the close entrance. Leo's red sandstone building was constructed over five levels and had been B-listed some time ago, after which point all its occupants were required to maintain their outer woodwork in black. The inside light with its ugly porcelain shade dimly lit the brown, cobwebby ceiling; this seemed morbidly depressing when viewed through the main door's misted upper window. The handle looked greasy and he produced a handkerchief to wipe it clean before entering. The close was cheerless and shadowy tonight, the flickering stair light barely illuminating the heavy wooden banisters, the art nouveau wall tiles and stained-glass upper windows. He thought he could detect the smell of cat urine on one of the landings, where a fuse box hummed and fizzed menacingly. He would try to remember to telephone the factor about the flickering light and the piss, and the electricity board about the fuse box. He reached his own lonely little landing and stepped into the vestibule with its damson walls and two-tone floor tiles. He unlocked his front door, which had a splendid depiction of a Greek urn frosted into the glass. Before going inside he closed the hefty black storm doors and drew the ancient bolts, as though to doubly shut out the corruptive influence of the outside world from the rarefied atmosphere within.

Leo's apartment was comfortable, secluded and filled with his beloved things. He loved his flat. It was his den, his inner sanctum, his own private Dalmatia. Whenever he closed that front door and turned the latch he was left in glorious solitude; no one could bother him or hurt him. He loved the fact that his rooms were located in an end attic of the tenement, which itself was on elevated ground, affording some of the best views of the River Kelvin and the West End, upon which he could gaze down unobserved.

Another thing he loved about the apartment was the fact that he owned it. Outright. One hundred per cent. No rent, no mortgage. This was the investment he had made after he had been rewarded by a wealthy family for a humanitarian task which he would have gladly done for nothing. But, as it happens, that task had proved so arduous and dangerous that he had earned such a reward. So the flat was his; not the bank's, not the building society's, not the council's, not some bloodsucking landlord's.

The windfall had also enabled Leo to furnish and adorn the property to his tastes. He took one of his little tours of the various rooms, an indulgent exercise he allowed himself from time to time, noting the treasures he had amassed over the years. The space in the dining room was dominated by a ten-foot William IV mahogany table upon which sat two sterling silver Queen Anne candlesticks, and a Georgian maple sideboard. The bookcase contained the cream of Leo's collection, including Boethius's *Consolation*, Cassius Dio's *Historia Romana* and Gibbon's *Rise and Fall*.

An archway communicated with the drawing room, with its elaborate ceiling cornicing, and bowed dormer with stained glass to the upper window panes. The impression of this room was of grandeur, antiquity and depth of colour. It was centred on the fireplace, which incorporated abstract floral-patterned tiles in three shades of green enamel. The surround was constructed from tooled hardwood, as was the mantelpiece, upon which rested a pair of French Empire urns, a Winterhalder & Hoffmeir pearl-dialled clock, an alabaster bust of Beethoven, a Qing dynasty ginger jar and a statue of the Sacred Heart. A large gilded overmantle mirror hung above. The suite was a pair of oxblood leather sofas, and an Egyptian rattan chair and a little octagonal bone-and-ebony inlaid shisham table occupied the west-facing oriel window. To pause there on a summer's evening was like occupying a bathyscaphe immersed in an ocean of liquid sunshine as one gazed downwards at the majestic pink granite bridge which spanned the Kelvin. Burnished walnut side tables bookended the sofas, two of which bore Tiffany lamps, one of which supported a nautical sextant, while the other bore a statue of

Minerva. A walnut Regency table sat in the centre of the room. The floor-boards were stained dark, and mostly covered by a spiral-patterned carpet from Damascus. The wallpaper was a heavy, green-dominated Morris & Co. design. On the walls hung two superb Hebridean land-scapes by William McTaggart, a wooded scene by John MacWhirter and a print of Raphael's *Madonna and Child*. A standard lamp stood in one corner, across from a cream-upholstered *chaise longue*. In another corner was Leo's stereo and music collection.

Block-printed linoleum ran over the polished boards of the hallway, which contained a head of a Greek man by Orazio Marinali in marble, a hatstand, a Victorian sea chest and a French console table, the surface of which was crammed with splendid trinkets and *objets d'art*. The walls were decorated in a patterned gold satin, and there hung two framed originals by Hannah Frank: whimsical black and white draw-ings of woodland nymphs at midnight. There was an arched window of leaded glass, which admitted refracted natural light from the next room, and a mid-nineteenth-century oval Florentine mirror with elab-orate cartouches.

The master bedroom was sparely attired; Leo believed neat order was conducive to sound slumber. There was a sleigh bed, a bow-fronted Edwardian wardrobe, a George III tallboy and a companion dressing table, all constructed from mahogany. The only adornments were a crucifix above the bed and a framed wedding photograph of his parents upon the nightstand. The little dressing room was now a study, housing a writing table by Gillows of Lancaster, upon which was a coromandel wood stationery box; it contained his holy of holies – perfumed letters from his long-lost love Maddi.

The bathroom contained a grand, claw-footed cast-iron slipper tub. The morning sun would gush through the window and ivy tumbled from atop the high cistern. Wright's Coal Tar Soap lay on the Burlington washstand.

The cheerful kitchen, with its ancient baby-blue refrigerator and Belfast sink, was at the rear of the property, next to the guest bedroom.

Later, Leo had stretched himself out upon one of the sofas in the draw-ing room, looking decidedly urbane in his silk Paisley dressing gown, his Turkish slippers and his plum velvet smoking cap, which was embroidered with little primroses of different colours and worn rakishly to one side.

He breathed deeply through his nose, enjoying the room's default background scent: a comforting blend of old wood, dusty books, varnish, Silvo and beeswax, further infused tonight with the sweet fragrances of burning coal, candle grease and Cuban tobacco smoke. Bach's Partita No. 4 in D major drifted soothingly from the cherrywood speakers, almost drowning out the sound of the grisly weather outside. Such was the altitude of Leo's rooms that in high winds the doors and windows creaked and groaned in their frames, like the rigging of a tall ship. He lounged listlessly as he surveyed the evidence of his various vices and wondered what to give up for Lent. A bottle of red wine, almost drained, sat upon the table, alongside a crystal goblet, his snuff box, an opened box of Orange Creams and a smouldering cigarillo from which blue smoke curled upwards.

Leo thought of Fordyce, sick at heart that they hadn't been in touch with each other again. Yet some undisclosed emotion stopped him from picking up the telephone. He placed a purple ribbon to mark his place and closed his book with a snap.

One aspect of the case in particular pestered him like a gadfly: the text sent from Robbie's phone to alert Craig that the 'killer' was on his way to St Fillan's Kirk that freezing night. Leo considered it for the hundredth time, now preferring his original theory that the sender was the real murderer trying to incriminate Lex or Robbie. Who had easy access to Robbie's phone? George Rattray was the obvious answer, as they lived in close proximity to each other. But Leo had seen Rattray on foot just before the Land Rover had been driven at him on the Kildavannan–Loch Dhonn road – surely by the killer, which would apparently rule him out.

Sighing with exasperation, Leo got to his feet and unhooked the poker from its berth. He pretended he was fencing with Helen's murderer.

'Take that, you vile blackguard,' he declared as he plunged the poker into his invisible foe.

The intercom buzzed rudely from the next room. Leo replaced the poker, excitedly swished through to the hallway and engaged the microphone: 'Hello?'

'Stephanie' came the glacial response.

After what seemed an age of listening to his friend's stomping footsteps echoing up the gloomy stairwell towards him, Leo relieved her of her dripping umbrella and raincoat, and installed her by the fire.

'Still wet out?'

'No, I emptied a chanty over myself,' she said mordantly.

'I love the rain.'

'That's because you're a complete weirdo.'

'I fail to see why one weather type is inherently inferior and less bonny than another. They all bring with them their particular aesthetic joys.'

'Pish! You prefer the rain 'cause you're a melancholic bastard. And anyway, the last time I was up here you were moaning about the dreich weather too. Now would you turn that racket off – it sounds like the kind of music Hannibal Lecter would dismember policemen to.'

Leo got the distinct impression that Stephanie wasn't in a sociable mood, so he obeyed and lifted the needle from the Bach.

'Can I get you something? Some wine, perhaps? I'm about to open another Château Ducru-Beaucaillou. I laid it down some time ago; a rather eminent year, I must say,' he said, gesturing towards the bottle.

'No, I don't want anything. I'm not staying. I just want to know how you managed to piss off DI Lang so much.'

Leo sat down solemnly on the opposite sofa to her, his elation at a rare visitor dissipating rapidly. 'I suspect that you are already aware of the reason.'

'I am, but I want to hear it from you.'

'He requested that I did not visit the Addison family. Unfortunately, it soon became evident that it was a wish with which I could not comply. I needed to meet them, in order to help stimulate my feeling for the case.'

'Did you warn Lang beforehand that you were going to visit them?'

'I did not.'

'Why not?'

'To be truthful it didn't occur to me. Because he would only have said no.'

'So you went ahead anyway, despite all the trouble I had gone to on your behalf. And then – and *then* – you *threaten* him with going to his superiors! Do you have any idea how important these professional relationships are to me? How much effort I have gone to in nurturing them? Lang and his pals won't ever do me a favour again. And it's not just that: I've been made to look ridiculous to all of these people. Recommending an oddity such as you.'

'Stephanie, I am beginning to take umbrage at your words.'

'I don't fucking care!' she snapped, growing more agitated. 'What's more, you were about as much use as Anne Frank's drum kit up there. So much for your magic powers.'

'Stephanie, I beg of you, please adjust your tone.'

She ignored his protestation. 'To think I had gone to the effort of arranging a date for you with Angela.'

'Angela of the wide jowls?'

'You cheeky bastard – she's beautiful!'

'On the contrary, she looks as though she's constantly trying to swallow a stick of Rothesay rock which has been inserted into her mouth sideways. I've seen hamsters with better-proportioned faces. That's something I've hitherto noticed about your gender: you are quick to describe a plain woman as beautiful because you don't feel threatened by her. Yet you seldom comment when true beauty walks into a room.'

Stephanie took a deep breath as she struggled to ride out her friend's chutzpah. 'Can I ask you something?'

'*Mais oui.*'

'Why do you dislike my darling husband so?'

Leo felt somehow crushed by Stephanie's sudden loyalty towards her man. She was right, of course; he didn't like Jamie. But the feeling was mutual. They were very different people: Leo, cerebral, eccentric and moody; Jamie, alpha male, outgoing, sickeningly attractive and with an ego that required – and received – gratification from more than one female at any one time. They did share in common their Irish-Catholic provenance, but Jamie was lapsed, 'with the dreary predictability of his type', a drunken Leo had once caustically remarked to Stephanie, concluding: 'How else would he fit in at all your West End dinner parties, where it is a given that all present are far too clever to hold with religious faith?'

She and Jamie had been hailed as the perfect couple: handsome, successful and popular. Indeed, it had been deemed inevitable that a man as indecently good-looking as he should win a catch such as the beautiful fiscal. Jamie was an accomplished stage actor who had recently broken into television drama with a supporting role. Occasionally, he had tried to trip Leo up in company, and on one such occasion, at an evening *soirée* at his and Stephanie's first flat, Leo had followed Jamie into the kitchen and threatened to forcefully ram a lignum vitae pestle (probably purchased by an evening guest from the couple's John Lewis wedding list), which was caked in ground cayenne pepper, up an unmentionable orifice, should he repeat the offence. Leo had noted that things were never quite the same between them after that.

'I find his moral certitude oppressive,' he replied, after a moment. It was at times such as this that being a perennial singleton made Leo feel isolated. So, characteristically, he opted upon attack as the best form of defence.

'Pardon?'

'He lacks . . . agnosticism. For example, he insists on possessing an opinion upon everything, and an unassailable, pre-rehearsed, pugnaciously delivered one at that.'

'You bloody hypocrite!' Stephanie exclaimed.

Yet Leo pressed on, unable to stop the terrible momentum that he had unfettered. 'He can defeat any argument because he claims to believe in absolutely nothing, apart from himself, and a vague, conveniently mutable set of live-and-let-live utilitarian principles; *ergo* he takes no position that can, in turn, be assailed. One can scarcely land a glove on him. He thinks his cynical view of life and the cosmos confers upon him a deep, weatherbeaten aspect. Furthermore, he looks upon politics and intellect as a fierce race, and is dreadfully afraid of being perceived as not being sufficiently informed or advanced.'

Stephanie glared at him, then stood up, turned and began striding towards the door.

But something malevolent had stirred within Leo and urged him to proceed, to wreck, to say things he only half meant. 'He is vain, sexist, aggressive, vulgar and self-absorbed,' he shouted at his retreating friend. His soul groaned in dread.

Stephanie slammed the front door.

'Well, you *did* ask,' he said after a moment, to the empty room.

Leo moved on to Scotch rather than more wine, and melancholically performed his weekly manicure – his least favourite ablution. And as he languished by the fire a startling notion dawned upon him: that this friendship, enduring and enriching as it had been, was starting to disintegrate. And he felt quite powerless to do anything about it.

He padded over to the rattan chair, trying to ignore the sense of vulnerability and fatalism that was mushrooming within him. He sat down at the shisham table and surveyed his beautiful room, crammed with the adornments he had carefully collected over the years, but felt empty, like Midas alone in his palace. He examined the chess problem he had constructed (which was based on the 1894 Lasker versus Steinitz game) with exquisite hand-carved chess pieces he had bought in St Petersburg, but couldn't rekindle his interest. He gazed out of the window. From the street below he could hear a staggering drunk lurch into the opening bars of a sad old mountain song. There was such an unnaturally thick, murky texture to the gloom outside that it was made brown-tinged by the electric lights; it was unspeakably enclosing and oppressive. Leo stood up and drew the heavy crimson damask curtains. He could hear the dull siren from a shipyard a mile or two to the south-west, grudgingly moaning at the back shift to take their supper.

Depression always made Leo feel wretched, weak and a little frightened, and he hated feeling weak or frightened, such was his hubris. What is this strange thing, consciousness? What is it for? For an instant, Leo couldn't discern a scintilla of meaning in the universe. All of his faith seemed so trite and contrived. The pointlessness of it all, of existence. The lack of any enduring, overarching moral structure, the cheapness of life, the random injustice of fate, the relentless, shaming tyranny of the inner voice, the apparent impossibility of conquering one's demons and insecurities, the banality of everything. All he wanted was to sleep; perchance not to dream.

Sighing, he checked his mobile phone for the fifth time that hour in the vague hope that Fordyce or anyone else had been trying to get in touch with him. He went back to his chess replication, quickly lost patience and then angrily tipped the board over, casting the ebony and burr walnut pieces everywhere.

He turned round and yelled at the impassive statue on the mantelpiece: 'Lord, it's never enough – You always want more!'

38

Leo's hangover was dismal. He checked the bottle, rather alarmed that he had downed almost a litre of spirit, to say nothing of the wine that had preceded it. He had awoken indecently late for breakfast, so he boiled some cabbage and potatoes – enjoying the honest, earthy odour of the noble root as it cooked – and fried three link sausages in a pan.

As he cooked, he listened to Radio 4 and tried to ignore the black dog that had now fully taken up residence within his consciousness. A spokesman for the British Retail Consortium was speaking about the target for sustainability by 2050, and it occurred to Leo that his default mode was not to believe a single word fellows such as this spoke. But what if he, and not the capitalist, was wrong? What if he was simply irrevocably prejudiced against all things free-market thanks to his socialist indoctrination? What if this spokesman was just a decent bloke, a family man perhaps, doing his job, living his life, speaking the truth as he saw it? Was it really necessary that one always perceived the world through a political prism, that one must always qualify the views of others within some structural context? Who could say for certain that capitalism can't be tamed, that sincere, clever people can't bring their will to bear for the general good? And how much had his cynicism impinged upon his enjoyment of life, of the way the world is, over the years? Leo sighed. Sometimes he truly felt as though the world had left him behind, politically and religiously. But what was the alternative? To believe in nothing? He'd rather jump in the Clyde. In a way, he marvelled at the burgeoning multitude of New Atheists, at their courageous ability to shrug off any notions of deeper meaning to their lives.

The kettle whistled shrilly. He switched off the wireless and brewed a pot of strong tea. He mashed the spuds with a knob of butter and noticed that the sausages were beginning to smoke, so he opened the window before the detectors could start shrieking. He shivered with the new air and poured a drop of brandy into his teacup, just a stiffener to take the morning chill from his bones.

As he climbed the Sixty Steps Leo felt glad of the obstinate drizzle; it, along with the oppressive, battleship-grey sky, provided the perfect atmosphere for a cheerless pub crawl. Bereft of further visions since arriving home, his relentless analysis of the case had proved fruitless and left his faculties cloudy and inert, and his spirits low. He considered what his erstwhile therapist, Brother Francesco, would extol about the importance of men reaching out and communicating when they felt under pressure, but some hoary old instinct kicked in and he resolved to keep a stiff upper lip. At least, he mused, he had resisted the temptation to indulge in corrosive romantic fantasies about Eva, effortlessly transmogrifying a nice Home Counties lass into a Madonna. He ordered half-and-a-halfs in a series of old-fashioned hostelries, Celtic ones mostly, where they still kept the floors bare and the gantries polished. He started west: the Smiddy, the Dolphin, Tennent's, the Star and Garter, the Carnarvon, the Avalon, Orwells; then moved into town for the Griffin; then over the river to Kelly's, Heraghty's and the Queen's Park Café. Occasionally, he would nip into a dripping, filthy lavatory to relieve himself, gazing at the rude slogans scrawled on the ancient Anaglypta and dreading the germs doubtlessly multiplying on the tap handles, or huddle outside to smoke a forbidden cigarette. His only detour was for egg and chips in a cheap diner, outside which he placed a ten-pound note into the supine palm of a poor soul who was sitting sodden on the pavement amid fag ends and streaks of spittle. Later, he sat in the bandstand in a gothic park, by the pond, where melancholy swans contemplated the rain. The tree trunks were slimy, the crooked branches black and skeletal against the foreboding sky. Every edge seemed gilded in a strange silver light. Did everyone else perceive this end-of-the-world weirdness? Much to his dismay, the war memorial, a rather beautiful creation with a wreath-bearing angel set upon a tall plinth of pink marble, had been sprayed with graffiti. 'Mark-M', whoever he was, obviously deemed it of critical importance that the neighbourhood know of his name. Leo hoped that Mark-M was simply too young and misguided to realise the incredible crassness of his choice of canvas.

If it hadn't been for the booze and the sense of despair that blurred Leo's senses and deadened his awareness, he might have perceived a black-clad creature standing under the trees, watching him. A vicious, ghastly, obscene presence that had been hollowed out and then deformed by years of self-pity.

The beast enjoyed watching its pathetic nemesis, feeling smugly superior as it observed his clumsy, inebriated movements, safe in the knowledge that its presence would be obscured by the dark forces it felt in full communion with, now that a perfect sacrifice had been made. The same forces it had petitioned to deaden Moran's extra-sensory powers. The same forces that would make it look like an accident when the moment came. The beast would be guileful and patient. It would wait for the optimum opportunity to present itself and then strike, like a viper.

The subway trains were surely less frequent than they had once been, Leo pondered, as he people-watched through an alcoholic lens. He was fed up waiting on draughty platforms. A surge of irritation welled inside him and he vowed to write a stern letter to some operative or other. By the time the initial rumblings of the train could be heard further up the tunnel, the platform had become uncomfortably busy with commuters and some high-spirited students undertaking the subway circuit pub crawl. Leo stepped out towards the edge, determined to stake his rightful claim to a seat; he had been here first.

The beast edged towards its enemy, its coat collar up, a hat brim pulled down over its brow. Moran was quite evidently oblivious to its presence. Perhaps it had overestimated his powers. Perhaps he wasn't worth swatting like a fly, after all. Still, it had come thus far, so why miss out on all the fun? The commuters straightened up in anticipation of the train's arrival, jostling slightly for position with the selfishness found among strangers. The beast could smell the booze from its target now; perfect – it would seem like so many other Glasgow drunks who had stumbled towards an inevitable early demise beneath hooves, charabancs, trams, trolleybuses and steel wheels . . .

The beast glanced right, towards the dumb mouth of the tunnel. The twin headlights of the train appeared, the noise now dramatic, portentous, cinematic.

Just one little push would be all it would take.

*   *   *

The toy clattered to the floor and bounced towards the platform edge and the abyss beyond. The nearby commuters ignored it, perhaps too tired, perhaps too self-consciously British to become the centre of attention. Yet it was instinctive for a gentleman such as Leo to stoop down and halt its progress. He brandished the trophy at the child's mother, who took it with a murmur of uneasy thanks (she, too, could smell the booze). The infant, a cute, plump, two-year-old boy with a thick head of dark hair, smiled mischievously at his chevalier. Leo gave an impromptu bow, then turned to watch the flashing of the train's side slow to stasis. He would never know how Buzz Lightyear had saved his life.

And the beast would never fully understand that there are forces at work in this world brighter and more powerful than the ones with which it had sought alliance.

39

L EO could experience euphoria amid his depressions which would burst into his consciousness like a skyrocket. The next morning, some peculiar chemical process had, perversely, stimulated his serotonin to cause a hypomania that made him feel as though he needed to take a dose of lithium carbonate, a substance of which he was currently bereft. So he began drinking again instead, uncorking a bottle of 1971 Solera before luncheon. He manically tidied and polished, regularly pinching little quantities of pulverised tobacco from a precious enamelled Hungarian snuff box and snorting it like a cocaine fiend.

By three o'clock, Leo had wheeled his television set from its closet and was sat upon a sofa amid a growing pile of pistachio shells, absent-mindedly watching DVD episodes of *Frasier* and sipping more and more dry sherry. He speculated for a moment upon a misplaced notion that unopened pistachio shells meant that their possessions were bad, as with mussels. Perhaps the seafood analogy made a lateral link, because he then called Rogano's and reserved a booth for a pre-theatre meal, and dressed for the evening.

The bar in the City Halls was deserted but for the ghost of Charles Dickens, who quaffed a gin punch in the corner. Leo was dressed magnificently in a two-piece charcoal lounge suit with an open-necked white shirt and a scarlet Paisley-pattern cravat. He smelled of spicy aftershave lotion and brilliantine. He had continued drinking through dinner (the scallops had been excellent) but felt relatively sober, the alcohol serving only to quell the ecstatic rushes of the daytime, and his senses were quite clear. He would slip into the auditorium during the forced applause for the opening piece, an atonal, discordant contemporary work. To Leo's ear it was about as musical as a piano falling down a flight of stairs. He smiled at his younger self, at a time when he had been so eager to form an opinion upon whatever seemed to him *moderne*.

Leo loved attending concerts. He loved the egalitarian way in which for little more than a tenner one could purchase a seat at any of the city's superb venues, to hear one of Scotland's, or indeed the world's, best chamber or symphony orchestras. He loved the internationalism of the events, the fact that the musicians came from near and far. He loved the genteelness of it all, the black ties and white gloves, the way the audience would gladly give of their applause, which the conductor and soloists would then humbly and generously share with the rank and file. All of them – beholder and performer – bonded by a mutual love of classical music, communing momentarily through the most wondrous of emotions which its live rendition evoked. Leo felt a surge of rapture as the pianist's fingers whirled up and down the keyboard; she barely had to glance at Chopin's notation. Then the tempo slowed, almost to a standstill, then built again before dissolving into its reflective phrase, the final notes gentle, poignant, beautiful. It was as though for a brief moment the planet slowed upon its axis to pause in beatific meditation.

Sometimes, when at home, Leo would put on his headphones and identify every line of instrumentation he could, then return his perception to the piece as a whole again, and somehow appreciate its beauty all the more. That was the crux of the genius of Mozart *et al*; this ability to pull disparate strands together and weave them into an overarching melodic theme. Some of these little narratives were barely audible, barely perceptible, unless one sought them out; perhaps, for example, simply the second violins gently shadowing the main phrase, light to the touch but no doubt adding some important nuance to the overall mix. Perhaps it went beyond genius – perhaps it was miraculous. Yet genius always struck Leo as precisely the same as a miracle anyway, in the same way that elegant, finely tuned physics governed dirty rainwater running in a gutter.

By interval time he was in good spirits. The first three of the *Études* had been brilliantly performed with much finesse and subtlety of emotion by the captivating young woman from Lithuania; Leo had already decided to send a spray of flowers to her hotel the next morning in gratitude, before she left town. Also, he had been most fortunate with his neighbours: no air-piano players, no programme leafers, no peppermint suckers, no bag handlers, no loud nasal breathers, no restless, floppy-haired children dragged along against their will because they were considered 'gifted' by their hopeful West End parents; indeed, no fidgeters whatsoever. Now he had his pre-ordered double Black Bottle and soda to look forward to, before the night's highlight.

He exchanged smiles with the white-haired lady beside him, and turned, ready to join the shuffling throng to the bar. As he did so, he happened to glance upwards, towards the balcony, drawn by some inexplicable instinct. A shadowy figure was making its way to the rear exit.

Leo knew instantly that it was the killer of Helen Addison – and what's more the killer knew that it had been spotted.

The audience ebbed forward and filtered into the lobby at an agonisingly slow pace. Leo excused himself as he pushed through the mostly elderly patrons, repeating the words 'sorry, emergency' as he did so. At this rate the murderer would be out of the upper circle and down the stairs before he could get out. Leo tried to control his breathing, anguished thoughts flashing through his mind as the lighted exit sign gradually drew nearer. 'Oh God, help me,' he whispered as he passed through the doorway.

On to the landing, a break in the crowd – the opportunity to dash down the stairs. He rushed towards the automatic doors. They opened on cue.

Into the cool, moist night air. He glanced left, then right. Nothing.

He made to dial Lang, with images of armed cops sealing off the area, but he knew it was too late. He cancelled the call, and then realised the unlikelihood of Lang dispatching a firearms squad on one of his whims anyway. He might not even have picked up when he saw the caller ID.

Not even the mouth-watering prospect of the young pianist and the marvellous Scottish Chamber Orchestra performing Mozart's Piano Concerto No. XXVII, the *Larghetto* of which Leo always found achingly moving, could dispel the evil that had invaded his evening. And so he strode through the Merchant City, then along Argyle Street, the shock gradually fading, his breathing steadying. He tried to find a suitable bar in which to soothe his nerves but they were all too busy, too noisy, too young. At last he found a little howff in Oswald Street, the kind of joint where no one asked your name. He availed himself of a large Scotch which he washed down with a pint of heavy. Then out, and the long walk home; he couldn't bear the prospect of a festive Glasgow taxi rank.

Rain drummed noisily on his umbrella and danced in the gutters while his leather soles click-clacked on the pavement, only the sodium light of the streetlamps and the birds' evening lullaby for company.

40

A DAY had expired since the beast had followed the sad Glaswegian to the City Halls. It had intended on disposing of him outside, after the concert had finished: a surreptitious blade in the ribs as it brushed by, then it would have slipped off like a shadow into the night. But its presence had been detected. Damn it, it would have been Shakespearian . . . operatic, even, to have left him bleeding to death on the steps. Never mind. He was out of the picture now anyway. And should Leo Moran ever return to Loch Dhonn the beast would share with him the little surprise he had just purchased.

The beast's thoughts then turned towards the stooge. It had enjoyed the power it had wielded over him, regularly spiking him with horse tranquilliser and even the odd handful of the magic mushrooms it had picked last autumn for good measure. It had worked a treat; the idiot was rendered even more docile and malleable than usual, and had started hallucinating and behaving more and more erratically, thus heaping more and more suspicion upon himself. What a joy it had been finding the unsent love letter! *What kind of a person would send such a thing to the home of a grieving family?* they would all ask. *What kind of beast!*

But the jewel in the crown of the strategy had been simplicity itself: get the dolt to help move a pile of scrap metal. Among that scrap metal plant a foot-long brass cylinder – the phallus still smeared by the consummation of Helen Addison with the dark lord – and watch to make sure the idiot handles it. All the while the beast had been fastidious to wear gloves.

The outstanding portion of the plan was also simple: borrow a boat and head over to Innisdubh for the rituals in order to coax that hippie bitch, who was next on the list, and the stooge out into the dead of night at the same time. Then row by the usual place and quickly stash the accoutrements of the black rites – best to travel light as there would be further to walk this time. Then replace the boat, kill the bitch and fuck her with the brass shaft (ensuring not to smudge the stooge's print); leaving the coppers to put two and two together and blame the wandering stooge who had clearly forgotten to wipe the rod clean – the strange hypnosis brought on by the rituals would seem like the murderous culmination of his recent anaesthetised, erratic state. The beast would stash the phallus somewhere nearby with the crucial evidence on its smooth surface, concealed, but not so well that it wouldn't be found. It would stash the knife with it, too. The beast would run back to the hidey-hole in order to stow the robes, and head for home. It would take a special ceremony to lure both of the targets, but it had been easy to procure the required precious items belonging to them both, and anyway, the beast believed it enjoyed its master's favour and had the thirteenth baron, who was of its own bloodline, to intercede on its behalf.

The beast fondly remembered the item it had used for Helen's rite – her first brassiere of adolescence – taken and cherished all of these years. Then it had swiped the little rag doll she was holding when she arrived for her sacrifice. Its white innocence was even stained by a dark splash of its owner's arterial blood.

The beast had already planted it in the stooge's abode, where the inevitable police search would uncover it.

Bombardier William John Minto regained consciousness, for the twenty-two hundred and twelfth time. He felt hardly any pain, just a strange sensation on his left side, as though dry ice had been applied to his nerve endings. He looked down. His uniform had largely disintegrated in the intense heat and much of the skin on his abdomen was pink or charred. He climbed out of the slit trench. The smoking remains of his comrades, like contorted mannequins, lay on the hillside, which had been shorn of snow in an instant. Some of the napalm fizzed angrily in the rough grass. One thing you cannot convey about warfare is its smell, which is the smell of death. And as the combined odours of burning petroleum, polystyrene and human flesh made Minto retch, he realised that this smell was a thing that he would never be able to convey to anyone; it was just too evil a thing.

He flinched as the American F86s, having realised their miscalculation, screamed overhead and lit the horizon with a gorgeous blossoming of orange flame, which contrasted vividly with the drab grey of the gigantic landscape.

I'm the only one left, thought Minto as he stumbled down the valley, the cold affecting him now, the brutal cold. I'm the only one.

He awoke in a sweat, panting, the experience so vivid it might have happened yesterday. The strange thing had been that the Yank medics at the MASH, then everyone in his unit back at base, then everyone back home in Scotland, had treated him as a conquering hero. Why? Because he had survived a bombardment and his pals hadn't? It was like lionising someone for rolling two sixes. Survivor guilt had gnawed at him over the years, and ever since he had longed to perform some gallant act to justify that undeserved adulation. But as time passed by, Shona's influence had worn down his resolve. Then came that filthy deal they had done with the baron. He had voiced his disapproval, but he was just as guilty. More guilty, in fact. At least Shona had had the guts to sign away her soul. He had simply walked out of the room.

Bill knew this feeling of insomnia like an old lover. It was the reason he and his wife didn't share a bedroom. There was no use fighting it; years ago he would have sunk enough White Horse to send himself into oblivion, but then had come Shona's ultimatum. She had been right on that score. Bill had been utilising the Scotch for more than just its sedative effects; he was self-medicating to ease the memories which stalked his sleep and showed no signs of abating as the 1950s and then the new decades of the 1960s and 1970s unfolded. And so he had made his pledge. Then – irony of ironies – he had found himself working behind a bar, his own bar. Still, he had not succumbed. Sometimes, in his dreams, he would revisit the nebulous sensation of whisky blooming out through his body like a warm, golden panacea. And as it flooded through his consciousness every ancient wound was healed, every inadequacy muffled, every faulty neural circuit repaired. Then he would wake, his mouth dry and vile, his nerves frayed, nausea sitting in his belly and gloom pressing upon his soul; hungover as though he had actually imbibed spirit the previous night. But these occasional crises were quelled by a meeting at a group he had discovered in Oban; never again had a drop passed his lips, not even so much as a scoop of sherry trifle.

Bill decided to go for a walk, an old trick the recent thaw made more palatable. He got out of bed, threw together winter apparel, and stole out of the hotel.

It was approaching three o'clock.

The thaw had indeed arrived, and yesterday's rain rendered the last snowfall a mere memory; only the odd stubborn patch of slush remained. Bill went southwards, down the Loch Dhonn–Kildavannan road. He felt blue as he marched, thinking about his dream and wondering if a man ever escapes his past. And then he thought about that poor lassie Helen, and about what had happened to her, and he wondered if the police would ever catch her murderer. And he wondered if her father Stuart, that nice family man who used to smile pleasantly as he waved a morning hello, would ever find any peace, or if he would remain like him, haunted forevermore by the tragedy of doomed youth, waking during the dead of night, eyes wide open, with no one to quell his desolation.

Yet Bill was about to receive some closure of sorts that very hour, upon that mean little stretch of byway, as he was presented with a truly bizarre sight.

About a hundred and fifty yards ahead a figure, wearing strange robes and a pointed hood which obscured the face, emerged from the path which led down to the loch near to the homestead where Robbie and George lived. This person, who had the build and gait of a man, strode away from Bill, oblivious to his presence. He was carrying something which glowed metallically in the faint light cast from the globe lamps near the Innisdara Inn.

Up ahead, shuffling forward, was someone else. Bill wiped his spectacles with his handkerchief and replaced them, and saw that it was the English lassie, Eva, from the Kildavannan community. Bill's initial reaction was one of complete bewilderment, even mild levity at the weirdness of this encounter, as though it was some pre-arranged, nocturnal mating rite. But this quickly gave way to profound concern when he noticed that the robed figure was now brandishing a knife, a fact that Eva seemed utterly unconcerned by.

Bill opened his lips to call out just as the robed man brought the weapon down in a vicious slashing motion. Bill yelled a threat and quickened his pace. This was Helen's killer, and whoever it was they likely had years on him, but Bill, strangely, was quite prepared to die.

He jogged forward only because he was unable to run nowadays, given the way his heart fluttered anxiously within his chest. What would you expect for a man this side of seventy? he asked himself. He was frightened, but he knew that courage wasn't not feeling scared – only psychopaths didn't feel scared – courage was feeling scared but doing the right thing anyway.

The image of the smouldering corpses of his buddies flashed into his mind. Then he remembered their faces, alive now, smiling.

He pictured himself only yesterday manoeuvring five-gallon barrels in the beer cellar with the sprightliness of a thirty-year-old. Sod it. I'll give him a smack in the mouth and go down fighting, he thought.

The robed figure turned, his pointed head tilted slightly to one side in surprise at the presence of a third party, hesitated for a moment, then ran down a different, narrower track from whence he had emerged, which plunged into the woods.

Bill reached Eva to find her quite catatonic, the left arm of her pyjamas darkening with blood which then dripped from her index finger and pattered upon the ground. Her bare feet were bloodless with cold. Bill's basic first aid training kicked in, and he hastily fashioned a ligature from his belt, then partly undressed and peeled off his cotton vest, which he applied to the area of the knife wound. He draped his heavy overcoat around Eva and appraised the situation. He hadn't brought his mobile phone with him, therefore he would have to approach the nearest abode for help. The inn was uninhabited at night-time as the landlord and his wife lived in a cottage in the village, so he began walking Eva along and then down towards George's house. He guided her as quickly as her altered state would permit, speaking softly to her to try and bring her round, all the time anxious that the assailant might be lurking in the shadows. Bill became more and more concerned about Eva's blood loss, so he opted to steer her towards George's converted washhouse which was slightly nearer, where Robbie lodged. He rapped upon the flimsy front door but Robbie was either out or dead to the world. Bill cursed with exasperation, and guided Eva towards the main house. A security light clicked on automatically when they came within the sensors, illuminating the clean white harling, and Bill hammered loudly upon the front door. About a minute later George answered, his sleepy face lined with concern.

'What on earth is going on?' he asked, blinking in an effort to discern the identities of his visitors.

'George, this lassie's been attacked. She's losing blood – I need to use your phone.'

George ushered them inside while Bill related an abridged version of events and deposited Eva on the settee. George brought in a first aid kit, then called 999. Bill frantically peeled back Eva's sleeve, and was relieved to discover that the wound was relatively superficial.

'I'd better check on Robbie, if there's a maniac on the loose,' said George.

'He's not answering. Just make sure the doors are locked and get a dram for her.'

41

A LMOST two full days had passed since Leo had glimpsed the beast at the City Halls, and the profound sense of dissatisfaction he felt over events at Loch Dhonn had not dissipated. The Mitchell Library had still been closed the previous week due to refurbishment, so he had had to wait until today, Monday, to follow up on his idea to research occult practices.

He took a cab to the grand, domed edifice that gazed down sadly upon the M8 motorway extension, which had ripped much of the heart out of the old city. He marched through a series of corridors with waxed chequerboard floors until he arrived at the enquiries desk within the library's modern extension, a comfortingly beige world of blond wood and muffling carpets. This was constructed upon the site of the old St Andrew's Halls which had burned down in 1962, along with a magnificent Austrian oak organ case, and Leo regretted never having had the pleasure of enjoying its legendary acoustics.

He was directed to the fourth floor, where there was a section on the occult. Two pale youths with hair dyed raven-black eyed him sourly as he entered their domain, then scuttled away. Leo took an armful of books to one of the massive reading tables and splayed them out. Jules-Bois, Anton LaVey, Aleister Crowley, all the usual tiresome scoundrels, he thought to himself as he flicked through the volumes. Some symbols he came across bore resemblance to the ones described to him by Helen that were on the killer's hood and robes, or the ones he had seen carved into the thirteenth baron's tomb on Innisdubh, which he had photographed. He traced them out with a pencil and jotted down some notes.

Leo then consulted the library's full catalogue using one of the public computer terminals. After a manly, if inexpert, struggle with the technology, he came across one entry that caught his eye, filled in a little chitty and handed it to the desk assistant, who scurried off to some dusty vault and fetched it. It was an ancient and more obscure text, published in the 1930s by some long-defunct Edinburgh press, entitled Satanic Rituals in Medieval Scotland, authored by one Oliver J. Gannt, QC. It detailed how witches and warlocks would use a specially adapted liturgy of the Black Mass to lure innocent maidens from their homes in the dead of night. The poor unfortunates would be inexorably drawn in the direction of the sordid ordinances in a kind of trance. Apparently, an item precious to the target had first to be procured for the ceremony. The victim was dispatched by a dagger, then the corpse violated by some revered phallus to manifest the woman's union with Satan. This climactic sacrifice was timed to occur at the witching hour of three a.m., which is the obverse of the miracle hour of three p.m., the time Christ had died on the Cross.

Leo snapped the musty covers shut as a shiver ran down his spine.

Outside the library he pondered his next move. He had a hankering for alcohol, but the previous morning, on the way to Mass, his mother had gently admonished him for his hungover state, and he had felt a burning sense of shame. However, he was a mere stone's throw from the Carnarvon, and Frederick Norvell (a family man whose wife was convinced that Leo was a bad influence upon him) would likely be in, having finished his shift at the Criminal Injuries Compensation Board; they could retire to one of the snugs with the pub's chess board. Leo felt lonely; he craved society and dreaded going home. Also, he wanted to see if Frederick was able to complete an endgame that had been vexing him, in which six of the remaining pieces were corralled into the bottom-right corner of the board, with one of his white knights watching from nearby. It was an easy enough problem, he supposed, but what deductive powers had survived the recent onslaught of booze had been used up on analysing the Helen Addison case. So try as he might, Leo simply couldn't figure out how to lure the black king.

To hell with it, he decided. I'll only have a couple of halves, just to be sociable.

He headed for the Carnarvon, but soon stopped abruptly and retraced his steps to regard the *Evening Times* billboard: LOCH DHONN – WOMAN RESCUED FROM SECOND ATTACK. ARREST MADE.

He grabbed a copy, telling the vendor to keep the change from a pound coin and declining the promotional companion tin of Irn-Bru. He scanned the front page and then turned to page three. No mention of who had been attacked or arrested – the story had clearly been slipped into the late edition at the last moment.

He withdrew his mobile phone and rang Stephanie. She let it ring four times, then picked up.

'Mr Moran,' she said languidly.

'Who is it?'

'Who?'

'The killer.'

'A guy called Robert McKee. I spoke to Lang on the phone briefly, earlier.'

'Who was the attack upon?'

'Some woman called Eva.' Leo's stomach sank to somewhere around his ankles. 'She's going to be OK.'

Leo almost collapsed with relief, and was oblivious to Stephanie as she warbled on. He tried to refocus on her monologue. 'Don't worry, you tried your best . . . The cops picked him up later, wandering around, disorientated . . .'

Leo's relief was suddenly replaced with a blooming sense of mortification. His *idée fixe* of Robbie's innocence had been misplaced all along. Somehow, Satan had obscured the truth from him. And Leo had indirectly helped him with his inveterate boozing. Still, over the coming days he would have to try and humbly focus upon the good news that the guilty man was in custody and unable to strike again.

'Steph, I've got to go,' he said, and rang off. The smirr came on as he sank down upon a little wall, the rush-hour traffic crawling homewards behind him through the quickening gloom. Leo considered for a moment how his entire consciousness seemed steeped in obstinate pride. 'Vanity – am I all and only vanity?' he panicked aloud.

He knew he was clutching at straws, but he rang Lang to ask anyway. By some small miracle the detective picked up. Presumably such was his elation at catching the murderer that he was happy to endure Leo one last time.

'Was Robbie in Loch Dhonn on Saturday evening?'

There followed an eternity. 'Yes, he was. I know because he was in the bar at the same time as me. We were watching the late match, Spurs v. Liverpool.'

A strange sense of reprieve descended upon Leo, followed quickly by the terrible realisation that this information meant that the real culprit was still at large.

'He was *definitely* there?'

'Yes. Why do you ask?'

'Because I believe the killer was in Glasgow. Watching me.'

'Why would he watch you?'

'Getting a kick, I suppose. Either that or . . .'

'Or what?'

'Or trying to kill me. After all, I was attacked at Loch Dhonn.'

'Once was probably by Kemp.'

Leo already knew for sure – Bill Minto had confirmed it – that it was indeed Kemp who had carried out the Innisdubh attack, to scare him off, but he wasn't about to muddy the waters with Lang by furnishing him with that information at this critical juncture.

'Granted, but what about the other time, when the Land Rover was driven directly at me that night? Whoever was behind the wheel was Helen's murderer, who wants me dead. Because he has an inkling as to my capabilities. He's on to me. After all, some malign force has been impeding my powers. He's been taking steps.'

'Look, Leo, you got it wrong. No one blames you.'

'Detective Inspector Lang, the fiend was in Glasgow on Saturday – I'll swear to it upon all that is holy. Robbie isn't the killer.'

'Who is, then?'

'I don't know.'

'Oh, Christ!'

'I'm coming back up.'

'I wouldn't bother. We've charged him. Now we're packing up and heading home.'

'What if he strikes again? Look here, I require a list detailing the whereabouts of every Loch Dhonn man on Saturday evening . . . Detective Inspector? Detective Inspector?'

But Lang had hung up, so Leo hailed a taxi on Berkeley Street. Horns sounded irritably as the cab braked abruptly.

Once he had told the driver his destination he tapped out a text to Stephanie: 'They've got the wrong man. Going back up.'

Ludwig sounded just as he was passing the grand towers of the

228

Kelvingrove Museum. 'U impossible bastard!!!' read the response. The Beethoven motif resonated in his mind. Fate knocking at the door, indeed.

Leo didn't feel as though he was being an impossible bastard as the taxi negotiated the darkening, rain-slick West End streets. He had never believed in Robbie's guilt, and now he was convinced that he had been right all along. He felt a compelling urge to get to Loch Dhonn as quickly as possible. He wouldn't be able to sleep tonight anyway. The killer was still abroad, as free as a bird, and it had to be made clear to him that not everyone accused Robbie McKee. Leo needed to get back on the trail before it went cold, and try to speak with Helen again before she disappeared beyond the veil forevermore. He had to clear Robbie, who after his arrest would be liable either to totally lose the plot or do himself a mischief, and find the real culprit, so that no other poor family would go through the Addisons' nightmare, perhaps not tomorrow, but five, ten years from now, in a different place, with a different MO to cover his tracks.

He paid the taxi driver, giving him an uncharacteristically meagre tip.

'Thanks,' grumbled the bemused cabbie. 'I'll be able to weigh mysel' twice.'

V

LOCH DHONN

42

L EO hastily packed some essentials, then wasted some considerable time checking and double-checking that all was switched off and in good order in his apartment. He would have been too late for the last Oban-bound train anyway, so he headed to the old roughcast lock-up at the end of the high-walled lane that ran behind his tenement. He generally disliked driving, apart from summertime jaunts in the countryside, and he somewhat dreaded the journey ahead.

The garage was cold but dry. It smelled of engine grease, creosote, motor oil and paint primer. He felt for the cord and the single light bulb clicked to life to reveal a Mark VI 1956 Humber Hawk, its two-tone paint job still glorious in turquoise and cream. It had been the Moran family's pride and joy as it was a vehicle well outside their budget; they had inherited it upon the passing of Great Uncle Pat, a beloved Donegal man of unearthly geniality who had amassed a small fortune as a scrap-metal dealer.

Leo lifted the bonnet and removed a stained old blanket from the engine. He then went to the boot and deposited his suitcase, and withdrew the starting handle. He opened the driver's door, put the key in the ignition and turned it. He pulled out the choke and waggled the gearstick to check it was in neutral. He got out and inserted the handle into the front of the vehicle, and crank-started the car, feeling a twinge in the damaged nerve endings of his right hand. The engine complained, then spluttered, then fired after only a few seconds, despite the length of time it had lain idle. Leo quickly leapt round to gun the accelerator and get the revs up. The pistons chattered noisily in the enclosed space. He savoured the familiar, pleasant odour of the car's upholstery, which evoked happy holidays from a past that seemed from another lifetime, another consciousness, another dimension. He switched on the headlamps and indicator, and did a quick check that everything was operational. He removed the starting handle and loaded it into the boot along with a jerry can of four star. He closed up the boot and bonnet with a satisfying clunk. Lastly, he draped his sterling-silver antique rosary from the rear-view mirror, before coaxing the stately old saloon into the night.

The journey northwards was stressful. Beyond Loch Long the mountains and dense fir, spruce and pine forests of Argyll seemed particularly bleak, and a downpour at the Rest and Be Thankful made Leo fearful of being swept away by a landslide. He had always disliked this gigantic, enclosing glen, even at the best of times, and tonight he found it particularly sinister. He felt a kind of faceless camaraderie with the drivers of the handful of nearby vehicles who found themselves huddled together in convoy. His flesh pined for booze. But a long-standing, sacred vow committed before the tabernacle never to drink and drive forbade him from swigging from the hip flask he had stowed in the glove compartment, and he had to make do with a Pan Drop instead. He eyed the rosary's crucifix, swaying slightly with the motion of the Humber as it ponderously toiled up the incline, and asked for safe passage. Leo dreaded a breakdown as he didn't get on at all well with engines. All those connecting rods and head gaskets tended to confound him, and he guessed that the membership represented by the chrome RAC emblem on the front grille had lapsed in the year 1978. Perhaps his prayers were answered because the faithful old car held the road steadfastly – even though its wipers struggled to keep up with the rain and the heater discharged only a meagre quantity of warm air – and soon he was on the final stretch northwards to Loch Dhonn. Just outside Inveraray he was overtaken by some irate flash Harry in a VW Golf to whom Leo jabbed a two-fingered salute. He endured a final duel with a massive articulated lorry, before bypassing Kildavannan. As he did so he thought about poor Eva and thanked God for her survival, and for his safe arrival.

43

IT was almost nine o'clock when Leo arrived at Loch Dhonn village. There were now enough parking spaces at the hotel as the media circus had moved on. The police presence had also diminished – only a handful of marked and unmarked cars remained. The Portakabin that had served as the incident room was still there, but a flatbed lorry sat alongside it, ready to whisk it away.

Leo checked in with Paul the barman, and the two were glad to meet in person to banish the bicycle debacle. Leo apologised profusely, while Paul explained that he felt embarrassed by his overreaction, and had been moved by Leo's parting gift. Leo enquired after Fordyce, and Paul told him that he had returned from Edinburgh but had then gone back again yesterday; apparently he had seemed disappointed by Leo's absence. He had, however, left a sealed envelope for Leo, lest he return.

Leo eagerly unpeeled it and unfolded the creamy high-grade paper within to reveal his friend's beautiful script. He fancied that he detected a faint suggestion of Lily of the Valley, but dismissed the notion as absurd. His blood ran cold as he read.

Leo,

Dreadfully sorry for my hasty retreat, please do forgive. I needed to spend some time in the 'Burg, not least to revisit certain key volumes in the National Library in order to brush up on my cryptographic skills.

Should this find you, then you have returned, and are in need of due warning. I have decoded the blurb from the tomb. The runes were written in cipher, as you rightly suspected; a fiendish but somewhat redundant old technique known as polyalphabetic substitution. My guess is that the thirteenth baron ordered the ghastly sepulchre long before he actually expired. The inscriptions are mostly tedious, self-aggrandising ramblings, but for one rather chilling paragraph:

'Heed ye my example of the dark crafts, the means required to satisfy the profound and unknowable Majesty. Emulate me, but beware an adversary who ventures northwards, in search of retribution.'

Take good care, old stick.

Yours affectionately,

F.

Leo deposited his suitcase in his familiar room, quickly freshened up and then went down to the bar, where a sandwich he had ordered was waiting for him. The Mintos were nowhere to be seen and the regulars were absent, no doubt traumatised by the recent arrest of their friend and neighbour, but the remaining police officers were there, providing a mood of muted celebration, or at least relief and satisfaction that the case was solved at last. Leo felt like the spectre at the feast.

DI Lang was present, drinking heavily and enjoying the company. It seemed odd to hear his laughter, to get a glimpse of the man and not the copper. Some of the colour had returned to his cheeks, and he looked as though he might survive the Helen Addison case after all. He noticed Leo, who had installed himself in a booth with his cheese sandwich and a pint of beer, as he walked by after using the gents.

'So you meant it,' he said, sitting down opposite Leo, 'about coming back up.'

'I just know it wasn't McKee. It's too obvious.'

'Murders usually are.'

'What happened to keeping an open mind? Do you have a confession?'

'He's not been lucid enough to make a statement.'

'I think he's been set up.'

'"I think" isn't good enough. You want to hear our case?'

'Certainly.'

First, Lang retold Bill's description of the attack upon and rescue of Eva, and then began relating what had happened in the aftermath: 'We found Robbie wandering around in the woods at five twenty-five a.m. He was wearing only jeans and a jersey, and he was barefoot. He was suffering from mild exposure and rambling incoherently; we think he's had some sort of a breakdown.'

'Did Bill notice if the attacker was barefoot?'

'No. He says the robes were long and covered the feet. We found the robes floating in the loch at first light, near to where we picked up Robbie. I'll give you this, Leo: you were right about the killer being into the occult – those robes were bloody weird. We then found the knife in the undergrowth nearby; a highly decorated thing, like an antique. It had Eva's blood on it from when she was slashed.'

'May I see it?'

'No, you may not. Alongside it we found a brass rod with Robbie's handprint on it. It was the same one used to violate Helen – Forensics have just rung to confirm it has her blood on it. You were correct about it having been lifted from Eva's workshop. It all fits perfectly.'

'Too perfectly. The first instinct of the criminal is to divert suspicion from himself, preferably by casting it onto someone else. Tell me, did you find Robbie's footprints where Eva was attacked?'

'No, because it occurred on tarmac.'

'Of course. What about nearby?'

'Robbie's footprints are all over those woods, including at the top of the path that leads to his home, which is where Bill saw the assailant emerge from, and the little trail he escaped down. Oh, and Robbie's a size nine, by the way.'

'That all proves nothing. Were any prints found on the knife handle?'
'No.'

'Did Bill say if the attacker was wearing gloves?'

'He says he was. We haven't found them yet.'

'So, you're saying the killer, having left his identifiable footprints everywhere, took the trouble to wear gloves to keep his prints off the knife, but for some reason decided to dispose of the brass rod having managed to leave a print on it?'

'Yes. You should have seen the state Robbie was in. He was in no fit state to act rationally.'

'I don't buy it. Remember, Helen's murder was well covered up, despite the high level of violence, and therefore committed by someone who was very clear-thinking, in his own cold-blooded way. For example, you took no incriminating fingerprints from the oars or the boat used by the killer before he attacked Helen. Why? Because he was wearing gloves, and I believe he would never have handled either weapon without wearing gloves. By the way, I bet you don't find those gloves, because the real attacker will have kept them in his possession; they're easily cleaned or disposed of.'

'They could be lost to the loch. Incidentally, his time no boat was found away from its usual berth,' interposed Lang.

'Probably because the boatyard was in the killer's direction of travel this time, on his way back from black rites at Innisdubh, as he journeyed south to intercept the entranced Eva on her long, solemn march from Kildavannan. So it made sense to return whichever vessel he had borrowed from whence he had taken it.'

'There were no clues on Innisdubh as to a Black Mass or anything else; my men have searched every blade of grass on that island,' said Lang.

Leo continued unabashed: 'The murderer would have previously got Robbie to unwittingly handle the rod, so that he could plant it and implicate him. Robbie does odd jobs all around this area, so he wouldn't have blinked if someone requested they help him move some scrap metal. The killer threw the robes into the water, probably in case any miniscule forensic traces of him remained on those items, assuming they would dissolve in the water. He would stash the knife and of course the rod, as this was the item with which he would frame Robbie.'

'There's something else,' said Lang. 'We searched Robbie's home and found Helen's rag doll there. It was streaked with her blood.'

'It could have been planted.'

'Look, Leo,' said Lang, getting to his feet, 'this is no time for denial, for vanity. It's too serious for that.'

The detective left a dejected Leo alone again. He withdrew his mobile phone and typed a simple text to Fordyce: 'Back at Loch Dhonn. This isn't over yet. Sorry I missed you. Thanks for the letter. Warning duly noted.' He hit send and waited until the icon confirming the message's successful dispatch appeared.

44

L EO ventured outside, despite the hour. The rain had gone off, but a damp texture still pervaded the atmosphere, and the waxing moon peered out from behind the clouds. He hoped for another visitation, and indeed he saw Helen standing on a little incline, which was covered in cushion and sphagnum moss, near to the folly where they had first met. She was gazing at the loch, out towards Innisdubh. Leo approached her and wordlessly stood by her side.

Over the last day, which in her dimension could have seemed like a minute or a month, Helen had finally faced up to thinking about her parents, her brother and Craig. She had at last dared to consider the agony they were enduring. How she longed to be held by Craig now, to feel protected by him, loved by him. But that would never happen again. *Never.* Up until now that fact had been incomprehensible to her, as though this state of affairs was some existential gag, a mere hiatus; soon justice would be done, soon she would be somehow reunited with her loved ones. But no – she had been cut down in her glory, just as she was blossoming, just as she was falling completely in love with that big lummox with his inner steel which she so admired and his pale green eyes which she thought were dreamy and beautiful. With that man whom despite her city experience she preferred because he embodied home, and everything fine and honest and rural and daft and gentle about it. The unnatural, premature, violent nature of her death was held up to her now, in all of its obscenity.

Leo was unnerved by the ghost's oddly disengaged demeanour. She turned to face him. Something terrible was happening to Helen Addison. Twenty-three pinpoints of blood had appeared on her nightdress, and were quickly expanding until they merged into a single mass of darkness. Helen's face was now splashed and streaked with the gore, her hair matted from a further wound on her scalp, her eyes sparkling with fury.

Then, horribly, her form began to levitate as she slowly raised her arms until they were perpendicular to her torso, as though to more fully display the stigmata of violence upon her.

'You men are all the same,' she said in a chilling voice.

'Helen!'

'All the same! What vicious filth do *you* fantasise about, Leo, you silly little man?'

'Helen, please, stop it!'

'Yet we have something in common, you and me,' she said, as she floated back down to the ground. 'Because we're both trapped, we're both stuck in a dungeon of visions and unreality, in this . . . in this fucking limbo! But at least you're *alive*, Leo, at least you have that. So whatever it is from your past that's trapping you, for Christ's sake forgive yourself and let it go, otherwise *I* won't forgive you. Look at you – here you are, thinking you can ride in like my knight protector, saving a girl who isn't even properly here!'

She turned and ran off. He didn't call after her. Then she stopped. Turned. And said, 'Oh, and tell that stupid policeman he's got the wrong man.'

She disappeared into the nothingness.

'I know,' he whispered.

45

L EO slept badly that night, shocked by the visceral encounter with Helen, deeply upset by her obvious anguish and horrified that he might in some way have contributed to it. No amount of alcohol could assuage his distress. The next morning, after a desolate breakfast, he went for a walk, hoping to figure out some plan of action.

He headed up to where the attack upon Eva had occurred, and examined the muddy ground at the top of the path from which Bill had seen the robed figure emerge. It was the same one where Bosco had found the ketamine vial. Despite the obliteration caused by the heavy police presence, a few of Robbie's footprints, travelling in the direction the assailant initially took, were still discernible, as were Eva's from when she had been escorted to safety by Minto. At one point her print was superimposed upon one of Robbie's, in keeping with the theory that he was the attacker, in that he had trodden here first. The path itself was of hardpan lined with compacted gravel, therefore only this glaur at the top was soft enough to receive a footprint. Leo examined the verge at either side of this area. On the northern flank he discovered a mere toeprint in a tiny, turfless patch of soil. It proved nothing, of course, but it might mean that the real attacker had kept to the edge lest his footprints be detected in the mire. It belonged to a moulded rubber sole with a basic grooved pattern, and the print looked of a recent vintage. It didn't match the design of shoe worn on the night of Helen's death which Leo had photographed a fortnight ago, but doubtless the killer wouldn't have set off wearing those same soles again. Crucially, it pointed eastwards, the attacker's direction of travel up this path. Leo took a quick measurement and photographed it with his mobile phone, stepped back onto the tarmac and walked further along, finding the little trail that was presumably the one down which the assailant had fled. This was a narrower, muddier track than its nearby counterpart, and there was some extraneous foot traffic here, probably belonging to policemen and before that anglers and ramblers. Again Leo found evidence of Robbie's soles. In fact, these prints went in both directions, possibly more than once, indicating a man wandering around in a trancelike stupor. Leo stooped down to examine a particular shoeprint. His phone and tape measure matched it with the toeprint by the other path, and it pointed westwards, the direction of the attacker's flight. It was a size nine, and soon Leo found another, and another, and another. It made sense that the attacker, surprised by Minto and having taken off at speed, would have been less cautious about where he stepped during his retreat than he had been in his approach. But Leo felt as though he was clutching at straws.

He daundered aimlessly and found himself down at the boatyard. A trailer had been wheeled to the lochside, to take the police launch away the next day. Leo gazed out towards Innisdubh. He considered if he should hire a boat; if another black ceremony had been held over there, the islet might yield some further clues missed by the police. As he deliberated, he absent-mindedly picked up a flat stone and tried to skim it across the water, but it bounced only once and promptly sank.

'That's nae good for the boats' keels; we try to keep the harbour free of rocks, ye fuckin' tumshie.'

Leo turned round to see Kemp grinning at him, wearing a sports jacket and no overcoat despite the time of year.

'Takes one to know one, I guess,' he responded.

Leo stepped up and over the jetty. Kemp moved to one side, as though to bar his path. Leo suddenly felt vulnerable, despite the daylight, despite the open space. He instinctively glanced up towards the hotel, hoping to see another human being.

'Can I help you with anything?' he asked Kemp.

'His lairdship's fashed that yer back poking around in his private business.'

'So?'

'So, he has tasked me with beating ye like a red-headed step-bairn,' grinned the hired thug.

'I must say you seem to enjoy your work, if that inane grin is anything to go by.'

'Oh, I do, don't ye worry about that.'

'That's nice for you, you big bully.'

'Ye remember this?' asked Kemp, brandishing a sand-filled sap. 'Oh, of course ye dinnae, 'cause ye didnae see it coming last time.'

'And what about my being run off the road last week, after the Innisdara Inn – that wasn't you, was it?'

'Nope. Not my style, pal.'

'I didn't think so.'

'Now, where were we?'

Leo stepped back, glancing over his shoulder in desperation and seeing only the empty grey expanse of Loch Dhonn. He gulped and turned to face his aggressor, who was theatrically slapping the cosh upon the palm of his hand.

'Come to Daddy!' Kemp stepped towards him.

Behind the boatsheds was a dense thicket of glossy-leaved deciduous shrubs, which suddenly burst with violent animation as the thick-set figure of Bosco rushed into the scene in a blur.

Kemp turned, jaw slack with surprise, but his expression quickly changed to one of aggression as he braced himself for the attack. He raised the sap and brought it down with immense power, but Bosco, his face livid with exertion, skilfully deflected the blow with a glance of his forearm; undoubtedly some simple but effective martial arts technique, thought Leo. Bosco then ripped the weapon from Kemp's grip and cast it aside as though it was a child's toy.

The two then engaged in a terrifying bout of unarmed combat, in which Kemp chiefly tried to land punches on Bosco's face, and Bosco tried to neutralise Kemp using various slaps and jabs with his hands, and by attempting to drag his jacket over his head. The duel was truly titanic; Leo felt as though he was watching two Tyrannosaurus Rex battling to the death upon some primeval stage. Mud, ice and gravel were thrashed up into the air, and the sound of the violence set Leo's nerves on edge. Suddenly, the thought occurred to him that perhaps he should intervene on Bosco's side. He deliberated upon his rudimentary knowledge of the honour code of the Glasgow 'square go'. This was Leo's – his – battle, but, then again, it was proscribed to 'jump in' and 'gang up' on a single fighter. And it wasn't as though he had asked Bosco to help. Then Leo recollected himself; this wasn't some crude street brawl. An assault – a crime – had been about to be committed, and Bosco had been sterling enough to intervene (Leo correctly speculated that Bosco's clandestine protectorate of him had been at the Grey Lady's direction). And so Leo, with a not insignificant amount of valour, stealthily approached the whirl-wind of violence, while hesitantly adopting a vaguely Victorian boxing posture. He then felt strangely self-conscious of this pugilistic pose, and couldn't seem to aim a fist on target. Therefore, he instead resolved to fashion a cudgel from a fallen bough. While he scanned the floor for a suitable potential weapon, he noticed that Bosco was now getting the better of his opponent. It was queer to see Kemp being dwarfed in terms of girth and sheer physical power by another man. In fact, Bosco now had Kemp on his knees, and was throttling him. Kemp's eyes were standing out on stalks and a horrible gargling sound was emanating from his larynx. Leo shouted out at Bosco to stop, before remembering that he was deaf, and so he approached the Maltese at close quarters and demonstra-tively mouthed his concerns in an attempt to avert disaster. Finally, after a moment which seemed like an eternity, Bosco relented and let Kemp's limp frame flop and then crash to the ground.

The victors left Kemp choking for breath, and walked to the hotel where Leo bought his rescuer a much deserved pint. In fact, Bosco quickly downed an entire gallon of ale, before wiping his wet mouth on his sleeve, shaking Leo's hand vigorously with one of his gargantuan paws, and heading off home to Fallasky House.

46

LEO dined alone, requesting that Ania seat him at the table furthest away from several canoodling couples. He enjoyed smoked salmon and asparagus soufflé, then cock-a-leekie soup, followed by a main of rustic mutton and cabbage, and finally Eve's pudding and egg custard, all washed down with a delightful bottle of Clos Saint Denis. As he sat masticating his dessert he brooded upon his ongoing chess problem. His knight, which sat detached from the cluster of the other remaining active pieces, was somehow the key, he felt sure. He just had to figure out how to force the black king to break cover. Then Leo wondered what on earth his next move would be regarding the case. His pondering continued through in the bar, which was devoid of other patrons. By the time he had drunk so much that he could no longer focus upon the text of the newspapers' reportage of the drama of two nights ago, he bid Paul goodnight and retired to his room. He fell asleep quickly, oblivious to the seminal events that were about to occur.

It was deep into the night when the vision unfolded.

Leo is looking upwards, as though from the bed of Loch Dhonn, watching someone working a splash net, the face blurred by the rippling surface. The person withdraws the net and puts it aside, then plunges a tightly wrapped bundle into the water, reaching downwards, and stashing it in an underwater cavity beneath the lip of the bank.

Then Leo again sees Helen and Craig together in the woods, making love, being watched by something malign lurking in the trees. The beast. Now Leo can see it, if only in profile. It is clutching something – an undergarment – something from Helen's childhood.

The image fades, and is replaced by one of a figure, its face obscured, digging a pit in the moonlight. A grave. The setting is familiar: Innisdubh. The figure puts the spade down and turns slowly towards Leo. The face

is featureless: no mouth, no eyes, no nose; just skin stretched out across a
blunt trestle of bone.

Leo awoke bolt upright, drenched with sweat, and exclaimed automatically, 'I have to save her!' He swung his feet to the floor, clicked on the
lamp, wrenched open the bedside drawer and grabbed the A4 copy of
the page from Helen's diary, then scanned it frantically: 'Tark cornered
me in the woods today. Must have seen me and Craig making love.
Gave me the creeps. Said we are meant to be together. Could not
fathom my refusal. Assured me is not pathetic, but we know differently, don't we?!'

The undergarment that the beast had been clinging to in the vision –
this must be the key to why it was considered 'pathetic'. Something
nagged at Leo, and he racked his brains furiously, trying to make a lateral
link with something someone had once said to describe Helen . . . then it
came to him: a throwaway sentence spoken by the hermit James Millar,
two weeks ago: 'It was as though she was a little . . . damaged, by something that was buried deep.'

So who in Loch Dhonn could have 'damaged' Helen when she was
younger? Just about anyone, potentially. And then, suddenly, Leo remembered the words of a man whom he had once seen working a splash net at
the banks of Loch Dhonn: 'I even babysat for Helen when she was wee.'

'It's Rattray,' he said aloud, into the night.

He grabbed his mobile phone and called Lang on speed dial. It rang
out to voicemail. Leo cursed as the detective's recorded voice drawled out
instructions to leave a message.

'Detective Inspector, it's Leo Moran. The killer – it's George Rattray.
I'm going to Innisdubh now. He's digging a grave there. I think he's about
to kill again. Or already has.'

Leo dressed in a whirl of activity, pulling just trousers over his pyjamas,
stepping into thick socks and outdoor shoes, then grabbing his sports
jacket. He picked up his rosary from the dressing table and, almost as an
afterthought, took out the flick knife, still left in the outer compartment
of his suitcase from when Rocco had insisted he pack it, and thrust it into
his trouser pocket.

He strode off quickly along the corridor, down the stairs, and out through
the front door of the Loch Dhonn Hotel. Outside, there was an odd, slightly

unpleasant sulphuric aroma hanging in the air, and the half moon lit the surroundings relatively well. There were no policemen standing guard any more, and Leo put a jog on down the incline towards the loch.

At the boatyard there was a coble tied to the jetty, its oars laid out invitingly in position. A wave of terrible fear washed over Leo. He untied the rope with ease, and stepped tentatively into the little vessel. He pushed off with an oar, then righted himself and found the rhythm of his stroke, steadily negotiating the stretch of cold black water between himself and Innisdubh.

As he rowed forth his arms began to ache with the task. He glanced over his shoulder and discerned two pinpoints of light coming from the island. He felt a new sensation of dread build within the pit of his stomach, so he prayed aloud: 'Saint Michael the Archangel, defend us in battle. Be our protection against the wickedness and snares of the devil.'

His eyes had adapted somewhat to the darkness by now, and he built up a little momentum before feathering the oars and drawing them in, and letting the coble slip between the rocks that guarded the islet. He clutched his elbows into his abdomen, as though this would reduce the overall width and ease his passage. But he glided through successfully and the keel crunched on the gravel below. Another rowing boat, which had presumably been commandeered to convey his *bête noir* to the island, sat on the shore. Leo stepped tentatively onto the cold rock of Innisdubh. He took a moment to catch his breath, then entered the pitch-black undergrowth and walked towards the points of light, towards the crucible of evil.

As he suspected, they were situated at the standing stones. They were two black candles which sat upon a makeshift altar, the large standing stone which had fallen on its side. An ancient human skull, a cornucopia containing various frightful items, two large occult books and an obscene chalice completed the ensemble. But where the priest for this foul ceremony?

Leo walked on, towards the keep, to where the skeletons of the wicked old barons were interred. 'Childe Roland to the Dark Tower Came,' he quoted under his breath.

It was then that he saw him.

Leo had to hand it to him – he had somehow propped up the enormous slab that had covered the Green Lord's remains for centuries. In the exposed earth he was digging a grave, just as the vision had foretold, and

Leo was suddenly aware of the considerable physical power of the man, despite his years. He was wearing a green gown decorated with various mystical symbols.

'Rattray,' said Leo.

'Who did you expect, the de'il himself?' said the man, barely looking up from his task.

'No, I expected a vulgar little acolyte such as yourself, Georgie Porgie.'

'How rude!'

'I see you've got yourself a new Hallowe'en costume. You do realise Black Masses are not widely regarded as a healthy hobby for grown men? Have you ever considered model railways instead?'

Rattray kept digging. 'I don't know. After all, Mr Toad did a grand job of luring out my Helen for three a.m., my master's hallowed hour. And your hippie girlfriend and the halfwit Robbie, although they were all a good deal less talkative than you. It took a while longer to awake you from your deep slumber, you pathetic drunk. But here you are; better late than never!' He looked up and smirked. 'All I needed was something that was precious to each one of you. Remember losing this?' he said, as he picked up and brandished the missing *Golden Treasury*. Leo stiffened. 'I saw it in the hotel lobby. I read the inscription and purloined it. I thought it might come in handy.'

Leo's voice came out low, trembling with anger. 'That belonged to the finest man I knew. Now put it thou *down*, unclean beast!'

Rattray casually tossed the book aside with a malevolent grin. It landed on the pile of earth he had excavated. He resumed digging.

'I'm surprised I didn't sense it was you. I think I did, at some level,' said Leo.

'No, you didn't,' replied Rattray. 'My prince convinced the world he doesn't exist. For him to cover my tracks was a mere parlour trick. But you've proved a real pain in the neck to have around, always sticking your nose in where it's not wanted. So I decided to take steps.'

'No, I think I did suspect you. It was the fire at Robbie's place; it troubled me somewhat. You started it, didn't you – in order that you could invite him to live in your washhouse, and thereby have him close by and under your thrall?'

'Yep. And then I fitted up that sad bastard good and proper. The ketamine worked a treat on him.'

'Poor Robbie,' sighed Leo mournfully. 'There's one final thing that puzzles me.'

'Ask away.'

'That night I was almost killed by Robbie's Land Rover – who was driving?'

'Why, me of course!'

'But that's impossible – I saw you not an instant before, still out searching for the vial.'

A puzzled look momentarily flickered upon Rattray's face. He leaned on his spade to digest this new information. Then he smiled horribly and turned to Leo. 'Ha! You *think* you saw me.'

'I distinctly recognised you.'

'No – who you saw was an ally from the other side, with whom I bear a strong familial resemblance, an entity whose actual self gave glory to these parts nigh on a century ago: my grandfather, the thirteenth baron of Caradyne.'

'Your *grandfather*?'

'Indeed. He enjoyed a seductive sway over women, including my own grandmother, who was a scullery maid in his employ. My late father told me his secret – that he was the offspring of the great man's loins; one of many, I should imagine.'

'Perhaps that is why you invoked the old scoundrel, in the desperate hope some of his sex appeal would rub off on you,' Leo jibed.

Rattray seemed to flinch slightly, before continuing: 'The sacrificing of Helen widened the channel with the other realm, and granted me a dispensation of power and favour such that my grandfather must have manifested himself to distract you at the critical moment. And should you have survived the collision you would think me as innocent. Oh, manifold and mysterious are the powers of the dark arts!'

Leo's flesh tingled and he felt a peculiar kind of despair. He recalled that freezing night on the Kildavannan road, and how the figure he had seen was wearing a peculiarly antique mode of dress. 'So, where is she?'

'Who?'

'The girl for this grave.'

'Ha, you still don't get it! This grave's for you, my friend. You see, I've become more than a little vexed by your interference, particularly as my late mentor forewarned me of your coming. I was particularly displeased when I heard you had made your return. Therefore you are to vanish off the face of the earth upon this very night; everyone will think you fell into Loch Dhonn, pissed. It will take days before anyone actually cares about your disappearance, by which time the trail will be cold. This loch is over three hundred feet deep; many bodies have been swallowed by it and never recovered. People always easily explain away the death of drunks, because secretly they are glad to be rid of them. You do realise you're known for being a drunk?'

'I'll get over it.'

'You certainly will. Your bones are about to spend eternity with the Green Lord. Just think about that!'

Leo fingered the flick knife in his pocket. He was surprised at how gladly he would plunge it into the black-hearted bastard's flesh. A rare sinew of raw Glaswegian drawled in his accent: 'How d'you work that one out?'

Rattray calmly placed the spade on the mound of earth and wiped his hands on his thighs. He fumbled under his robes, at his waistband. Produced something.

A flashback to visions that occurred some time ago. Leo leaned back, out of the trajectory of the bullet. He turned and ran, the next two shots fizzing past his right ear then crashing through the branches above his head. A grunt of frustration from Rattray.

Leo dashed across Innisdubh, terror seizing at his heart, adrenaline and a sheer will to survive driving him onwards. He ran for the rowing boat, but quickly realised that he would be a sitting duck out on the water alone. Rattray only strode forward purposefully, calm in the knowledge that he would be able to cut down his prey at will. He had fitted a silencer to the pistol, so there was no chance the report could be heard up at the hotel. Leo dashed onwards, considering whether simply to risk it and dive into the freezing loch. His right foot stuck in a bog. Panic rose in his chest. He hauled himself free, then sprinted into the woods that separated him from the landing shore. A shot thudded into the tree ahead, and, *at that precise moment*, Leo tripped on a root and crashed spectacularly into a thicket that was so dense he remained upright. From Rattray's perspective the bullet had clearly struck his adversary – which was exactly what Leo, who let his body go limp, now hoped – and so he arrogantly sauntered towards him now, savouring the melodrama of the moment.

Those were the longest thirteen seconds of Leo's life. Would Rattray put a slug in him from a distance to make sure, or would he first of all get close, just close enough? The breath stopped in his lungs, and he felt the blood crawl in his veins as a hundred sensations flickered through his mind, all of them, for some reason, connected to summertime in north Glasgow during his childhood.

The echo of his plimsolls smacking the bitumen as he joins a hundred shouting children at play in a street lined with 1950s maisonettes which blush vanilla in the teatime sun. Asian groceries on the corners, painted bright green or blue with bubblegum machines outside. Ice-cream van chimes echoing surreally across the waste ground which separates the sentinel prefab towers. There is a vague haze of dust. The evening sun's rays glinting upon milk bottles and litter scattered amid the housing schemes: Riley's Salt & Vinegar, Dunn's Limeade, Matlow's Rainbow Drops. The air a heady mixture of fish and chips, cooling pavements and grass pollen. Zephyrs and Cortinas emerging from the mouth of the new tunnel as they return from trips down the west coast, their rears crammed with sun-tired kids. In the distance the Campsies, the foothills of the West Highlands, slowly turn from resplendent gold to darkness as the sun fades. The hills' contours and ravines and corries suddenly become the malignant black fingers of night. Creeping slowly south from Ben Nevis and the wilderness they reach and stretch inexorably downwards through the vast and shadowy mountains. The dusk sky enveloping the high-rise vista; a particular contrast of clean white concrete set against electric blue. Then the sodium streetlights come on and cast the shadows of tree branches onto the flagstones, the ether heavy with the abundance of the season.

Leo felt his bowels turn to water and the skin on his back and neck go cold and then tighten, as though tensing itself for the coming impact.

'God . . . help . . . me!'

But the impact did not come.

Instead, Rattray got so close that Leo could detect his feral stench.

He reached into the thicket.

Placed his hand on Leo's shoulder.

Hauled him around to face him.

And as he did so Leo, in a single movement, engaged the flick knife's blade and plunged it into the throat of the beast. A surge of pain shot up his arm from his damaged hand.

Rattray, his eyes bulbous with sheer surprise, staggered back a few paces, then collapsed to his knees, dropping the pistol. He momentarily touched his throat as the last moments of his pathetic life dissipated, accompanied by a strange bubbling sound of blood frothing from the fatal wound. Then he fell forwards, and lay face down on the soil.

Leo dropped the bloody knife in disgust, took the rosary from his pocket, and kissed the little crucifix. He became aware of the approaching gnaw of the police launch's outboards. Through a gap in the trees he could see three patrol cars cruising silently in the boatyard, their emergency lights rippling blue.

The pitch of the boat's throttle dropped an octave, then ceased altogether, the only sound the wash lapping the shore. Now Leo could see that it was Lang piloting the launch, coasting it through the rocks with the aid of a powerful fore light. There was no one else on board. The policeman wrested the light from its mounting, leapt from the gunwale to the shore, then dashed up to find Leo sitting on a mossy rock. The lamp cast a wide beam, illuminating the surroundings. Lang stopped and stared at the costumed body, then the knife, then the pistol, then the body again. He knelt down and turned it over to reveal George Rattray's countenance, forever locked in a death mask of utter amazement.

Automatically, he felt for a pulse.

'That is one dead Satanist,' observed Leo darkly.

'You OK?' asked Lang as he stood up.

'Aye.'

'It's a hell of a thing, to kill a man.'

'Fuck 'im,' muttered Leo, the unfamiliar note of street-Glasgow still sounding in his throat.

Lang noticed that Leo was shivering, so he took off his Berghaus and draped it over his shoulders.

'Give us a fag, for Christ's sake.'

'In the pocket.'

Leo lit up.

'You realise I can't rule out Robbie's involvement at this stage?'

But Leo ignored him, and gazed to the east as the sky flushed peach with the first new light of dawn.

47

L ANG had been lodging at the police house in Fallasky. He had acci-
dentally left his phone on silent mode and slept through Leo's call,
but awoke soon afterwards with a thirst. As he got up to fetch a glass
of water the screen had glowed lime to indicate the waiting voicemail
from Leo.

Now he hastily set up a makeshift incident room in the library of the
hotel, where Leo, quite exhausted but fortified sufficiently by a gallon of
strong tea, had to make a lengthy statement about what had taken place
on Innisdubh. He then sank a large Hennessy Napoléon, wearily climbed
the stairs and collapsed into his luxurious bed. All of the cares and
worries of the last few weeks evaporated, and in the last instances of
consciousness he felt the profound peace of the saint before slipping into
a sumptuously deep, dreamless sleep.

He awoke briefly in the late evening during a torrential rain shower,
hunger pangs urging him to order some supper. He swung his legs to the
floor and clicked on the bedside lamp.

Helen Addison was sitting on the end of his bed. 'Hey, stranger.'

'Helen!' He was delighted to see her.

'You've been sleeping all day. No wonder, after your ordeal. I was
nearby, this morning at Innisdubh. I could scarcely bear to watch. I've
never felt so helpless.'

'The battle against evil has rather enervated me,' Leo declared dramat-
ically, before yawning and stretching. 'Nonetheless, good has prevailed
and my powers will return, ready to vanquish Satan's cohort again.
Strong and cunning as the devil is, he cannot undo the miracles of God.
Not for ever, anyway.'

'Earlier, when he . . . George . . . was conducting that horrible Black
Mass thing, there were . . . others present. I could see them.'

'How do you mean, "others"?'

'I mean . . . *entities*.' Leo visibly shivered. 'Although there was another visitor,' Helen continued. 'A spirit of light.'

'My guardian angel, I expect.'

Helen looked away. 'Leo, I'm sorry about the other night. I shouldn't have taken things out on you.'

'You were so upset . . . I was worried I had done something wrong.'

'You're a decent man, Leo. Do not underestimate what that means.'

'I'm not sure I know what it means to be a decent man any more,' he said disconsolately as he stared at the carpet. 'The definition seems to change with the breeze, ever since Monsieur Derrida wrote his little treatises and made everything a shade of grey. And where does this so-called decency get you, anyway?'

'Perhaps it will get you to heaven one day. Perhaps being a decent man is just about trying your best, searching for the truth in your own way. I kind of get the feeling that most of the time you do that.'

Leo cleared his throat of emotion. 'You never mentioned bringing your rag doll out with you on the night of your murder.'

'Oh, of course, little Emily. Yes, I remember now, I was holding her when I was watching George row the boat towards me.'

'I take it that he was this Tark fellow you wrote about in your diary?'

'Yes. It was a childish anagram. Total Arse Reeks of Koffee. He had coffee breath, you see. And I used to think coffee was spelled with a "k", when I was a kid.'

'Why didn't you tell me about him?'

Helen began to fade into the ether.

'Helen, Helen, don't go – not yet! He did something to you, didn't he?'

She nodded.

'When you were young?'

She nodded again. Leo reflected inwardly that the worship of Satan is invariably connected in some way with sexual attacks upon children.

'And you've kept it locked away ever since. I'll wager you never even told Craig?'

She made a clicking sound in her throat that he took to be a yes. She composed herself, and her spectral form fully solidified again.

'He spied on us a few months ago . . . Craig and I, when we were in the woods . . . together. He waited for me and told me that he had been watching. I could sense his anger, his envy. He said he wanted us to be together, that it was fated. Obviously, I said no. But I didn't know it was him who had killed me. I don't mean just because he was wearing a hood; I just didn't think he was capable. I thought he was kind of pitiful, really. I certainly didn't realise he was into worshipping the devil! He really got inside my head as a kid, made me think that what we were doing together was normal. More than that, that it was actually, like, special. I never totally shook the idea off, and that made me feel all the more ashamed. Also, he somehow fooled me into thinking that he was still actually a nice man, although it was weird . . . some of the time I hated his guts. Sounds silly and pathetic, doesn't it?'

'No, nothing of the kind. It sounds exactly like the type of psychological trick that abusers play. And the victim is never to be blamed for falling for it, because they are a *child*, for goodness' sake.'

She nodded, her brow furrowed with thought. 'I think I believe that . . . now. Oh, some good news – the girls the thirteenth baron killed: they tell me they expect to pass over soon. That they will be at peace at last.'

'I am immeasurably gladdened to hear it. And what about you, Helen? Will you be all right?'

'Yes, Leo. Please tell my parents that. And Craig.'

Tears began to stream uncontrollably down Leo's face. 'Well, make sure you put in a good word for me,' he spluttered.

'Thank you, Leo. Thank you, my friend.'

And then Leo caught a glimpse in the dressing-table mirror of himself sitting beside no one at all, and for a moment he wondered if the ghost of Helen Addison had ever actually visited him. He wondered if all along he had just been experiencing some new, waking form of his second sight, a sort of conscious dream in which he tuned in with an imagined version of the girl or indeed some metaphysical imprint of her actual essence refracted towards his mind by whichever unknowable seraph governed such things. Not Helen *in persona*, but neither not Helen at all.

48

THE next morning Leo awoke with the first early spring sunshine pouring gorgeously through his bedroom window. He opened the curtains to reveal Loch Dhonn in all its magnificence, its surface glittering, beneath a cold, burnished azure sky. An exultant songbird hailed the glory of the morning and Ben Corrach gazed beneficently down the loch. Leo hoped that the new season would purge him of the foul humours of winter and perhaps even restore a little portion of innocence to these once cloistered glens.

It was singularly odd: for a man of sensitivity, Leo was strangely unaffected by his killing of Rattray. Not that he approved of executions or vigilante-style justice; it was simply that the circumstances had ultimately proven clear-cut: *a time to kill*. Certainly, he was left shaken and exhausted in the aftermath, but it was apparently nothing a balloon of brandy and a comfortable bed couldn't soothe. Leo had been forced to act in self-defence, plain and simple. There was no alternative *but* to dispatch Rattray. Moreover, there was something fitting, poetically just and perhaps even fated about the precise nature of the man's demise. He who had viciously stabbed poor Helen nearly two dozen times was himself fatally pierced by a cold blade upon a bleak, cold night at Loch Dhonn.

Nonetheless, he couldn't help but wonder if he would come to realise that some territory within the kernel of himself had shifted forever.

Leo showered, feeling like a new man as the rushing water revived his body and mind. He thanked God for His protection, and for answering his entreaties that justice be served. He took care over his toilet, wishing to look his best for his victory parade. He slipped his little chess computer into his overcoat pocket, in case the fanfare didn't materialise and he was forced to appear nonchalant.

As though the morning couldn't get any better, his friend was waiting for him at breakfast.

'Fordyce!'

'Ahoy there, old stick! I've saved us the best table.'

They shook hands warmly, then Leo embraced his friend, such was his joy at their reunion.

Fordyce, who had arrived from Edinburgh the previous night having heard about Leo's duel with Rattray, had of course reserved the best table, set within the dining room's bay window, with a fine view over the lawns, the rhododendron walks and then the loch itself.

Ania and Paul were serving, and they both came over to congratulate Leo for his result, and to thank him for his persistence and courage. Ania even pecked Leo upon the cheek, much to his delight.

Leo's meal was prodigiously hearty. He ordered kippers, followed by a full Scottish breakfast, with double egg, double haggis, double fruit pudding, a tattie scone, a full rack of toast and a large pot of coffee. For the purposes of invigoration he allowed himself two fingers of The Glenlivet and was informed that it arrived with the compliments of the house.

'So, who'd have thought it: old George, a ruddy Satanist,' observed Fordyce, with the understatement typical of his social class.

'The devil takes many forms,' replied Leo through a mouthful of toast and Dundee marmalade.

Leo's mobile phone sounded with Ludwig's iconic four-note motif: Stephanie.

'Well done u!!!'

'Thanks,' he responded.

He paused for a moment. Then tapped at the buttons again and sent an additional message.

'For everything.'

49

AFTER breakfast Leo made his way to the front doors and was dumb-founded by the sight outside. A scrum of media people had descended upon Loch Dhonn, even more than before, such was the high drama of the latest developments.

Leo whistled softly. 'This has gone international, my friend,' he said to himself.

Constable Shorty had been posted on the door; the Mintos had decided to keep the hotel press-free this time. Leo disappeared back inside before any of the pack noticed him.

He slipped out by a side door and took a daunder up by the Addison place. The air was sharp, and fragrant with the beginning of nature's renewal. The media had been told by Lang in no uncertain terms to stay away from the family, and apparently they – unlike Leo – had respected his wishes. Leo hesitated at the gate, meandering in a circle for a minute before resolving to stride up the path and knock on the door.

He needn't have worried. Leo had already attained the status of a folk hero in this house, and he was made more than welcome. Mr and Mrs Addison were now Stuart and Lorna. It was encouraging to see the latter dressed and downstairs, looking a good deal more together than previously.

The aunts – Grace from before and Joanne, a plump, quiet little woman with a gentle demeanour – prepared morning coffee while Leo ribbed young Callum about his preference for Hibernian FC and tried in vain to convert him to the Celtic cause, much to Stuart's amusement. Leo, ever the old-fashioned gentleman, rose from his chair when the aunts came in. They then left the guest alone with Helen's brother and parents.

'To think I had that animal as a babysitter!' fulminated Stuart, forget-ting Callum's presence for a moment. 'Can you imagine? God knows what he did to her!'

'Mr Addison, Stuart, my instincts tell me that no abuse took place back then,' Leo lied, keen to mollify the poor man's anxiety.

'Thank God for that,' sighed Lorna.

'Nonetheless, I should have been there to protect her . . . that night,' fretted Stuart. 'Or at least have realised afterwards that he was the killer.'

'Stuart, people like George Rattray, who now inhabits that realm where the worm never dies, succeed precisely because they are effective at aping decency, and at manipulating the decency and trust of other folk for their own nefarious ends. We cannot allow them to make us question our own sincerity and good faith.'

For a moment all that could be heard was the sound of teaspoons stirring coffee.

'Leo, you are obviously an insightful man, what with your special gift and all,' started Lorna. 'What I mean to say is . . . do you think we will ever see her again?'

Leo glanced at all three expectant faces. He cleared his throat and stood up. This would be his last address to the family.

'Lorna, Stuart, Callum. What I believe is very simple, and I tell you it with all humility. And I swear upon all that is sacred that what I tell you is the truth, and not something fabricated to give you succour. What I believe is that Helen is at peace now. And all of you will be reunited with her one day.'

Leo shook Stuart and Callum's hands, and Lorna insisted upon escorting him to the front gate. A blackbird greeted the new season with a song of profound and heartfelt joy.

'Gosh. This is the first time I've stepped outside since it happened,' said Lorna, drinking in the air and gazing up at the clear blue sky with almost childlike wonder. Her eyes glittered with tears, then she blinked them away.

Leo was silent, refraining from the temptation to utter some trite cliché.

'Leo, there's one other thing . . . You'll be aware that the police have released Helen's body?'

'Yes, I heard.'

'Well, the minister has been by, and we're ready to make arrangements. The point is, we'd really like it if you came to the funeral. Of course, we understand that it's a lot of trouble for you to come back here, but –'

'Lorna,' Leo interrupted, 'it would be a singular honour.'

He stepped forward and kissed Lorna Addison on the cheek, then turned and walked off.

Craig Hutton was easy to find. He was fishing at the same little broken-down pier where Leo had happened upon him a fortnight before.

'I'm sorry I got you arrested,' he said.

'Ach, don't be daft. I was an eejit. You saved me from myself.'

'I take it the charges have been dropped?'

'Aye.' Hutton expertly cast his line into the water, then steadily reeled in the spinner. 'She's at peace now, isn't she?' he asked. 'I can feel it.'

'Yes, I believe so. And I believe she loves you, Craig. So be worthy of her. And strive to be happy.'

50

L EO headed back up to the road, cutting back down to the lochside by the rhododendron walks, enjoying the novel warmth from the sun which bated the underlying freshness of the air. What a country, he mused. Rain and misery one day, heavenly sunshine the next!

There was a precise purpose to this part of his journey. He stopped at the mouth of the burn where he had first encountered George Rattray more than two weeks ago, removed his overcoat and jacket, rolled up his sleeves, pulled on a pair of latex gloves, knelt down and leaned over the water's edge. After much strenuous reaching and rummaging he hauled out a bundle, bound tightly in thick green oilskin. He set it upon the turf, opened it gingerly with some tools he had withdrawn from his detective's kit, and gazed inside with the aid of his little pencil torch, before carefully sealing the watertight wrapper once again. He nodded with solemn satisfaction.

He tidied himself up, pulled his outdoor garments back on, hauled the dripping parcel over his shoulder and plodded back up to the hotel, the stonework of which looked lovely in the sunshine. In the car park he paused to admire the towering Wellingtonia. It looked majestic in the golden light against the verdant backcloth of the wooded hill, a gallery of lime-lucent grottos. His attention was arrested by the sight of a hand-cuffed Lex Dreghorn, who pretended not to have seen Leo as he was frogmarched towards a squad car by two burly policemen. Leo resisted the petty temptation to call out to him.

Lang appeared alongside him, brandishing a sealed plastic envelope, inside of which was Leo's *Golden Treasury*.

'I got some of the boys from the lab to clean it up for you.'

'Thank you,' said Leo, eagerly taking the package and regarding the book with a sentimental smile. 'It belonged to my beloved father, now in Paradise.'

'I know,' said Lang. 'We saw the inscription.'

Over Lang's shoulder Leo noticed a priest wearing a clerical collar standing nearby, chatting with a WPC.

'What have you got there?' enquired Lang, gesturing towards the bundle.

'All in good time, Detective Inspector, all in good time.' He nodded towards the police car, which was crunching slowly over the gravel towards the road. 'What's that all about?'

'Our Lex has been a naughty laddie. He was dealing drugs. It's not just an urban crime, you know.'

'Ah, the last piece in the jigsaw.'

'Meaning?'

'I'll wager it was Lex from whom George bought the ketamine.'

'Possibly.'

As Leo watched that vain, self-serving man being transported away, his face set grimly ahead lest he make eye contact with his adversary, a tragic little miracle occurred. The sunlight that funnelled through the bare branches of a row of elms which sat upon the ridge above the road glanced upon Dreghorn's face, and in doing so bladed his features, which despite the healthy outdoors complexion were revealed as thin and old and tired. This was a man who had successfully shut out the world with his pride, yet in doing so had lost his place in it. And then Leo detected something else: almost imperceptibly, Dreghorn's tongue flicked out to moisten his lips, and a glint of something like fear flashed in his eyes. For a moment he was not old at all, as a trace of some long-hidden youthful vulnerability inhabited his countenance. Leo Moran had witnessed Lex Dreghorn's humanity, and his feeling of self-satisfaction instantly receded, leaving only a remote sensation of sadness. He looked at the rear profile of Dreghorn's head, somehow rendered pathetic and child-like, as the car reached the main gate, indicated, then joined the road and disappeared out of sight. Dreghorn had constructed a persona for himself many years ago and cemented innumerable thin layers to it over those years, and one day soon he would waken in a Barlinnie cell and realise in a panic that he had forgotten what his real soul actually looked like. Leo didn't envy the man his forthcoming epiphany.

His attention was arrested by Dreghorn's Border Collie, which had appeared beside him and was whining sorrowfully. Leo crouched down and attempted to make friends with it, but the animal ran off and disappeared into the rhododendrons.

Lang took a drag from his cigarette and exhaled. 'So, Leo. I'll see you at the inquiry.'

'Of course,' Leo gasped, 'I'll be called to an inquiry. Damn and blast, twice and thrice.'

'Well, you *did* kill a man.'

'Yes, I suppose there is that.'

'Will you mention your . . . visions and everything?'

'Detective Inspector,' Leo said, fixing Lang in the eye, 'I'll be giving testimony under oath. And when I raise my hand to the Almighty I'll be swearing to tell the whole truth, every last bit of it. There is no force in this universe that could compel me to do otherwise.'

'I thought so,' said Lang rather grimly. 'Anyway, Leo, you did well.'

'*Veni, Vidi, Vici,*' he replied serenely.

'Will you have a drink with me? I think I owe you one.'

'I'd be proud to, Detective Inspector. Scotch and soda, please, and make it a large one. I'll get you inside in a minute.'

'Large Scotch and soda coming up,' said Lang, walking towards the hotel.

'Good man,' said Leo. Then he thought for a moment, turned and called out, 'I mean that, Detective Inspector. You are a good man.'

Uncharacteristically, Lang flashed a grin and gave Leo a thumbs-up.

Leo lit a cigarillo and at that moment the priest he had seen earlier walked by. Leo greeted him and engaged him in conversation.

The priest, one Monsignor Mulvey, was aged about fifty and in possession of an earnest but kindly countenance and a magnificent head of jet-black hair. It transpired that he was a regular visitor to Lady Audubon-MacArthur, and on that very morning she had requested that he go over and cleanse Innisdubh, to save her having to contact the bishop in Oban and instigate a prolonged clerical process. The WPC Leo had seen conversing with Monsignor Mulvey was a former parishioner of his, and she had obtained permission from DI Lang to convey him to the island for a brief, supervised visit. The priest confided to Leo that it had been one of the most unpleasant purifications he had ever had to conduct.

'In what way, Monsignor?'

'It is hard to put into words. It was a sensation I had, a chill in my soul. It felt like something profane was mocking me and entreating me to despair. It was as though the very soil and stones of that place resented my being there. As though the island had been steeped in evil for a thousand years.'

51

A T a booth in the hotel bar Leo held court and pontificated at length to Lang and Fordyce.

'George was getting anxious. He didn't underestimate my powers, as you did, Detective Inspector, warned as he was by the runic words on the thirteenth baron's tomb.' At this point Leo slid Fordyce's translation towards the policeman, who scanned it rapidly. 'Therefore he tried to kill me, not just the other night – with a handgun probably purchased in Glasgow at some point – but also when he drove me off the road in Robbie's Land Rover. I also believe that he was stalking me in Glasgow, with a view to disposing of me there.'

'And he framed poor Robbie?' asked Fordyce mournfully.

'Yes. He needed a fall guy, and who better than the village idiot? A man of immense physical strength, some psychological problems and a dubious episode in his history concerning the opposite sex. The first thing he did was burn down McKee's house. That meant he could offer him somewhere to live, where he could control him better and easily plant evidence when the opportunity arose. George had him entirely in his thrall. He gradually drove him into a stupor by spiking his food and drink – we know they shared meals together – with horse tranquilliser. The process would no doubt have been aided by the little pills I saw McKee taking in the bar the first night I arrived here. They were probably some sedative to treat his anxiety. This doping not only subdued Robbie, it also made hime behave in a suspect manner.

'Rattray stole a length of brass from Eva's workshop. She leaves it unlocked, and he had legitimate reason for access anyway, to check on his boat which she was repairing. That was the item used upon poor Helen.

'Now, Robbie, the simple man, *did* feel strongly for Helen. He was in love with her. And when George found an unsent letter, undated, addressed to Helen and declaring said love for her, it was too good an opportunity to pass up. So he kept it in reserve, and waited for the optimum moment to send it to the dead girl and place Robbie further into the frame.'

'What about the handprint on that beastly brass rod?' enquired Fordyce.

'It's easy to trick someone into touching something. It is my belief that George kept it along with the occult robes and the knife, and all his other props such as the profane instruments used in his black rites, sealed and ready for action, stashed underneath the bank where you and I saw him working the splash net. There's a natural hidey-hole there, below the waterline, underneath the lip of the bank. No mortal man would ever have guessed at its existence. Apart from me,' he added grandly, as he hauled up the oilskin parcel and slammed it melodramatically upon the table. 'For you, Detective Inspector. Inside you will find personal items belonging to Helen, Eva and Robbie.'

There was a pause as Fordyce and Lang gazed dumbly at the thing.

'So, what about the other night, with Eva and Robbie?' asked Fordyce.

'George performed a black rite to lure Eva, his victim, and Robbie, his patsy, out into the open, just as he had with Helen, and just as he tried with me. Both were shoeless, wearing only the garments they had gone to bed in. He had purloined an item precious to each one of us – the things inside that bundle, and my Palgrave's *Golden Treasury*, to use in his squalid wizardry. After the ceremony to draw out Eva and Robbie, he would first have rowed to the hidey-hole using the boat he had borrowed and stashed the occult paraphernalia there, before hunting down his prey.'

Leo noticed that Lang's eyes seemed to lose focus at this talk about the power of black rites, but he pressed on regardless. 'George would slaughter and then violate Eva, and render the disoriented Robbie the obvious culprit. Helen's bloodstained rag doll was already planted in Robbie's home, to inevitably be found by the police. When he was interrupted by Bill, he simply scooted down towards the loch, dumped the brass bar in some undergrowth – such that it would be found and further implicate Robbie – along with the bloody knife, then chucked his robes into the water, and scuttled on home, presumably along the shore where he couldn't be seen from the path. He wouldn't have originally planned on dumping the robes but due to the arrival of Bill he didn't have time to conceal them in his usual nook, and he didn't want to bring them home that night to hide at a later date because the police would soon be crawling all over the vicinity because, of course, Robbie lived on his property. The fact was that a robed figure had been seen attacking Eva so it made sense to leave the garments in full view so that the police didn't get suspicious over a loose end. And dumping them in the loch made sense because hopefully the water would dissolve any of his DNA which may have been deposited thereon, while of course there would be no tell-tale hairs left in the hood portion, because Rattray is – or rather was – as bald as an egg. He would have kept the gloves as they were more likely to have retained forensic evidence, either disposing of them or cleaning them later. He also took care, on his approach to attacking Eva, not to leave obvious footprints so that the police would only focus on Robbie's prints; although he obviously used different shoes that night to the ones worn on the night of Helen's murder anyway. Incidentally, before attacking Helen and Eva he would have changed footwear in the boats so as not to leave the same footprints at the crime scenes as on Innisdubh, because he wanted his business on the island to remain secret. After killing Helen he would have changed back again in order that the police couldn't track him – he never got the chance to change after attacking Eva, because Bill had interrupted him, but the police, as he hoped, were engrossed only by Robbie's footprints. The shoes worn for the murder, and the ones worn for the attack on Eva, will have since been destroyed by George, probably by fire; he burned wood to heat his home. Also, after he had killed Helen, George would have deposited the robes, the ceremonial paraphernalia, the knife and the brass rod in his hiding place. I think he waited a while to do this so that he could head straight home after the murder; perhaps that's what he was up to the day I first met him by the lochside.

'Anyway, back to George's attempted murder of Eva: by the time Bill had walked her to his front door Rattray was already changed into his pyjamas, to make it look as though he had recently been abed, like a regular human being. Regarding his attempt to lure me to my death, his plan had a fatal flaw: he couldn't have guessed at my superior mental resilience. He would have banked upon my coming to him in a trance just like the others, thanks to his vulgar little ordinance. Instead, I arrived in a perfectly lucid state, and had already tipped you off. Even if I had nobly perished at George's hand, I had already identified him as the real killer. You see, it was not the awful magnet of the black rites that had drawn me from my bed, but my extrasensory gift, which is bequeathed by an entirely benign source.'

'What about all that nocturnal business up at St Fillan's I heard about?' asked Fordyce.

'George knew Robbie and Lex were planning to go up there to steal lead. He had probably heard them converse, or simply sneaked a look at Robbie's text messages. So he made Robbie ill by tainting the curry he served him. That cleared the way for him to send Craig a text from Robbie's mobile phone, telling him that Lex was the killer and that he was heading up to the kirk. Perhaps George guessed that Craig already believed Lex was the guilty man. Either Craig would succeed in claiming his wild justice, such that some suspicion would fall on a now dead and therefore silent Lex, or the text message itself would mean that the suspicions forming around Robbie would intensify. The police would figure Robbie was manipulating Craig into killing Lex in order to cover his own tracks. George was clever enough to delete the text after it had been sent, in case Robbie saw it on his phone and realised that he had been set up.'

Lang then admitted that he couldn't quite shake the suspicion that Robbie may have been an accomplice. The man had been admitted to Gartnaval Royal Hospital in Glasgow, but his lawyer was now insisting that the charges against him be dropped, and the door of his room be unlocked.

'As I already told you in my statement, Detective Inspector,' said Leo a little wearily, 'George himself gleefully informed me how he had framed Robbie. I can assure you the fellow is quite innocent.'

'But you told me you saw George immediately prior to the Land Rover trying to run you down that night. Meaning that someone else must have been driving.'

'I was mistaken. I did not, in fact, see George,' replied Leo truthfully, a chill running down his spine as he remembered. 'It was someone else. There is another, final matter of which you should be made aware: Rattray's late father was the thirteenth baron's illegitimate son.'

'By Jove!' exclaimed Fordyce.

'Are you sure?' protested Lang.

'Rattray himself told me. I believe he had come to dedicate his life to emulating his grandfather. Perhaps evil can lurk in the bloodline, like some congenital poison.'

The three men stood up and shook hands with each other warmly. Yet Leo had the feeling that his and Fordyce's adventures together were only just beginning.

DI Lang yawned and glanced at the mantle clock: 12.51 a.m. He poured himself a large Johnnie Walker. He had toiled hard to construct a version of events more rational than that offered by Leo, yet as he read over his notes one last time it was with a distinct sense of dissatisfaction. He signed off the report and re-read the final paragraph: 'As for the cooperation of Mr Leomaris Moran, I can only commend his perceptiveness. I cannot reasonably account for all of the information he brought to bear on the case, however, I would recommend his utilisation in future operations.'

The sleepwalking phenomenon that had broken out at Loch Dhonn of late was an exasperating loose end in the case. Lang's concerns about Robbie McKee had abated since his final conversation with Leo. The man's state of mind was so disturbed that he had been unable to interview him. Lang now believed that the poor bastard would easily have been persuaded or frightened into leaving his home in the middle of the night of the attack on Eva Whitton, in order to place him in the frame. Rattray was spiking him with ketamine hydrochloride and also, it turned out, probably a natural psychoactive – some traces of unusual fungi found in the killer's bin had been sent for analysis. In addition, it had now been confirmed that McKee was being prescribed benzodiazepine by his GP for his anxiety. However, Lang's theorising regarding Helen and Eva's night-time walks seemed tenuous; not least he doubted that an individual could indeed be enticed from their slumber by prior covert hypnosis, but hopefully further elucidation would emerge from psychologists skilled in the field.

Then an idea occurred to him: what if the notion of some audible trigger had been implanted by George Rattray into Helen and Eva's minds, which when heard would draw them from their beds? Could such a sound have been remotely controlled, for example a ringtone or a text message? No, neither victim's mobile phone had been contacted immediately prior to the attacks. What about an external sound? Both women had slept with their windows slightly open for fresh air – in true Highland fashion – which would have made any noise from outside more audible.

Could George have produced such a trigger himself? Possibly, but such an added complication to his strategy might have risked his being detected. And Lang couldn't think of any obvious long-range audio device that the searches of the killer's abode or the countryside had thrown up. So what if he had utilised an existing, recurring external sound, such as a scare gun or a siren of some sort? Lang and his colleagues had calculated the approximate time at which the women would have left their respective homes – between 2.33 and 2.43 a.m. was the range. He put down his whisky glass, deciding to refrain. He switched on the television to kill an hour and settled into an easy chair.

DI Lang woke with a start to trash, dead-hour broadcasting murmuring from the set. He glanced at the clock: it was just leaving two a.m. He would have to hurry. He switched off the TV and the two-bar electric fire, grabbed his coat, cigarettes and keys, and left.

He rolled the unmarked Mondeo all the way down the track that led from the Loch Dhonn Hotel to the boatyard, mildly enjoying the rumbling noise of the tyres against the rough hardpan and the way the full beam raked the branches of the trees by the waterside. He parked, turned the engine off, killed the headlights and got out. This was a spot open enough such that any notable sound issuing from anywhere in the wide vicinity would be easily discerned. He lit a fag. Walked up and down a bit to keep warm. At precisely 2.34 a.m. he heard it: the ghostly, two-note horn of the milk train as it crawled out of the Lairig Lom at Stob's Bend. Incredibly clear in the still night air, it could have been fifty yards away. Lang smiled, and as he walked back to the car rebuked himself for the relish he already felt at disabusing Leo of his supernatural theories.

As he drove the lonely few miles back to Fallasky, DI Lang felt satisfied and perhaps a little relieved at how his rational method had produced an explanation which chimed with his worldview. Sure, he had to accept that Leo's 'visions' had delivered certain key information about the case, but if the man indeed possessed unorthodox powers of perception then they were simply natural human facets as yet unexplained by science.

Lang pondered awhile upon Leo and his religious outlook. He remembered a quote from Carl Jung he had once learned by heart: 'One does not become enlightened by imagining figures of light, but by making the darkness conscious.' The awfulness of episodes such as the killing of

Helen Addison is too much for sensitive folk to bear, therefore they posit it within a grand metaphysical struggle between forces of light and darkness. It is comforting to do so because it imbues such occurrences with a hope for some kind of meaning. But really, that's just our controlling nature taking over. We can either face that down, and man up and call this world out for what it really is – chaotic and shitty – or we can refuse to grasp that core reality and carry on deluding ourselves, hiding under the covers like frightened children.

It was 3 a.m. when the detective arrived back at the police house. As he wearily approached the front door a gust of wind picked up suddenly, moaning as it passed through a strip of bare woodland to his right. Lang happened to glance up at the sky as a drifting cloud passed over the moon. Then, somewhere in the middle distance, something – a nocturnal animal perhaps – screeched horribly, and a chill ran through him momentarily, a kind of grating fear which seemed to jar somewhere deep inside, and as he quickened his pace slightly and scrabbled in his pocket for his keys the sense of smugness within him dampened somewhat, like the wick being turned down on a hurricane lantern.

'Daft bugger,' he chided himself, as he closed the door firmly behind him.

52

EARLIER that day, after taking his leave of Fordyce and Lang, Leo strolled out of the bar – Paul had parted the French doors which opened on to the terrace – and lit another mini Cohiba; he felt he had earned it.

He wandered over to the balustrade and gazed at the splendid surroundings. At that moment Eva happened by with a male companion.

'All hail the conquering hero!' she said, as they ascended the steps to the patio. She pecked Leo on the cheek. He felt a little thrill, which was quickly quashed when she introduced her friend by name. This was Ryan, the member of the Kildavannan community she had spoken so warmly of during their dinner date. He was a handsome fellow in his thirties who hailed from Western Australia.

Eva read the crestfallen expression on Leo's countenance. She would have preferred to have spared him the ignominy of meeting her with this man whom he would doubtless perceive as her new boyfriend, but had she walked on by Leo would likely have seen them anyway, and she didn't want him to think her rude. She cursed herself for being in the vicinity, but she had presumed that Leo would have left Loch Dhonn by now. And, as it happened, she had actually decided against any relationship with Ryan (they merely happened to be scheduled for firewood forage together that day); the dinner date with Leo had caused her to analyse whether she wanted anyone in her life right now, and she had concluded that she did not. The attack upon her person by George Rattray had consolidated her decision; as was her independent way, she wanted time by herself to come to terms with what had happened. She could still barely believe that George was Helen's killer, and that he had tried to murder her, too. She would wear a livid red scar down her left arm for the rest of her life as a reminder of how close to death she had come, of how intimately evil had brushed against her.

Anyway, she could hardly begin to communicate all of these facts to Leo, whom she now felt sorry for. Eva also felt a misplaced sense of shame. Misplaced because theirs had only been a dinner date and she had hardly led him on. But dates were patently rare for both of them these days, and she had used the mention of Ryan to fend off Leo's advances, and having now rejected both of them she felt vaguely insincere.

Life can be cruel at times by what must be left unsaid, and Leo, despite assuming that Eva and Ryan were indeed lovers, wished that he could soothe the discomfort that was written on her face. He didn't consider her in the least unjust.

Ryan, a man of considerable sensitivity, excused himself and left Eva and Leo together.

'How are you, Eva?'

'Scarred, but still here.'

'I feel in some way responsible. Not having detected him before you were assaulted.'

'My knight protector had retreated to Glasgow and let me down!' she teased.

Leo smiled, a little embarrassed. Helen's ghost had used the same term, 'knight protector', to injure him only three nights ago; it was as though she had heard Eva, whom she had looked up to, once use it, and had stored it away for future use. Leo cringed inwardly as he recalled a vestigial hope he had fleetingly entertained in the shower that morning that perhaps his heroics on Innisdubh would draw a swooning Eva into his arms.

'Sometimes even a gallant paladin must withdraw to heal his wounds and sharpen his blade,' he joked.

Leo considered momentarily that his banishment to Glasgow had actually proved key to cracking the case in that it had drawn the emboldened George to approach the city. If it wasn't for Leo sensing the killer's presence at the concert on the same night as Robbie was drinking in the same bar as DI Lang forty miles away, he may never have questioned Robbie's alleged guilt quite so emphatically after the arrest. 'Anyway, I felt dreadful when I heard you had been attacked,' he went on. 'I was very worried about you.'

She patted his arm affectionately.

'Eva, I realise that this is somewhat from left field, but I believe you have lost something precious recently. A certain item of jewellery.'

'How on earth did you know that? Just this morning I noticed my jade brooch was missing. My late grandmother gave me it before she passed away. You may remember I wore it to dinner that evening. Afterwards, I saw that the silver mounting was a little tarnished, so I had brought it down to my workshop, meaning to give it a polish.'

Leo wistfully recalled the thrill he had felt at how bonny she had looked in the hotel that night.

'George stole it from you, doubtless dropping by your workshop with some convenient pretext at hand in case you were in. He will have utilised it in his Satanic litany, to lure you out that night. Anyway, the good news is that I have recovered it for you. What's more, I enlisted a passing priest – such are the ways of Providence – to bless it, and hence remove the foul malediction of that man's sorcery. Have a word with DI Lang – I'm sure he will restore it to your possession in good time.'

'Thank you, Leo. It's odd: I don't actually remember leaving the house, or even the attack itself. The first thing I remember is sitting in George's . . . in *his* house, with a glass of whisky being forced upon me. To think that Bill took me directly to the killer's lair!'

'Bill, like everyone else round here, was entirely taken in by George's nice-guy act. Even I was fooled, if only a little.'

'Do you know he once propositioned me?

'Really?'

'Oh, he was the perfect gentleman, but looking back on it now it was kind of inappropriate. He must be twenty-odd years my senior and was more or less offering to take care of me, financially speaking, as though I was some feral dropout who needed taming. I told him no, of course.' Eva noticed the thoughtful expression on Leo's face. 'A penny for them,' she said.

'It explains why he targeted you. Both you and Helen rejected him; for that you were to pay with your lives. And while disposing of you he would also deflect the blame onto poor Robbie.'

'You mean to say that because I turned him down he meant to kill me? I find that hard to believe.'

'Your refusals were merely the straws that broke the camel's back. Eva, it would be unwise and frankly pointless to spend too much time speculating upon how a fellow like George Rattray became as twisted and violent as he did; that is a job for psychologists and theologians. Suffice to say it took years for his inadequacy to find its full expression as cruelty. My guess is that he brooded upon his hatred for women – his hatred for people – for so long that he gradually descended into depravity. Thought precedes action just as lightning precedes thunder, so if a wicked notion comes to one's mind, better to do as the Buddhists and brush it aside or watch it float away of its own accord, rather than obsess upon it. Or better still, take it captive and make it obedient to Christ, as Paul recommended. From such bitter little seeds a terrible harvest is reaped. But we live in a historical moment in which one's selfish appetites are exalted. Our concern for what is right, rather than what feels good, has been sacrificed upon the altar of individualism.'

Eva didn't happen to concur with Leo's hell-in-a-handcart analysis of society – she more or less subscribed to the epigram, 'The more things change, the more they stay the same' – but now wasn't the time for philosophical dispute, so she kept her counsel.

They strolled together for a while, down the path that led towards the loch. At the Victorian folly where Leo had first met Helen, he bade Eva *adieu*, bowing magnificently and kissing her hand. As he watched her walk away he took a surreptitious swig from his hipflask. Yet somehow on this morning – on this glorious day – he wasn't going to allow the familiar feelings of loneliness to overcome him. Suddenly, the phrase Eva had used about the knight protector withdrawing to Glasgow flashed into his mind. 'Eureka!' Leo exclaimed and he sat down upon a mossy stump and eagerly withdrew his chess computer. He once again addressed the endgame that had been so vexing him. The bottom-right three squares contained, left to right, white king, black bishop, white knight. Immediately above were black pawn, white pawn, black king, with Leo's remaining white knight on king4. Instead of the direct attack he had been fixated upon, he withdrew this cavalier knight to bishop6. The chess engine walked into the trap, taking Leo's other knight with its king. Leo now turned round his retreated knight, advancing it to knight4. The computer moved its bishop to rook7. Leo smiled as he played the killer move, his knight taking the black pawn. *Checkmate.*

He relit his little cheroot and ambled down towards the boatyard, drawn by sounds of human activity.

53

O N rounding the boatsheds Leo was presented with a remarkable sight. A minibus bearing the crest of Glasgow University and the initials GUARD was parked up. The far end of the jetty was swarming with activity. A dozen men, aged from eighteen to sixty, almost all of whom sported beards and woolly jerseys, were manoeuvring a small JCB digger onto a support vessel.

At the waterside, the baron was shouting hysterically at his man Kemp, whose neck was a range of crimson hues following his unsuccessful bout with Bosco. The puce-faced baron saw Leo and glared at him; he was met with a satirical bow. Kemp noticed Leo's arrival, too, but for once he didn't shoot him an ironic grin.

Another altercation was taking place. Bill Minto stood impassively with his arms folded watching the festivities, while his wife Shona lectured him in stern tones. Leo walked over to them, and his presence seemed noxious to Shona, who strode off huffily.

'So, what's going on, Bill?' Leo asked, after they had exchanged congratulations for their respective nocturnal heroics.

'Ach, I just decided to put a few things right,' the hotelier replied.

They took a few steps together, slowly walking a circle as Bill related his news. After Leo had confronted him the previous week, Bill had undergone something of a crisis of conscience. Following a couple of days of rumination he resolved to tell the Grey Lady the truth about Innisdubh's dark secrets, about the girls who were buried there. He did this without Shona's knowledge, lest she try to dissuade him. The Grey Lady was most kind and understanding, and the pair decided to have the place properly surveyed. Bill would then approach the police with their findings and come clean about the whole cover-up. Serendipitously, this team of archaeologists happened to be excavating a Bronze Age burial cairn located on a strip of land owned by the Grey Lady down towards

Kilmartin Glen. She therefore requested that they investigate the mausoleum and they were happy to help due to her generous cooperation with their dig. They were supposed to have gone over to Innisdubh yesterday, but the police had sealed the island after George's demise. However, they agreed to allow access today under strict supervision.

Bill changed tack, and began speaking about the occult temple he and his wife had discovered beneath Ardchreggan House several years ago. 'The thing is, just before I bricked off the entrance to it I took one last look round. And I noticed that certain items we had discovered were no longer there – some robes and some books, maybe some other paraphernalia as well. I had forgotten all about it until just yesterday. And it occurred to me that it was probably George who swiped them. He must have known about and visited the temple when Ardchreggan House was lying derelict.'

A man in a business suit called over, and Bill waved back in acknowledgement. The man walked off, leaving two police constables behind to keep the peace.

'That's the Edinburgh lawyer the Grey Lady and I hired. I think he's cleared up any misunderstanding with his lairdship regarding ownership rights for these islands.'

'Good for you, Bill,' said Leo.

'Those archaeologist bods have been using X-ray apparatus in the old mausoleum and they've detected six distinct voids beneath the floor. There was a Catholic priest here earlier. I had a word with him. He's going to give them a decent funeral.'

Leo was glad of this opportunity to part company with Bill on friendly terms, and they bade each other a warm farewell.

Leo then ambled northwards, following the bank. He came across a male mallard strutting and quacking his way around his territory, his glossy bottle-green head and bright yellow beak gorgeously vivid. Leo smiled; something in the creature's portentous demeanour put him in mind of himself.

Once he had come abreast with Innisdubh he stopped and gazed up the loch towards Ben Corrach, which was gilded with the light of the late morning sun. Then he looked over to the isle and imagined that it looked a little less ugly today and somehow more at peace. And he thought about Helen Addison, and the evil that men do. And he wondered what it was like before the Fall, before cruelty was poured into people's hearts. And for a moment he fancied that a little piece of Eden still prevailed, over there to the west, over the mountains, among the islands where the Gaels lived peacefully, softly speaking their strange, poetic language beneath sunsets so beautiful they could make you weep.

ACKNOWLEDGEMENTS

Three people deserve particular thanks. Martin Greig and Neil White of BackPage Press, for their early belief in the book and their invaluable help and support thereafter, and my cousin Madeleine Tait for her early edit which made the manuscript remotely publishable. Also thanks to her and George for loans of their holiday house, which inspired the setting of Loch Dhonn. To David Toner and Des Mulvey for being sounding boards for certain key plot points, and to Pete Burns for championing the book. Finally, thanks to everyone at Polygon for their sterling work, especially my editor Alison Rae who did a superb job.